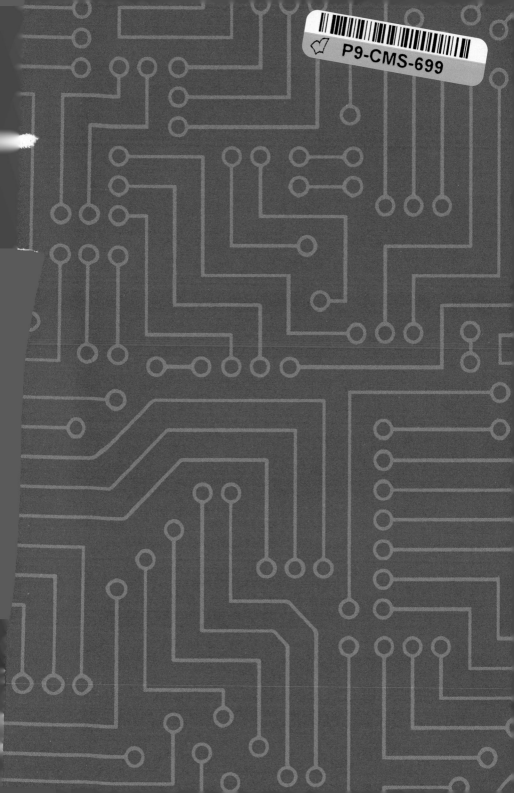

A CHRISTOPHER ELIOPOULOS PRODUCTION

COLORED BY REBECCA NALTY

MONSTER MAYHEM

DIAL BOOKS FOR YOUNG READERS

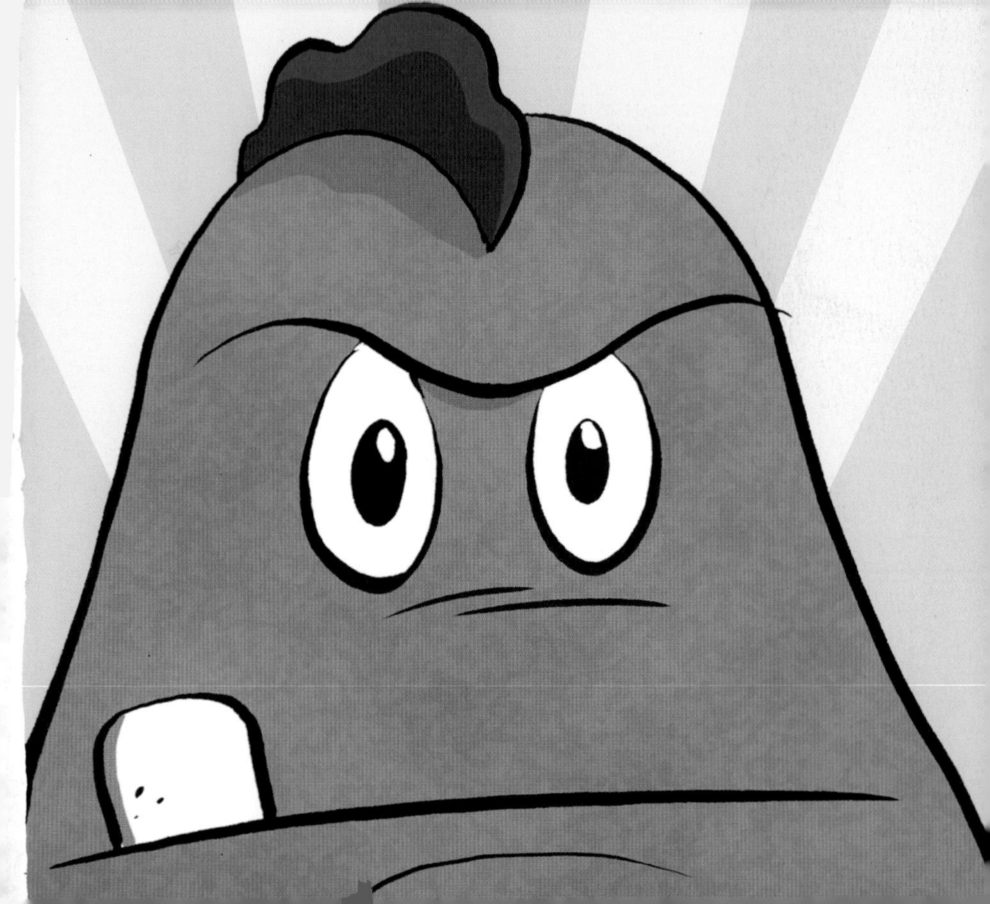

For Jeff, Tommy, Xan, Matt, Nick, Mike, Joey,
Brendan, Eva, Chloe, Lucine, Anna, Kelsey,
Caroline, and Susy. Jeremy and Justin are
lucky to have you as friends.

DIAL BOOKS FOR YOUNG READERS
PENGUIN YOUNG READERS GROUP • An imprint of Penguin Random House LLC
375 Hudson Street • New York, NY 10014

Copyright © 2018 by Christopher Eliopoulos

Library of Congress Cataloging-in-Publication Data
Names: Eliopoulos, Chris, 1983- author, illustrator. • Title: Monster mayhem / Christopher Eliopoulos.
Description: New York, NY : Dial Books for Young Readers, [2018] | Summary: "Science-obsessed Zoe finds herself trapped in one of her favorite monster movies and needs to invent her way out of a disaster while also saving the monster who has become her friend"— Provided by publisher. • Identifiers: LCCN 2017059554 | ISBN 9780735231245 (paperback) • Subjects: LCSH: Graphic novels. | CYAC: Graphic novels. | African Americans—Fiction. | Monsters—Fiction. | BISAC: JUVENILE FICTION / Science & Technology. | JUVENILE FICTION / People & Places / United States / African American. • Classification: LCC PZ7.7.E44 Mon 2018 | DDC 741.5/973—dc23
LC record available at https://lccn.loc.gov/2017059554

Printed in China • 10 9 8 7 6 5 4 3 2 1

Design by Jason Henry • The artwork for this book was created digitally.

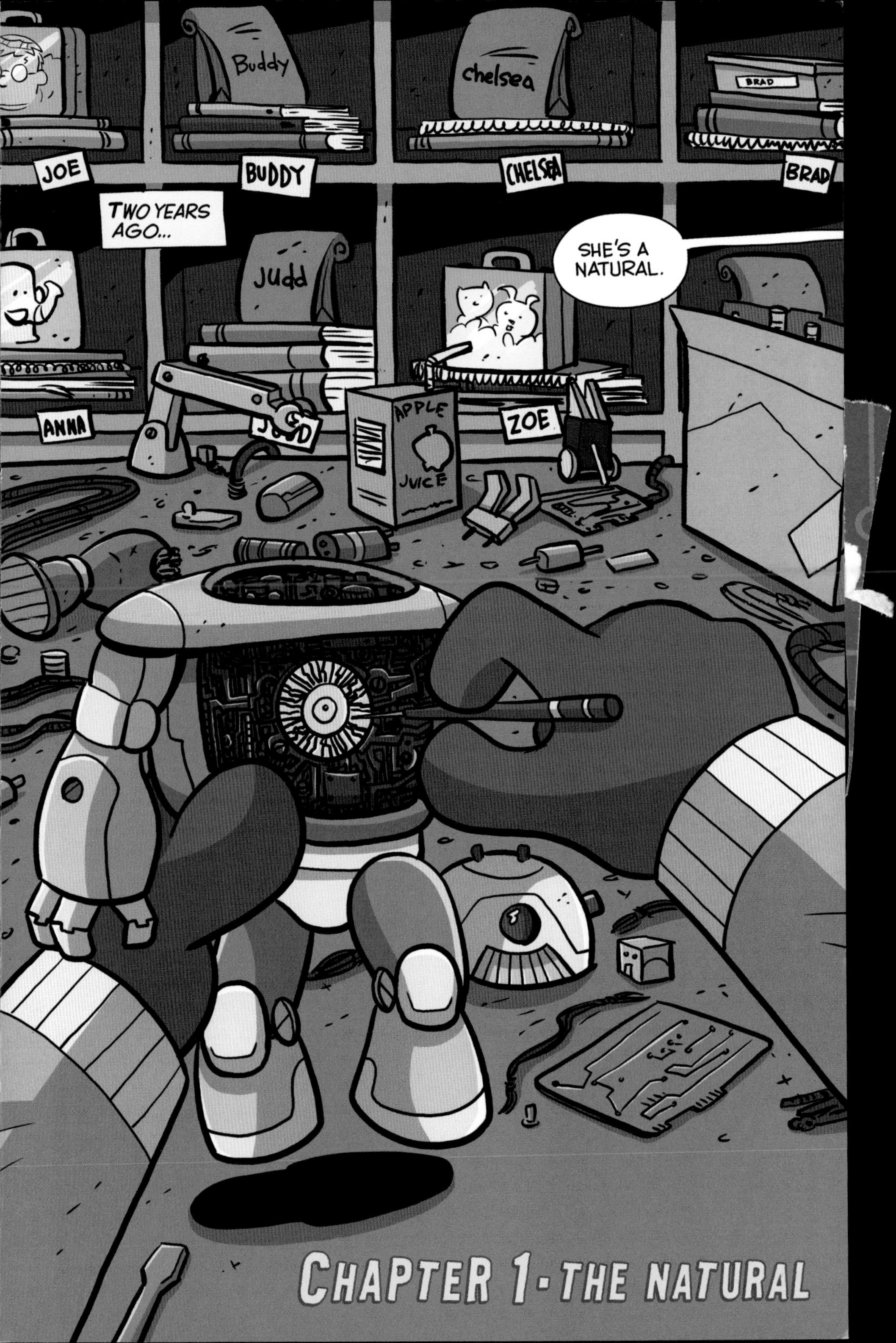
Buddy
chelsea
BRAD
JOE
BUDDY
CHELSEA
BRAD
TWO YEARS AGO...
Judd
SHE'S A NATURAL.
APPLE
JUICE
ANNA
JUDD
ZOE

CHAPTER 1 - THE NATURAL

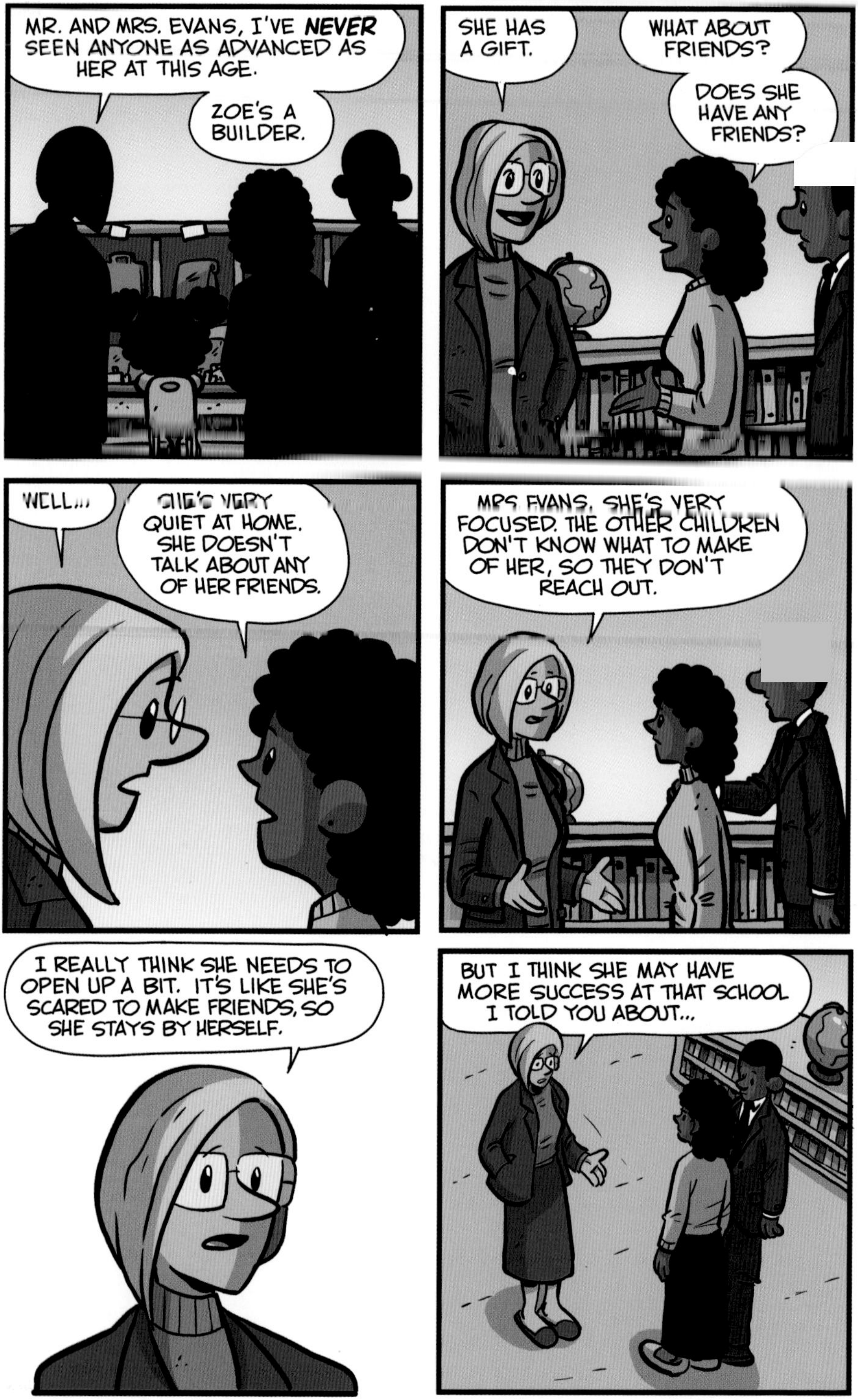
MR. AND MRS. EVANS, I'VE **NEVER** SEEN ANYONE AS ADVANCED AS HER AT THIS AGE.
ZOE'S A BUILDER.
SHE HAS A GIFT.
WHAT ABOUT FRIENDS?
DOES SHE HAVE ANY FRIENDS?
WELL...
SHE'S VERY QUIET AT HOME. SHE DOESN'T TALK ABOUT ANY OF HER FRIENDS.
MRS EVANS, SHE'S VERY FOCUSED. THE OTHER CHILDREN DON'T KNOW WHAT TO MAKE OF HER, SO THEY DON'T REACH OUT.
I REALLY THINK SHE NEEDS TO OPEN UP A BIT. IT'S LIKE SHE'S SCARED TO MAKE FRIENDS, SO SHE STAYS BY HERSELF.
BUT I THINK SHE MAY HAVE MORE SUCCESS AT THAT SCHOOL I TOLD YOU ABOUT...

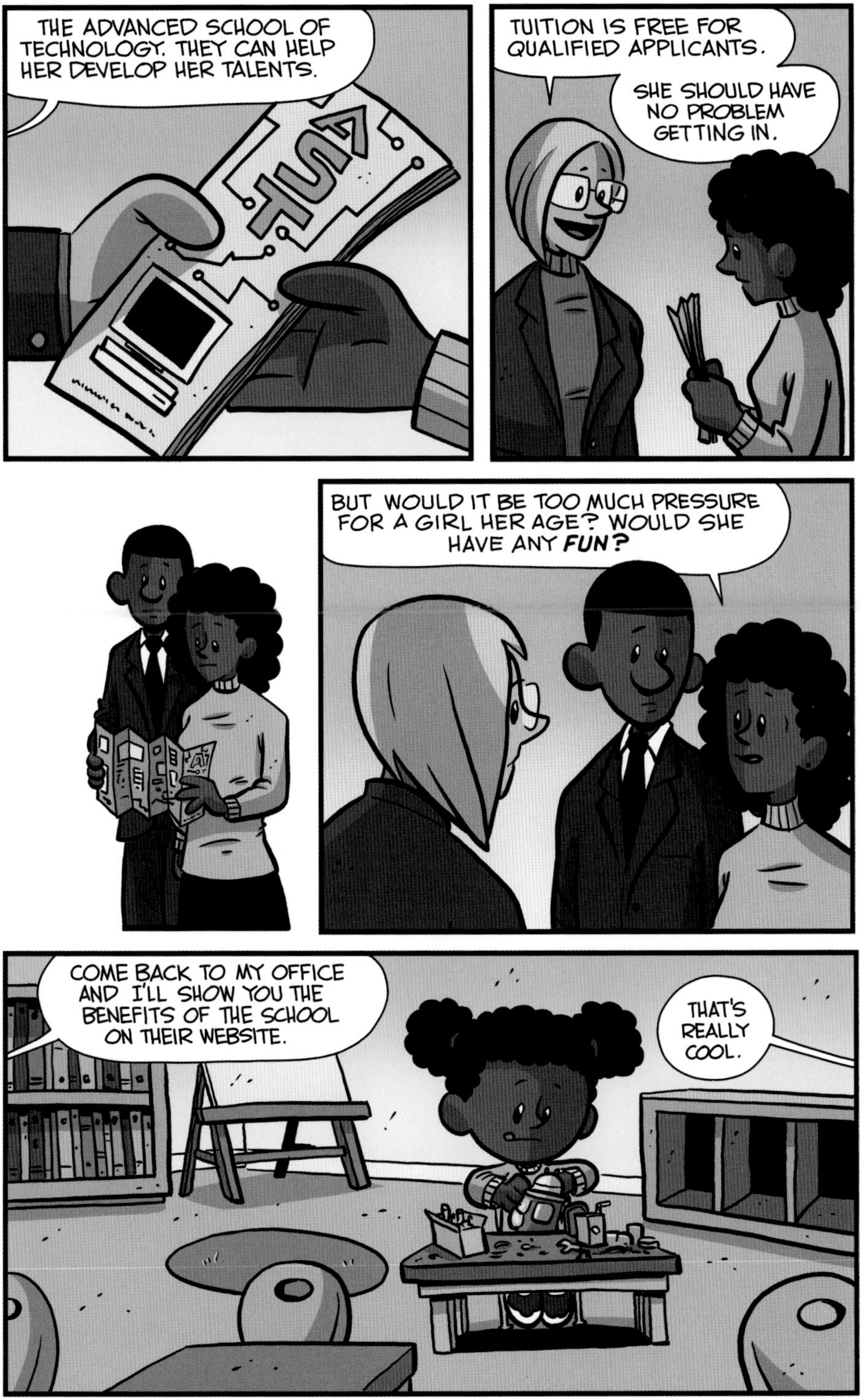
THE ADVANCED SCHOOL OF TECHNOLOGY. THEY CAN HELP HER DEVELOP HER TALENTS.
AST
TUITION IS FREE FOR QUALIFIED APPLICANTS.
SHE SHOULD HAVE NO PROBLEM GETTING IN.
BUT WOULD IT BE TOO MUCH PRESSURE FOR A GIRL HER AGE? WOULD SHE HAVE ANY *FUN*?
COME BACK TO MY OFFICE AND I'LL SHOW YOU THE BENEFITS OF THE SCHOOL ON THEIR WEBSITE.
THAT'S REALLY COOL.

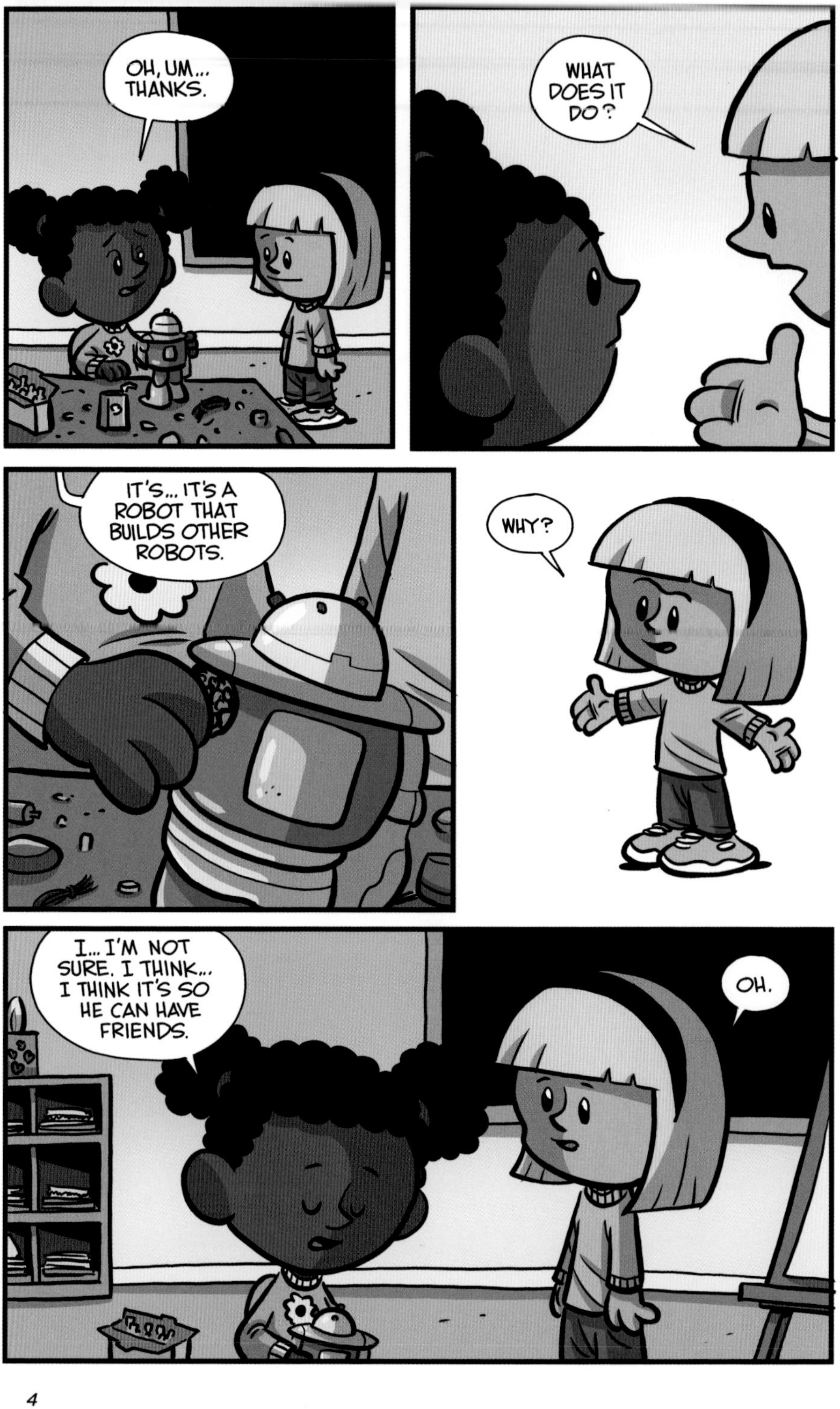
OH, UM... THANKS.
WHAT DOES IT DO?
IT'S... IT'S A ROBOT THAT BUILDS OTHER ROBOTS.
WHY?
I... I'M NOT SURE. I THINK... I THINK IT'S SO HE CAN HAVE FRIENDS.
OH.

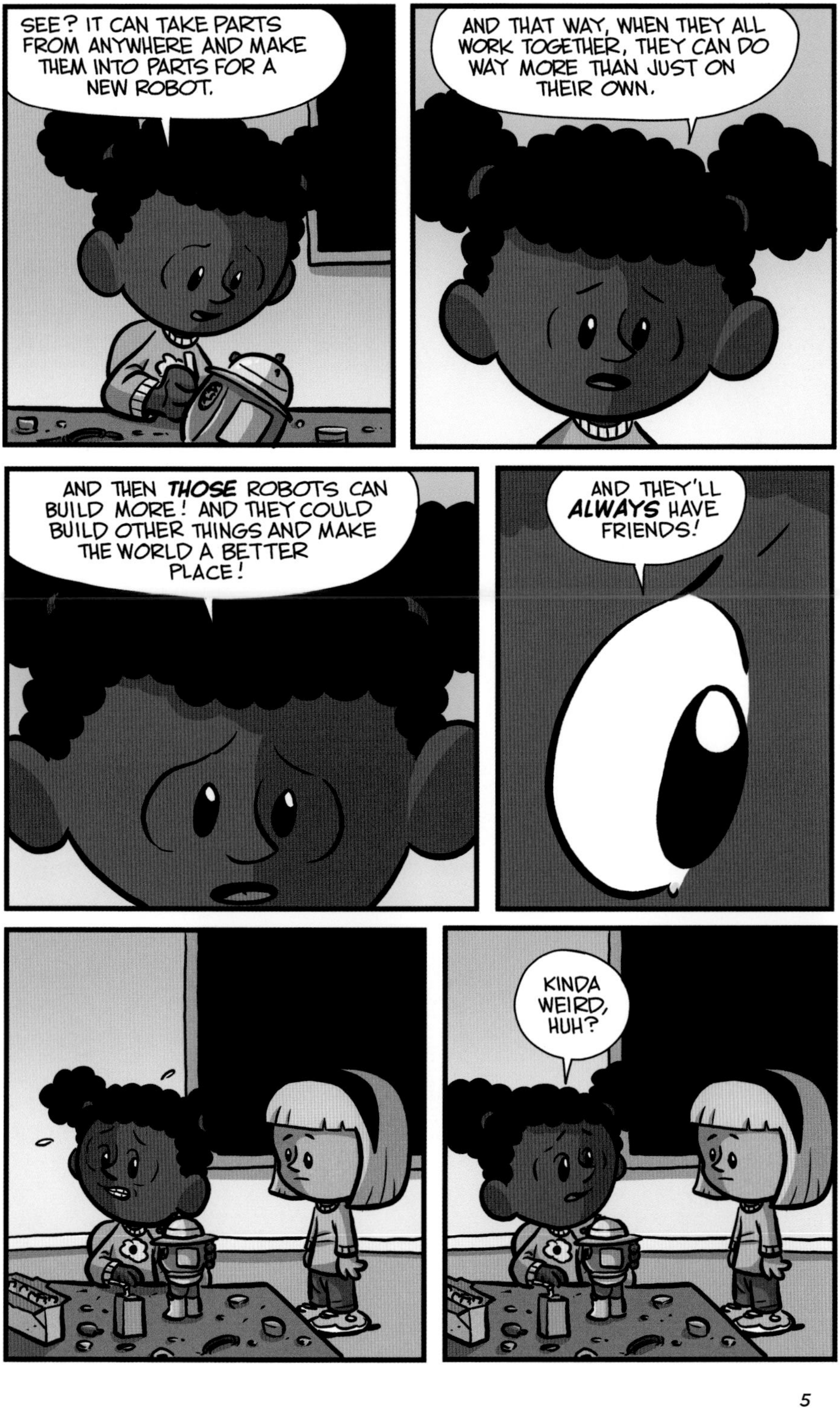
SEE? IT CAN TAKE PARTS FROM ANYWHERE AND MAKE THEM INTO PARTS FOR A NEW ROBOT.
AND THAT WAY, WHEN THEY ALL WORK TOGETHER, THEY CAN DO WAY MORE THAN JUST ON THEIR OWN.
AND THEN THOSE ROBOTS CAN BUILD MORE! AND THEY COULD BUILD OTHER THINGS AND MAKE THE WORLD A BETTER PLACE!
AND THEY'LL ALWAYS HAVE FRIENDS!
KINDA WEIRD, HUH?

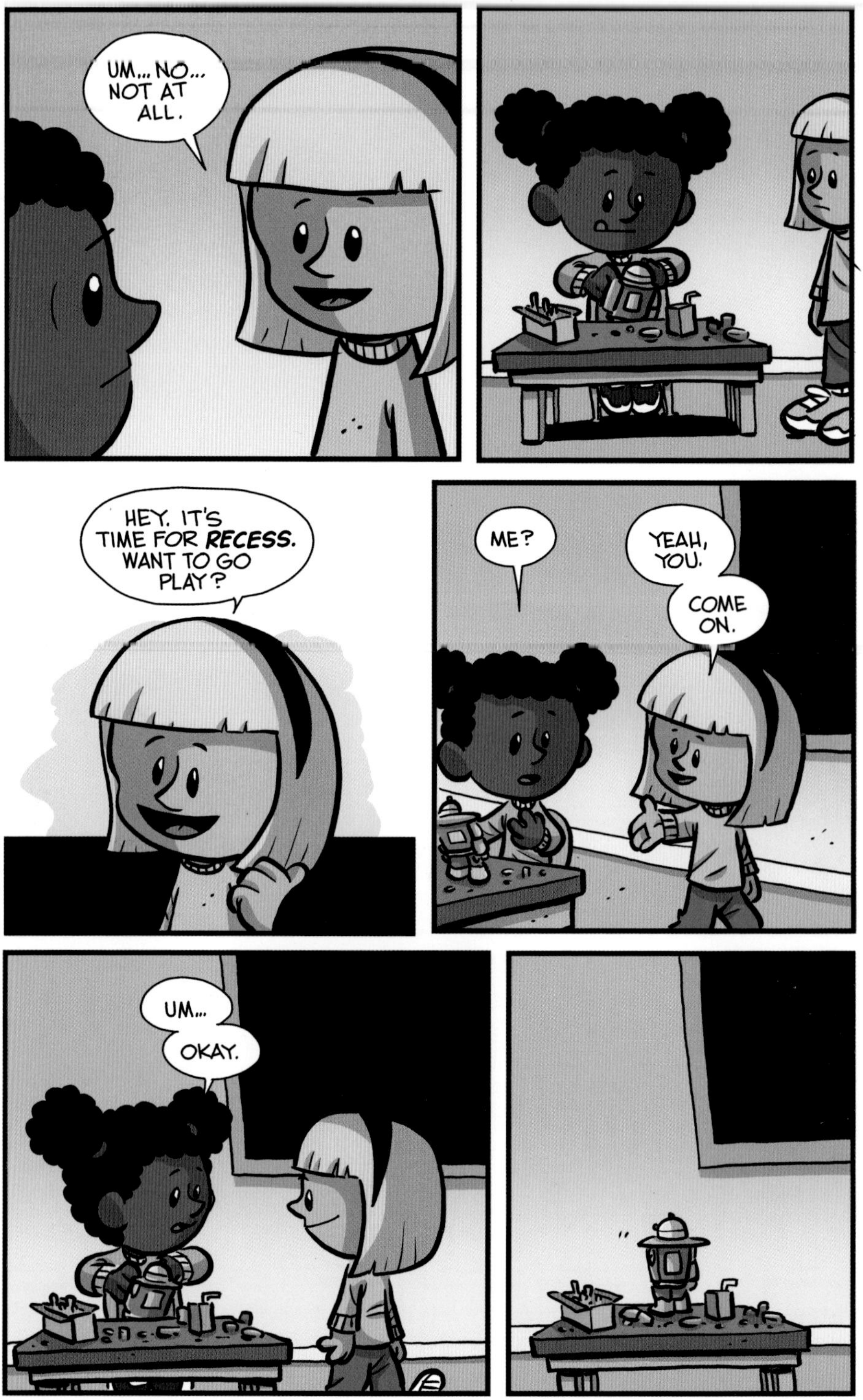
UM... NO... NOT AT ALL.
HEY. IT'S TIME FOR **RECESS.** WANT TO GO PLAY?
ME?
YEAH, YOU.
COME ON.
UM...
OKAY.

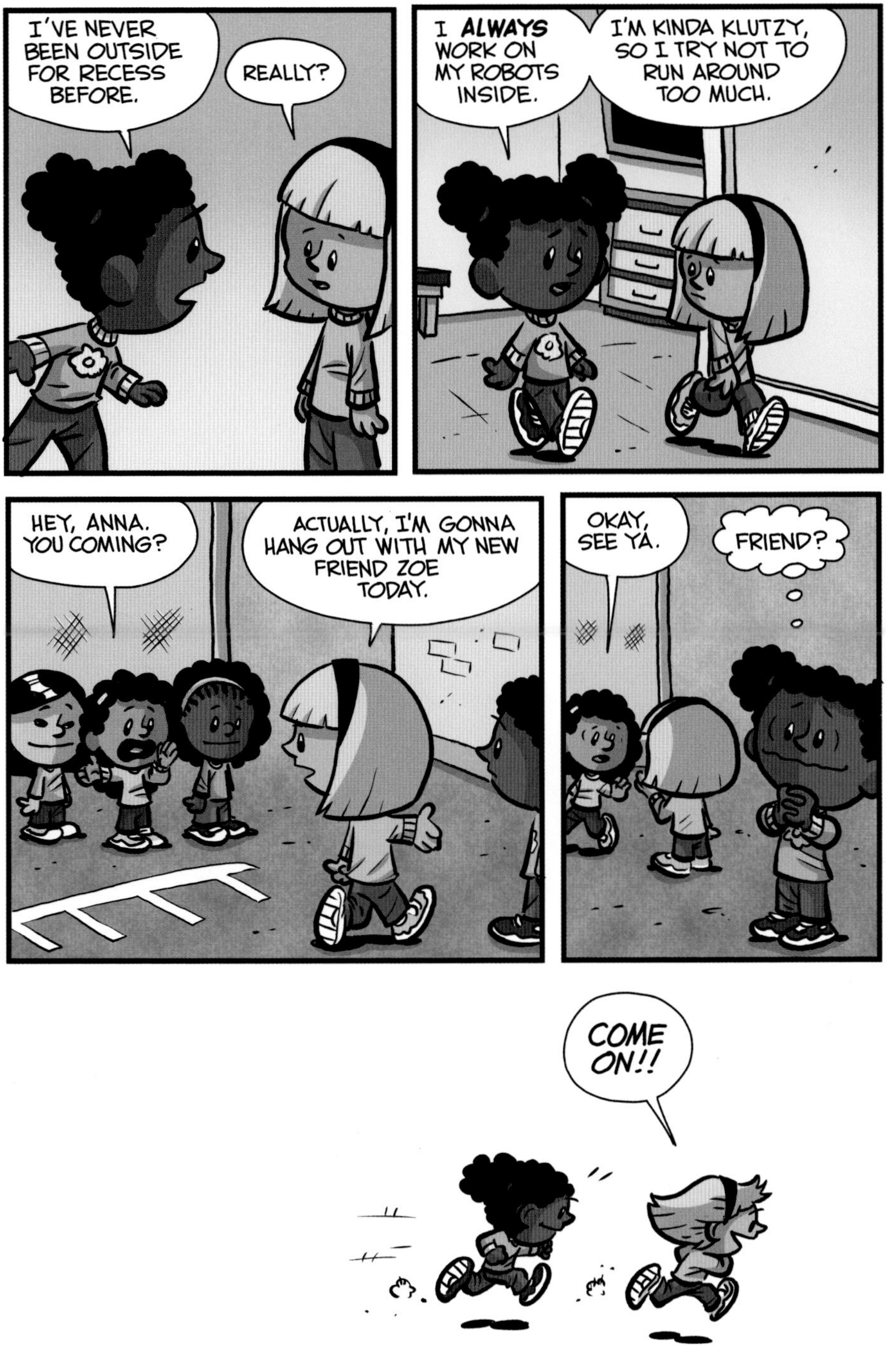
I'VE NEVER BEEN OUTSIDE FOR RECESS BEFORE.
REALLY?
I **ALWAYS** WORK ON MY ROBOTS INSIDE.
I'M KINDA KLUTZY, SO I TRY NOT TO RUN AROUND TOO MUCH.
HEY, ANNA. YOU COMING?
ACTUALLY, I'M GONNA HANG OUT WITH MY NEW FRIEND ZOE TODAY.
OKAY, SEE YA.
FRIEND?
COME ON!!

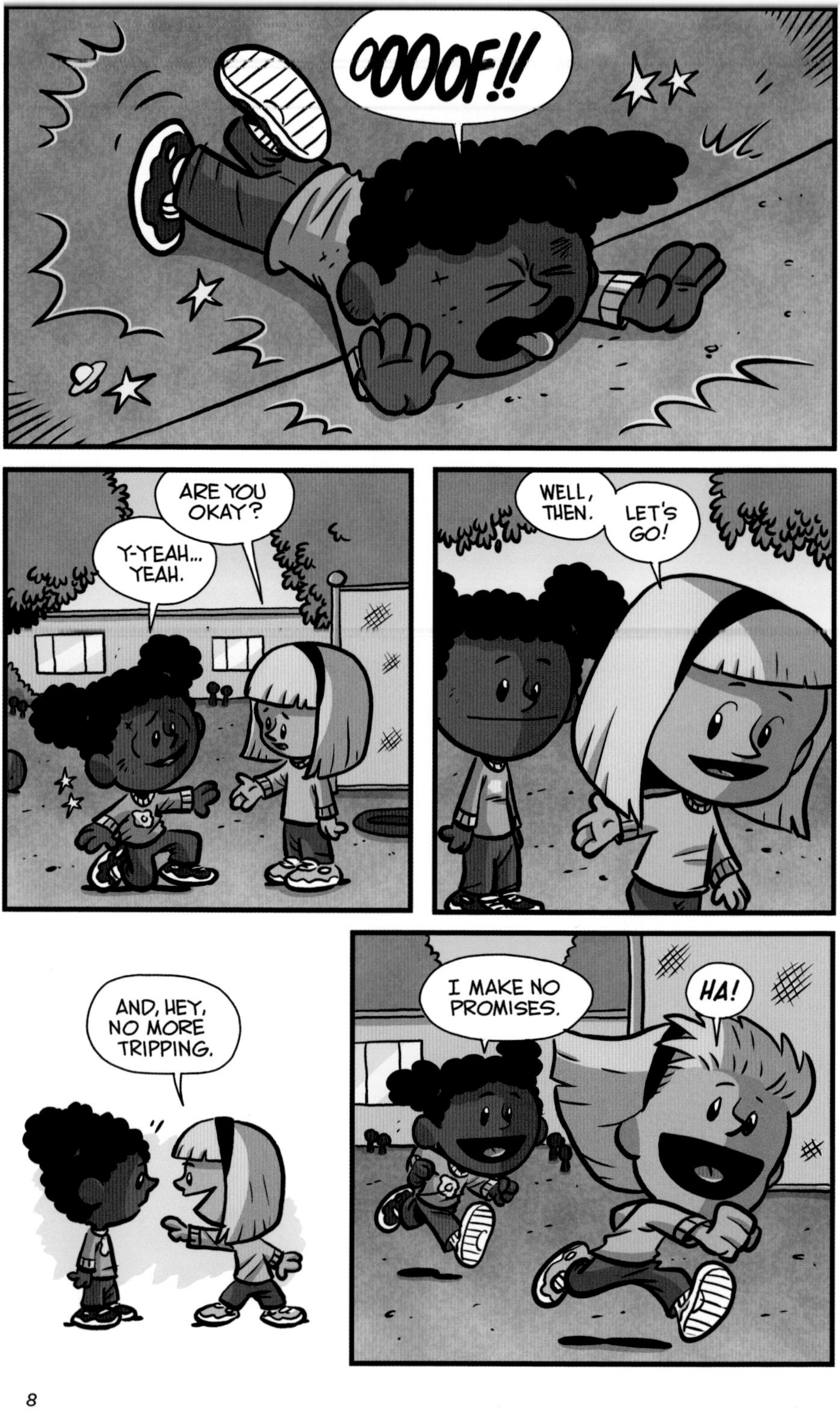
OOOOF!!
ARE YOU OKAY?
Y-YEAH... YEAH.
WELL, THEN.
LET'S GO!
AND, HEY, NO MORE TRIPPING.
I MAKE NO PROMISES.
HA!

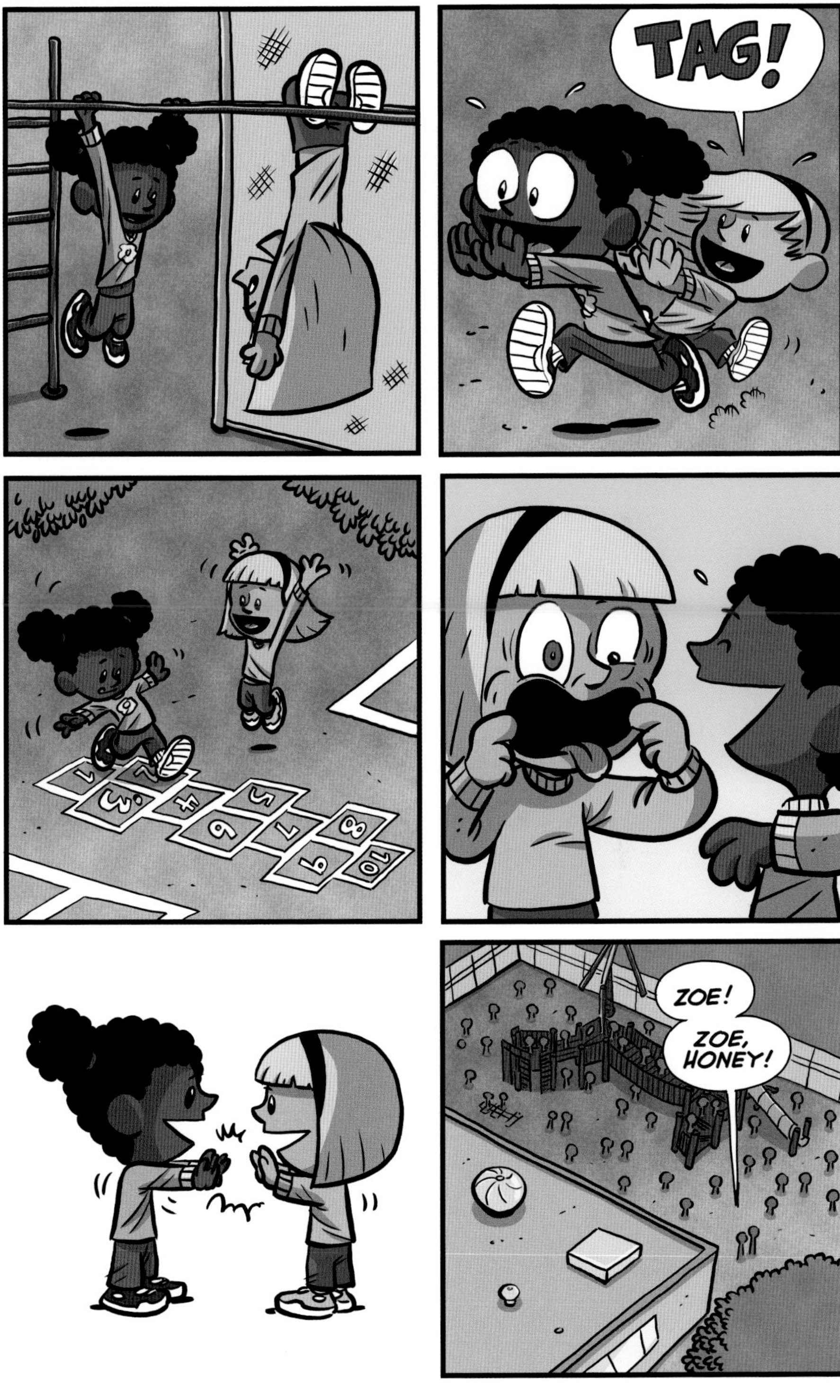
TAG!
ZOE!
ZOE, HONEY!

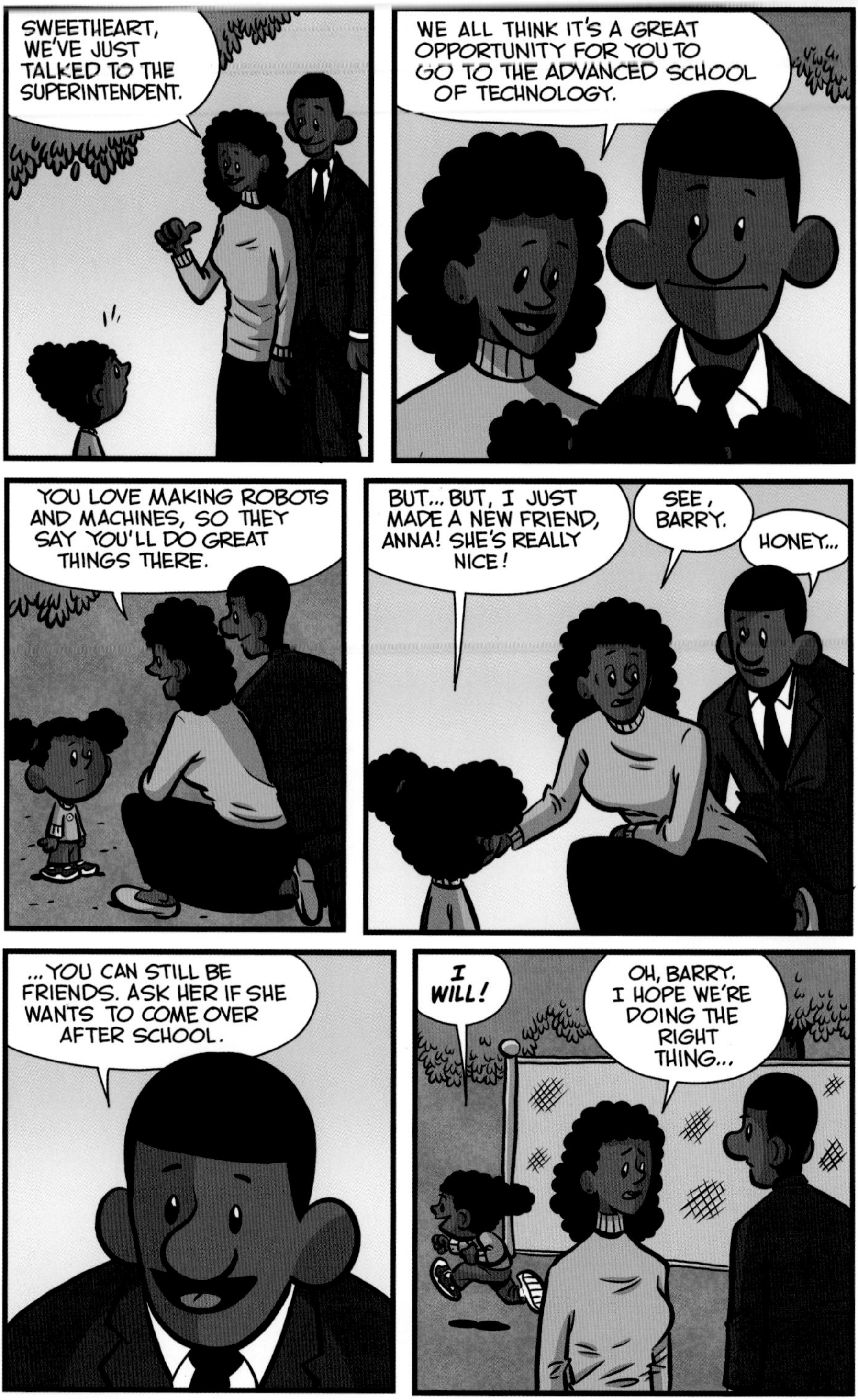
SWEETHEART, WE'VE JUST TALKED TO THE SUPERINTENDENT.
WE ALL THINK IT'S A GREAT OPPORTUNITY FOR YOU TO GO TO THE ADVANCED SCHOOL OF TECHNOLOGY.
YOU LOVE MAKING ROBOTS AND MACHINES, SO THEY SAY YOU'LL DO GREAT THINGS THERE.
BUT... BUT, I JUST MADE A NEW FRIEND, ANNA! SHE'S REALLY NICE!
SEE, BARRY.
HONEY...
...YOU CAN STILL BE FRIENDS. ASK HER IF SHE WANTS TO COME OVER AFTER SCHOOL.
I WILL!
OH, BARRY. I HOPE WE'RE DOING THE RIGHT THING...

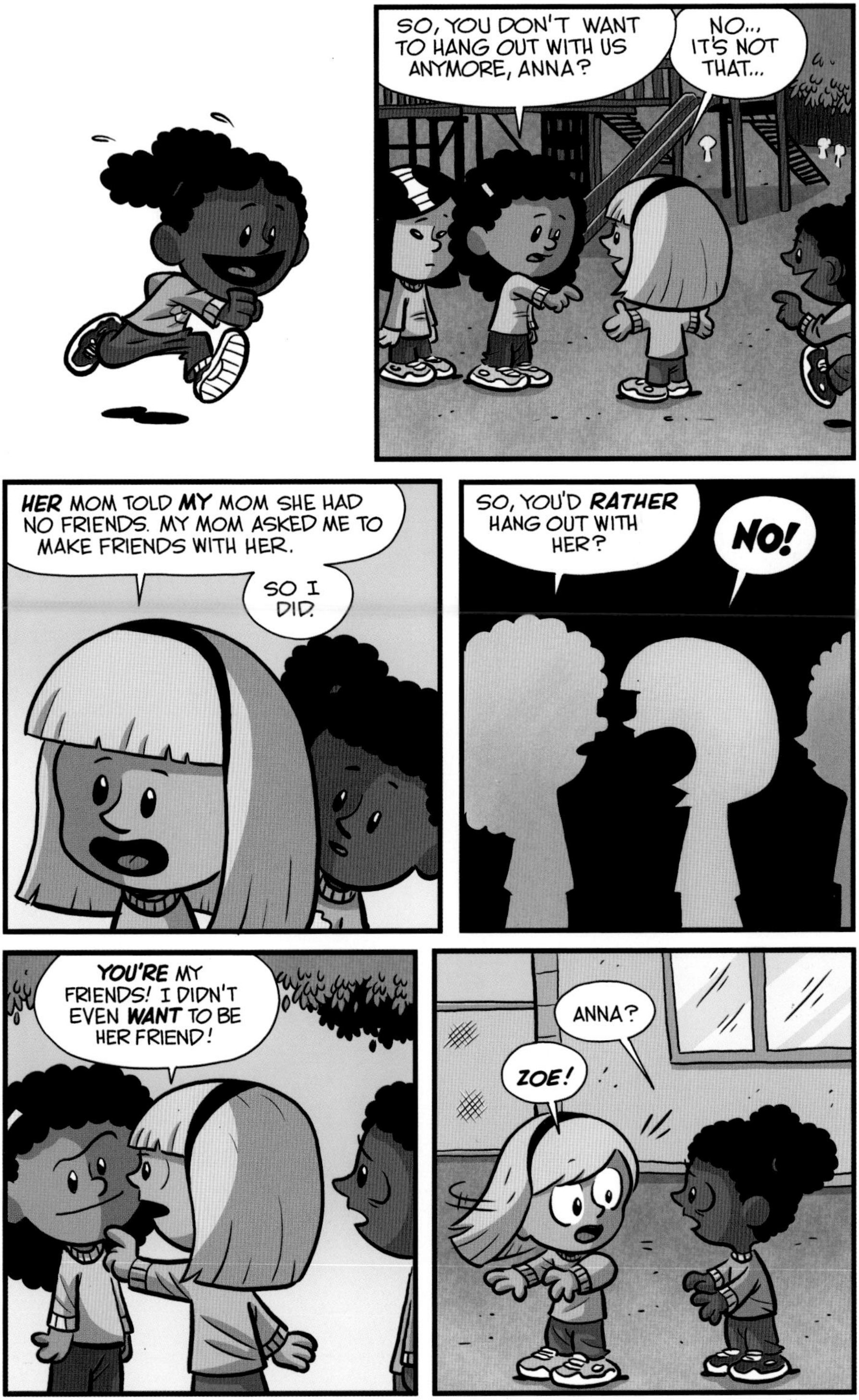
SO, YOU DON'T WANT TO HANG OUT WITH US ANYMORE, ANNA?
NO... IT'S NOT THAT...
HER MOM TOLD MY MOM SHE HAD NO FRIENDS. MY MOM ASKED ME TO MAKE FRIENDS WITH HER.
SO I DID.
SO, YOU'D RATHER HANG OUT WITH HER?
NO!
YOU'RE MY FRIENDS! I DIDN'T EVEN WANT TO BE HER FRIEND!
ANNA?
ZOE!

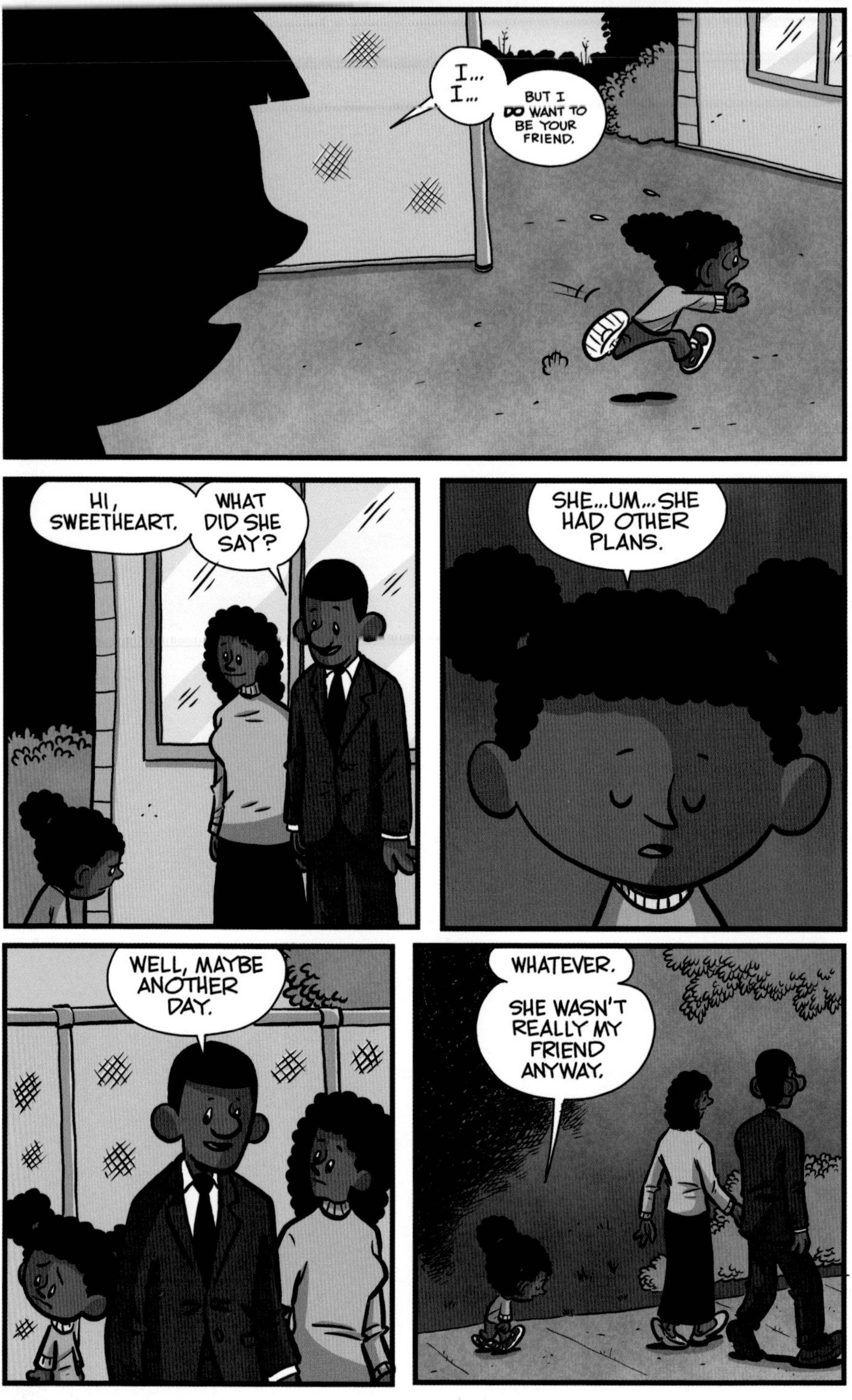
I... I...
BUT I DO WANT TO BE YOUR FRIEND.
HI, SWEETHEART.
WHAT DID SHE SAY?
SHE...UM...SHE HAD OTHER PLANS.
WELL, MAYBE ANOTHER DAY.
WHATEVER.
SHE WASN'T REALLY MY FRIEND ANYWAY.

CHAPTER 2 • KAIJU

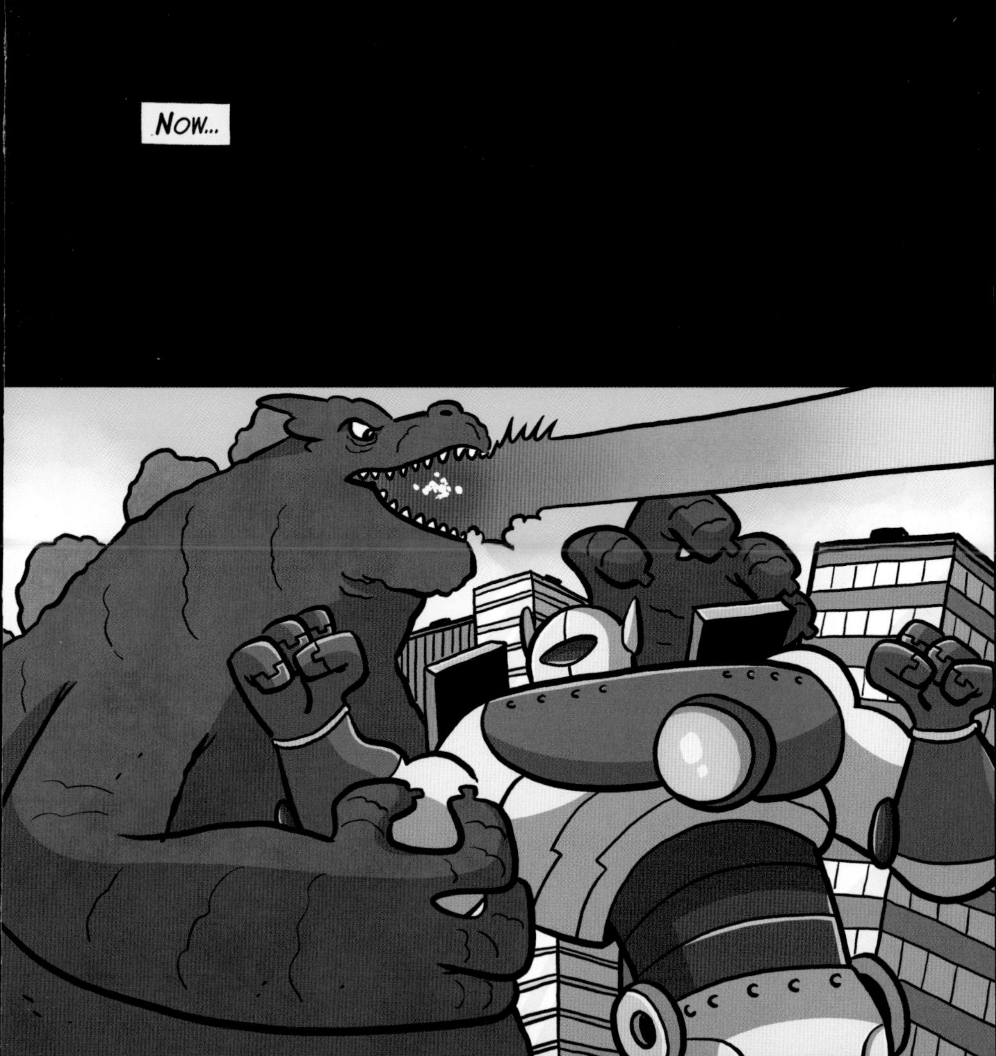
NOW...

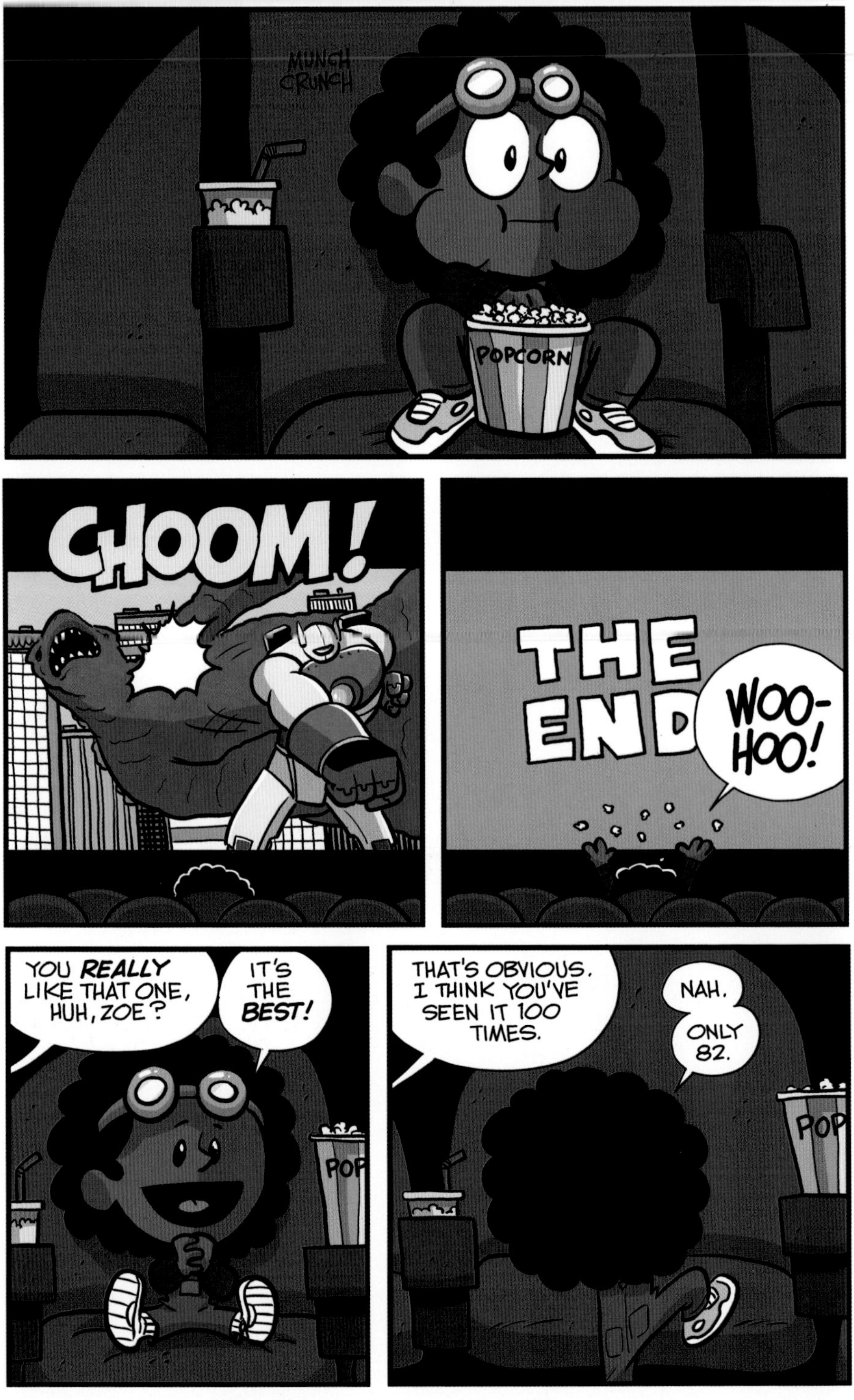
MUNCH CRUNCH
POPCORN
CHOOM!
THE END
WOO-HOO!
YOU *REALLY* LIKE THAT ONE, HUH, ZOE?
IT'S THE *BEST*!
THAT'S OBVIOUS. I THINK YOU'VE SEEN IT 100 TIMES.
NAH.
ONLY 82.
POP

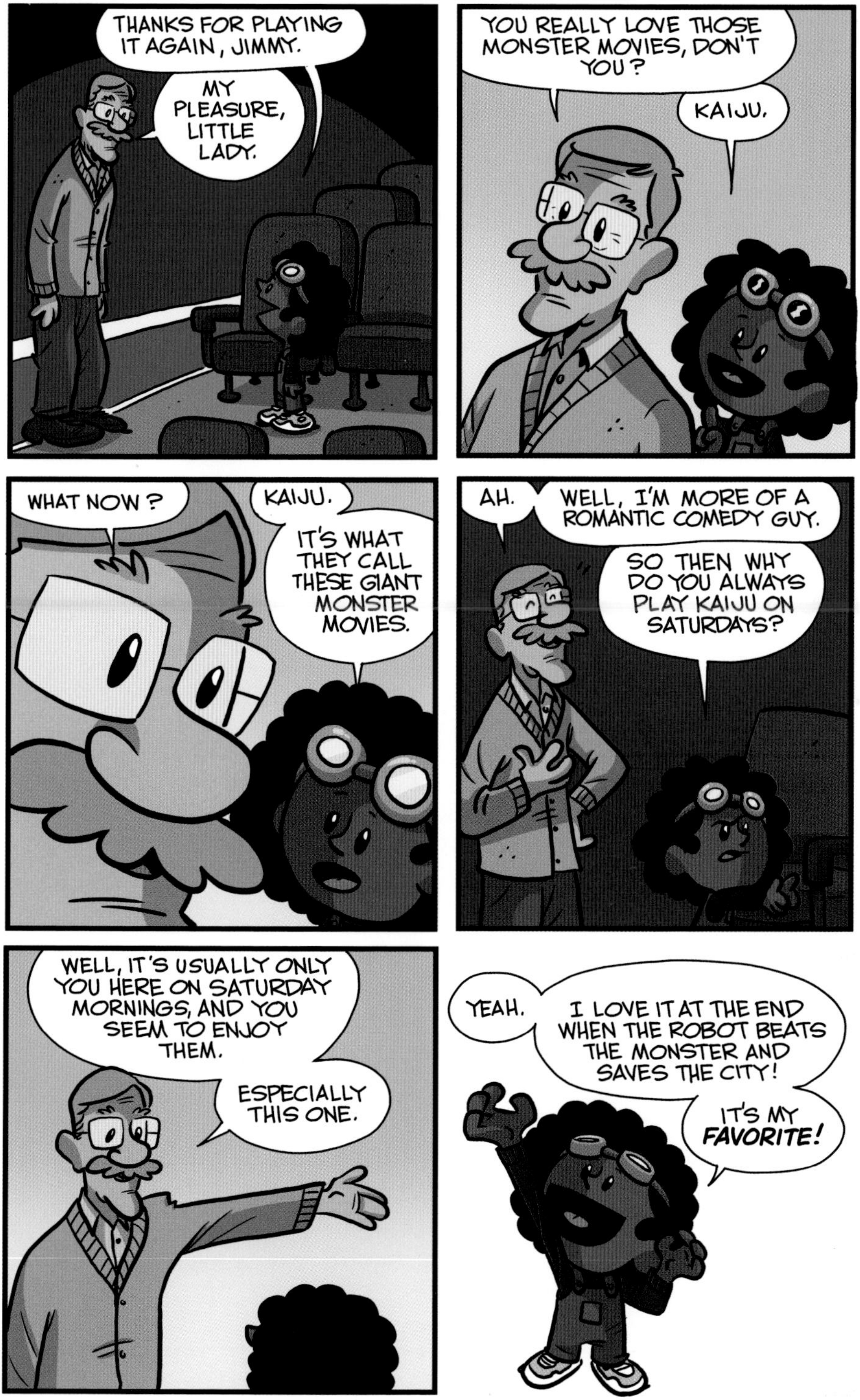
THANKS FOR PLAYING IT AGAIN, JIMMY.
MY PLEASURE, LITTLE LADY.
YOU REALLY LOVE THOSE MONSTER MOVIES, DON'T YOU?
KAIJU.
WHAT NOW?
KAIJU.
IT'S WHAT THEY CALL THESE GIANT MONSTER MOVIES.
AH.
WELL, I'M MORE OF A ROMANTIC COMEDY GUY.
SO THEN WHY DO YOU ALWAYS PLAY KAIJU ON SATURDAYS?
WELL, IT'S USUALLY ONLY YOU HERE ON SATURDAY MORNINGS, AND YOU SEEM TO ENJOY THEM.
ESPECIALLY THIS ONE.
YEAH.
I LOVE IT AT THE END WHEN THE ROBOT BEATS THE MONSTER AND SAVES THE CITY!
IT'S MY **FAVORITE!**

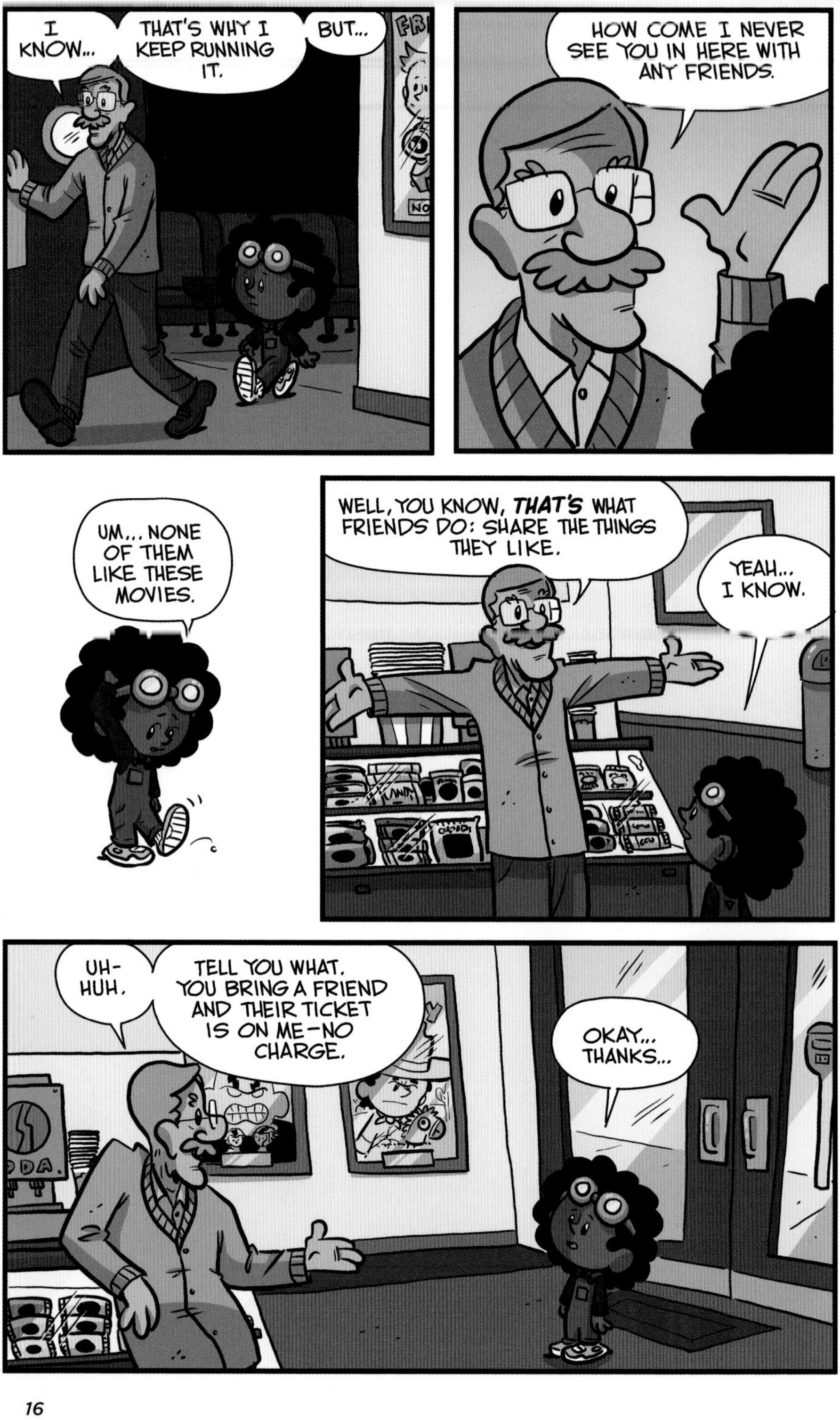
I KNOW...
THAT'S WHY I KEEP RUNNING IT.
BUT...
HOW COME I NEVER SEE YOU IN HERE WITH ANY FRIENDS.
UM... NONE OF THEM LIKE THESE MOVIES.
WELL, YOU KNOW, *THAT'S* WHAT FRIENDS DO: SHARE THE THINGS THEY LIKE.
YEAH... I KNOW.
UH-HUH.
TELL YOU WHAT. YOU BRING A FRIEND AND THEIR TICKET IS ON ME—NO CHARGE.
OKAY... THANKS...

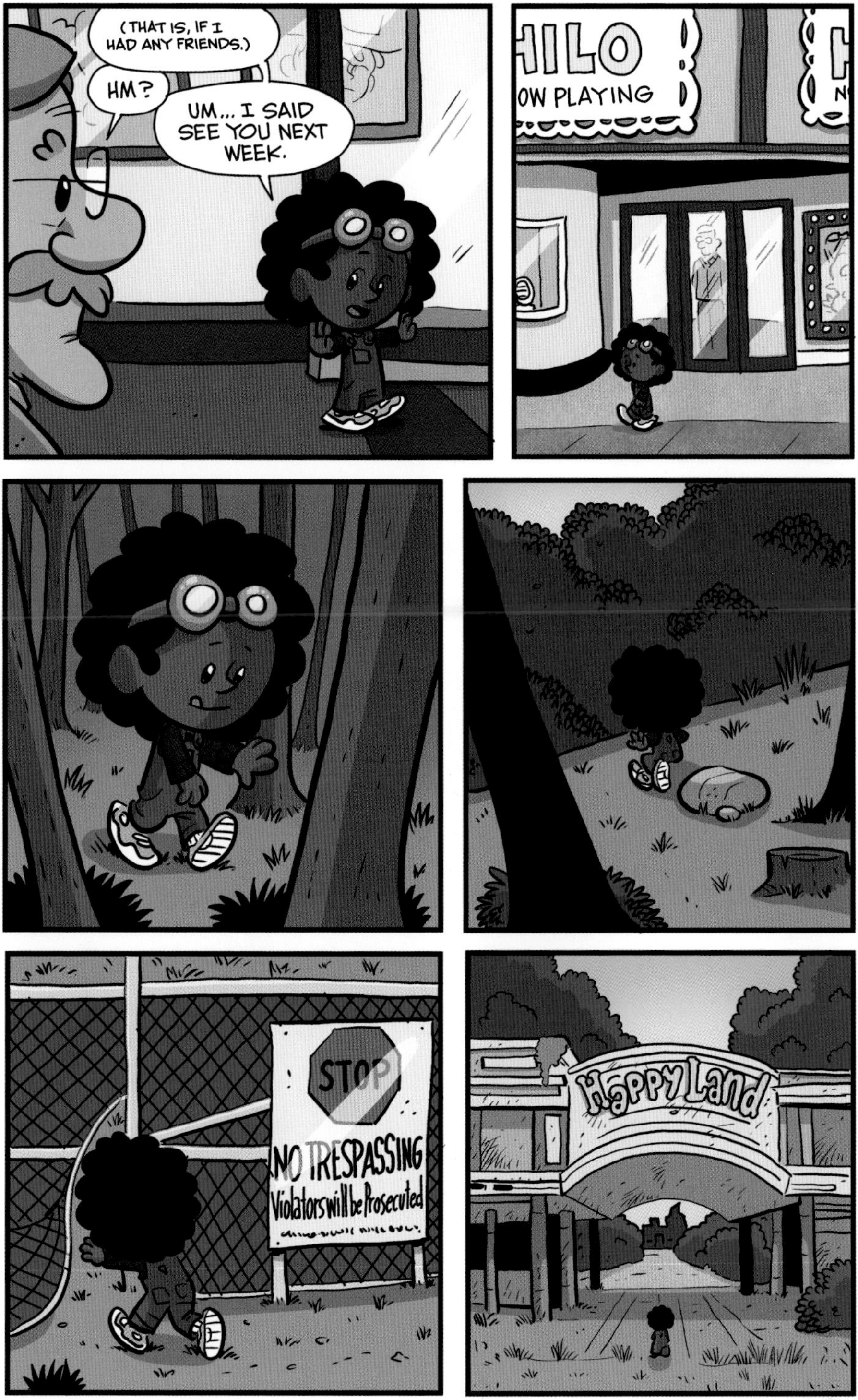

(THAT IS, IF I HAD ANY FRIENDS.)
HM?
UM... I SAID SEE YOU NEXT WEEK.
HILO
OW PLAYING
STOP
NO TRESPASSING
Violators will be Prosecuted
Happy Land

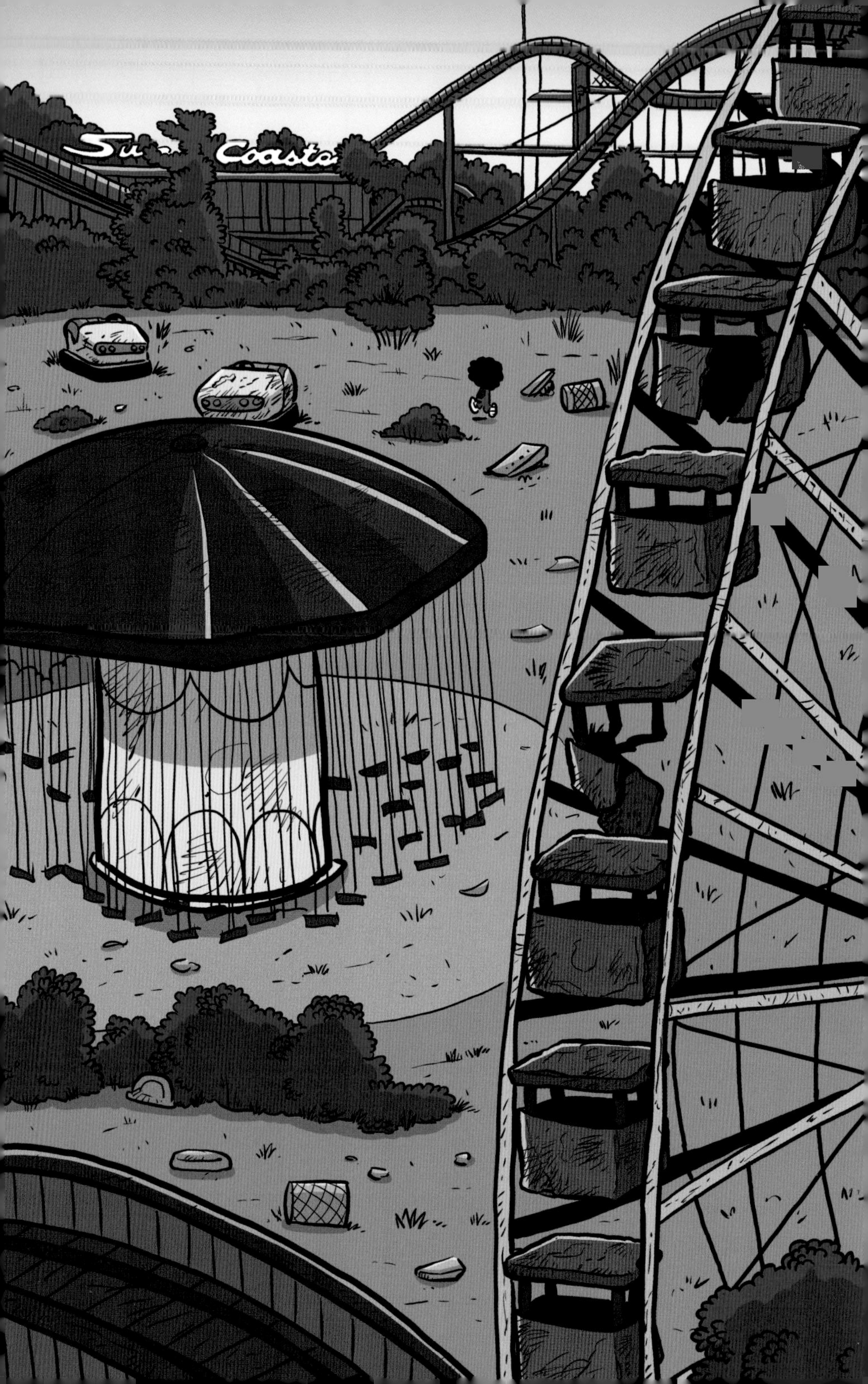

AHHHHHHHHHHHHHHHHH!

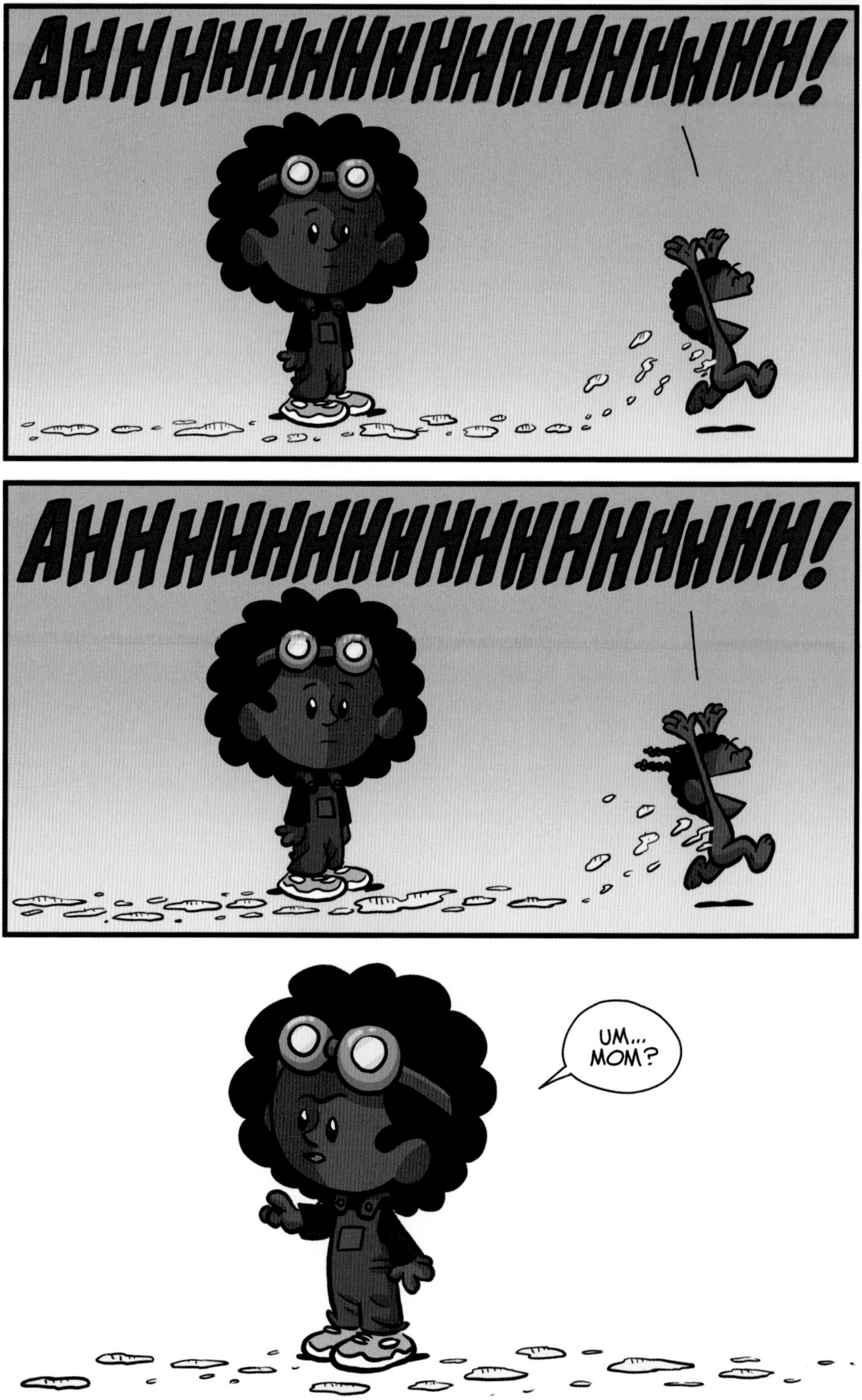
AHHHHHHHHHHHHHHHHHHH!
AHHHHHHHHHHHHHHHHHHH!
UM... MOM?

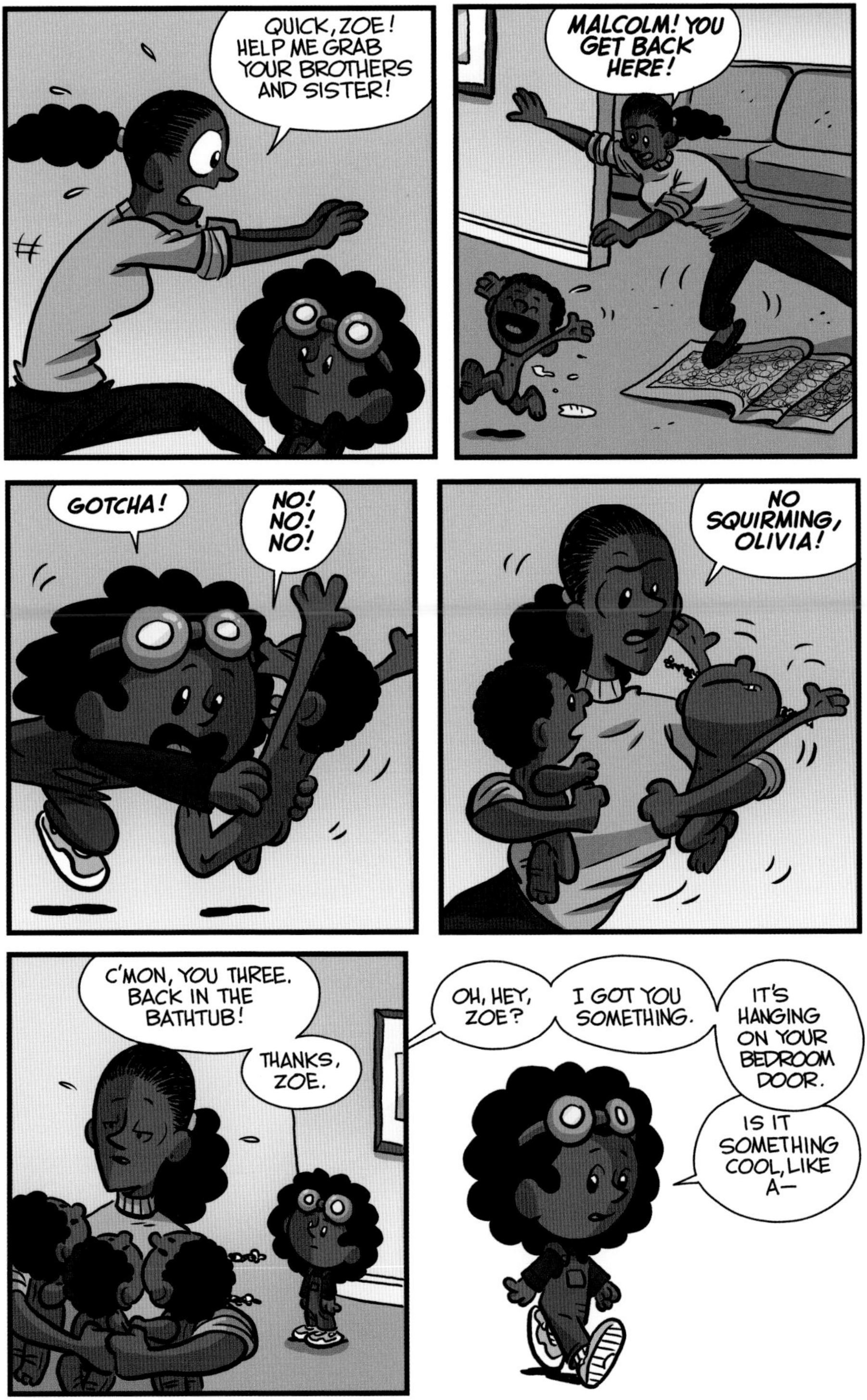
QUICK, ZOE! HELP ME GRAB YOUR BROTHERS AND SISTER!
MALCOLM! YOU GET BACK HERE!
GOTCHA!
NO! NO! NO!
NO SQUIRMING, OLIVIA!
C'MON, YOU THREE. BACK IN THE BATHTUB!
THANKS, ZOE.
OH, HEY, ZOE?
I GOT YOU SOMETHING.
IT'S HANGING ON YOUR BEDROOM DOOR.
IS IT SOMETHING COOL, LIKE A—

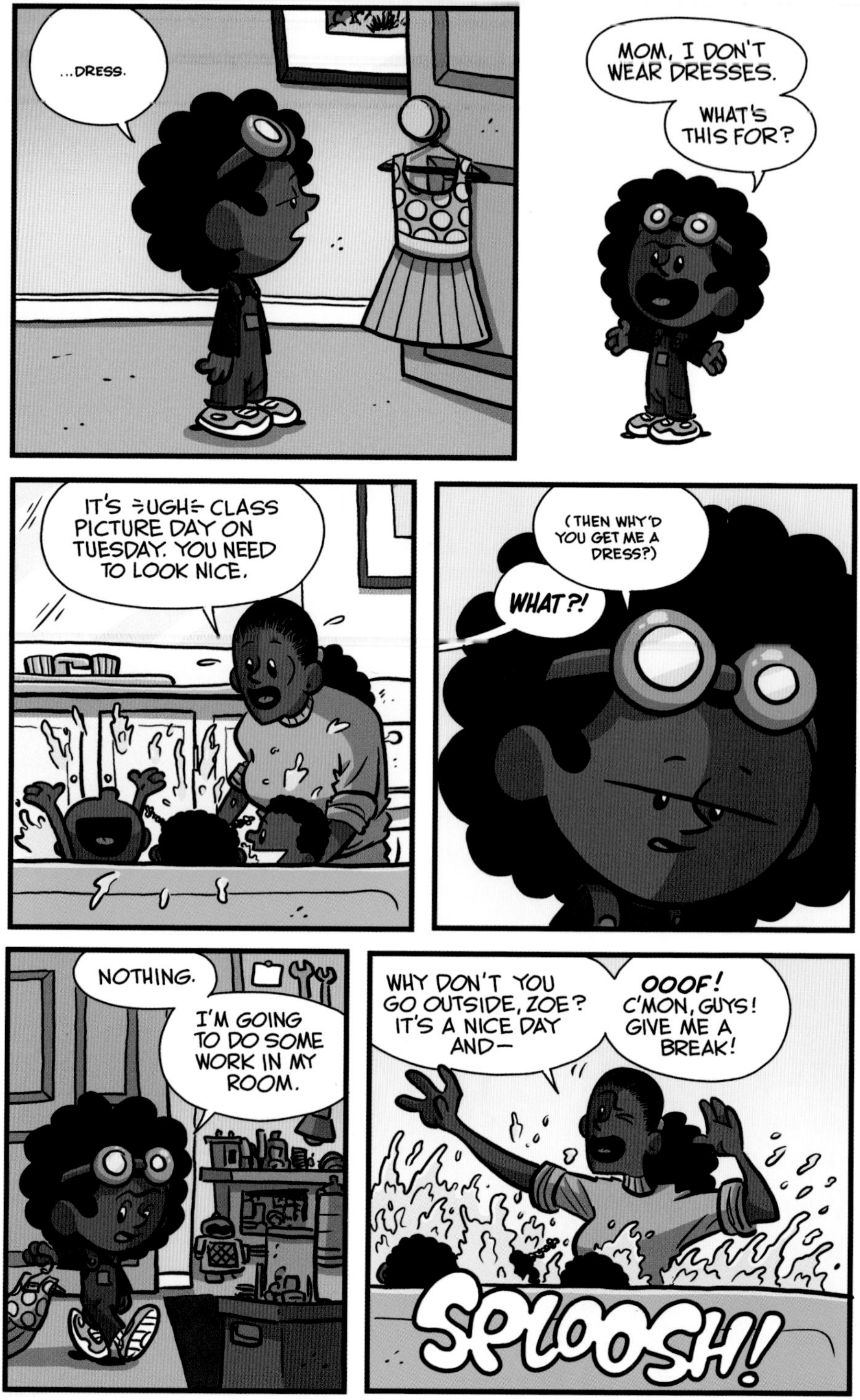
...DRESS.
MOM, I DON'T WEAR DRESSES.
WHAT'S THIS FOR?
IT'S =UGH= CLASS PICTURE DAY ON TUESDAY. YOU NEED TO LOOK NICE.
(THEN WHY'D YOU GET ME A DRESS?)
WHAT?!
NOTHING.
I'M GOING TO DO SOME WORK IN MY ROOM.
WHY DON'T YOU GO OUTSIDE, ZOE? IT'S A NICE DAY AND—
OOOF! C'MON, GUYS! GIVE ME A BREAK!
SPLOOSH!

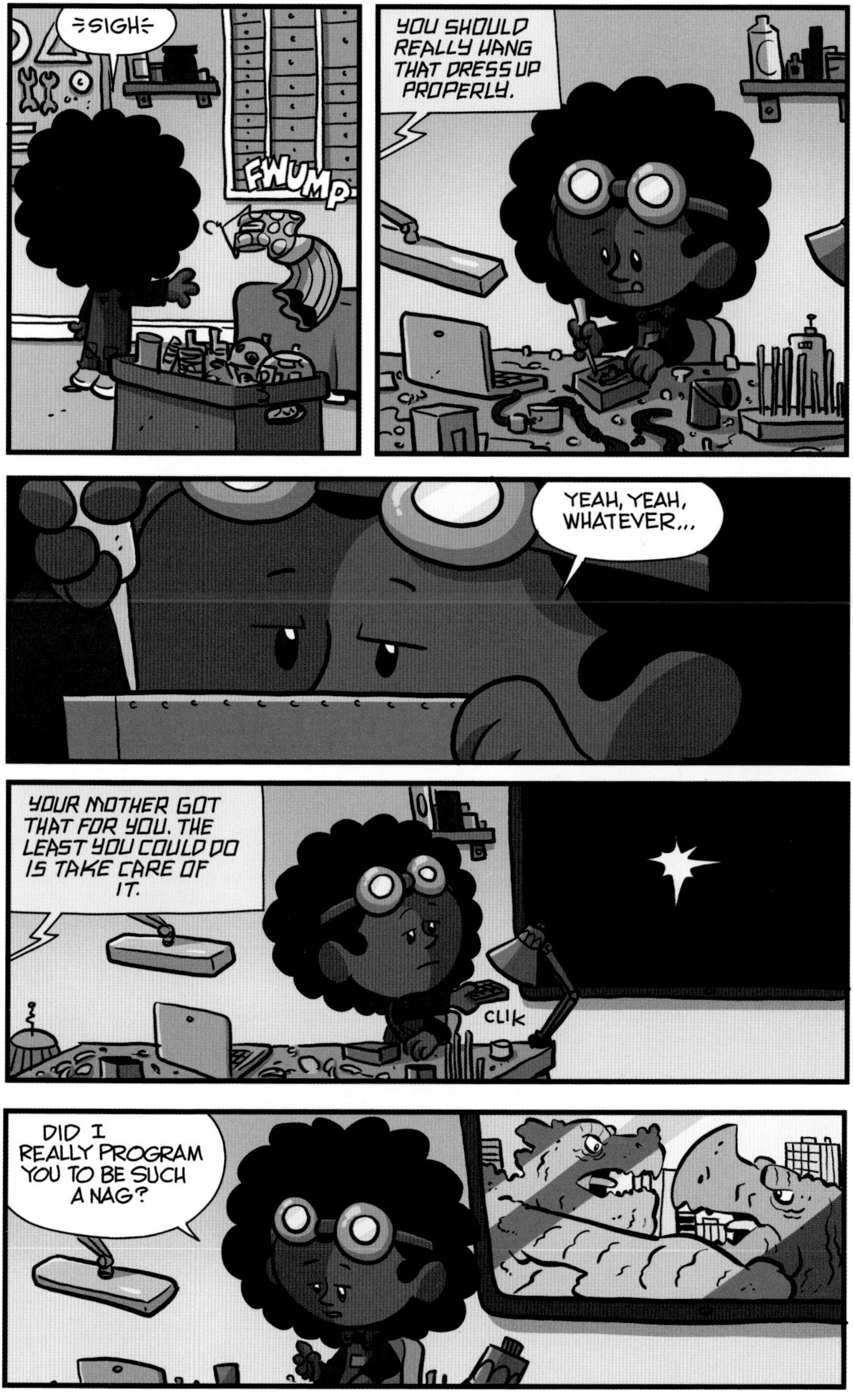
SIGH
FWUMP
YOU SHOULD REALLY HANG THAT DRESS UP PROPERLY.
YEAH, YEAH, WHATEVER...
YOUR MOTHER GOT THAT FOR YOU. THE LEAST YOU COULD DO IS TAKE CARE OF IT.
CLIK
DID I REALLY PROGRAM YOU TO BE SUCH A NAG?

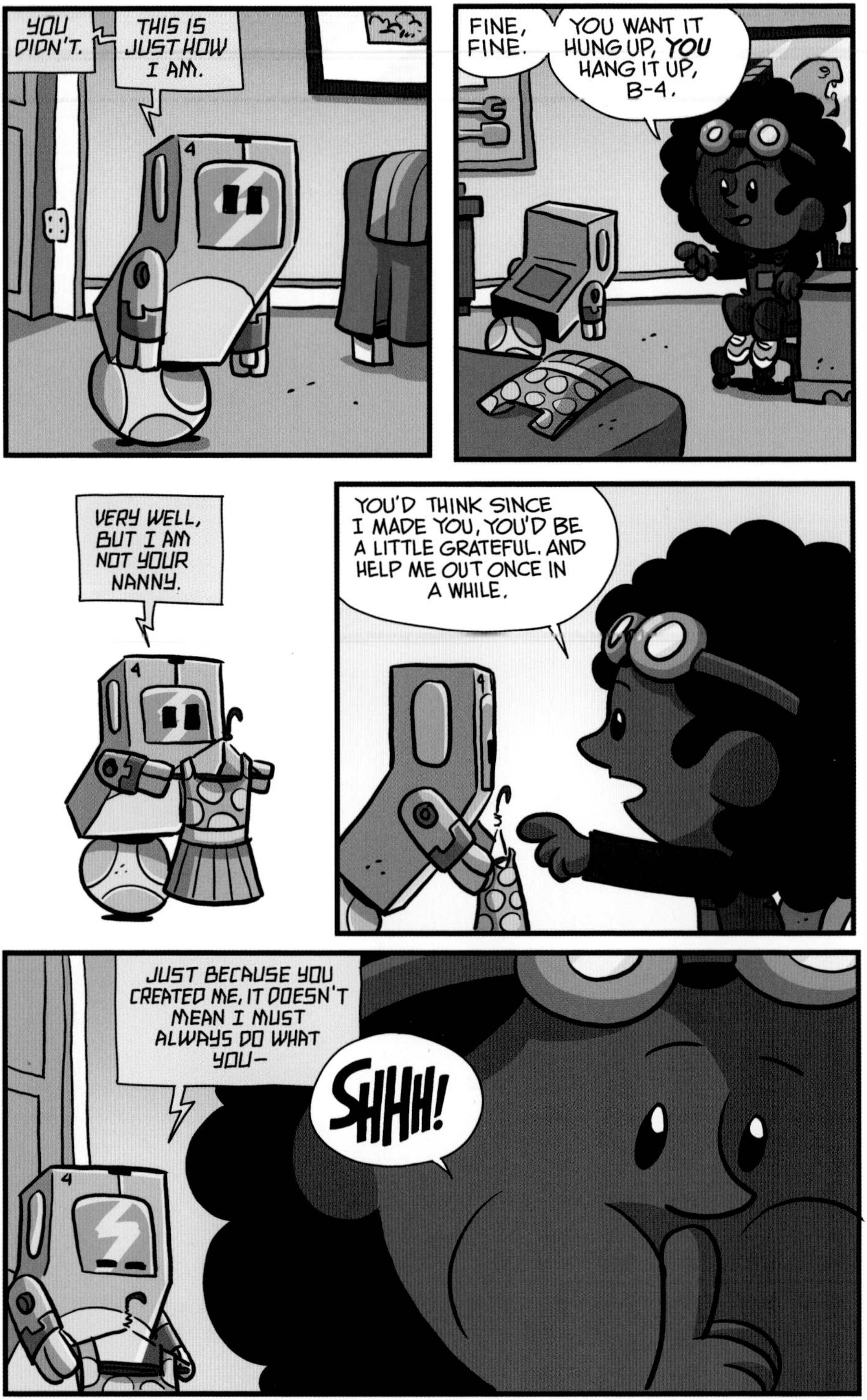
YOU DIDN'T.
THIS IS JUST HOW I AM.
FINE, FINE.
YOU WANT IT HUNG UP, YOU HANG IT UP, B-4.
VERY WELL, BUT I AM NOT YOUR NANNY.
YOU'D THINK SINCE I MADE YOU, YOU'D BE A LITTLE GRATEFUL. AND HELP ME OUT ONCE IN A WHILE.
JUST BECAUSE YOU CREATED ME, IT DOESN'T MEAN I MUST ALWAYS DO WHAT YOU—
SHHH!

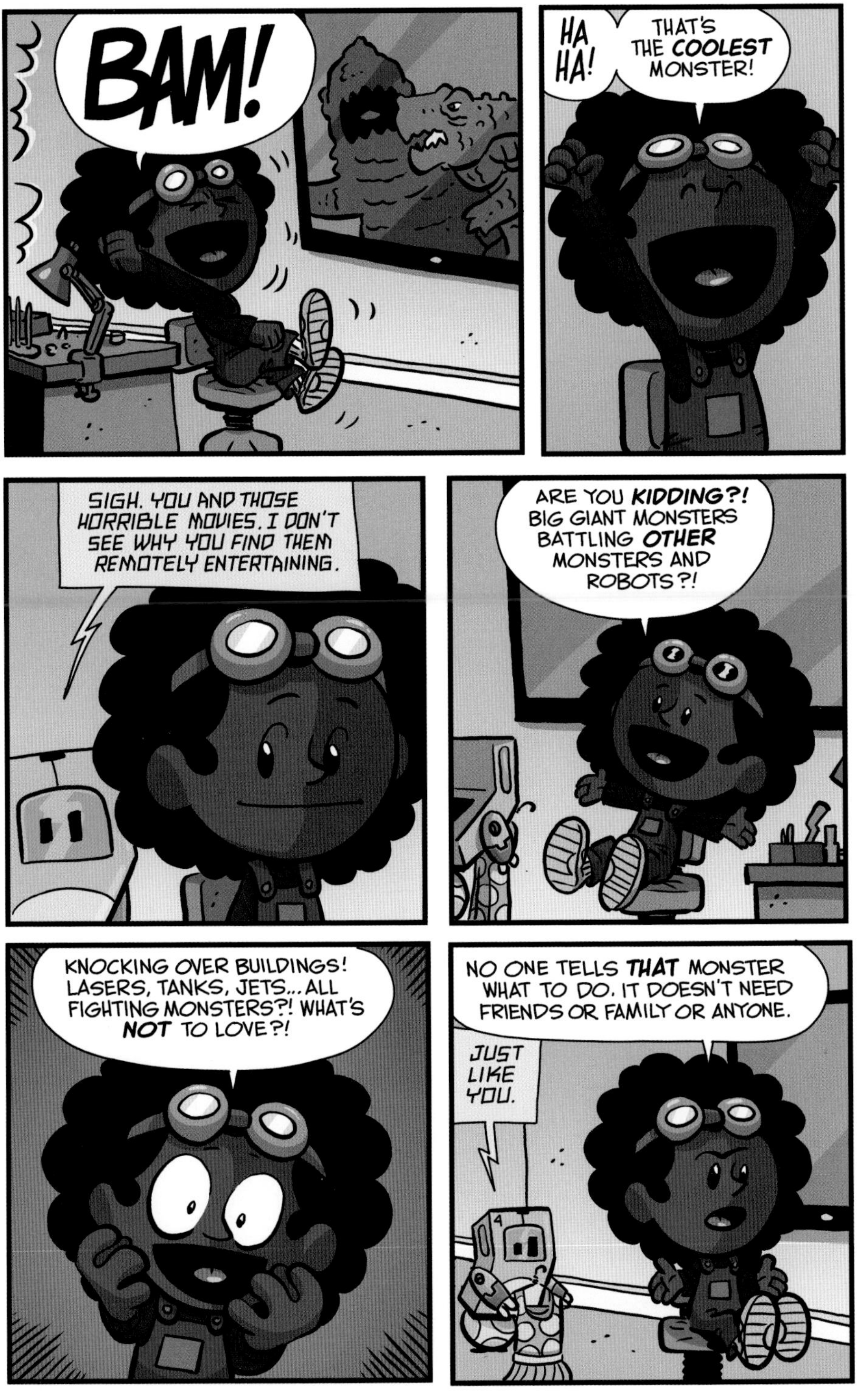
BAM!
HA HA!
THAT'S THE COOLEST MONSTER!
SIGH. YOU AND THOSE HORRIBLE MOVIES. I DON'T SEE WHY YOU FIND THEM REMOTELY ENTERTAINING.
ARE YOU KIDDING?! BIG GIANT MONSTERS BATTLING OTHER MONSTERS AND ROBOTS?!
KNOCKING OVER BUILDINGS! LASERS, TANKS, JETS... ALL FIGHTING MONSTERS?! WHAT'S NOT TO LOVE?!
NO ONE TELLS THAT MONSTER WHAT TO DO. IT DOESN'T NEED FRIENDS OR FAMILY OR ANYONE.
JUST LIKE YOU.

YEAH. NOW GO HANG UP THE DRESS.

GUESS YOU *DO* NEED ME.

OH, BE QUIET.

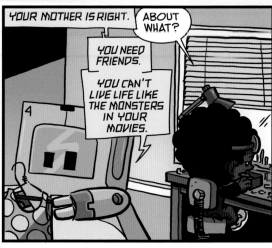

YOUR MOTHER IS RIGHT.

ABOUT WHAT?

YOU NEED FRIENDS.

YOU CAN'T LIVE LIFE LIKE THE MONSTERS IN YOUR MOVIES.

IT IS NOT HEALTHY FOR A YOUNG PERSON TO SIT ALONE IN *HER* ROOM WORKING ON ROBOTS AND WATCHING MONSTER MOVIES.

YOU KNOW WHAT? I DON'T NEED FRIENDS. ALL THEY DO IS *HURT* YOU. I DON'T NEED THEM!

I'M FINE ON *MY* OWN!

AND BESIDES, IF I *DIDN'T* SIT HERE ALL THE TIME...

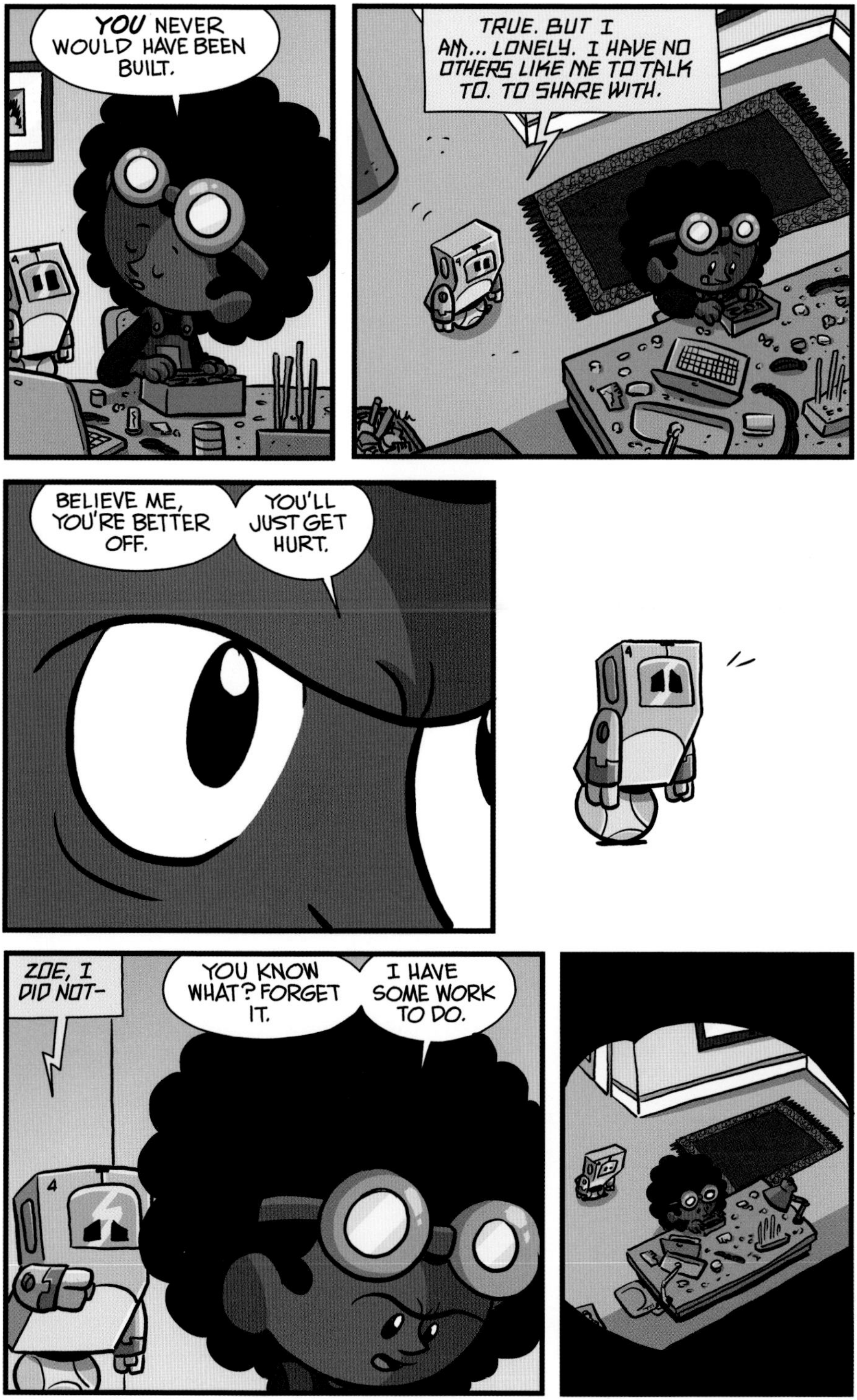
YOU NEVER WOULD HAVE BEEN BUILT.
TRUE. BUT I AM... LONELY. I HAVE NO OTHERS LIKE ME TO TALK TO. TO SHARE WITH.
BELIEVE ME, YOU'RE BETTER OFF.
YOU'LL JUST GET HURT.
ZOE, I DID NOT-
YOU KNOW WHAT? FORGET IT.
I HAVE SOME WORK TO DO.

CHAPTER 3 - GO BIG OR GO HOME

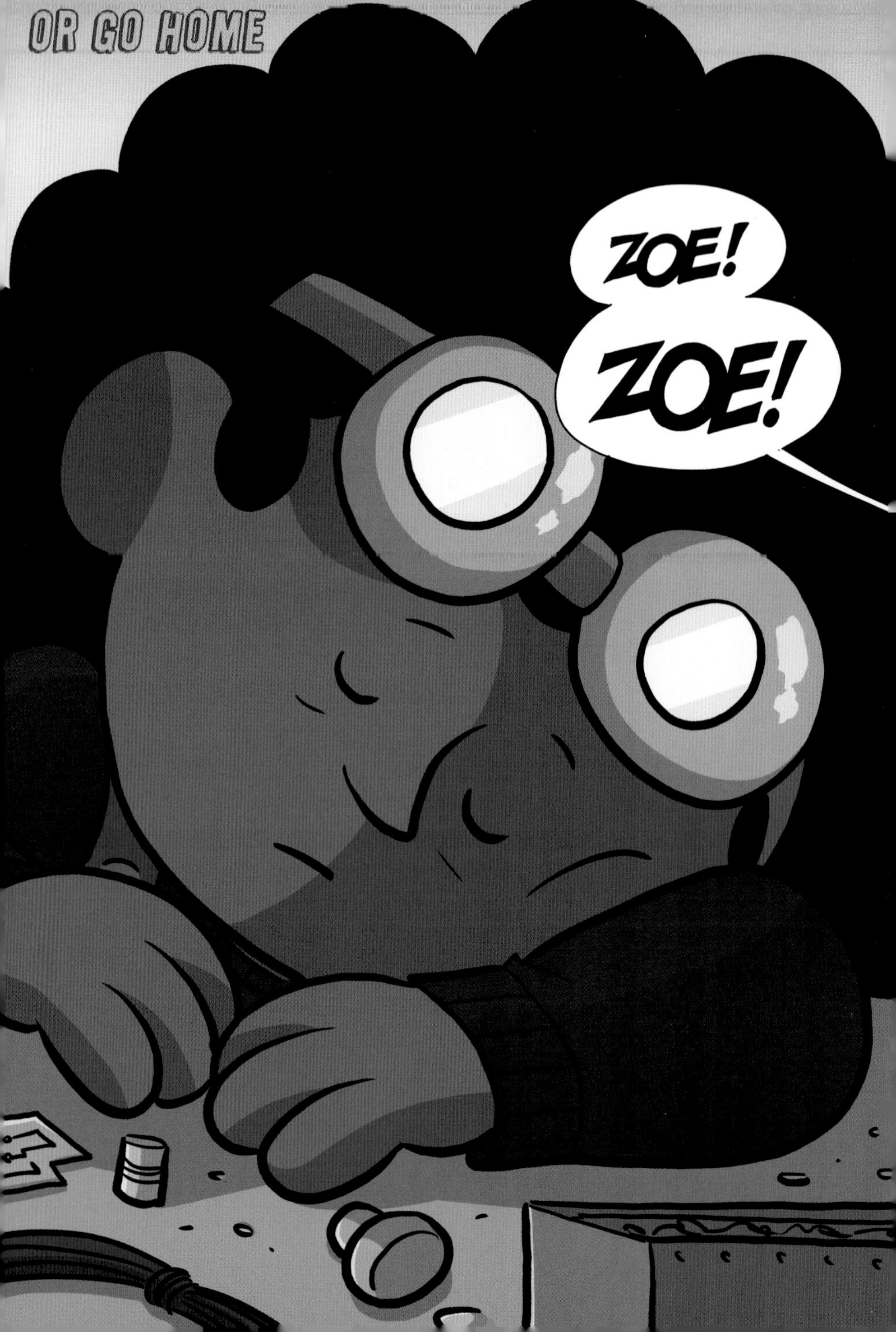
ZOE!
ZOE!

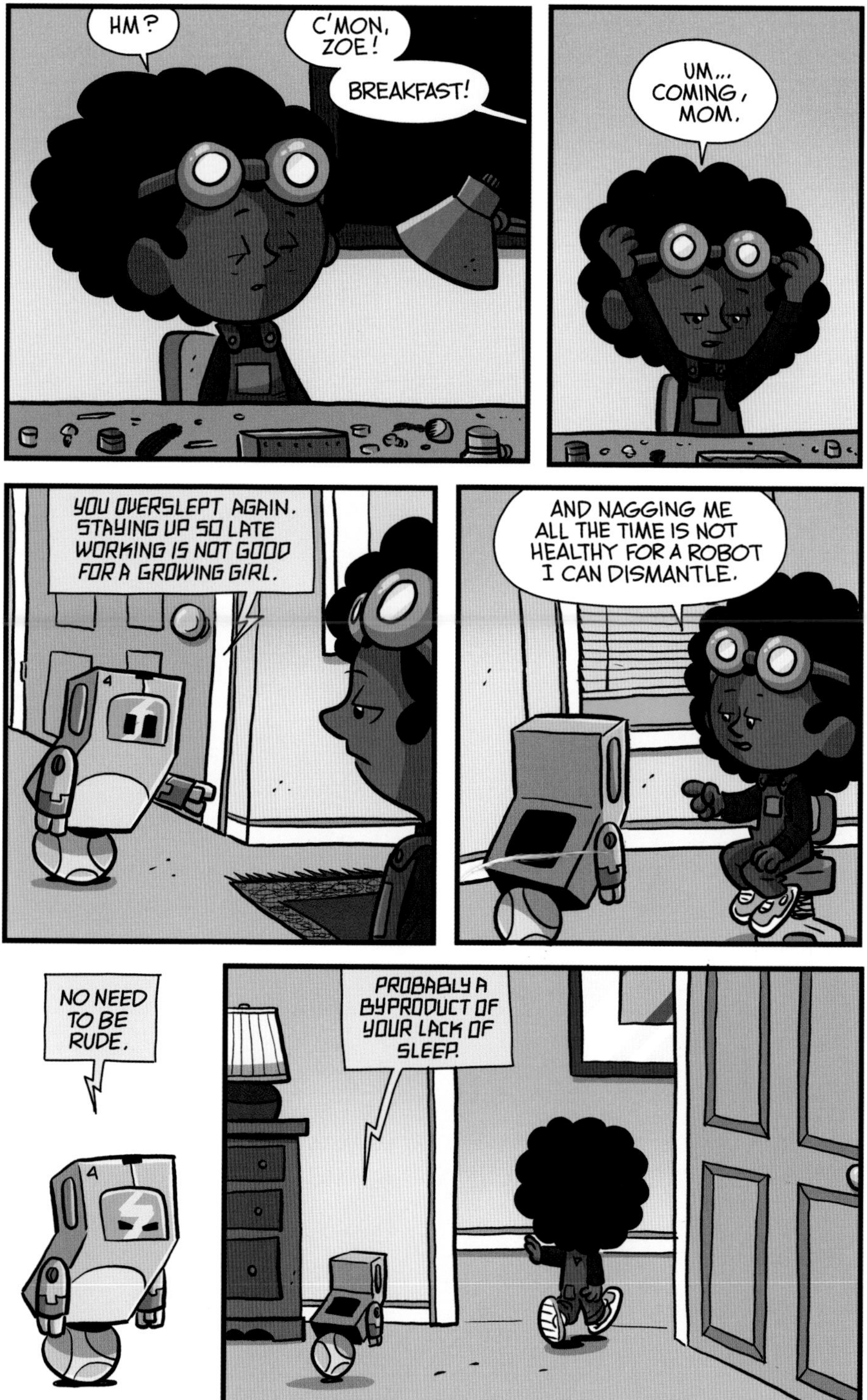
HM?
C'MON, ZOE!
BREAKFAST!
UM... COMING, MOM.
YOU OVERSLEPT AGAIN. STAYING UP SO LATE WORKING IS NOT GOOD FOR A GROWING GIRL.
AND NAGGING ME ALL THE TIME IS NOT HEALTHY FOR A ROBOT I CAN DISMANTLE.
NO NEED TO BE RUDE.
PROBABLY A BYPRODUCT OF YOUR LACK OF SLEEP.

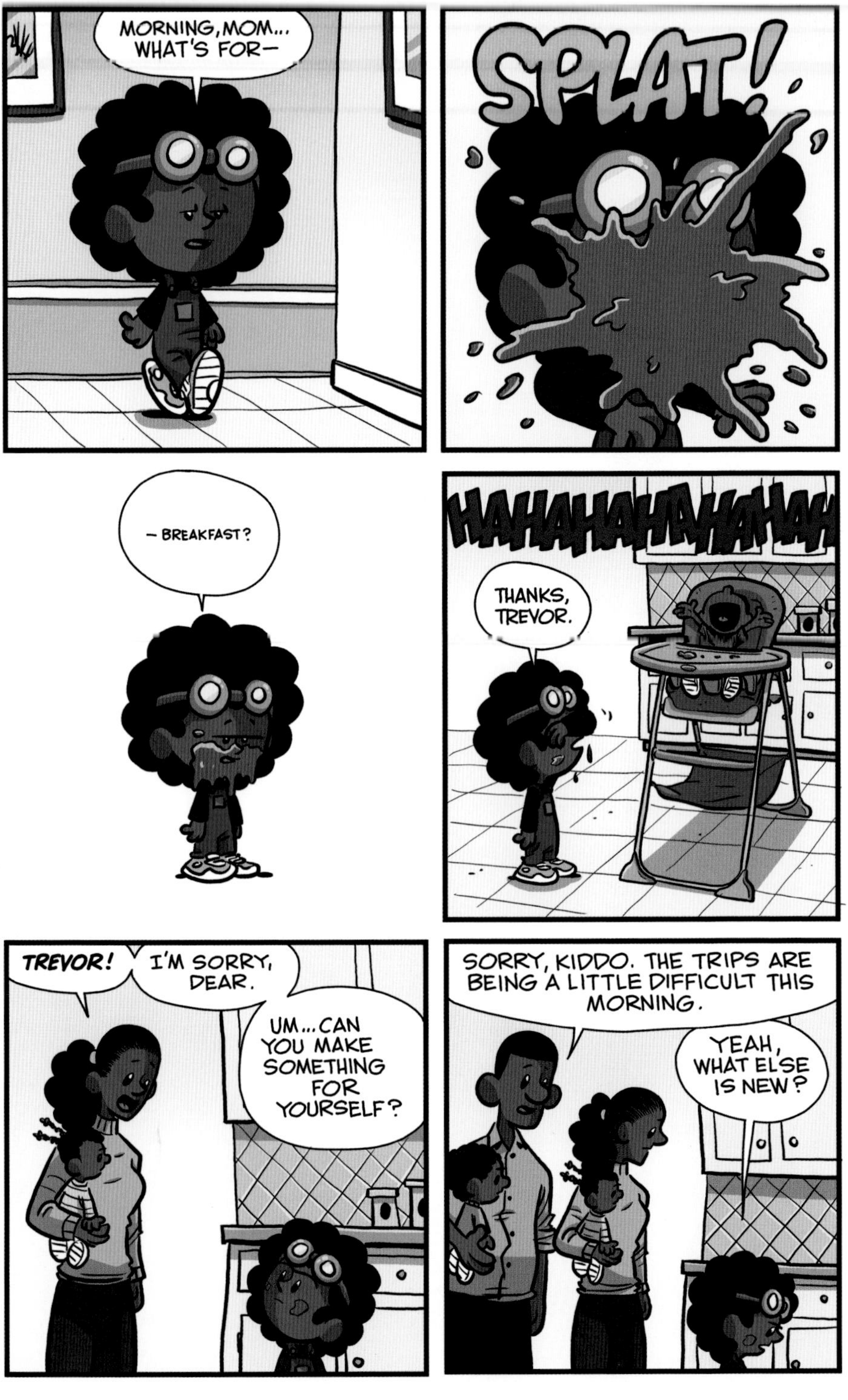
MORNING, MOM... WHAT'S FOR—
SPLAT!
— BREAKFAST?
HAHAHAHAHAHAHAH
THANKS, TREVOR.
TREVOR!
I'M SORRY, DEAR.
UM... CAN YOU MAKE SOMETHING FOR YOURSELF?
SORRY, KIDDO. THE TRIPS ARE BEING A LITTLE DIFFICULT THIS MORNING.
YEAH, WHAT ELSE IS NEW?

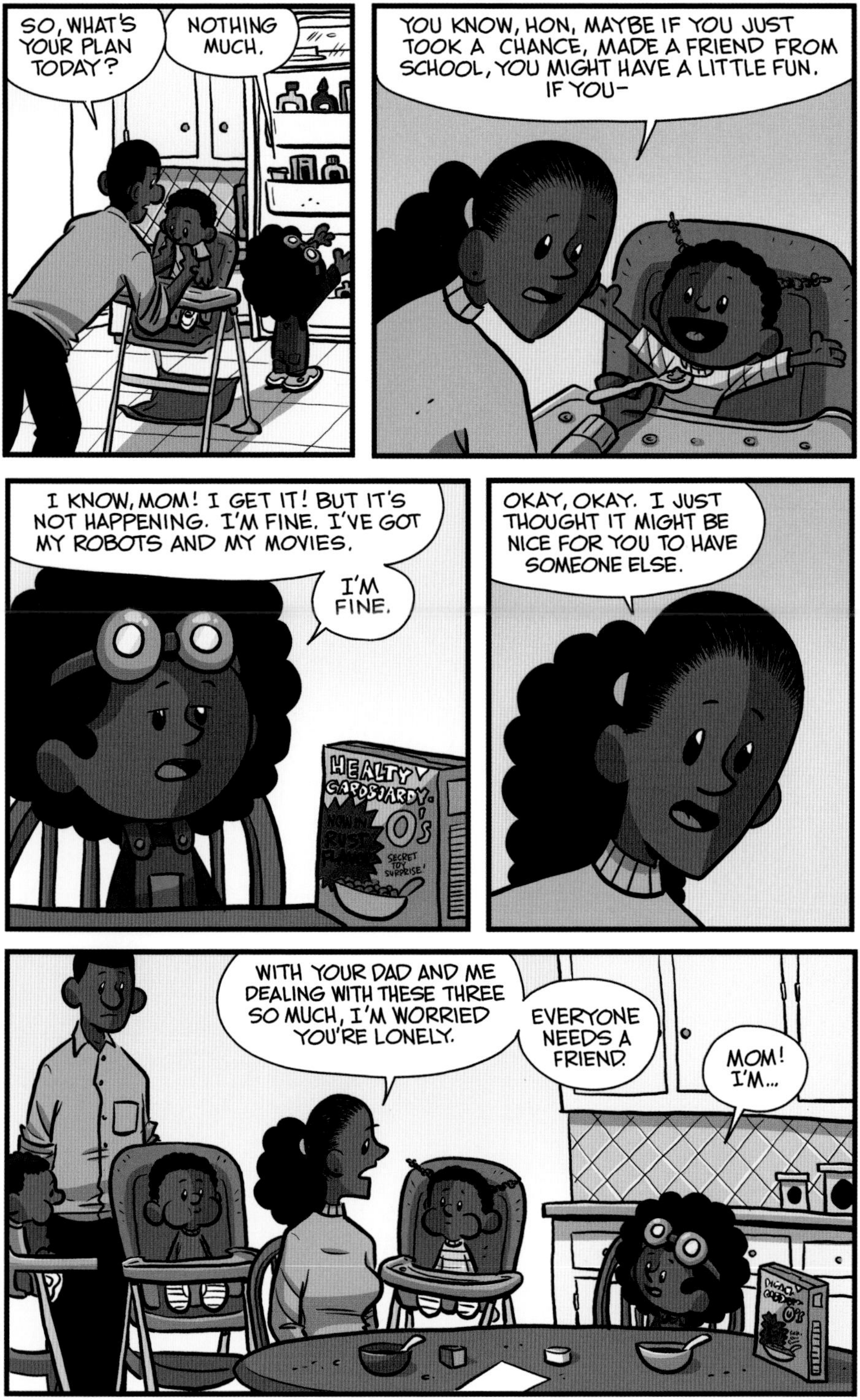
SO, WHAT'S YOUR PLAN TODAY?
NOTHING MUCH.
YOU KNOW, HON, MAYBE IF YOU JUST TOOK A CHANCE, MADE A FRIEND FROM SCHOOL, YOU MIGHT HAVE A LITTLE FUN. IF YOU-
I KNOW, MOM! I GET IT! BUT IT'S NOT HAPPENING. I'M FINE. I'VE GOT MY ROBOTS AND MY MOVIES.
I'M FINE.
HEALTY
O's
SECRET TOY SURPRISE!
OKAY, OKAY. I JUST THOUGHT IT MIGHT BE NICE FOR YOU TO HAVE SOMEONE ELSE.
WITH YOUR DAD AND ME DEALING WITH THESE THREE SO MUCH, I'M WORRIED YOU'RE LONELY.
EVERYONE NEEDS A FRIEND.
MOM! I'M...

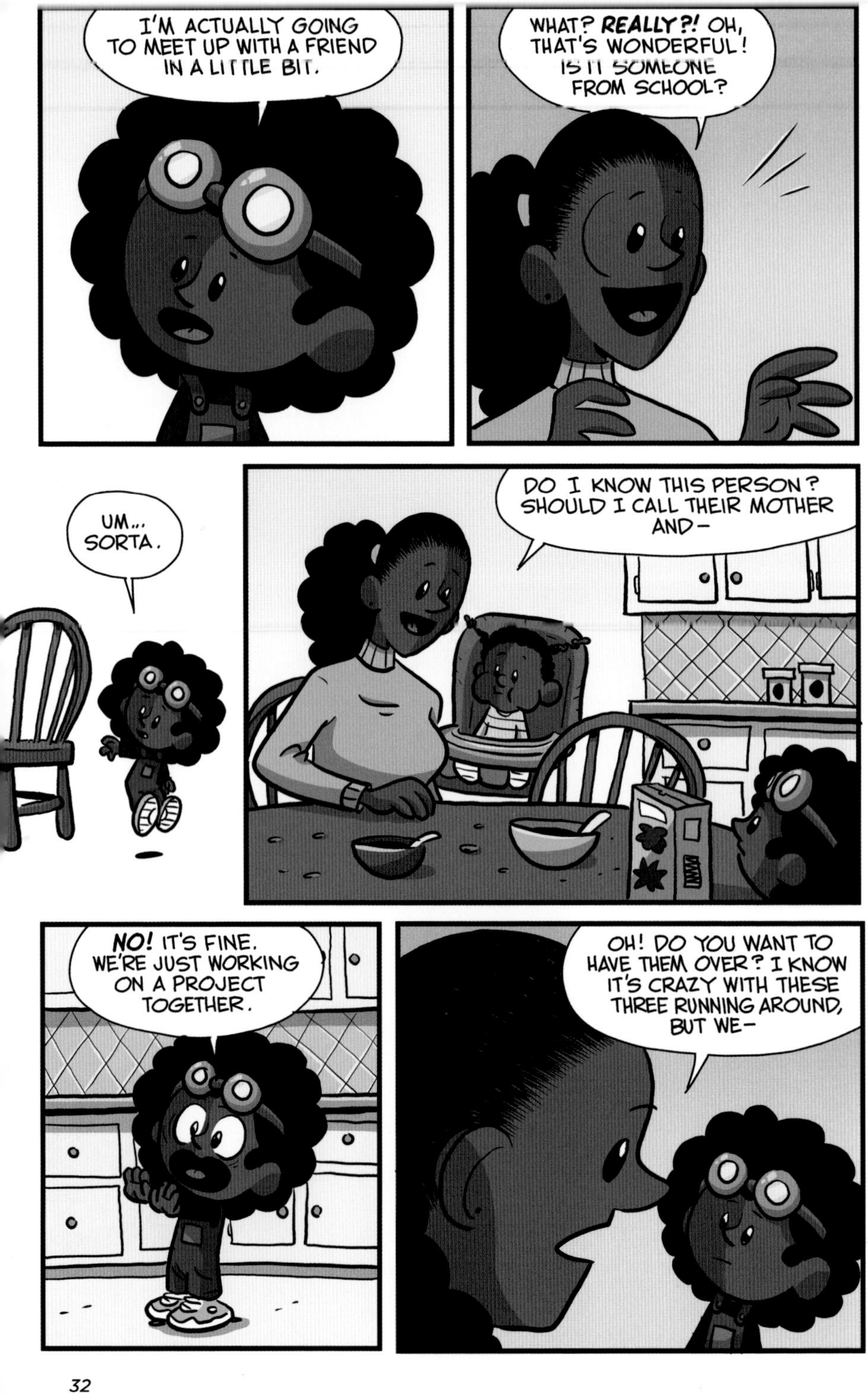
I'M ACTUALLY GOING TO MEET UP WITH A FRIEND IN A LITTLE BIT.
WHAT? **REALLY?!** OH, THAT'S WONDERFUL! IS IT SOMEONE FROM SCHOOL?
UM... SORTA.
DO I KNOW THIS PERSON? SHOULD I CALL THEIR MOTHER AND–
NO! IT'S FINE. WE'RE JUST WORKING ON A PROJECT TOGETHER.
OH! DO YOU WANT TO HAVE THEM OVER? I KNOW IT'S CRAZY WITH THESE THREE RUNNING AROUND, BUT WE–

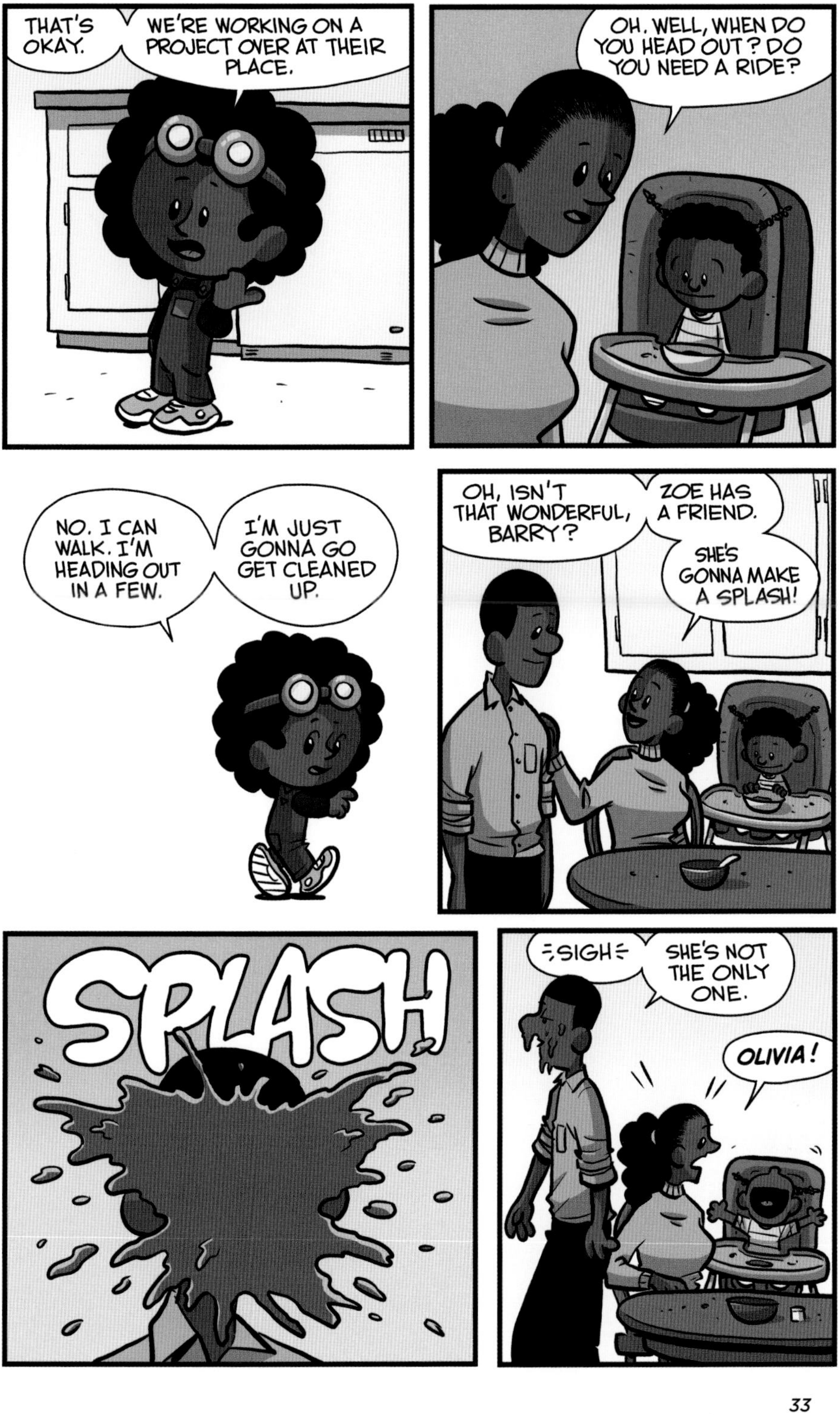
THAT'S OKAY.
WE'RE WORKING ON A PROJECT OVER AT THEIR PLACE.
OH. WELL, WHEN DO YOU HEAD OUT? DO YOU NEED A RIDE?
NO. I CAN WALK. I'M HEADING OUT IN A FEW.
I'M JUST GONNA GO GET CLEANED UP.
OH, ISN'T THAT WONDERFUL, BARRY?
ZOE HAS A FRIEND.
SHE'S GONNA MAKE A SPLASH!
SPLASH
SIGH
SHE'S NOT THE ONLY ONE.
OLIVIA!

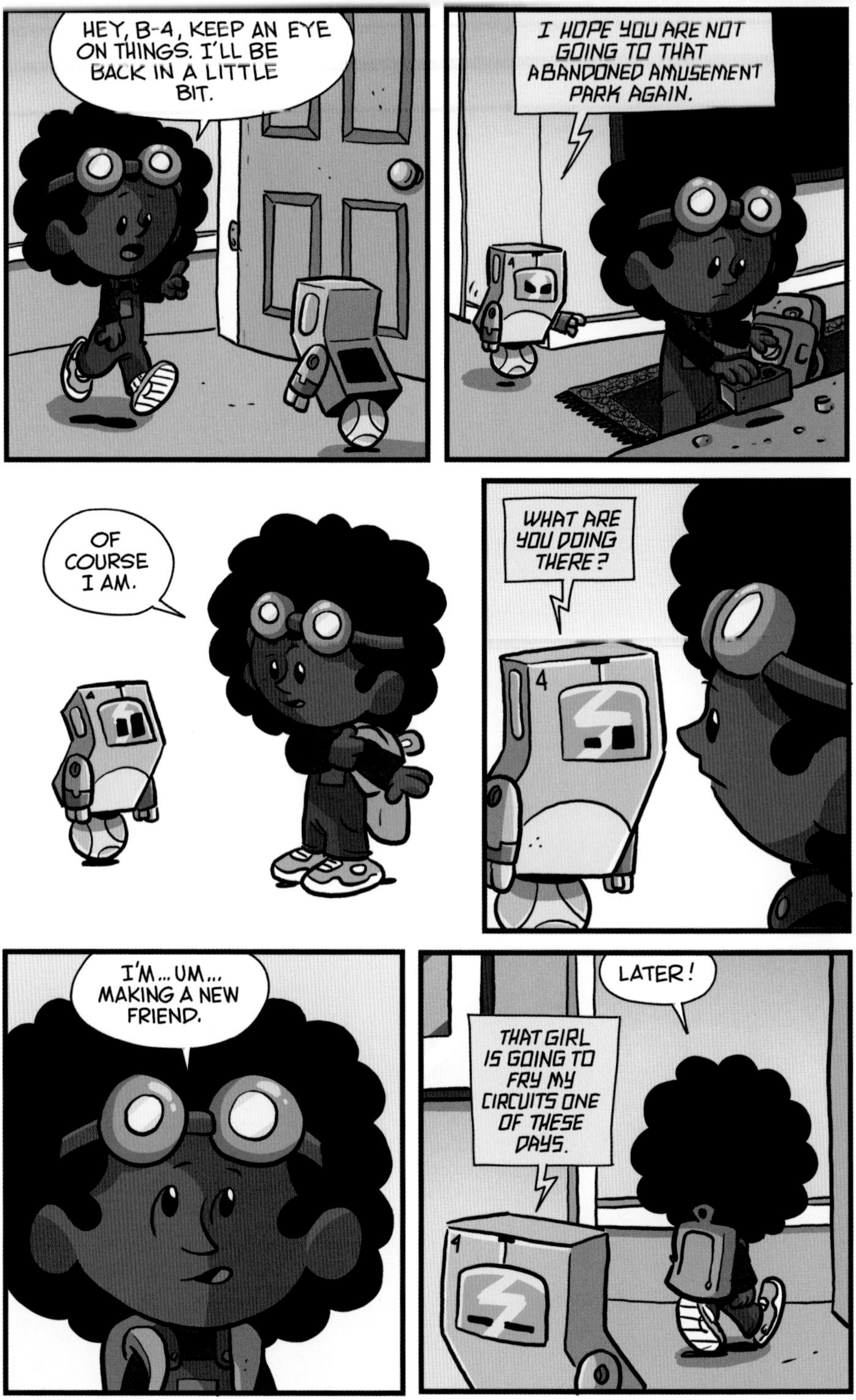
HEY, B-4, KEEP AN EYE ON THINGS. I'LL BE BACK IN A LITTLE BIT.
I HOPE YOU ARE NOT GOING TO THAT ABANDONED AMUSEMENT PARK AGAIN.
OF COURSE I AM.
WHAT ARE YOU DOING THERE?
I'M... UM... MAKING A NEW FRIEND.
LATER!
THAT GIRL IS GOING TO FRY MY CIRCUITS ONE OF THESE DAYS.

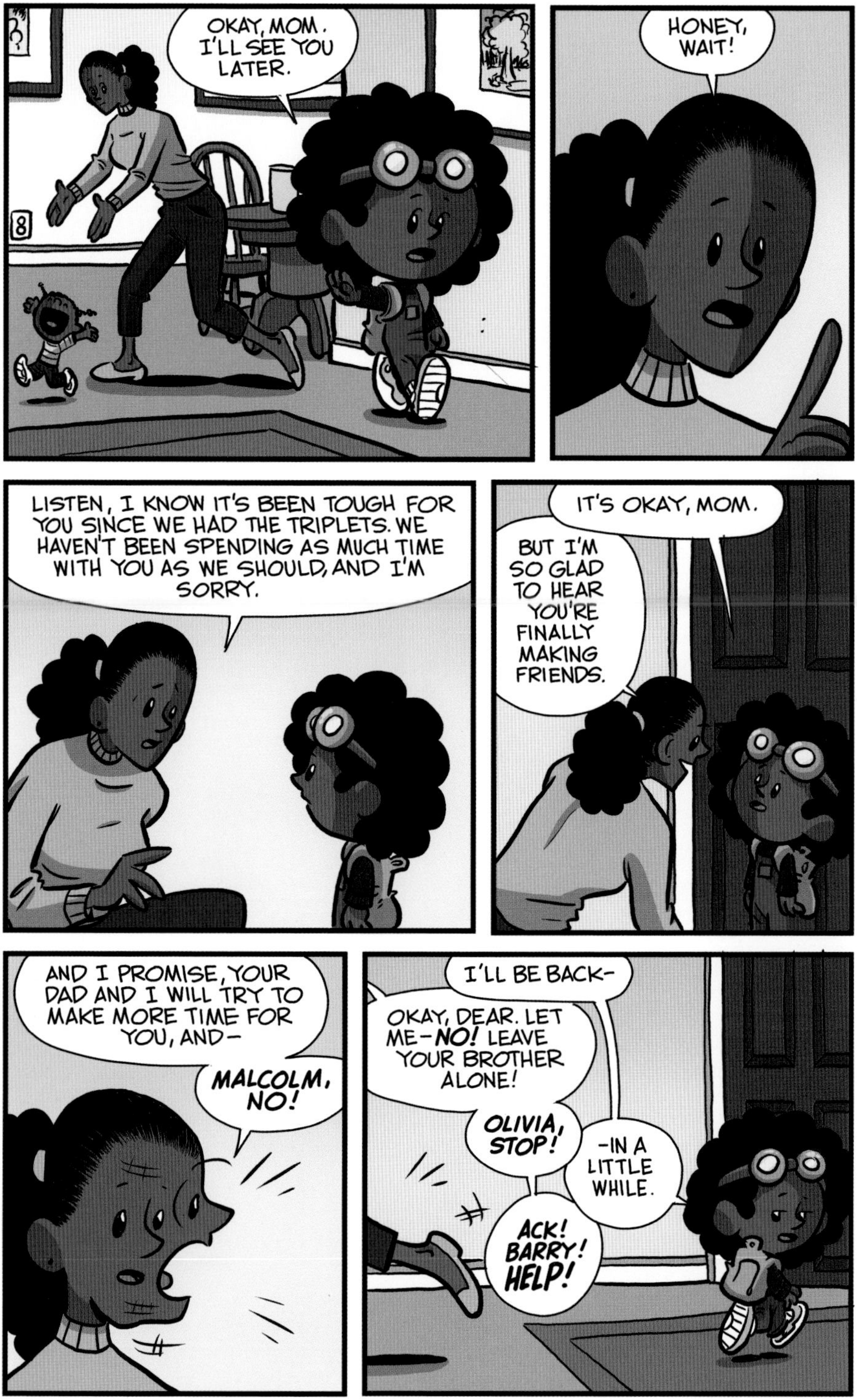

8
OKAY, MOM. I'LL SEE YOU LATER.
HONEY, WAIT!
LISTEN, I KNOW IT'S BEEN TOUGH FOR YOU SINCE WE HAD THE TRIPLETS. WE HAVEN'T BEEN SPENDING AS MUCH TIME WITH YOU AS WE SHOULD, AND I'M SORRY.
IT'S OKAY, MOM.
BUT I'M SO GLAD TO HEAR YOU'RE FINALLY MAKING FRIENDS.
AND I PROMISE, YOUR DAD AND I WILL TRY TO MAKE MORE TIME FOR YOU, AND—
MALCOLM, NO!
I'LL BE BACK-
OKAY, DEAR. LET ME—NO! LEAVE YOUR BROTHER ALONE!
OLIVIA, STOP!
-IN A LITTLE WHILE.
ACK! BARRY! HELP!

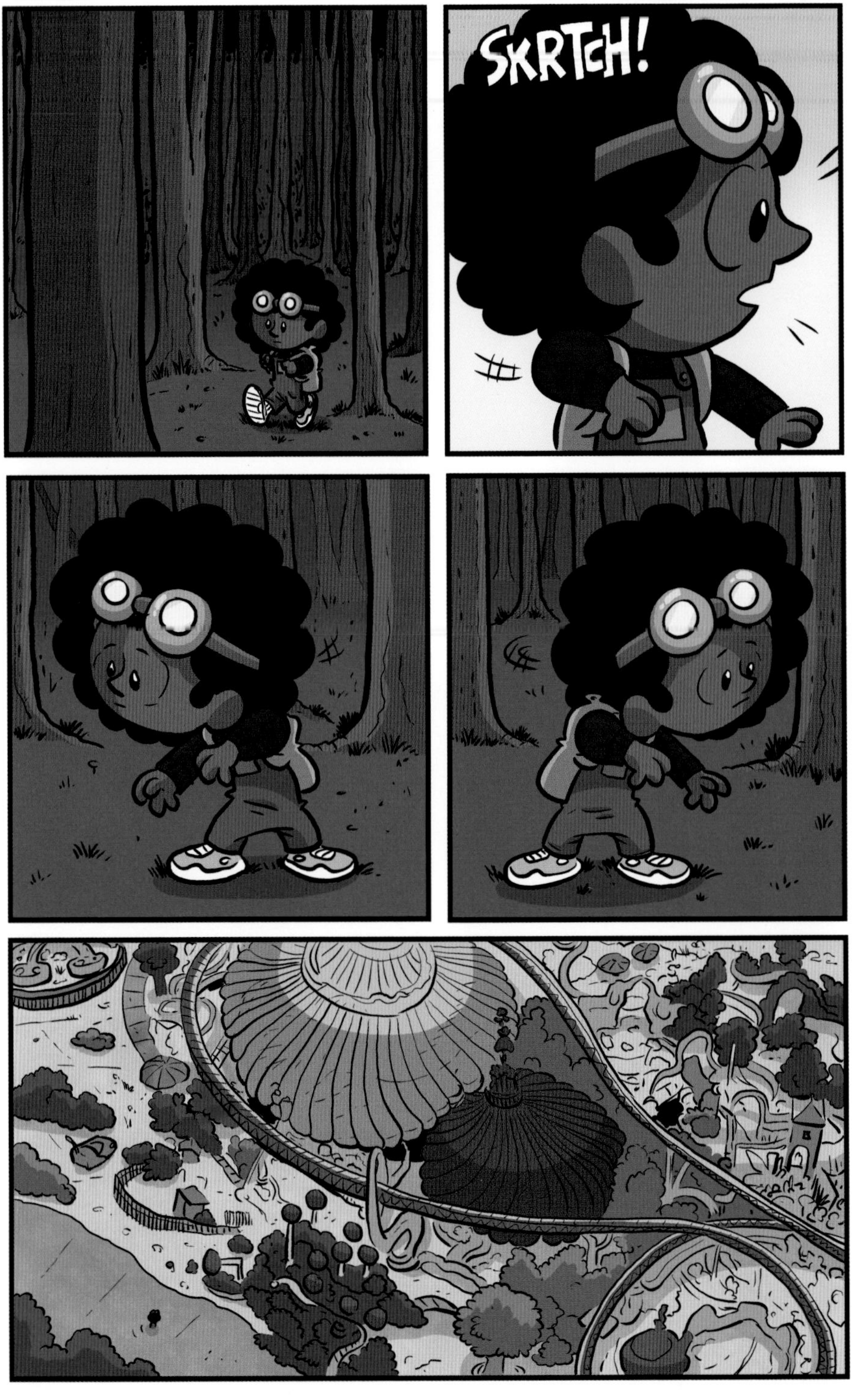
SKRTCH!

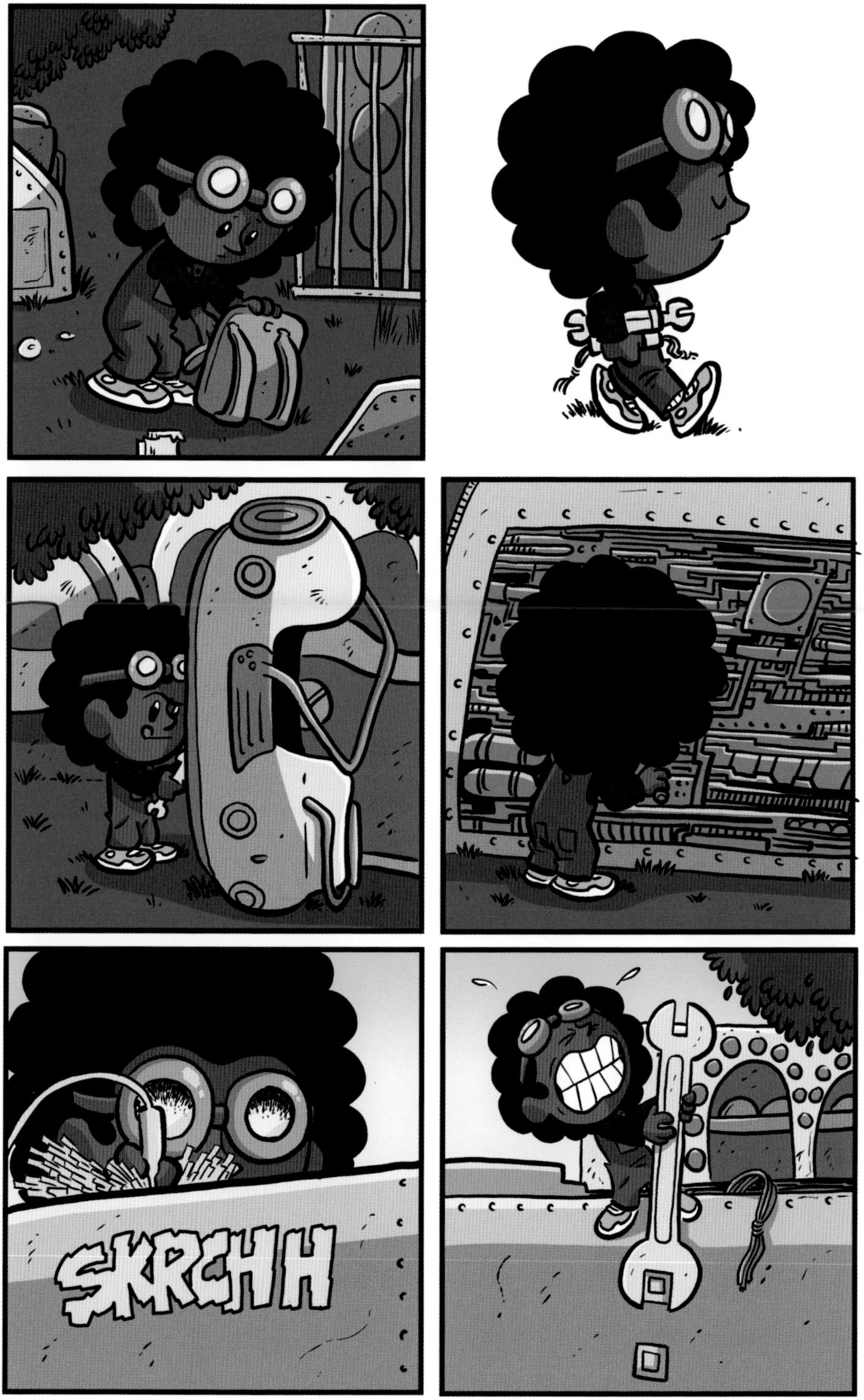
SKRCHH

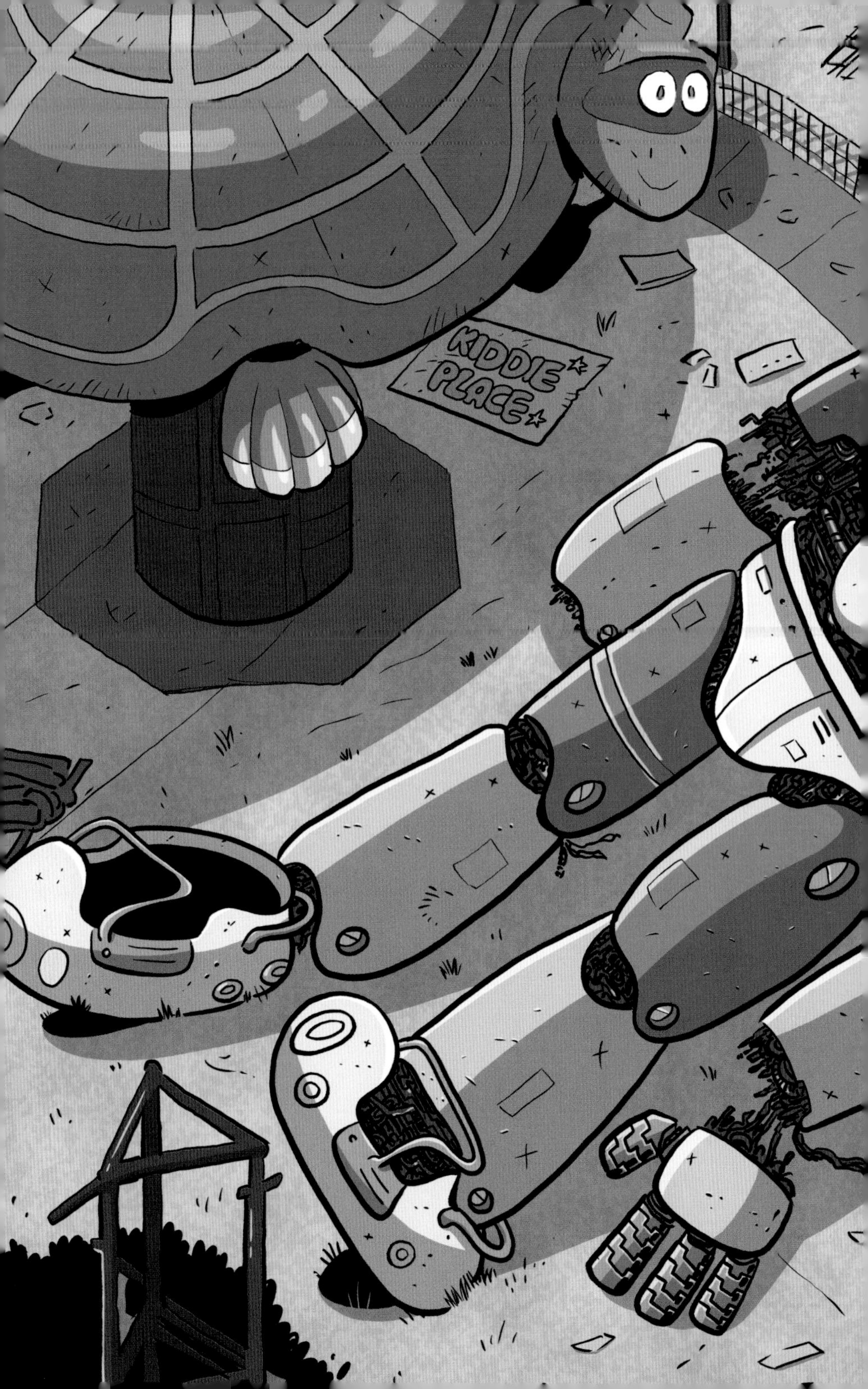
KIDDIE PLACE

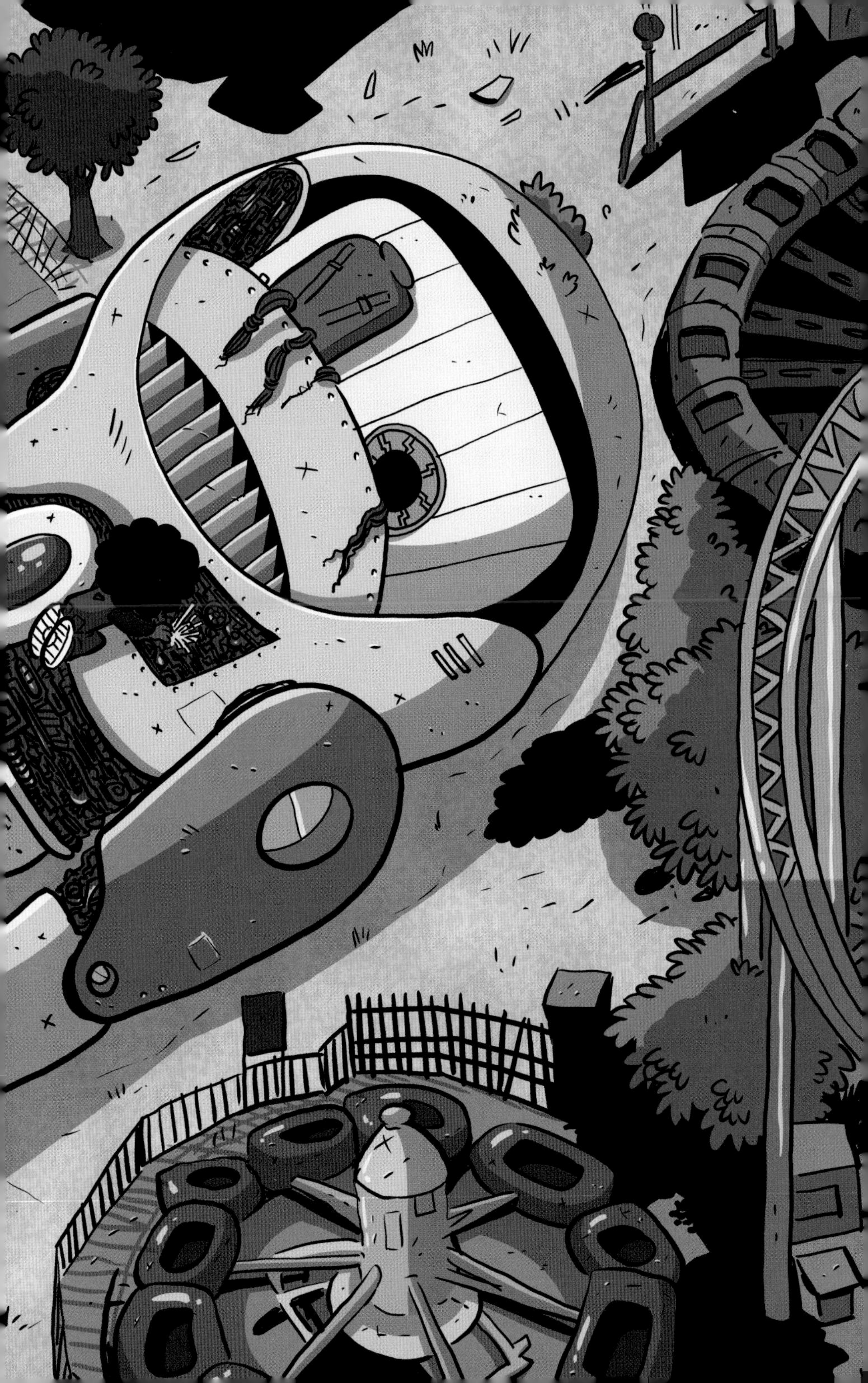

CHAPTER 4 - PICTURE DAY DISASTER

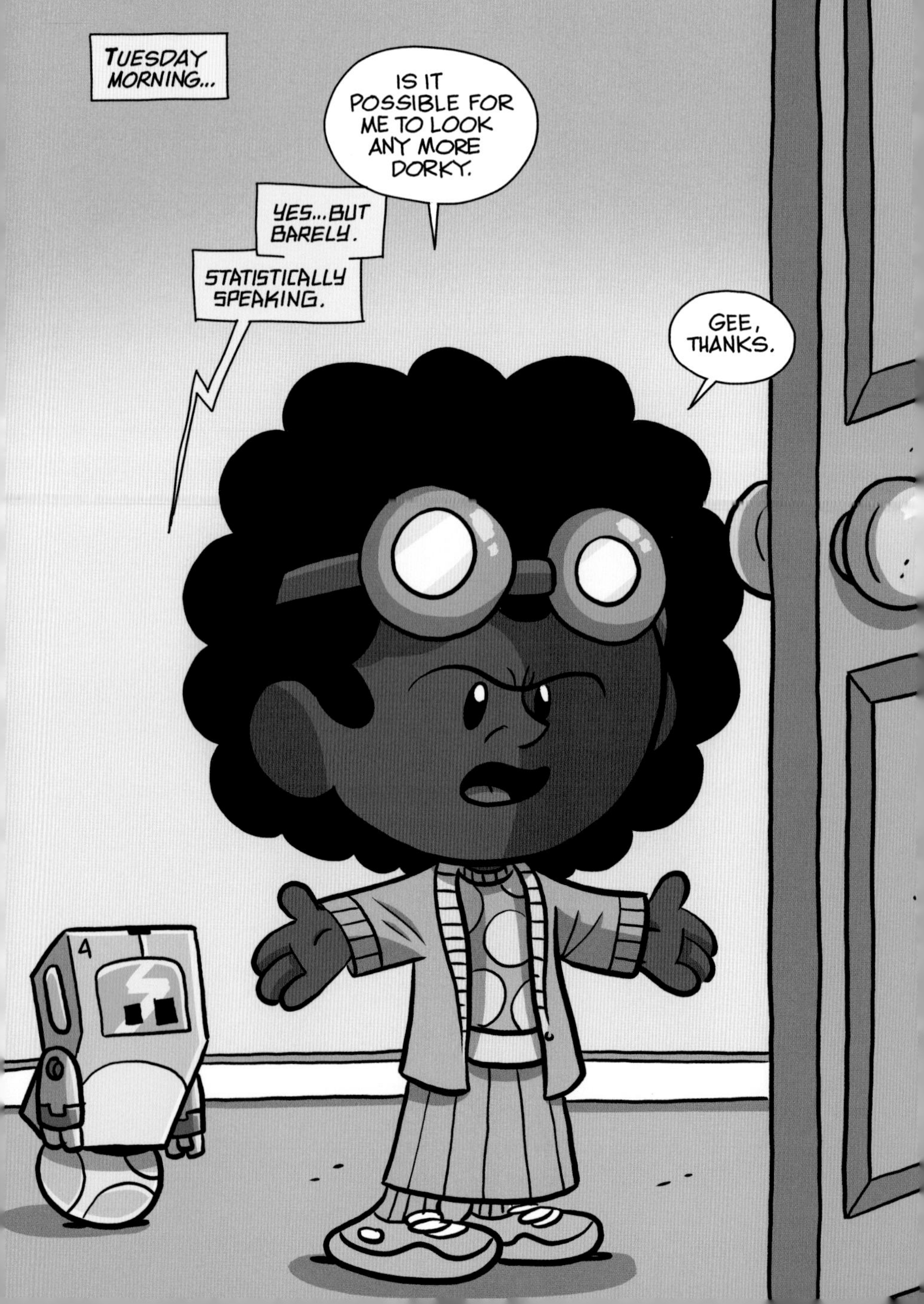
TUESDAY MORNING...
IS IT POSSIBLE FOR ME TO LOOK ANY MORE DORKY.
YES...BUT BARELY.
STATISTICALLY SPEAKING.
GEE, THANKS.

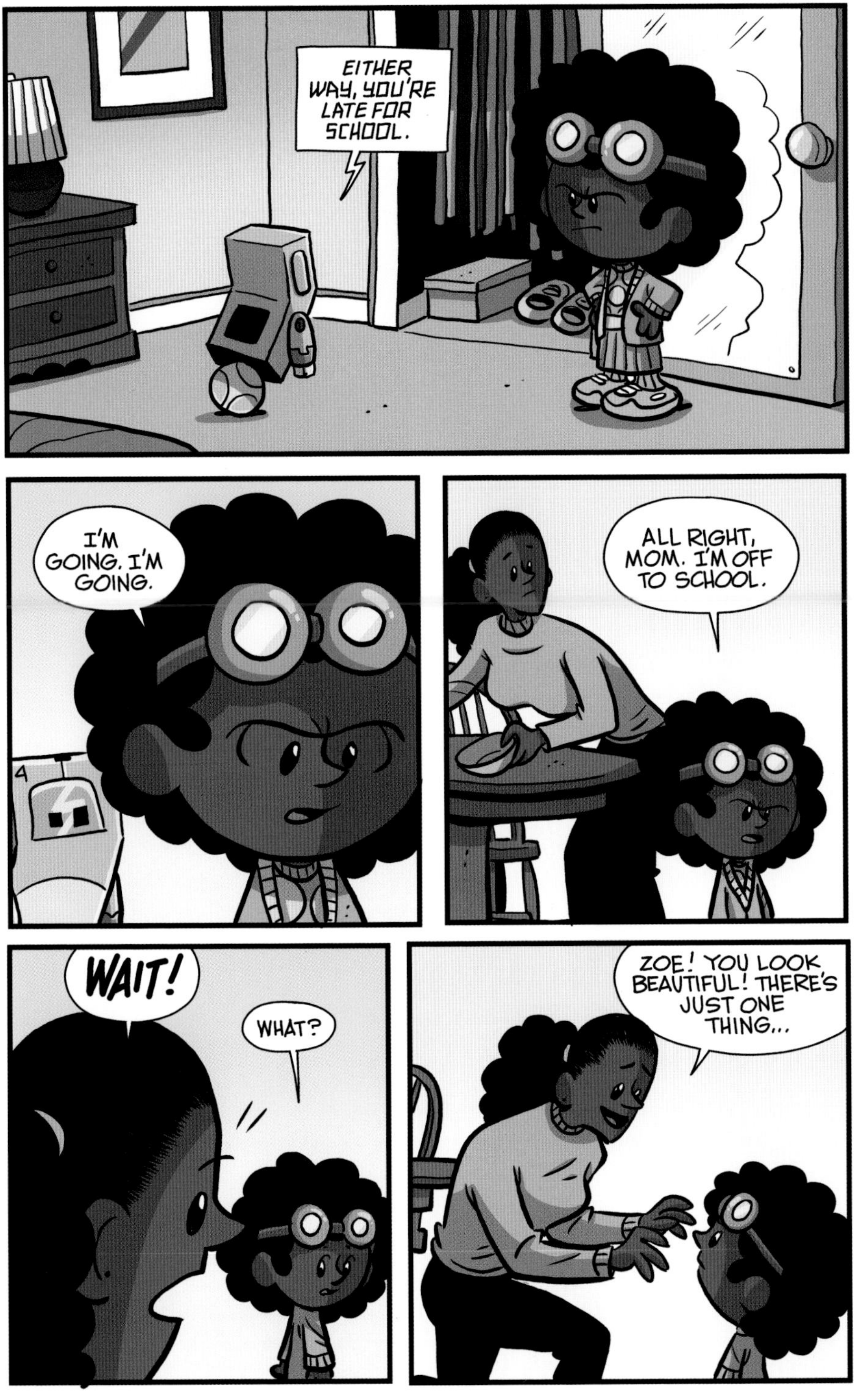
EITHER WAY, YOU'RE LATE FOR SCHOOL.
I'M GOING. I'M GOING.
4
ALL RIGHT, MOM. I'M OFF TO SCHOOL.
WAIT!
WHAT?
ZOE! YOU LOOK BEAUTIFUL! THERE'S JUST ONE THING...

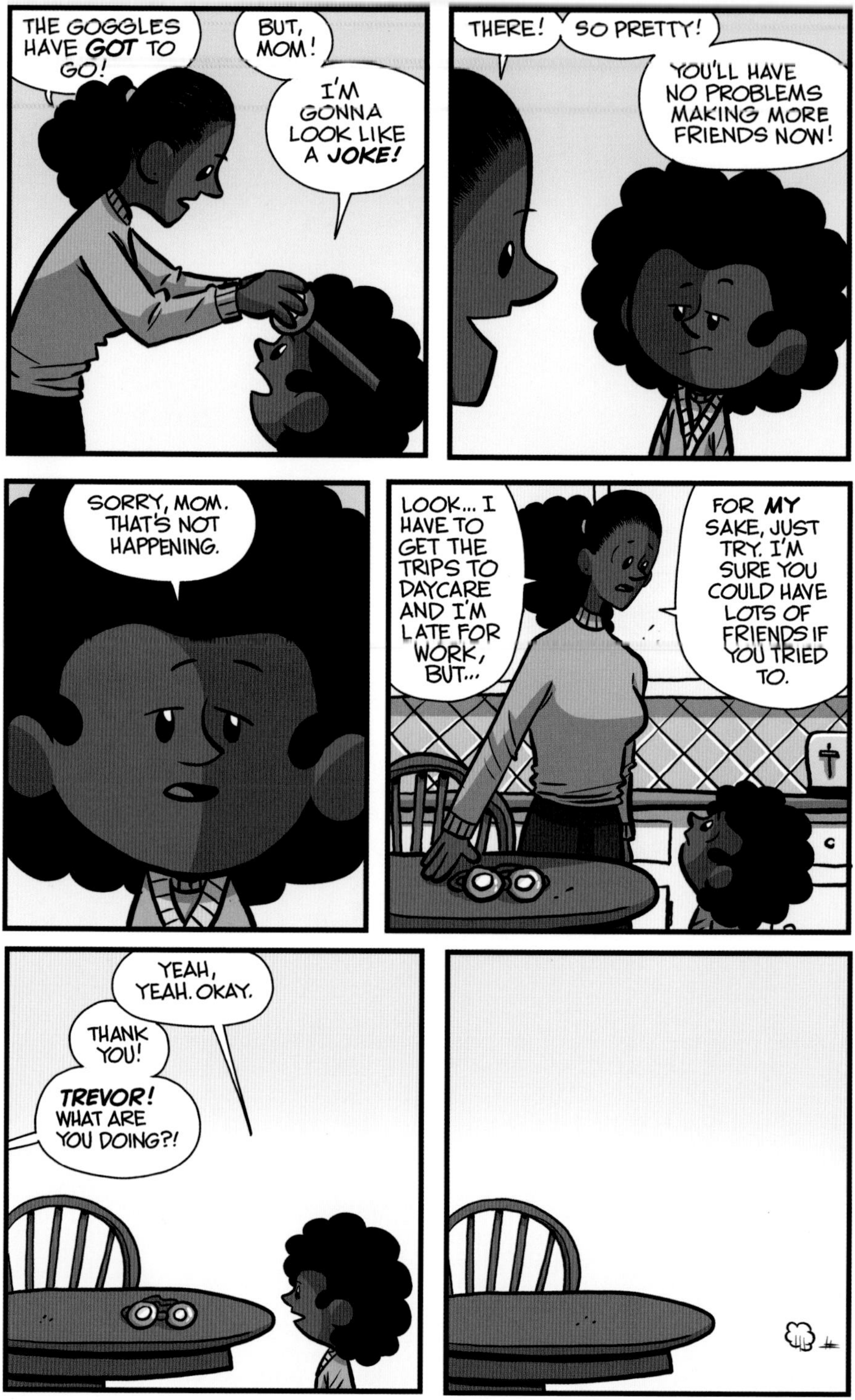
THE GOGGLES HAVE **GOT** TO GO!
BUT, MOM!
I'M GONNA LOOK LIKE A ***JOKE!***
THERE!
SO PRETTY!
YOU'LL HAVE NO PROBLEMS MAKING MORE FRIENDS NOW!
SORRY, MOM. THAT'S NOT HAPPENING.
LOOK... I HAVE TO GET THE TRIPS TO DAYCARE AND I'M LATE FOR WORK, BUT...
FOR **MY** SAKE, JUST TRY. I'M SURE YOU COULD HAVE LOTS OF FRIENDS IF YOU TRIED TO.
YEAH, YEAH. OKAY.
THANK YOU!
TREVOR! WHAT ARE YOU DOING?!

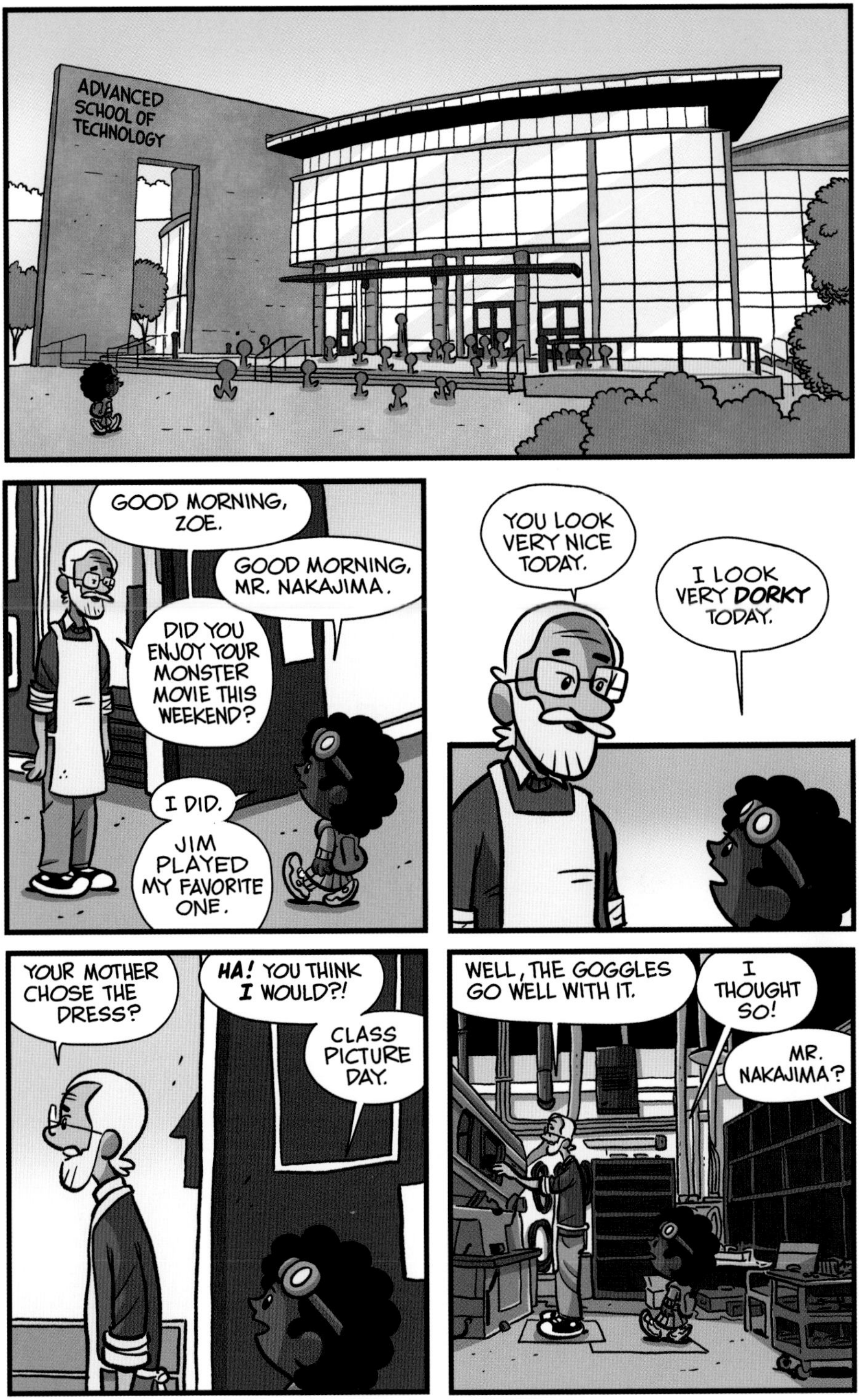
ADVANCED SCHOOL OF TECHNOLOGY
GOOD MORNING, ZOE.
GOOD MORNING, MR. NAKAJIMA.
DID YOU ENJOY YOUR MONSTER MOVIE THIS WEEKEND?
I DID.
JIM PLAYED MY FAVORITE ONE.
YOU LOOK VERY NICE TODAY.
I LOOK VERY **DORKY** TODAY.
YOUR MOTHER CHOSE THE DRESS?
HA! YOU THINK ***I*** WOULD?!
CLASS PICTURE DAY.
WELL, THE GOGGLES GO WELL WITH IT.
I THOUGHT SO!
MR. NAKAJIMA?

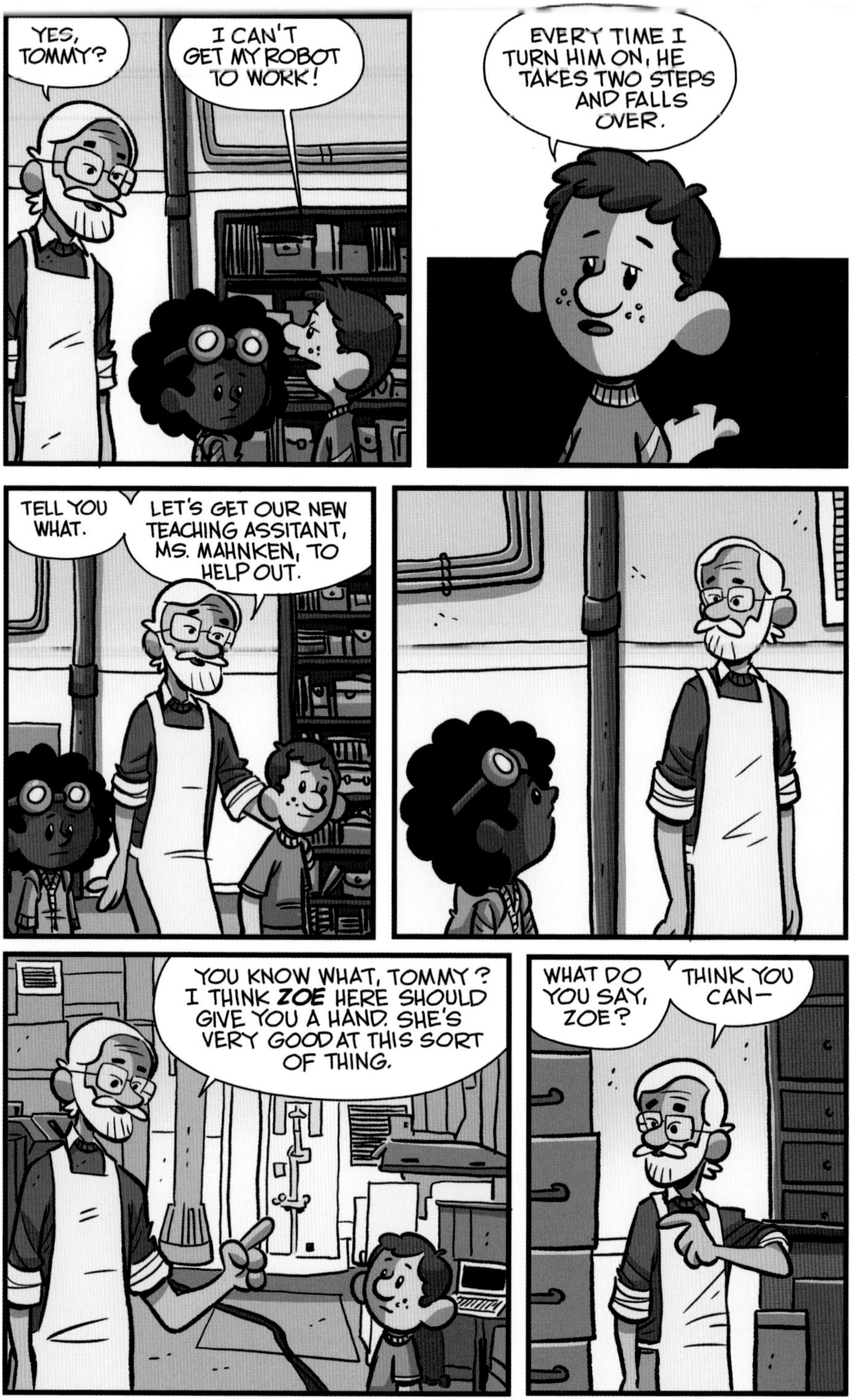
YES, TOMMY?
I CAN'T GET MY ROBOT TO WORK!
EVERY TIME I TURN HIM ON, HE TAKES TWO STEPS AND FALLS OVER.
TELL YOU WHAT.
LET'S GET OUR NEW TEACHING ASSITANT, MS. MAHNKEN, TO HELP OUT.
YOU KNOW WHAT, TOMMY? I THINK ZOE HERE SHOULD GIVE YOU A HAND. SHE'S VERY GOOD AT THIS SORT OF THING.
WHAT DO YOU SAY, ZOE?
THINK YOU CAN—

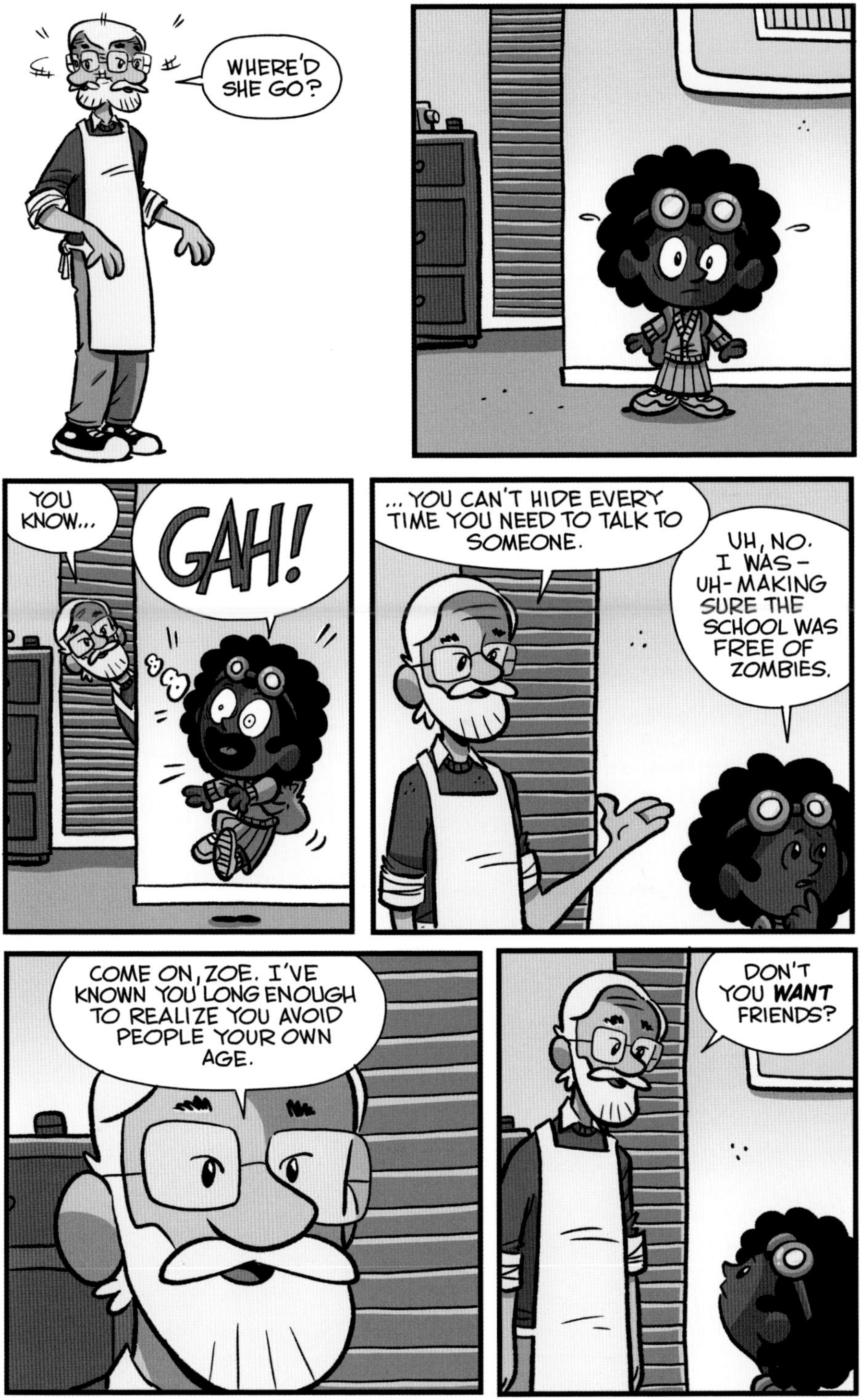
WHERE'D SHE GO?
YOU KNOW...
GAH!
... YOU CAN'T HIDE EVERY TIME YOU NEED TO TALK TO SOMEONE.
UH, NO. I WAS- UH- MAKING SURE THE SCHOOL WAS FREE OF ZOMBIES.
COME ON, ZOE. I'VE KNOWN YOU LONG ENOUGH TO REALIZE YOU AVOID PEOPLE YOUR OWN AGE.
DON'T YOU **WANT** FRIENDS?

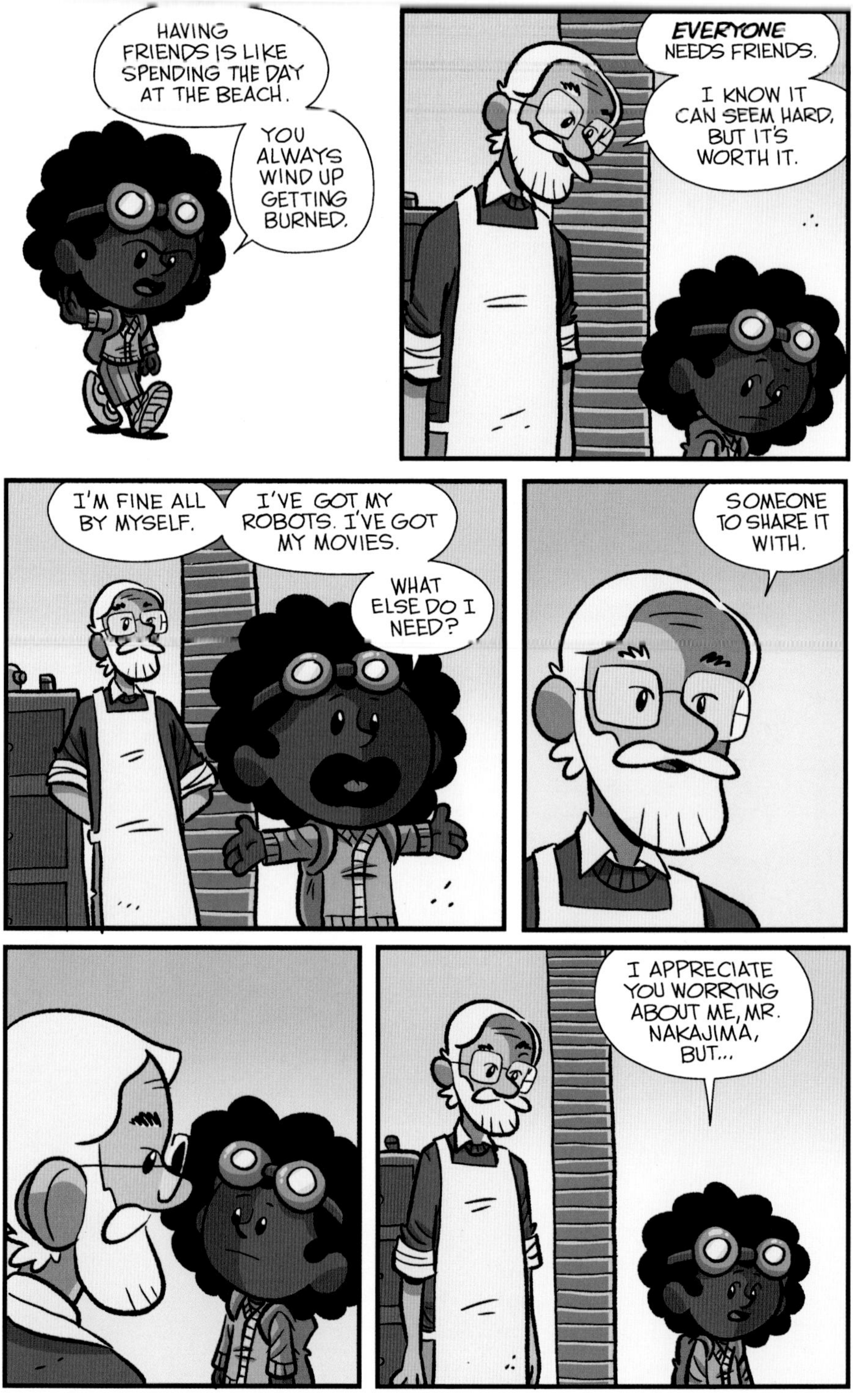
HAVING FRIENDS IS LIKE SPENDING THE DAY AT THE BEACH.
YOU ALWAYS WIND UP GETTING BURNED.
EVERYONE NEEDS FRIENDS.
I KNOW IT CAN SEEM HARD, BUT IT'S WORTH IT.
I'M FINE ALL BY MYSELF.
I'VE GOT MY ROBOTS. I'VE GOT MY MOVIES.
WHAT ELSE DO I NEED?
SOMEONE TO SHARE IT WITH.
I APPRECIATE YOU WORRYING ABOUT ME, MR. NAKAJIMA, BUT...

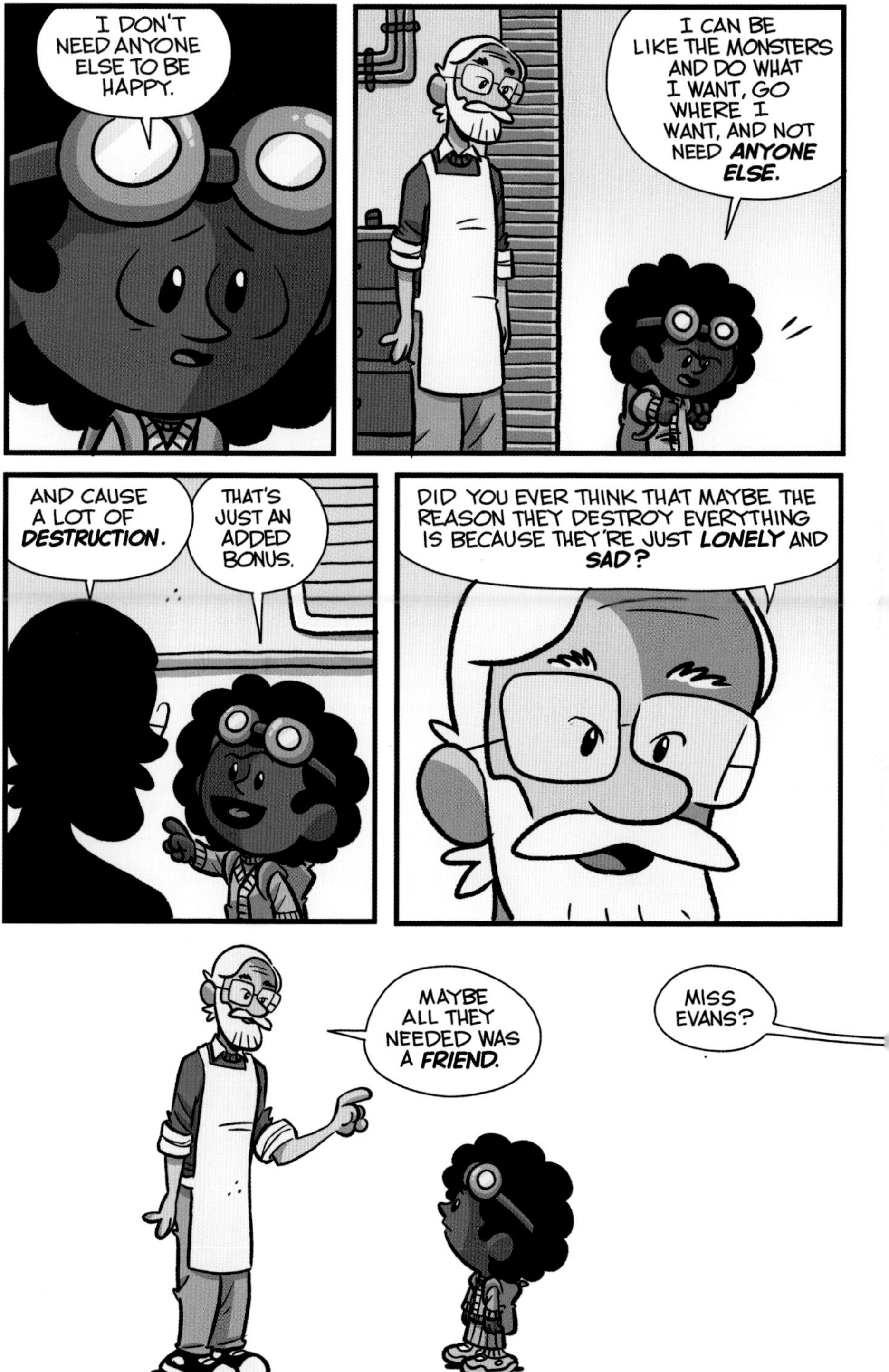
I DON'T NEED ANYONE ELSE TO BE HAPPY.
I CAN BE LIKE THE MONSTERS AND DO WHAT I WANT, GO WHERE I WANT, AND NOT NEED **ANYONE ELSE.**
AND CAUSE A LOT OF **DESTRUCTION**.
THAT'S JUST AN ADDED BONUS.
DID YOU EVER THINK THAT MAYBE THE REASON THEY DESTROY EVERYTHING IS BECAUSE THEY'RE JUST **LONELY** AND **SAD?**
MAYBE ALL THEY NEEDED WAS A **FRIEND.**
MISS EVANS?

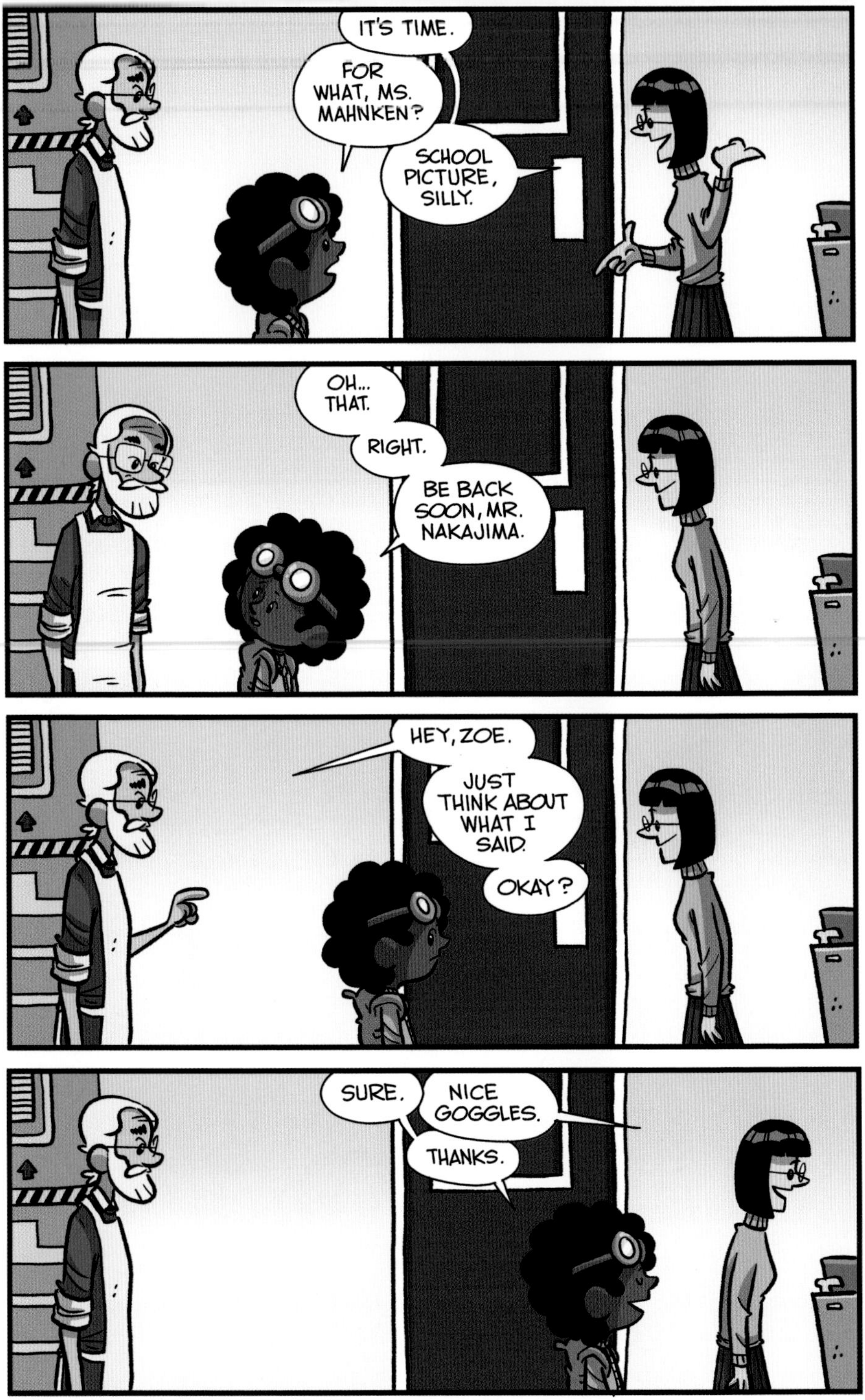
IT'S TIME.
FOR WHAT, MS. MAHNKEN?
SCHOOL PICTURE, SILLY.
OH... THAT.
RIGHT.
BE BACK SOON, MR. NAKAJIMA.
HEY, ZOE.
JUST THINK ABOUT WHAT I SAID.
OKAY?
SURE.
NICE GOGGLES.
THANKS.

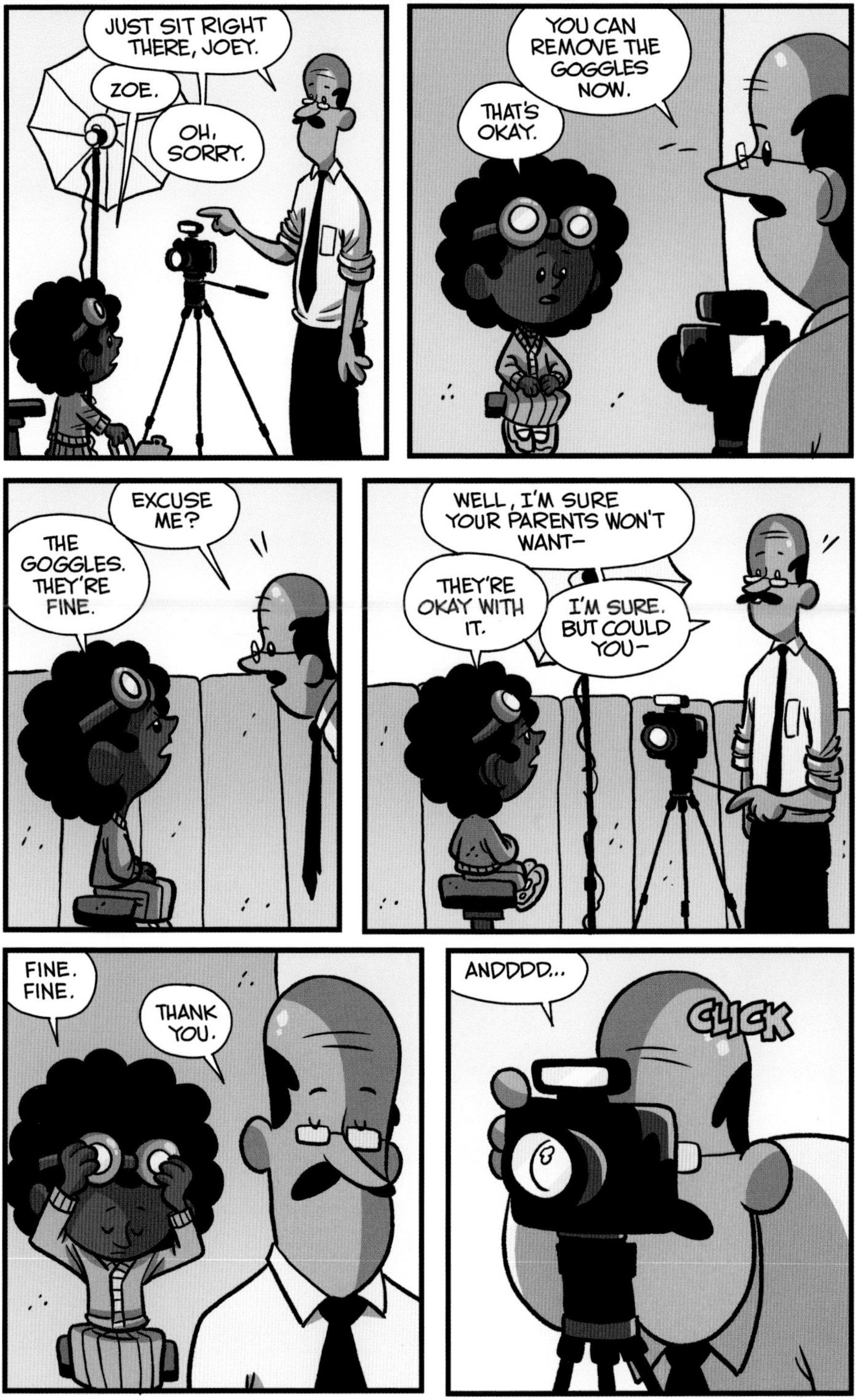
JUST SIT RIGHT THERE, JOEY.
ZOE.
OH, SORRY.
YOU CAN REMOVE THE GOGGLES NOW.
THAT'S OKAY.
EXCUSE ME?
THE GOGGLES. THEY'RE FINE.
WELL, I'M SURE YOUR PARENTS WON'T WANT–
THEY'RE OKAY WITH IT.
I'M SURE. BUT COULD YOU–
FINE. FINE.
THANK YOU.
ANDDDD...
CLICK

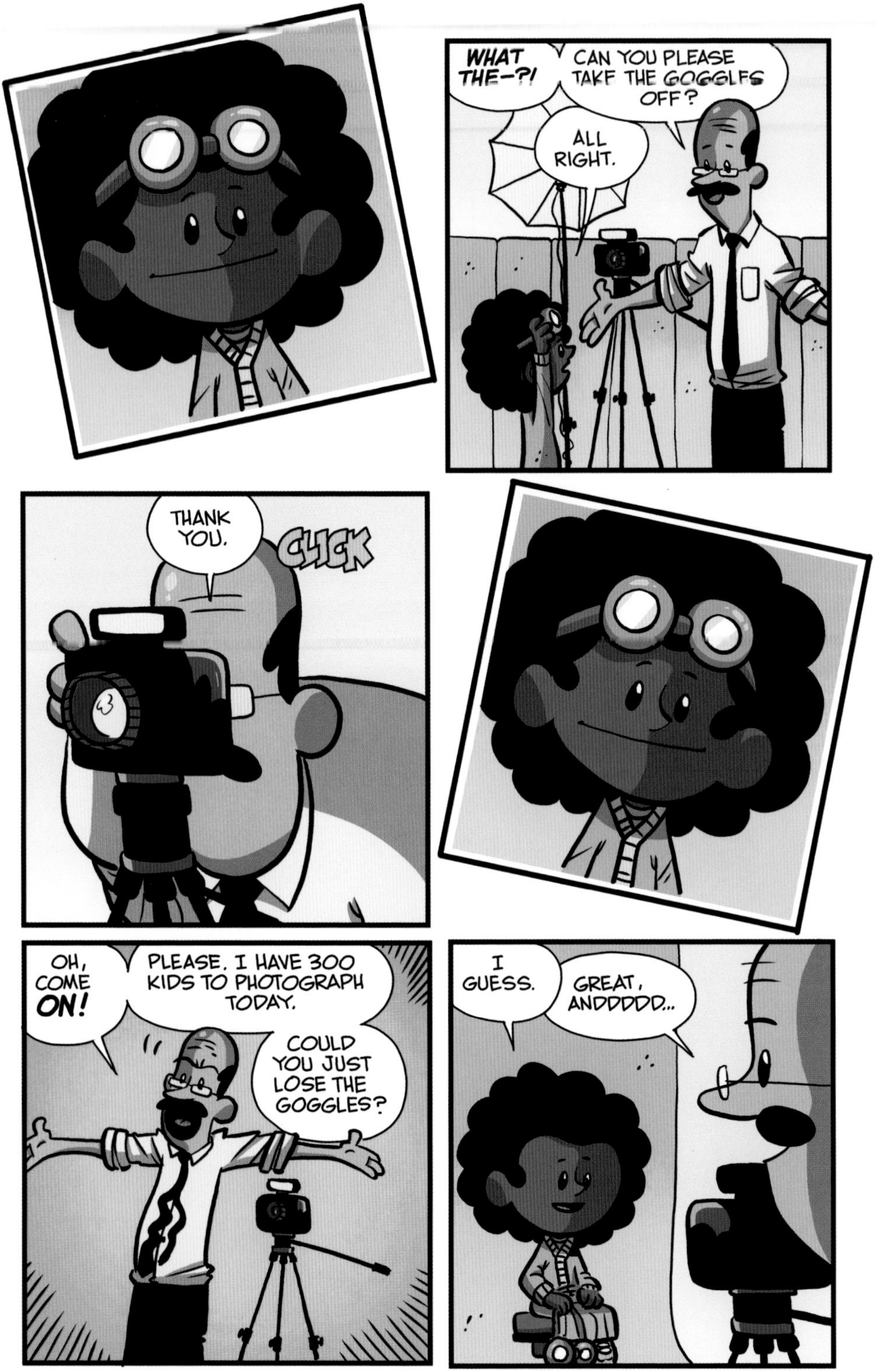

WHAT THE-?!
CAN YOU PLEASE TAKE THE GOGGLES OFF?
ALL RIGHT.
THANK YOU.
CLICK
OH, COME ON!
PLEASE. I HAVE 300 KIDS TO PHOTOGRAPH TODAY.
COULD YOU JUST LOSE THE GOGGLES?
I GUESS.
GREAT, ANDDDDD...

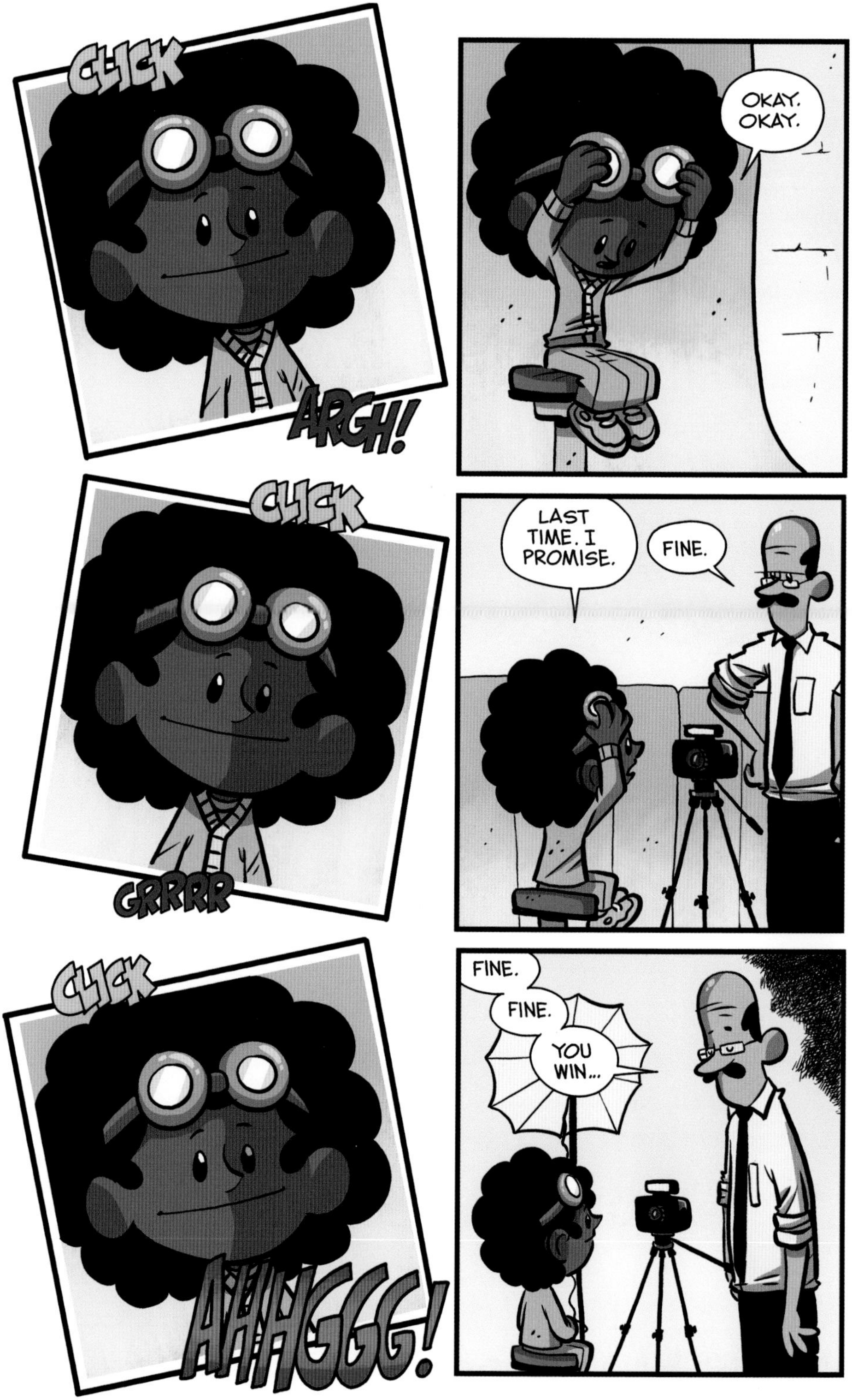
CLICK
ARGH!
OKAY. OKAY.
CLICK
GRRRR
LAST TIME. I PROMISE.
FINE.
CLICK
AHHGGG!
FINE.
FINE.
YOU WIN...

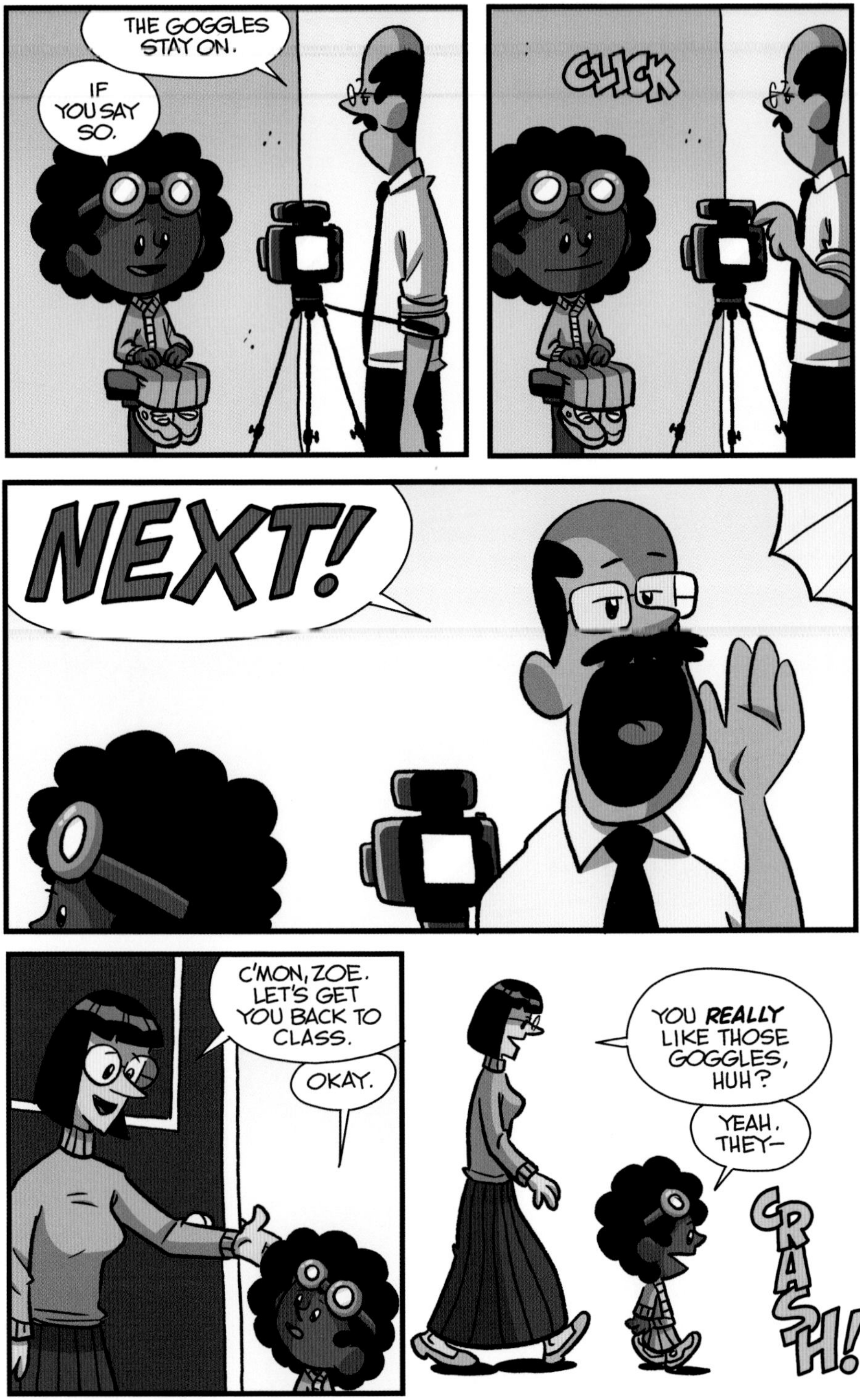
THE GOGGLES STAY ON.
IF YOU SAY SO.
CLICK
NEXT!
C'MON, ZOE. LET'S GET YOU BACK TO CLASS.
OKAY.
YOU **REALLY** LIKE THOSE GOGGLES, HUH?
YEAH. THEY—
CRASH!

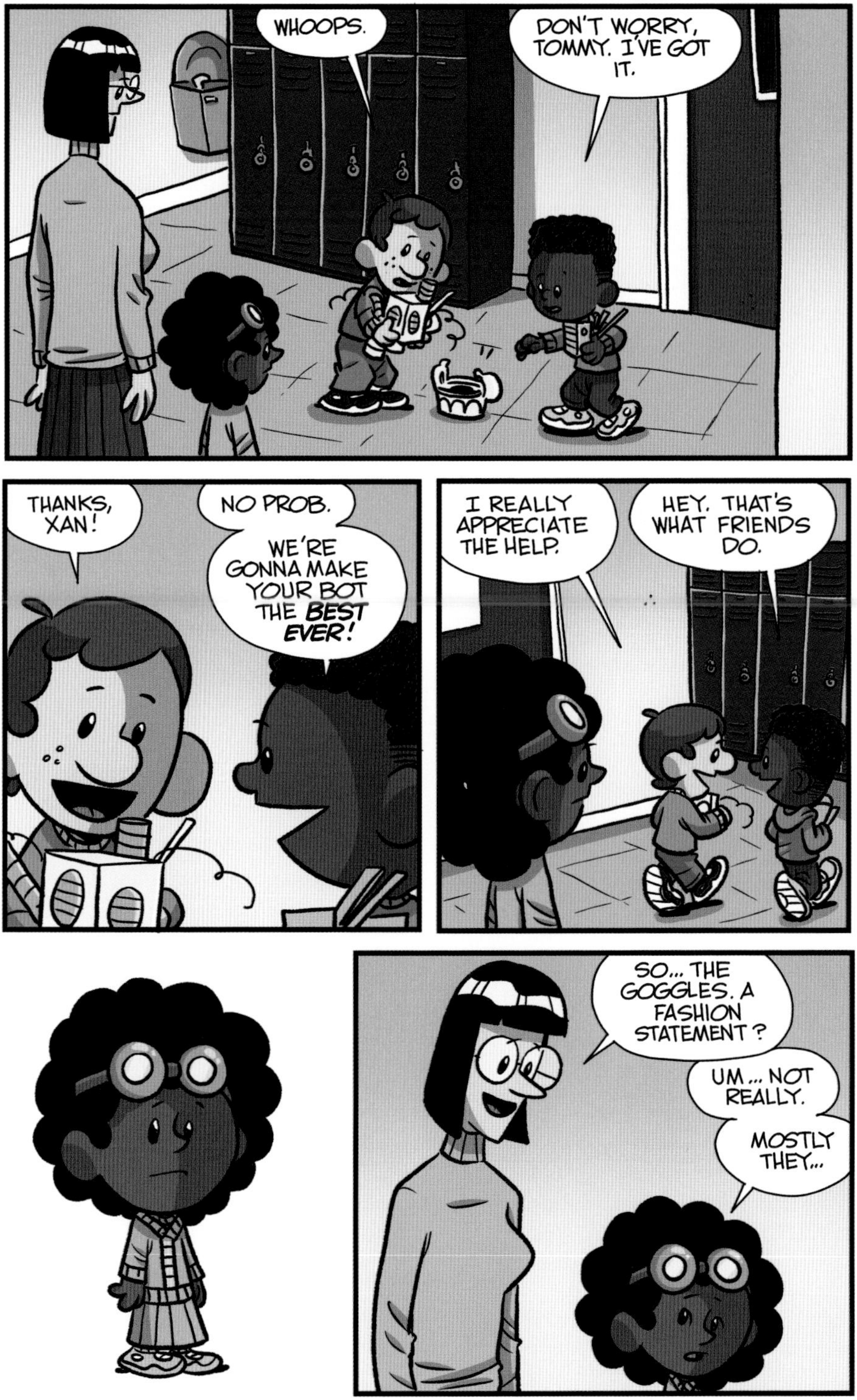
WHOOPS.
DON'T WORRY, TOMMY. I'VE GOT IT.
THANKS, XAN!
NO PROB.
WE'RE GONNA MAKE YOUR BOT THE BEST EVER!
I REALLY APPRECIATE THE HELP.
HEY. THAT'S WHAT FRIENDS DO.
SO... THE GOGGLES. A FASHION STATEMENT?
UM... NOT REALLY.
MOSTLY THEY...

THEY HELP WITH MY WORK.

OKAY, CLASS.

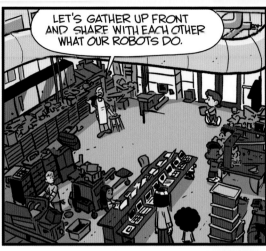

LET'S GATHER UP FRONT AND SHARE WITH EACH OTHER WHAT OUR ROBOTS DO.

XAN?

MY ROBOT FOLLOWS DOGS AROUND AND PICKS UP THEIR DOO.

THAT'S ONE POOPY JOB.

VERY NICE.

EVA?

MY BOT WILL TIE YOUR SHOES FOR YOU.

"KNOT" BAD.

NEAT.

JEFF?

MY ROBOT WILL BRUSH YOUR HAIR.

A STYLISH DESIGN.

GREAT.

AND ZOE, WHAT ABOUT YOU?

UM...

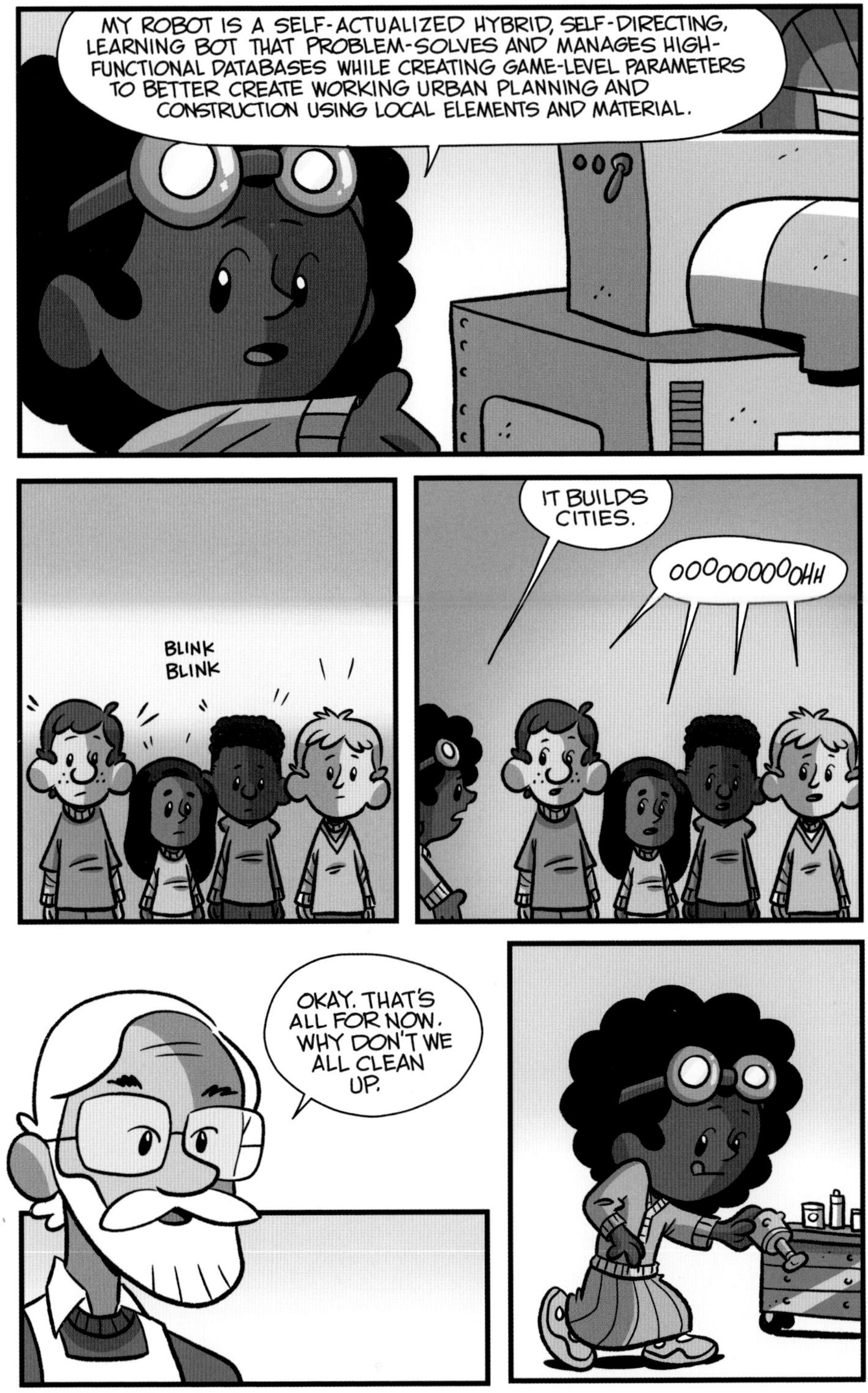

MY ROBOT IS A SELF-ACTUALIZED HYBRID, SELF-DIRECTING, LEARNING BOT THAT PROBLEM-SOLVES AND MANAGES HIGH-FUNCTIONAL DATABASES WHILE CREATING GAME-LEVEL PARAMETERS TO BETTER CREATE WORKING URBAN PLANNING AND CONSTRUCTION USING LOCAL ELEMENTS AND MATERIAL.
BLINK BLINK
IT BUILDS CITIES.
OOOOOOOOOHH
OKAY. THAT'S ALL FOR NOW. WHY DON'T WE ALL CLEAN UP.

ZOE!

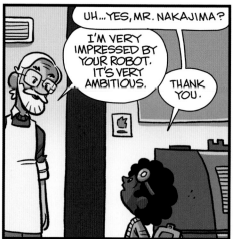
UH...YES, MR. NAKAJIMA?

I'M VERY IMPRESSED BY YOUR ROBOT. IT'S VERY AMBITIOUS.

THANK YOU.

PERHAPS YOU CAN GET ONE OF THE **OTHER** STUDENTS TO WORK WITH YOU.

NO!

I MEAN, UH, I'D RATHER WORK **ALONE.**

YOU KNOW, ZOE, WE CAN'T **ALWAYS** DO EVERYTHING ALONE. SOMETIMES WE NEED **HELP.**

I...

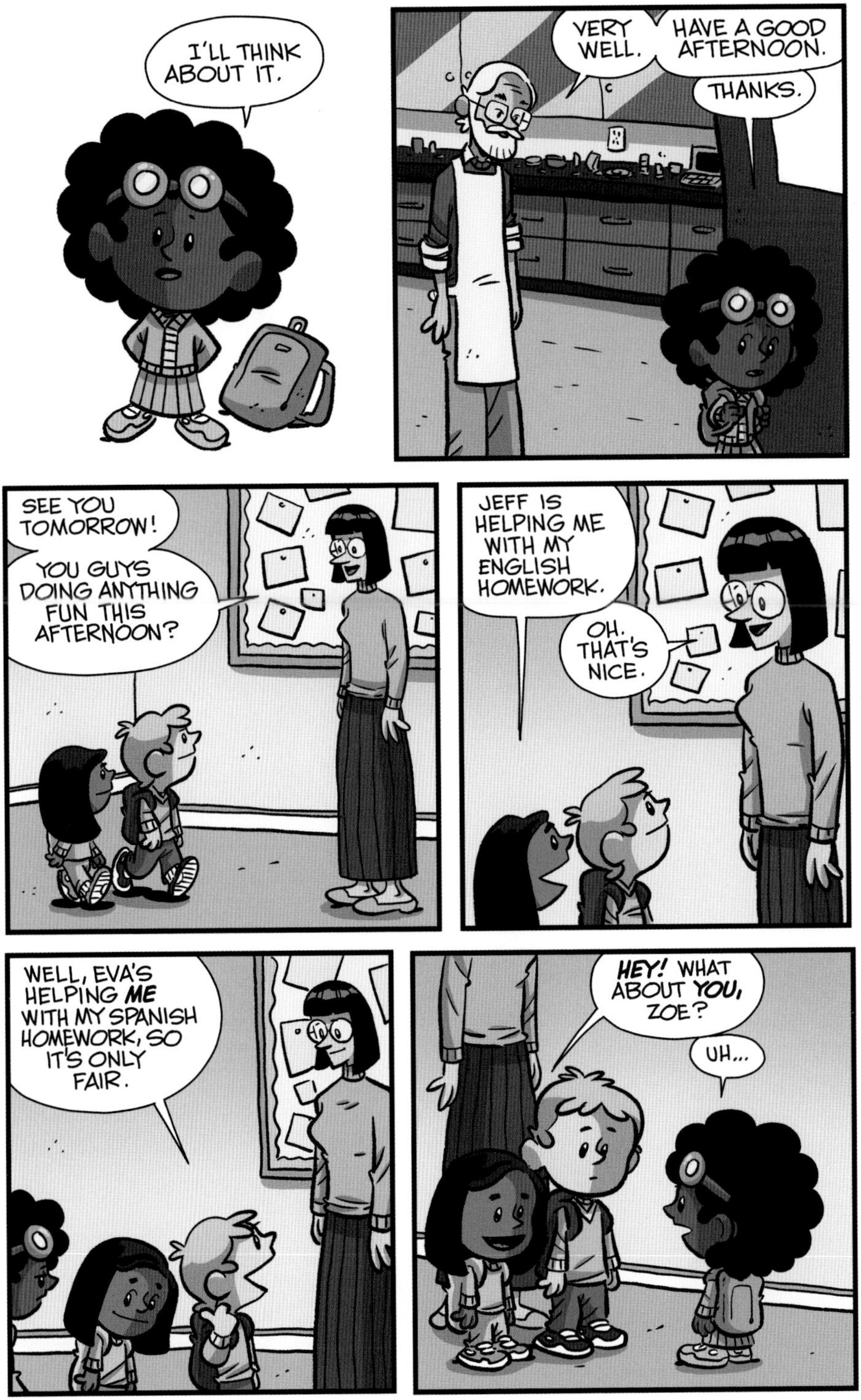
I'LL THINK ABOUT IT.
VERY WELL.
HAVE A GOOD AFTERNOON.
THANKS.
SEE YOU TOMORROW!
YOU GUYS DOING ANYTHING FUN THIS AFTERNOON?
JEFF IS HELPING ME WITH MY ENGLISH HOMEWORK.
OH. THAT'S NICE.
WELL, EVA'S HELPING **ME** WITH MY SPANISH HOMEWORK, SO IT'S ONLY FAIR.
HEY! WHAT ABOUT **YOU,** ZOE?
UH...

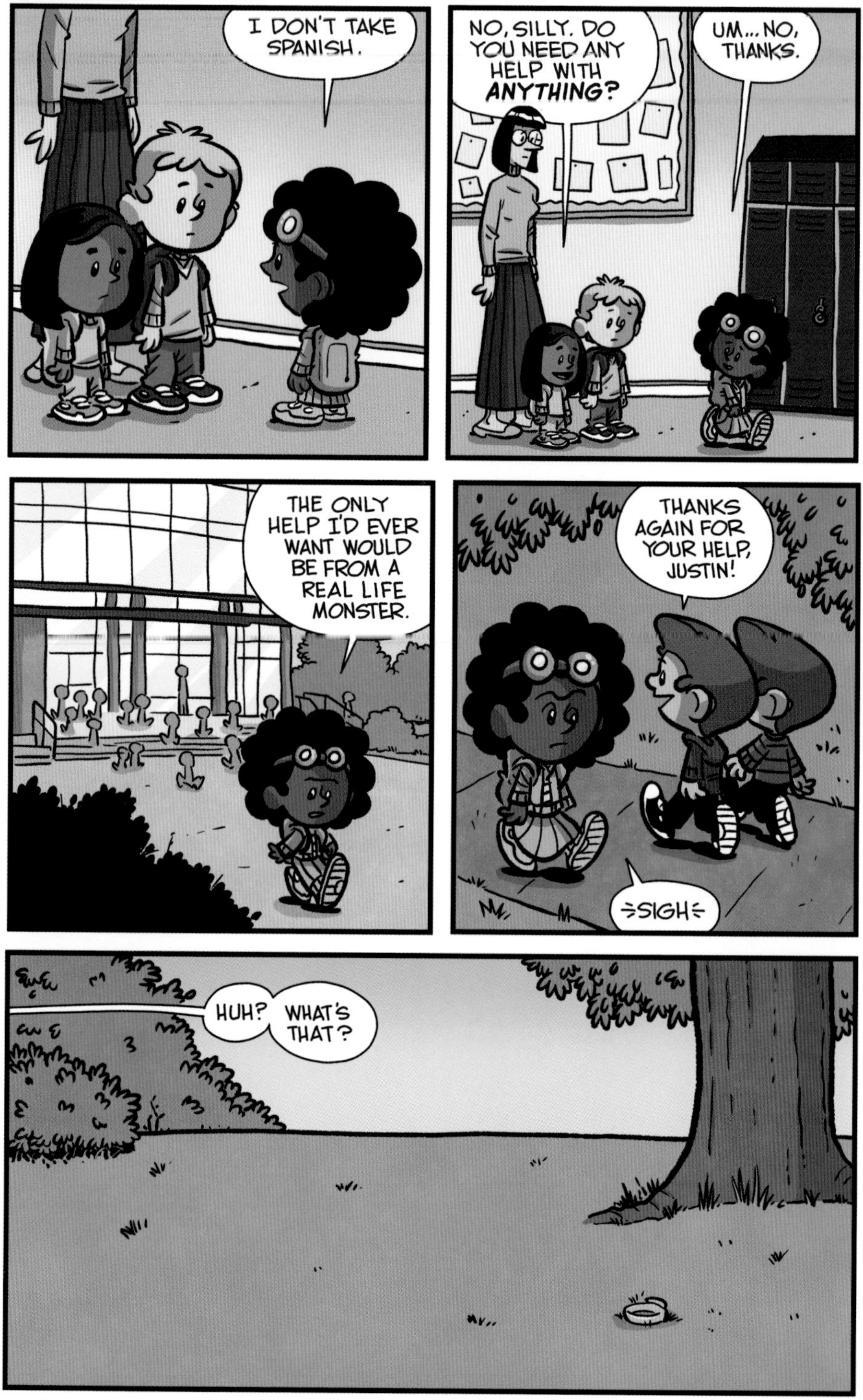
I DON'T TAKE SPANISH.
NO, SILLY. DO YOU NEED ANY HELP WITH **ANYTHING?**
UM... NO, THANKS.
THE ONLY HELP I'D EVER WANT WOULD BE FROM A REAL LIFE MONSTER.
THANKS AGAIN FOR YOUR HELP, JUSTIN!
SIGH
HUH?
WHAT'S THAT?

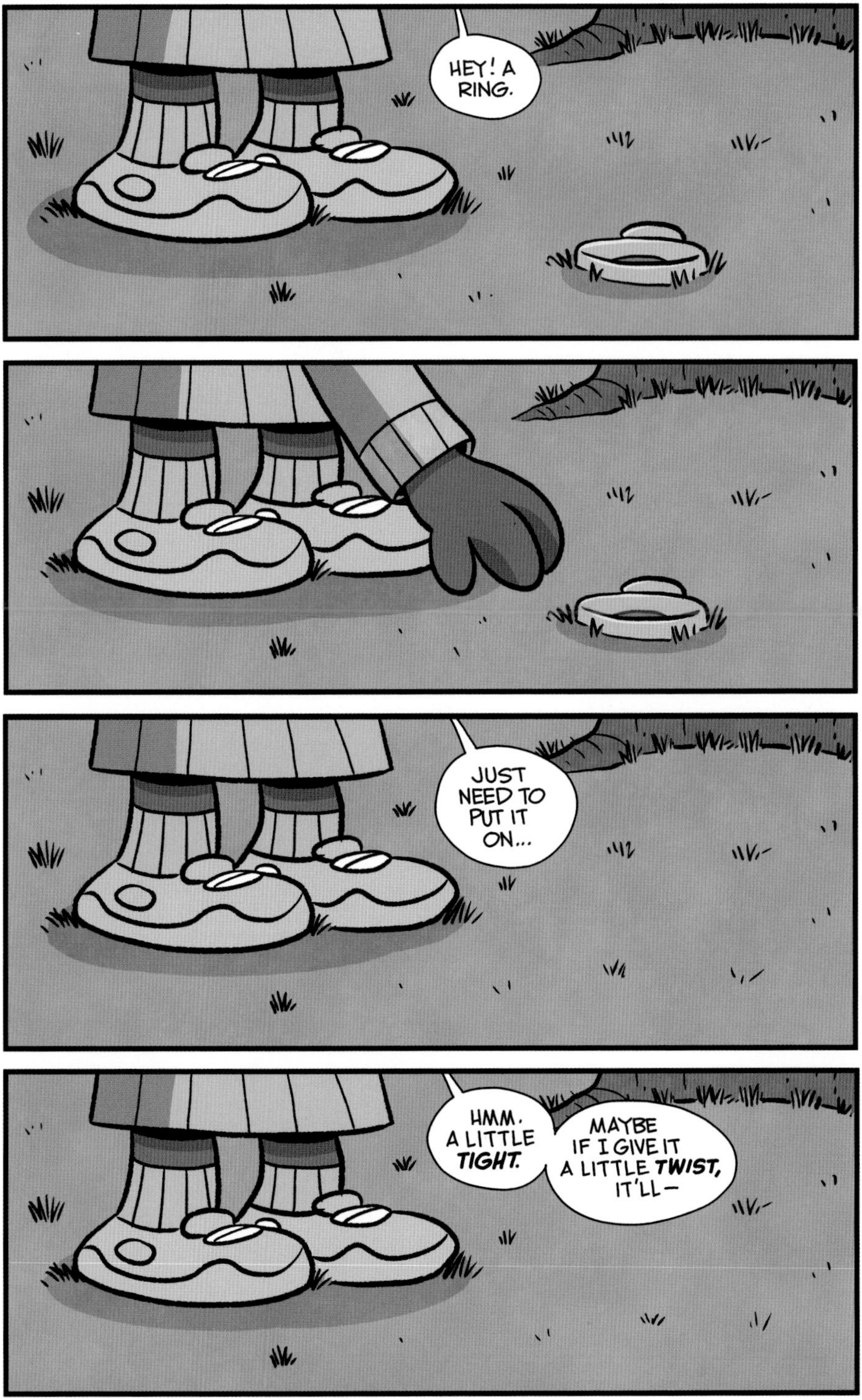
HEY! A RING.
JUST NEED TO PUT IT ON...
HMM. A LITTLE TIGHT.
MAYBE IF I GIVE IT A LITTLE TWIST, IT'LL—

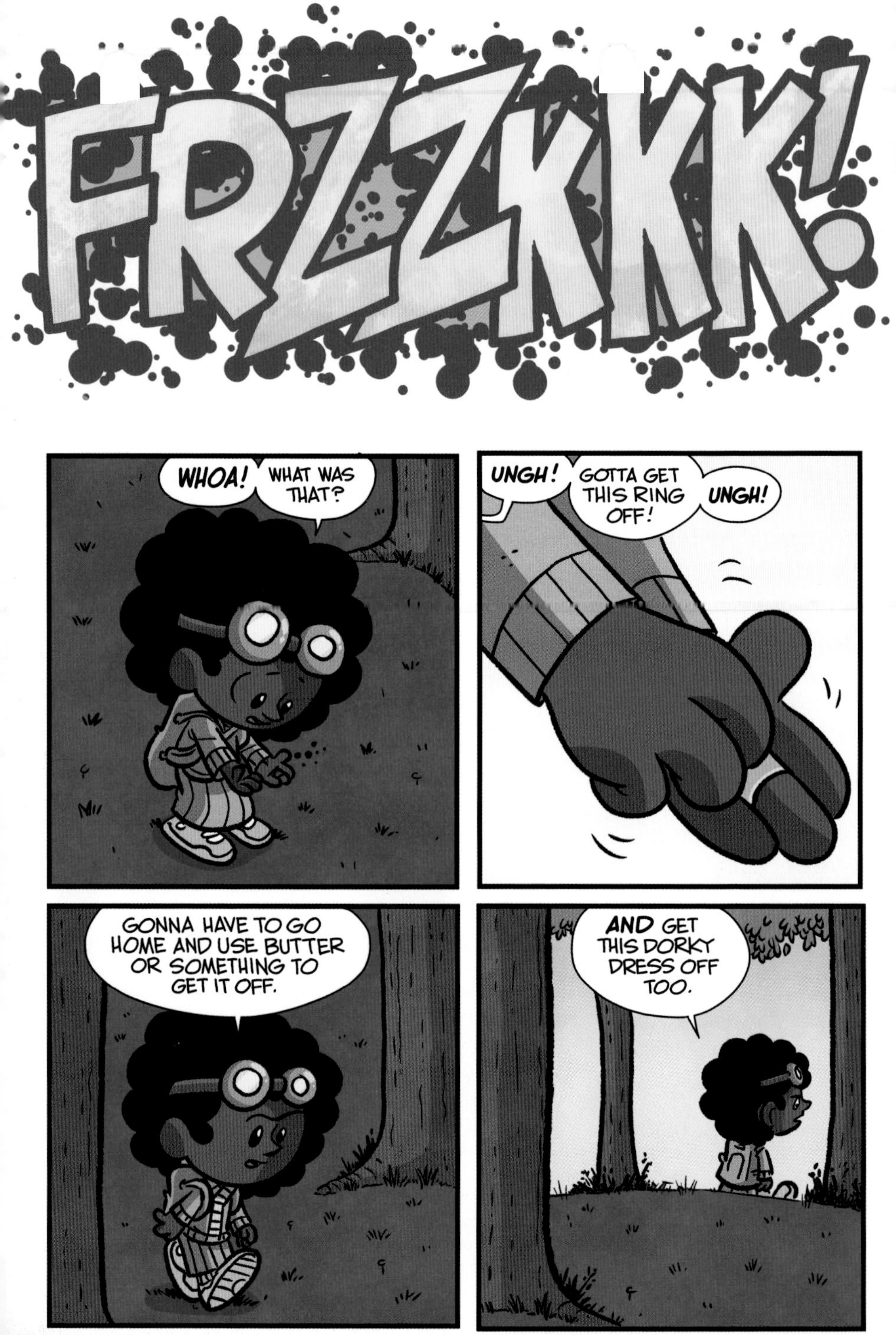
FRZKKK!
WHOA!
WHAT WAS THAT?
UNGH!
GOTTA GET THIS RING OFF!
UNGH!
GONNA HAVE TO GO HOME AND USE BUTTER OR SOMETHING TO GET IT OFF.
AND GET THIS DORKY DRESS OFF TOO.

Chapter 5 - A Monstrous Day

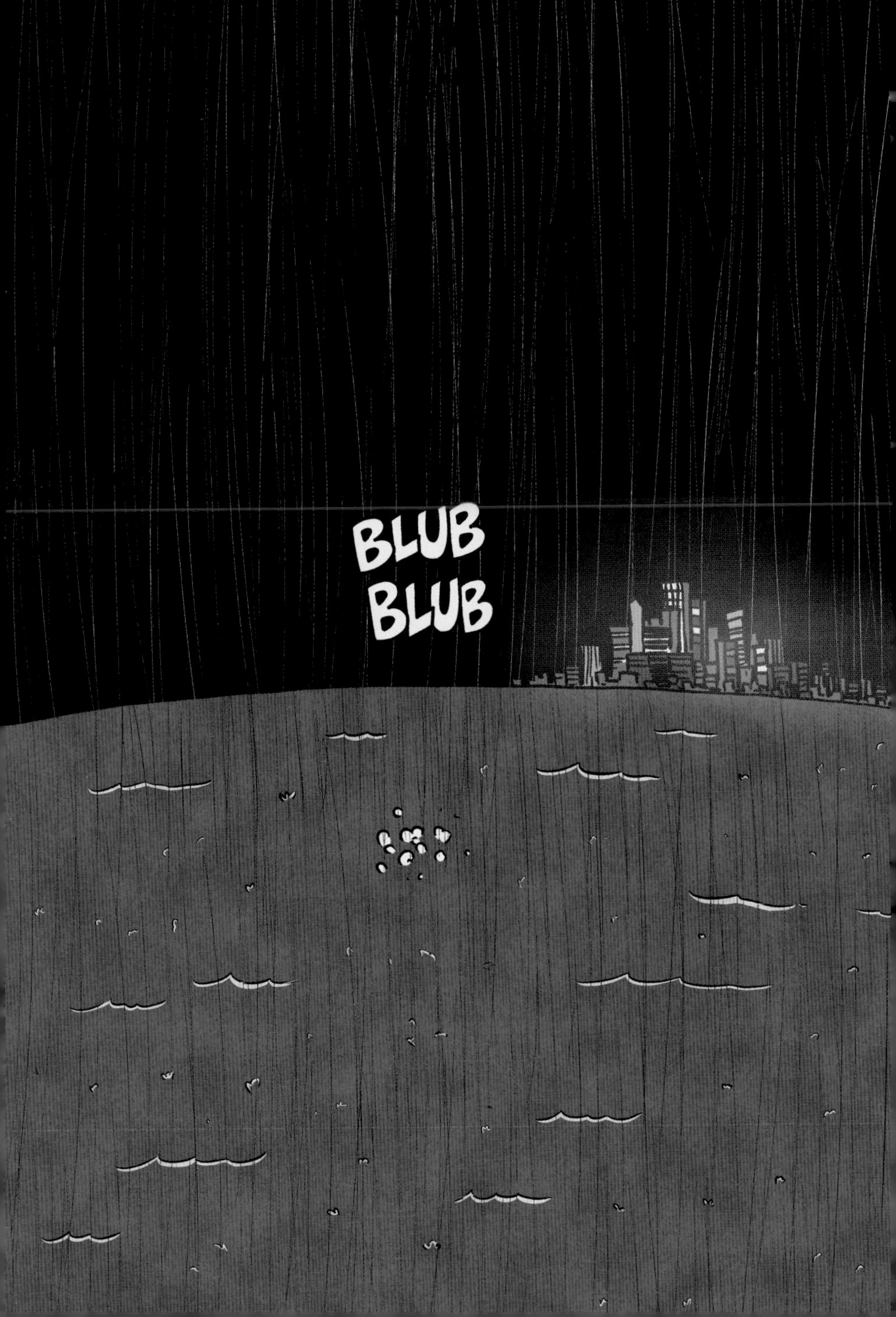

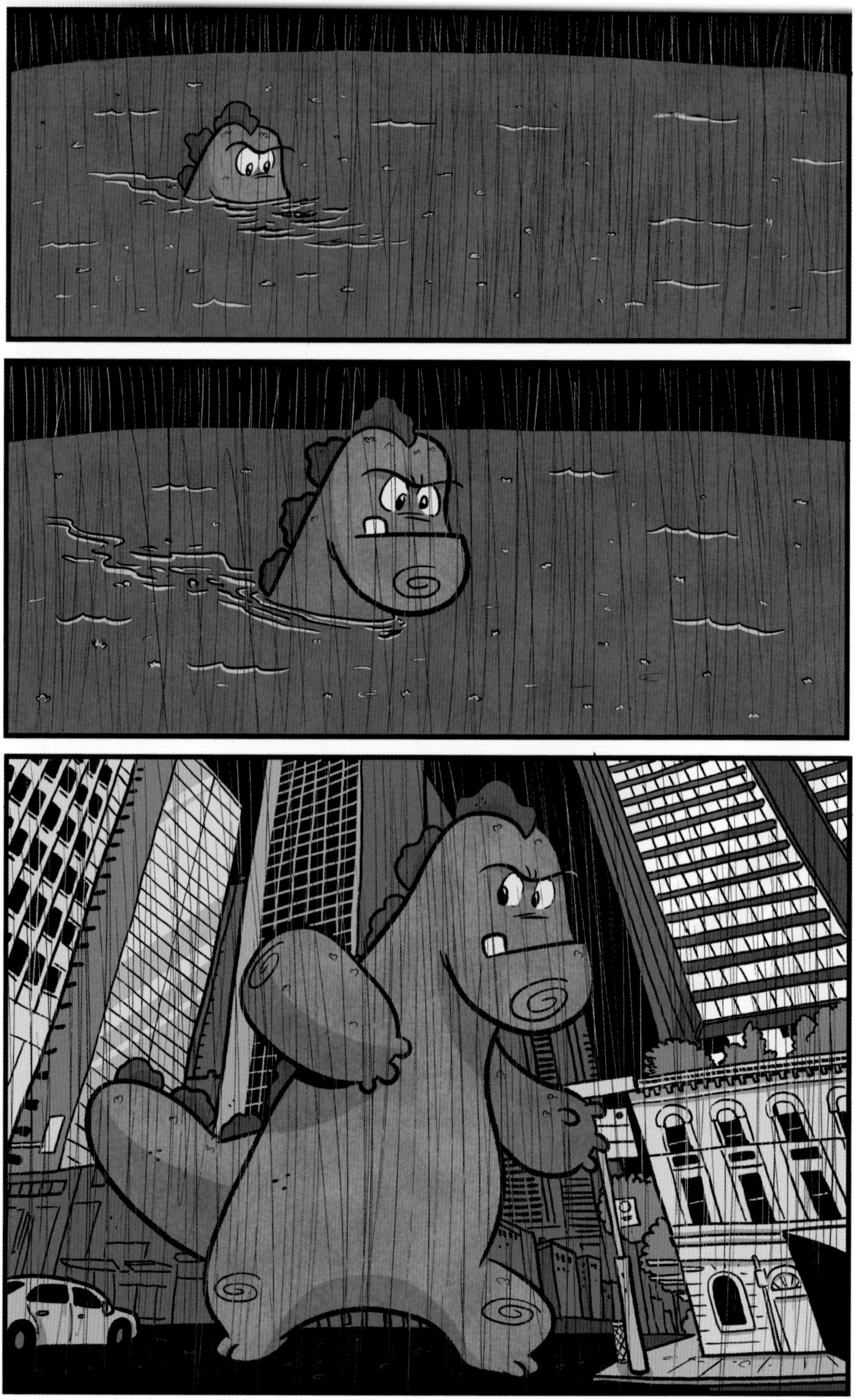

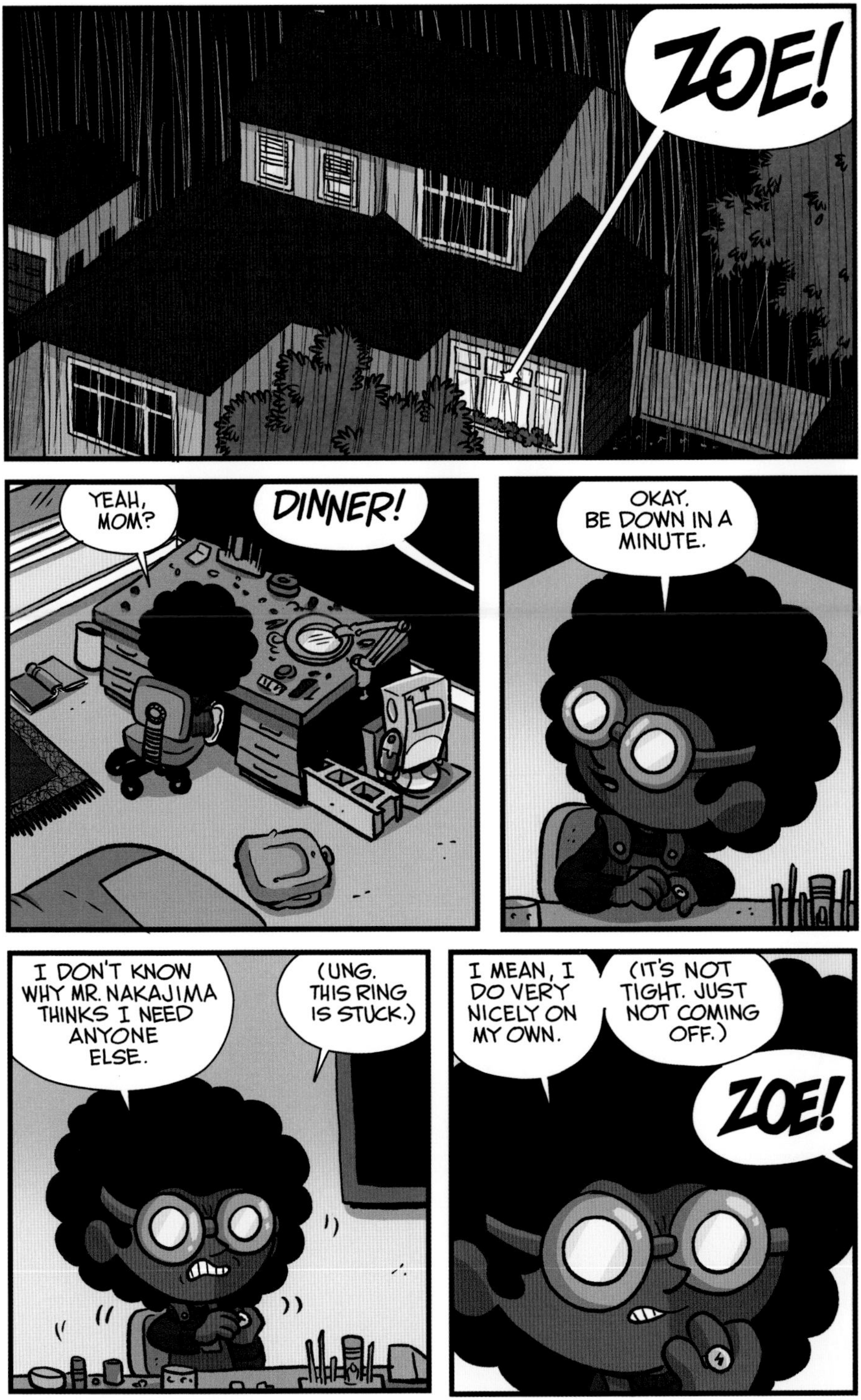
ZOE!
YEAH, MOM?
DINNER!
OKAY. BE DOWN IN A MINUTE.
I DON'T KNOW WHY MR. NAKAJIMA THINKS I NEED ANYONE ELSE.
(UNG. THIS RING IS STUCK.)
I MEAN, I DO VERY NICELY ON MY OWN.
(IT'S NOT TIGHT. JUST NOT COMING OFF.)
ZOE!

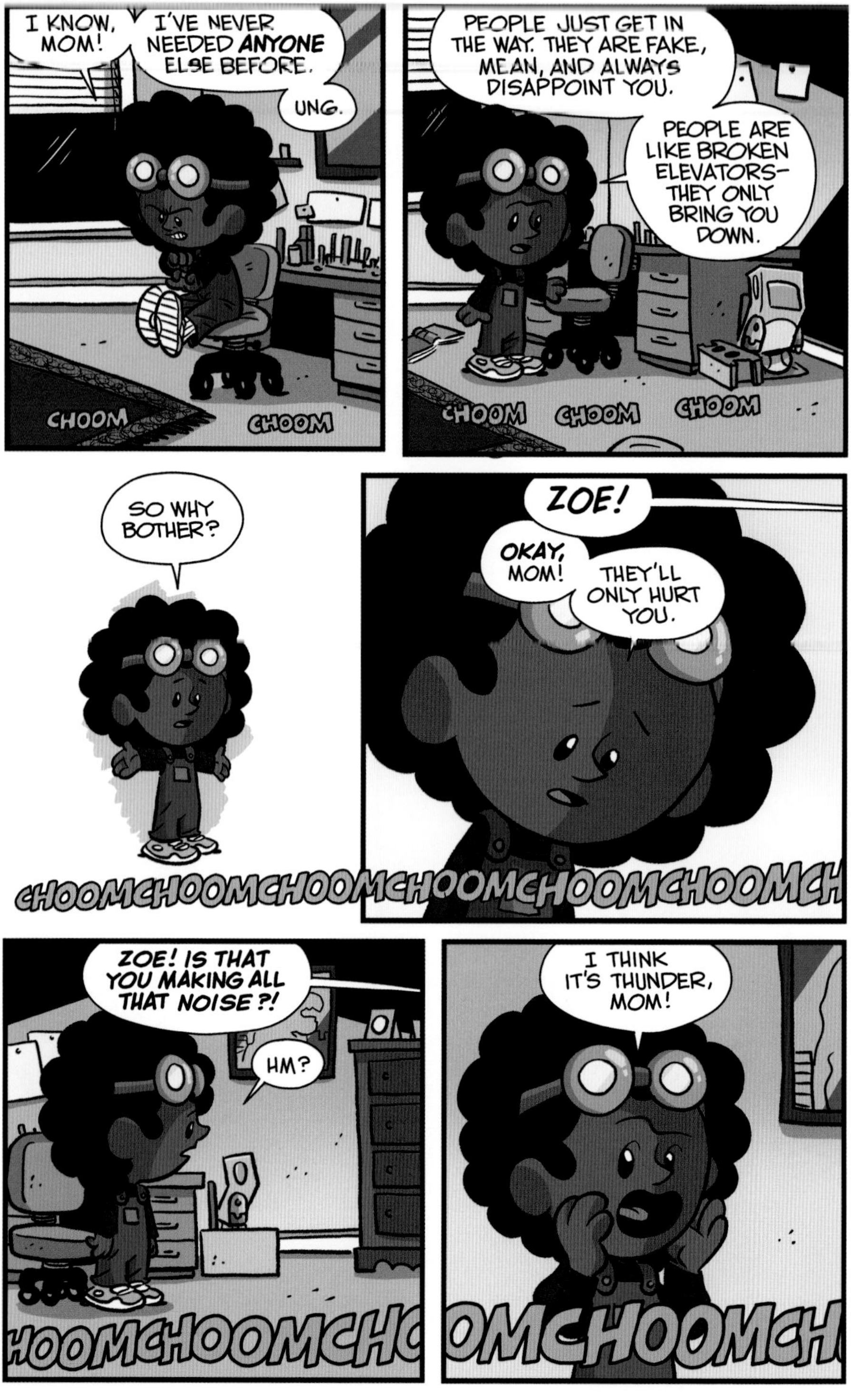
I KNOW, MOM!
I'VE NEVER NEEDED ANYONE ELSE BEFORE.
UNG.
CHOOM
CHOOM
PEOPLE JUST GET IN THE WAY. THEY ARE FAKE, MEAN, AND ALWAYS DISAPPOINT YOU.
PEOPLE ARE LIKE BROKEN ELEVATORS- THEY ONLY BRING YOU DOWN.
CHOOM CHOOM CHOOM
SO WHY BOTHER?
ZOE!
OKAY, MOM!
THEY'LL ONLY HURT YOU.
CHOOMCHOOMCHOOMCHOOMCHOOMCHOOMCH
ZOE! IS THAT YOU MAKING ALL THAT NOISE?!
HM?
I THINK IT'S THUNDER, MOM!
HOOMCHOOMCHC OMCHOOMCH

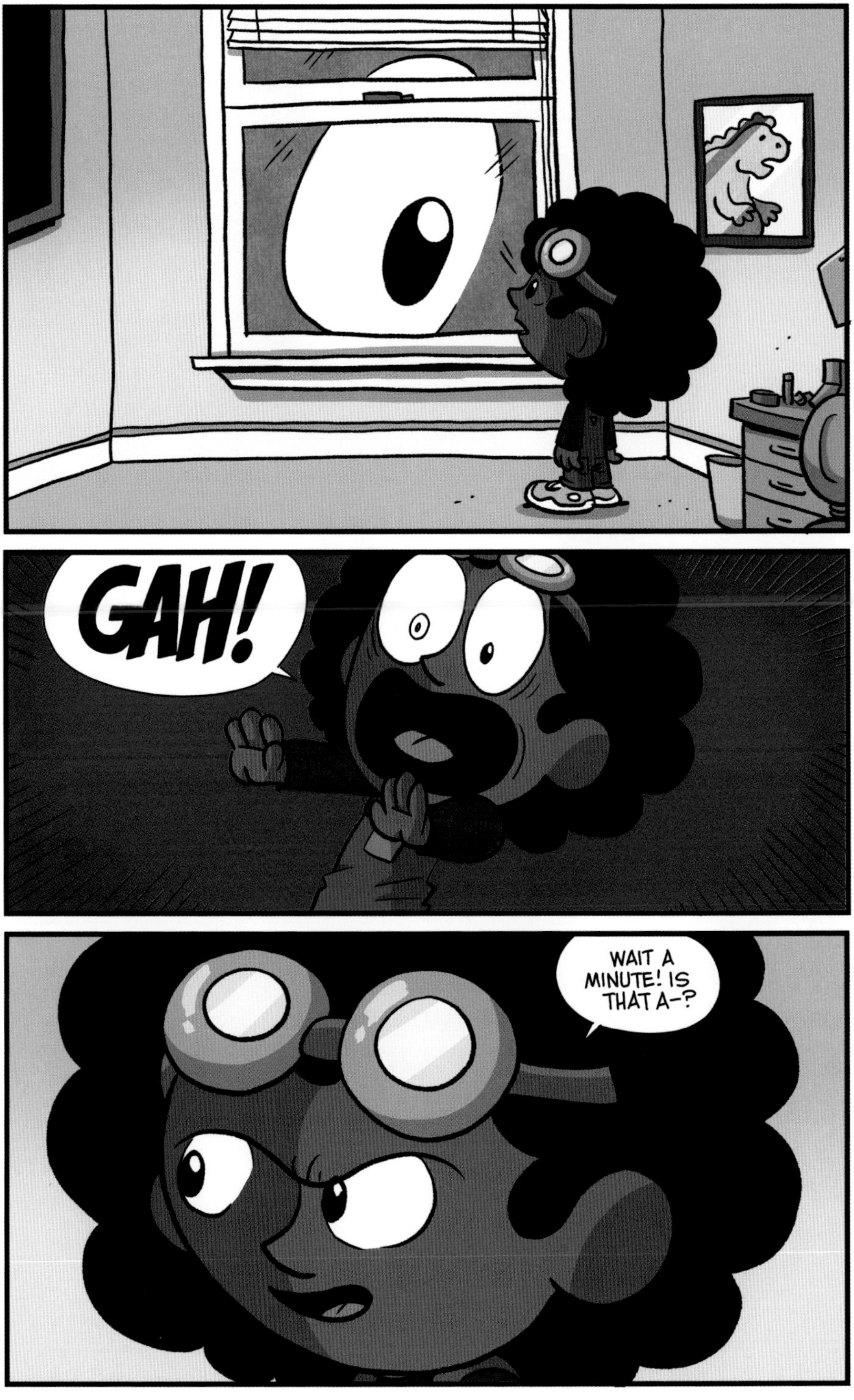
GAH!
WAIT A MINUTE! IS THAT A-?

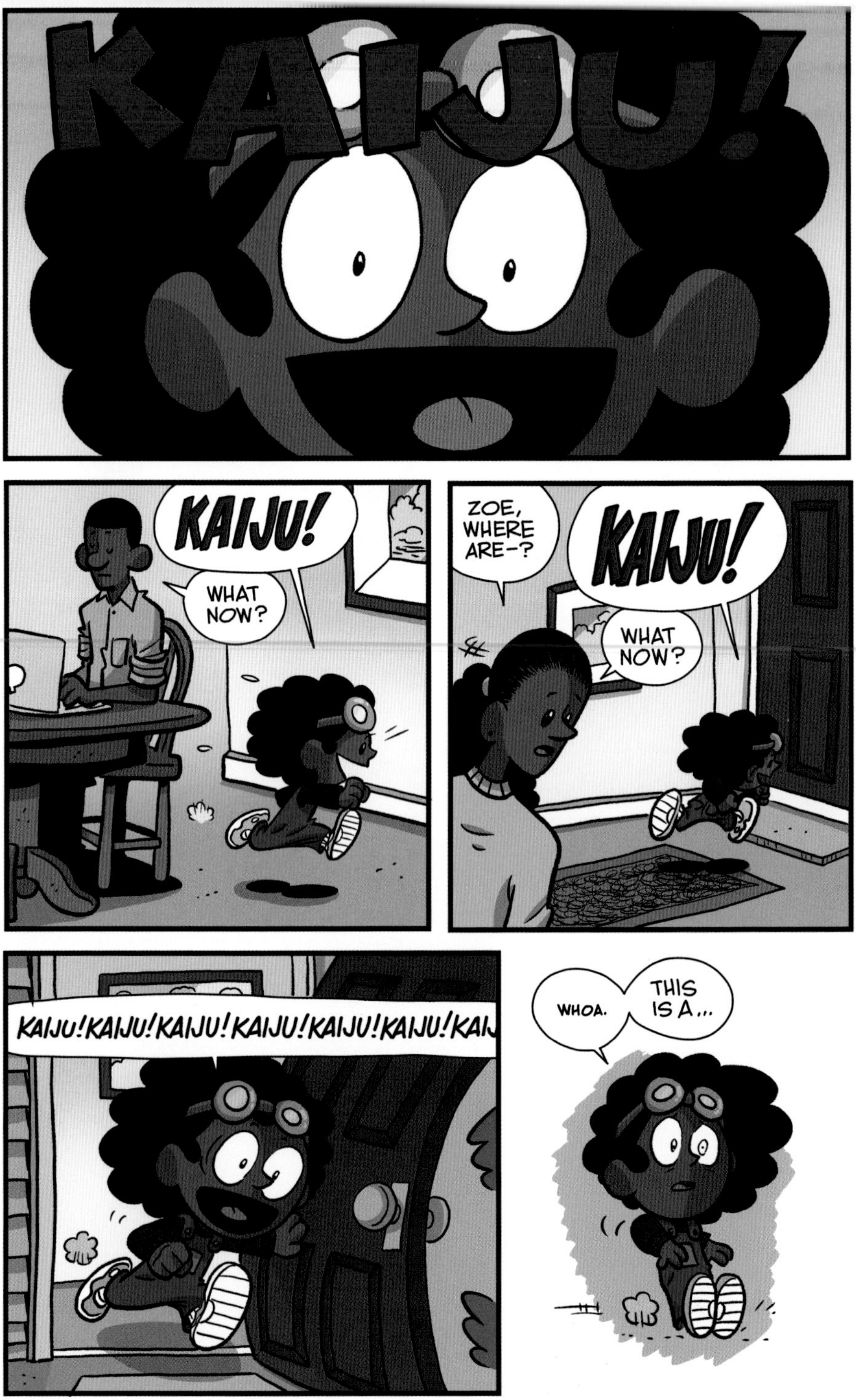
KAIJU!
KAIJU!
WHAT NOW?
ZOE, WHERE ARE-?
KAIJU!
WHAT NOW?
KAIJU!KAIJU!KAIJU!KAIJU!KAIJU!KAIJU!KAI
WHOA.
THIS IS A...

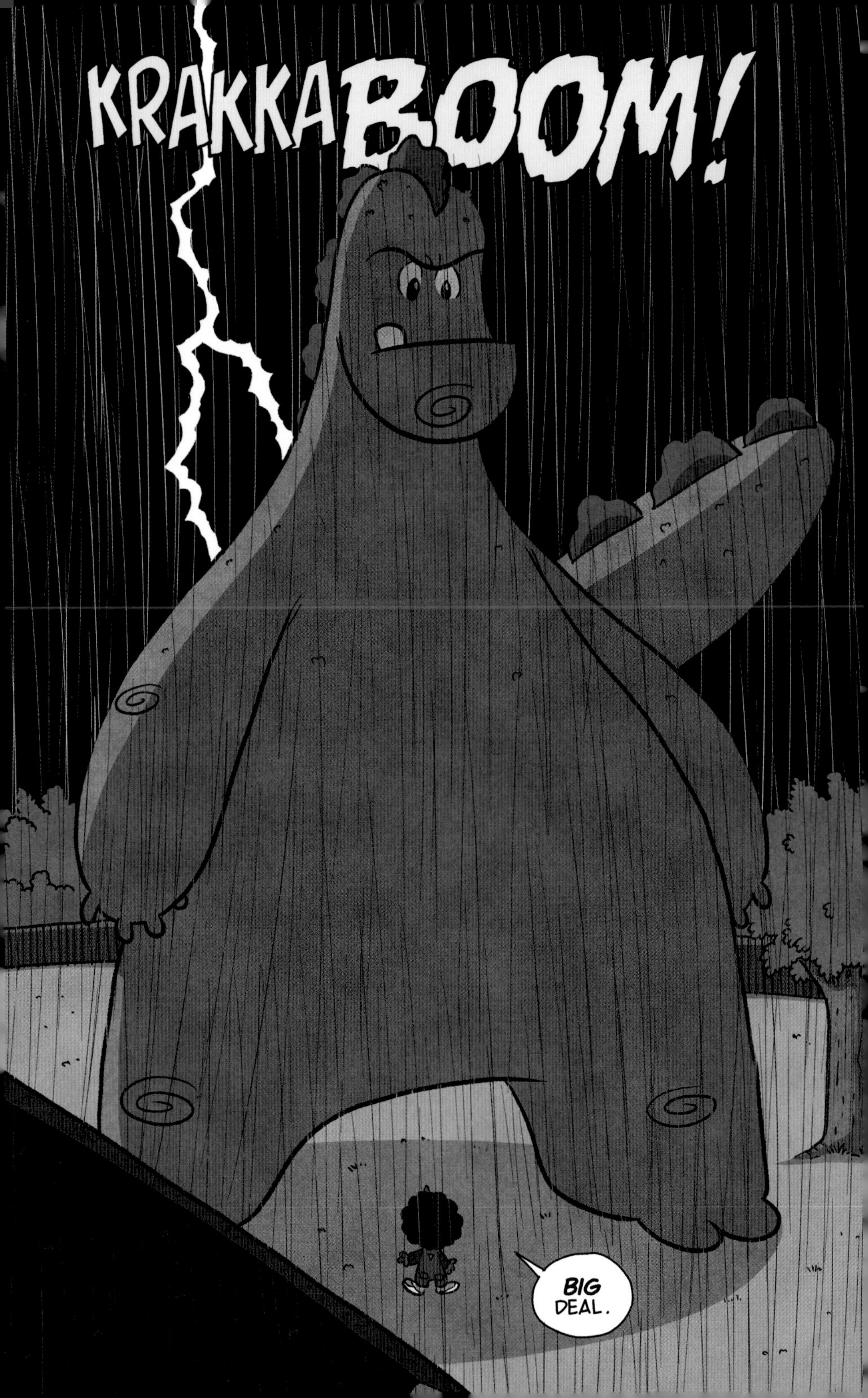
KRAKKABOOM!
BIG DEAL.

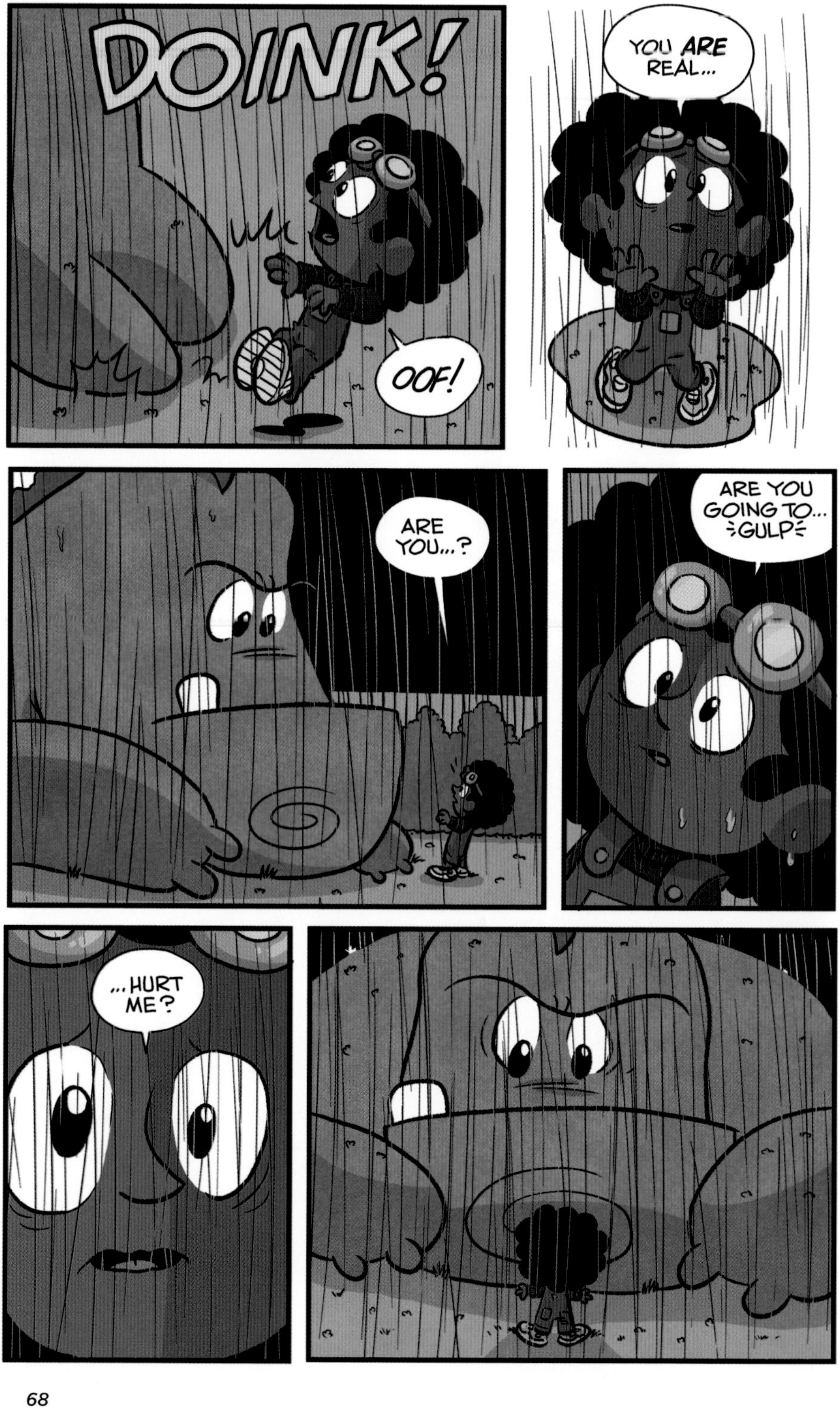
DOINK!
OOF!
YOU ARE REAL...
ARE YOU...?
ARE YOU GOING TO... GULP
...HURT ME?

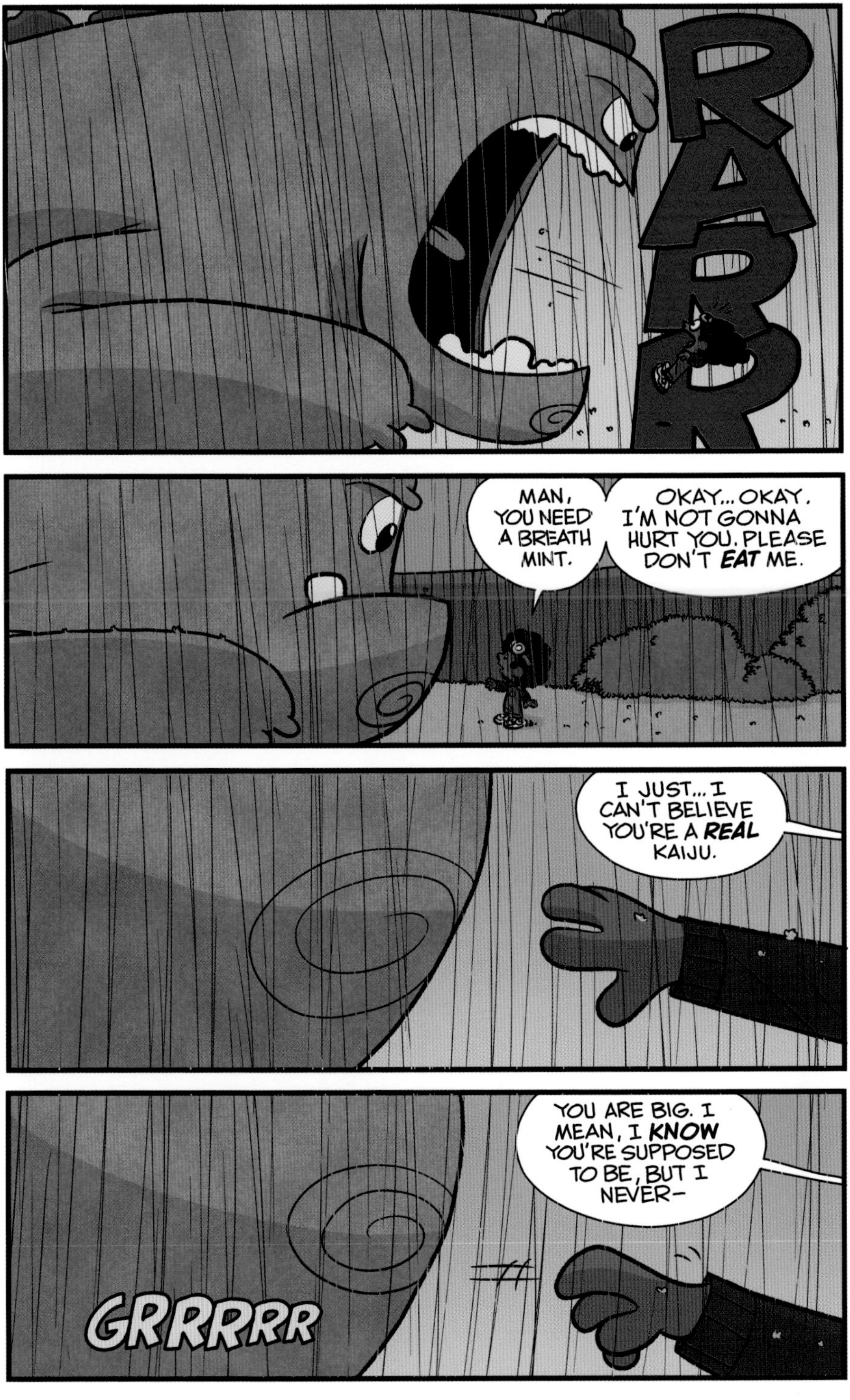
RARRR
MAN, YOU NEED A BREATH MINT.
OKAY... OKAY. I'M NOT GONNA HURT YOU. PLEASE DON'T **EAT** ME.
I JUST... I CAN'T BELIEVE YOU'RE A **REAL** KAIJU.
YOU ARE BIG. I MEAN, I **KNOW** YOU'RE SUPPOSED TO BE, BUT I NEVER–
GRRRRR

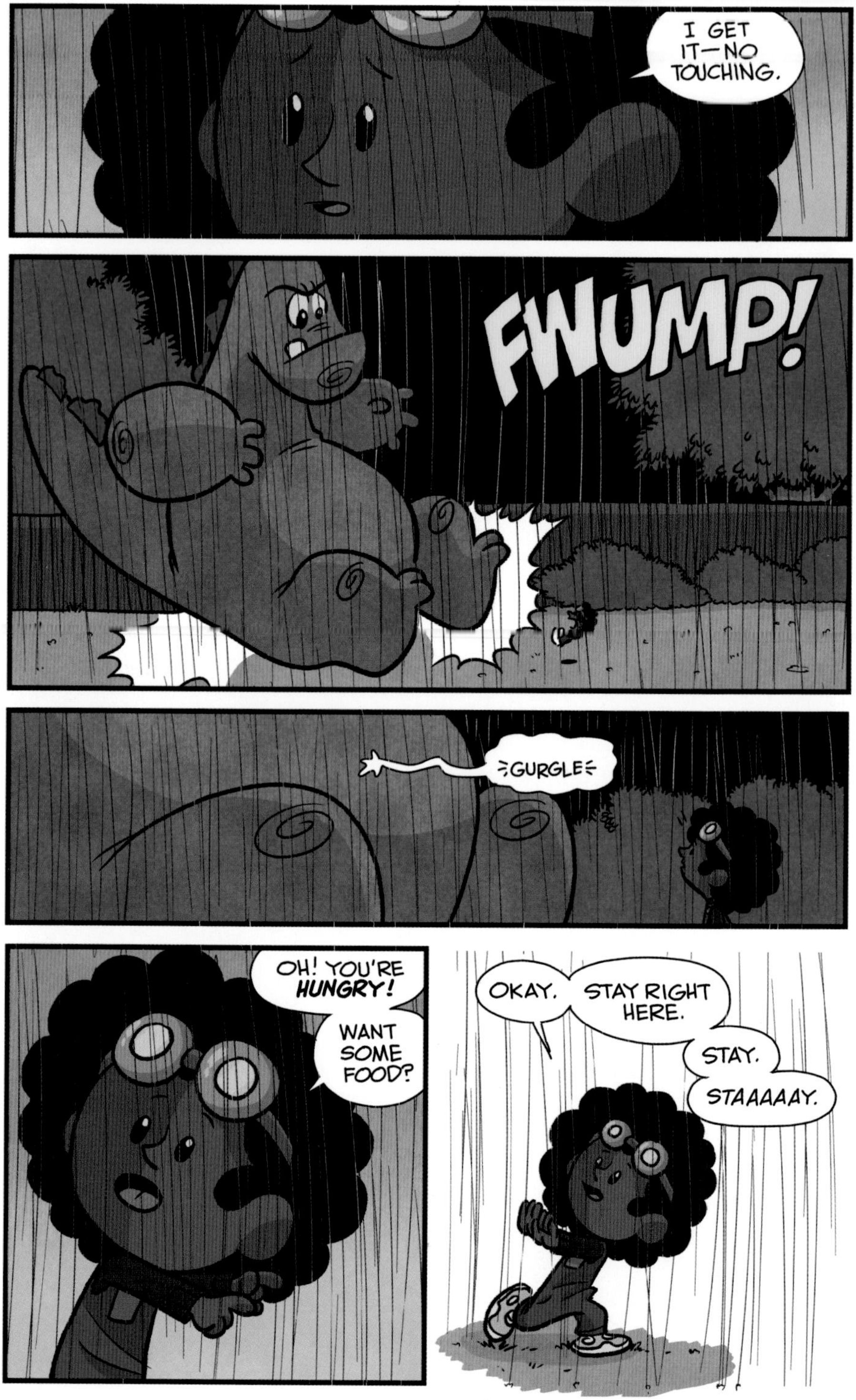
I GET IT—NO TOUCHING.
FWUMP!
GURGLE
OH! YOU'RE **HUNGRY**!
WANT SOME FOOD?
OKAY.
STAY RIGHT HERE.
STAY.
STAAAAAY.

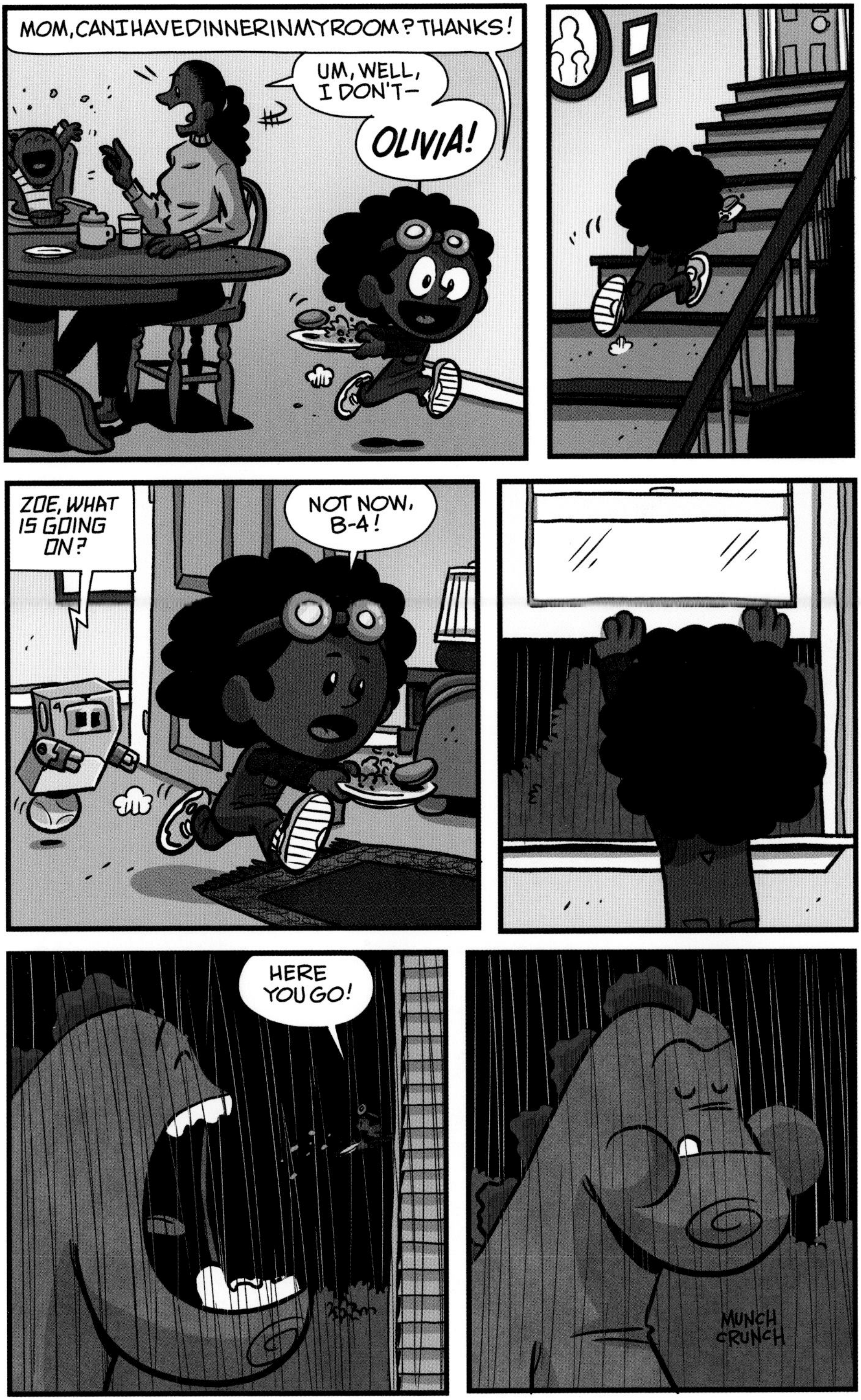

MOM, CANIHAVEDINNERINMYROOM? THANKS!
UM, WELL, I DON'T—
OLIVIA!
ZOE, WHAT IS GOING ON?
NOT NOW, B-4!
HERE YOU GO!
MUNCH CRUNCH

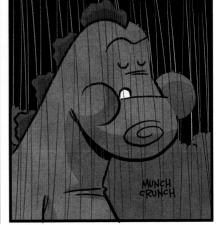

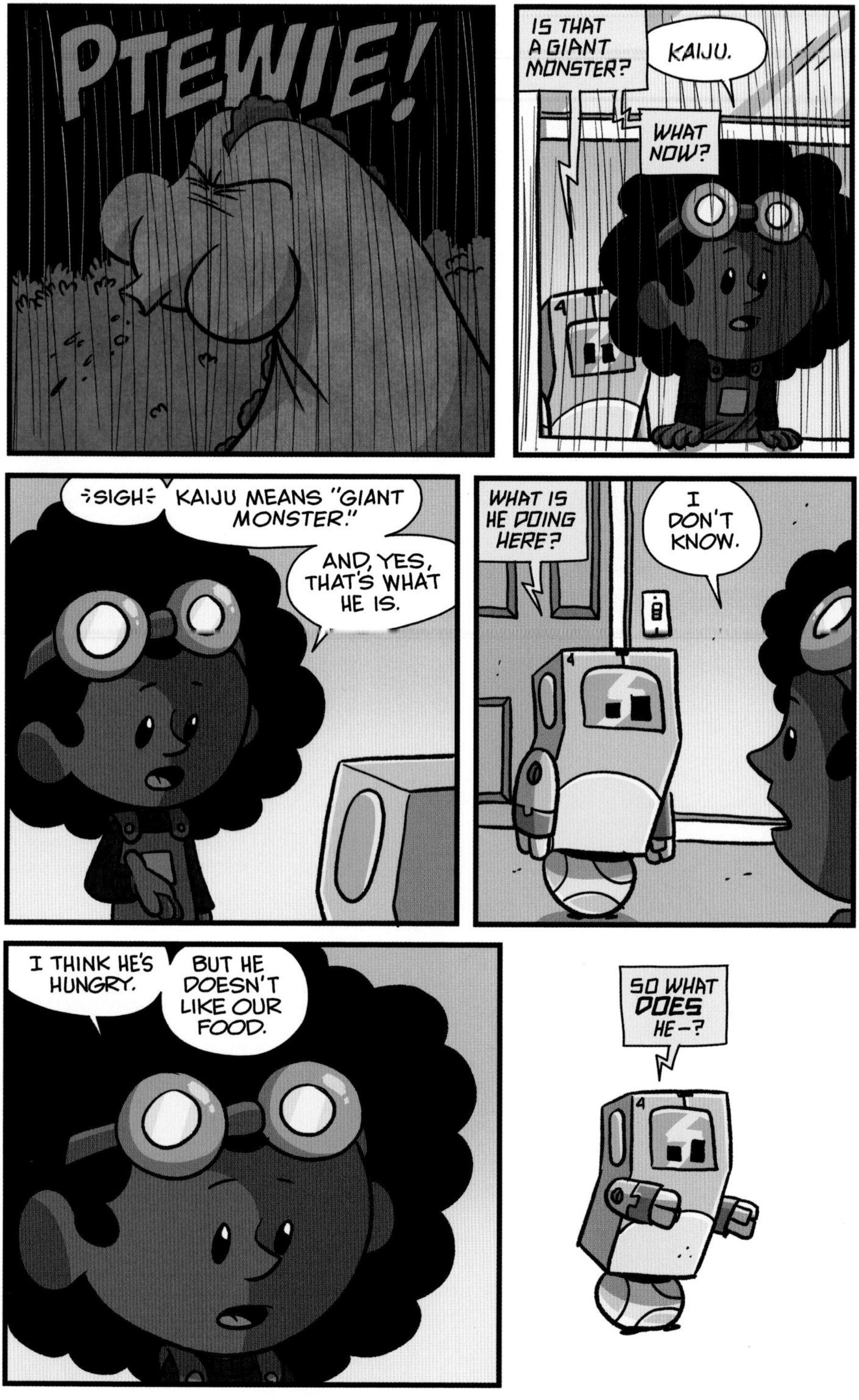
PTEWIE!
IS THAT A GIANT MONSTER?
KAIJU.
WHAT NOW?
⁼SIGH⁼ KAIJU MEANS "GIANT MONSTER."
AND, YES, THAT'S WHAT HE IS.
WHAT IS HE DOING HERE?
I DON'T KNOW.
I THINK HE'S HUNGRY.
BUT HE DOESN'T LIKE OUR FOOD.
SO WHAT DOES HE—?

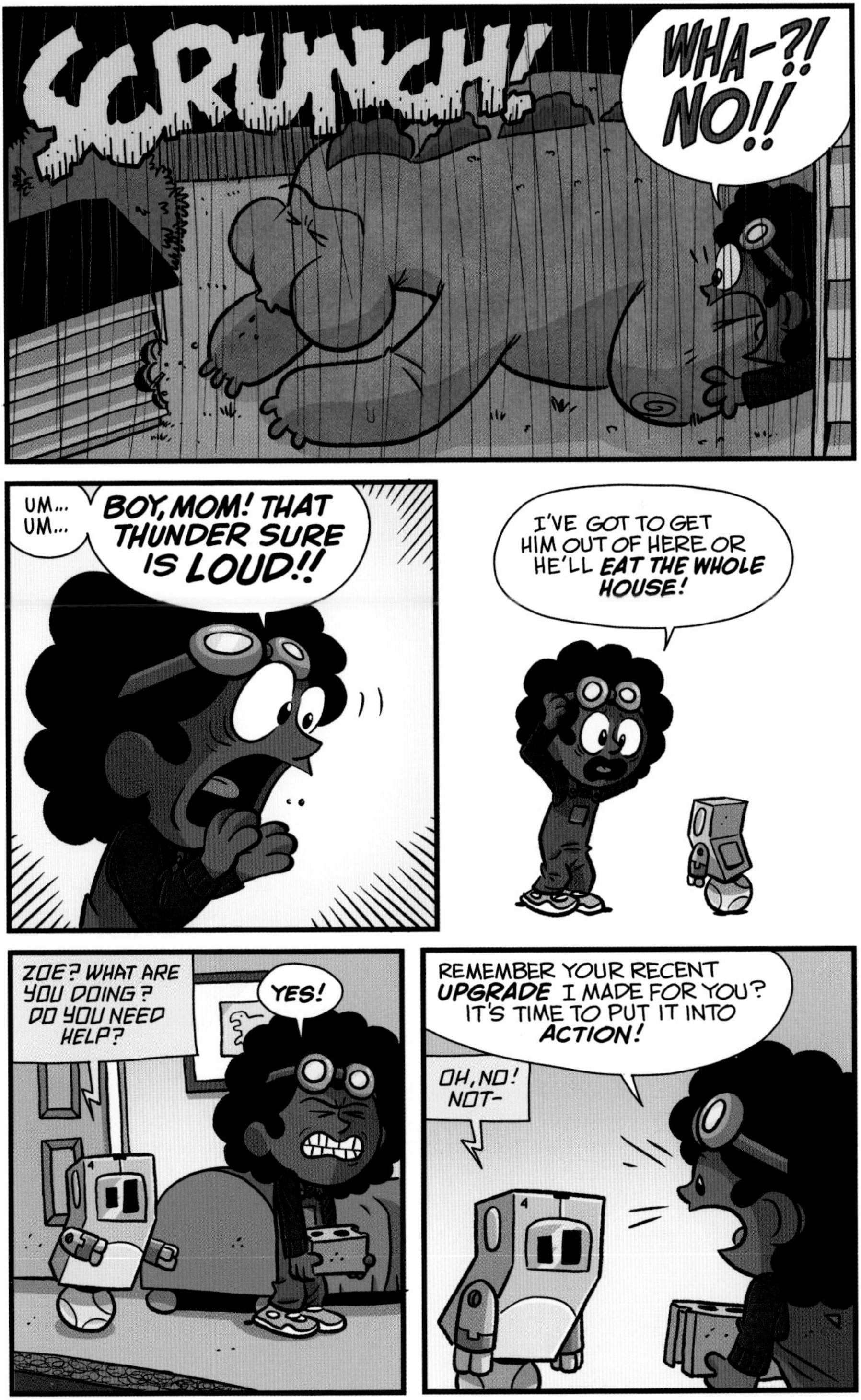
SCRUNCH!
WHA-?! NO!!
UM... UM...
BOY, MOM! THAT THUNDER SURE IS LOUD!!
I'VE GOT TO GET HIM OUT OF HERE OR HE'LL EAT THE WHOLE HOUSE!
ZOE? WHAT ARE YOU DOING? DO YOU NEED HELP?
YES!
REMEMBER YOUR RECENT UPGRADE I MADE FOR YOU? IT'S TIME TO PUT IT INTO ACTION!
OH, NO! NOT-

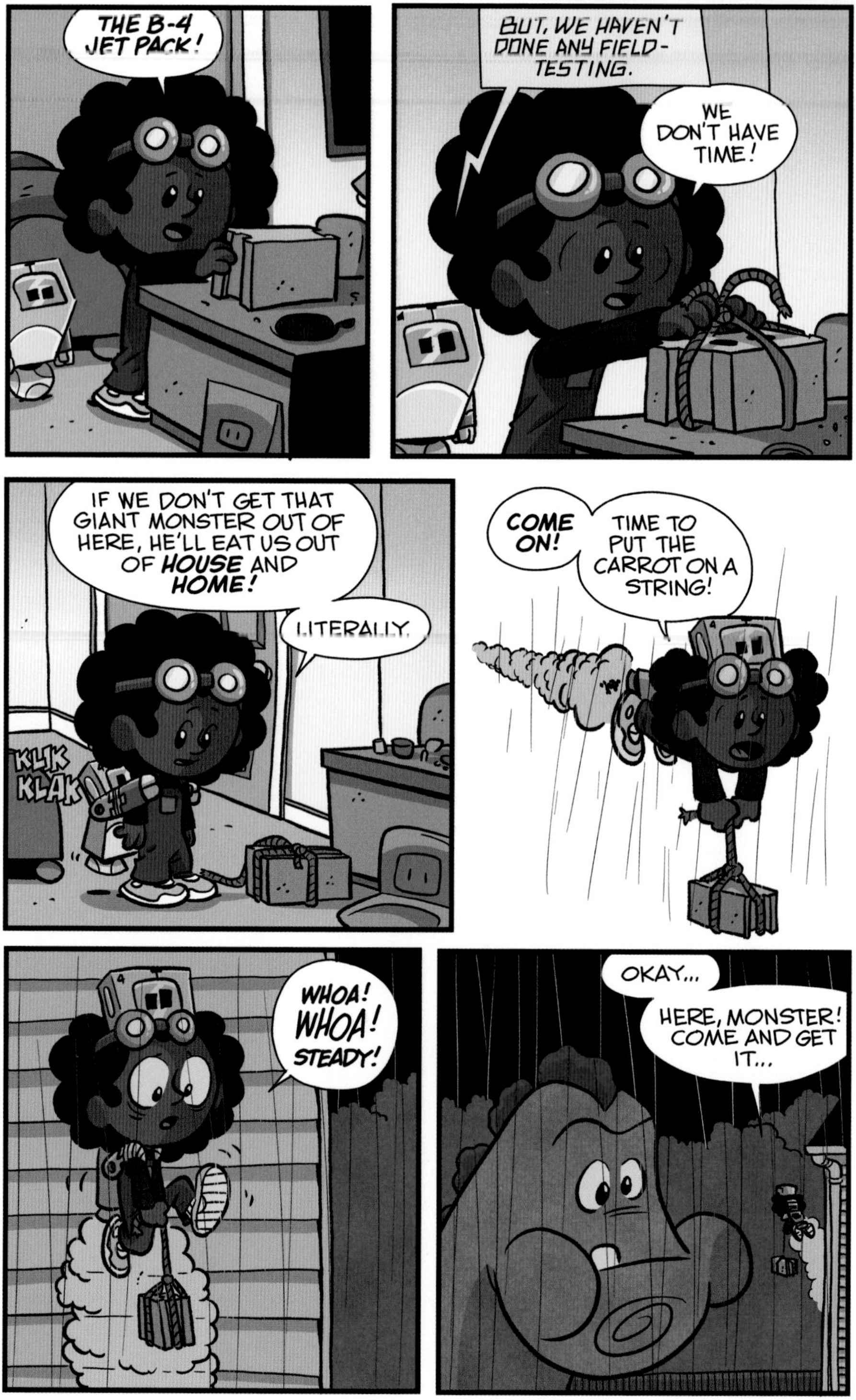

THE B-4 JET PACK!
BUT, WE HAVEN'T DONE ANY FIELD-TESTING.
WE DON'T HAVE TIME!
IF WE DON'T GET THAT GIANT MONSTER OUT OF HERE, HE'LL EAT US OUT OF **HOUSE** AND **HOME**!
LITERALLY.
KLIK KLAK
COME ON!
TIME TO PUT THE CARROT ON A STRING!
WHOA! WHOA! STEADY!
OKAY...
HERE, MONSTER! COME AND GET IT...

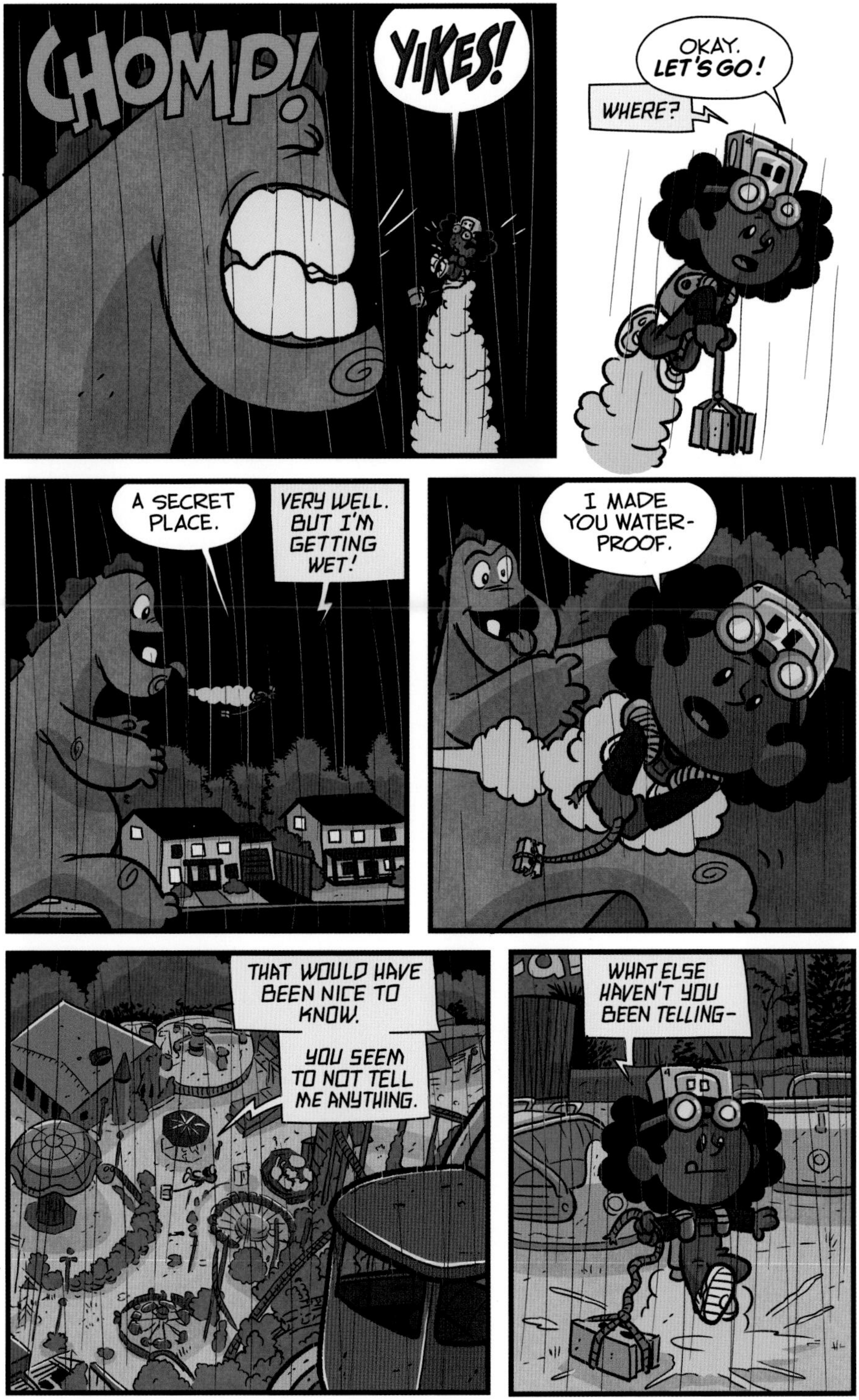
CHOMP!
YIKES!
WHERE?
OKAY. LET'S GO!
A SECRET PLACE.
VERY WELL. BUT I'M GETTING WET!
I MADE YOU WATER-PROOF.
THAT WOULD HAVE BEEN NICE TO KNOW.
YOU SEEM TO NOT TELL ME ANYTHING.
WHAT ELSE HAVEN'T YOU BEEN TELLING-

ZOE!

YOU'RE BUILDING A GIANT ROBOT?!

NO.

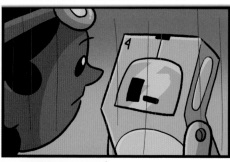

I'M BUILDING A GIANT *EXO-SKELETON.*

CALL IT WHAT YOU WANT. BUT WHAT ARE YOU GOING TO DO ABOUT *HIM?*

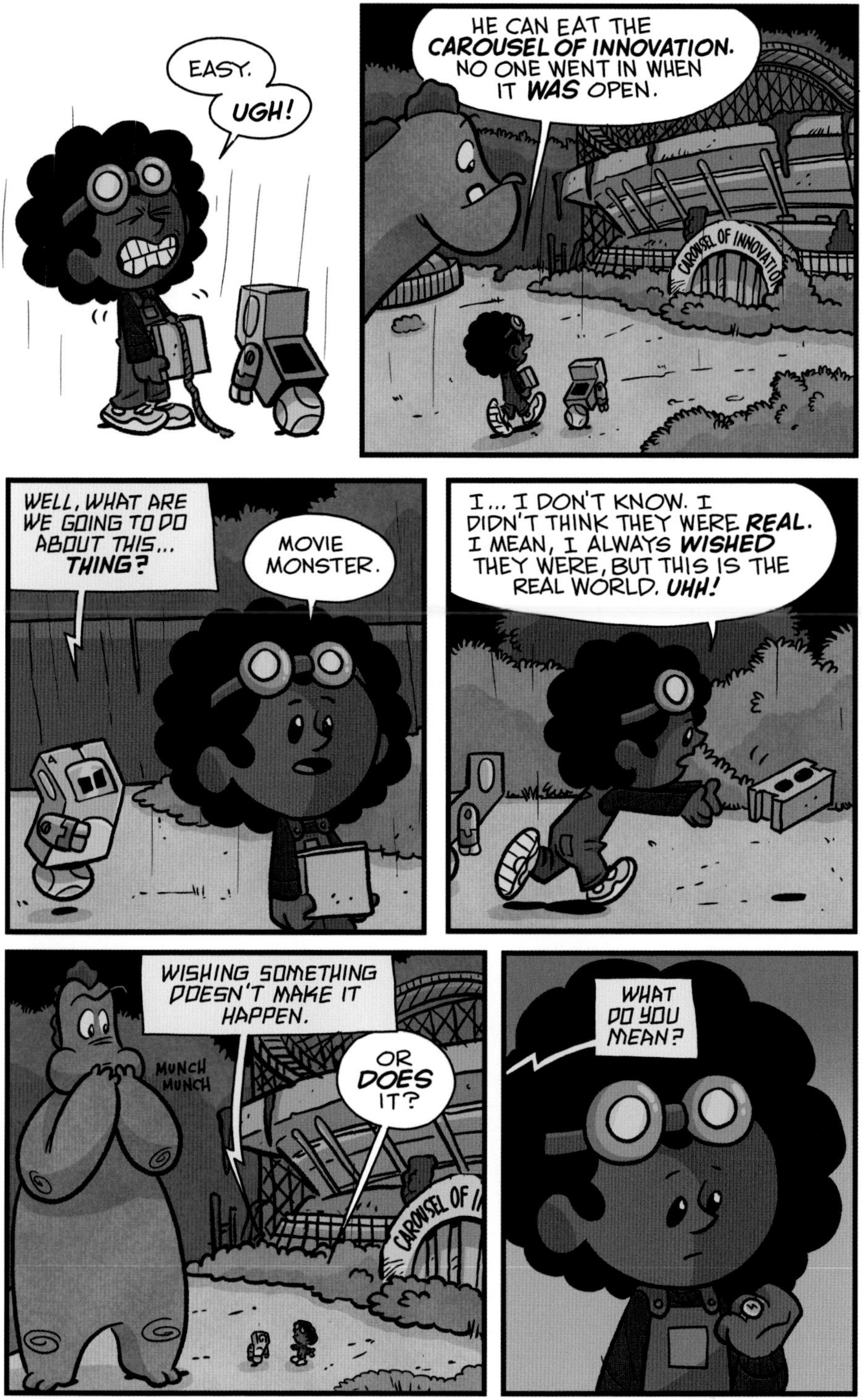
EASY.
UGH!
HE CAN EAT THE CAROUSEL OF INNOVATION. NO ONE WENT IN WHEN IT WAS OPEN.
CAROUSEL OF INNOVATION
WELL, WHAT ARE WE GOING TO DO ABOUT THIS... THING?
MOVIE MONSTER.
I... I DON'T KNOW. I DIDN'T THINK THEY WERE REAL. I MEAN, I ALWAYS WISHED THEY WERE, BUT THIS IS THE REAL WORLD. UHH!
WISHING SOMETHING DOESN'T MAKE IT HAPPEN.
MUNCH MUNCH
OR DOES IT?
WHAT DO YOU MEAN?

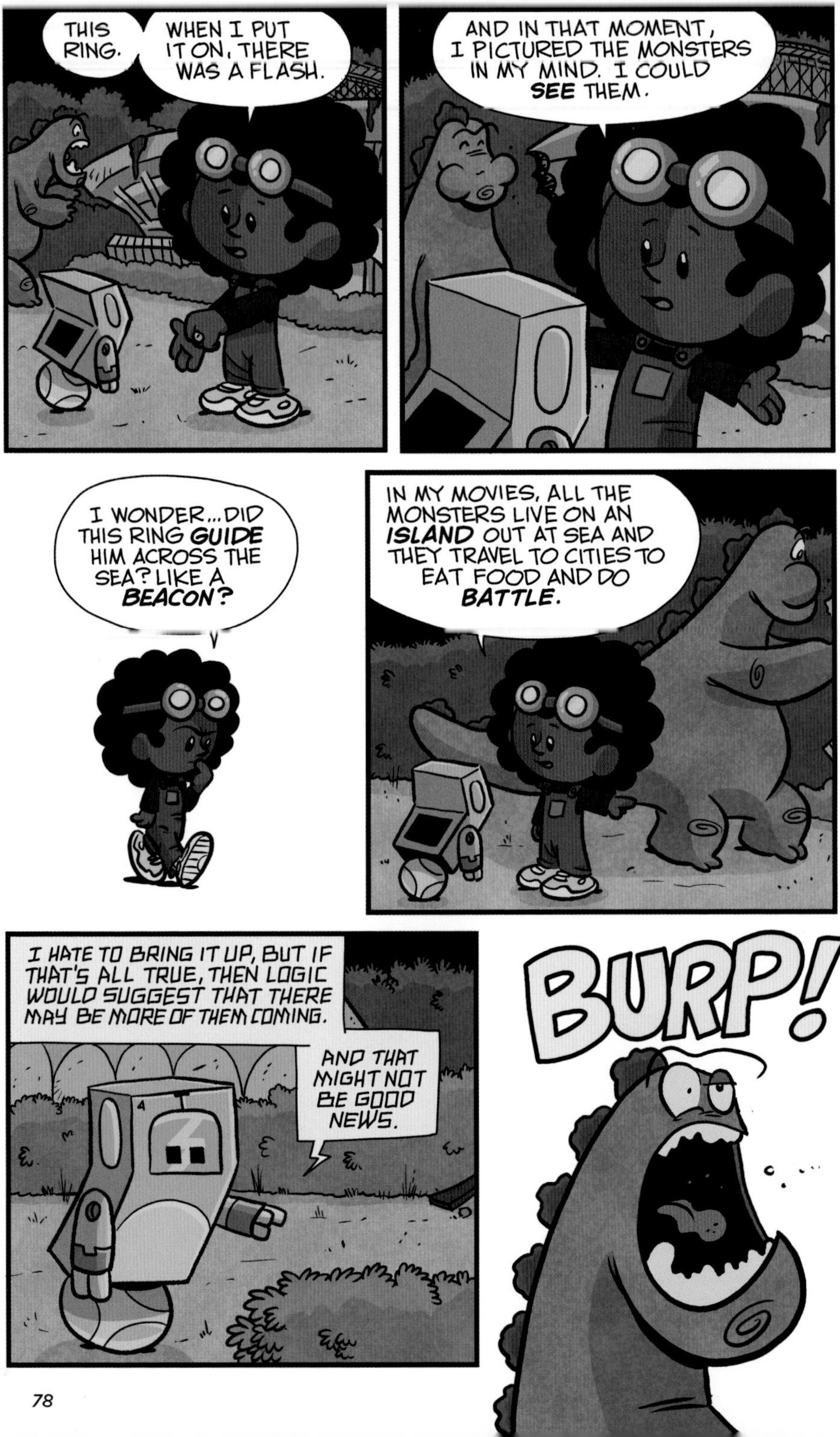
THIS RING.
WHEN I PUT IT ON, THERE WAS A FLASH.
AND IN THAT MOMENT, I PICTURED THE MONSTERS IN MY MIND. I COULD SEE THEM.
I WONDER...DID THIS RING GUIDE HIM ACROSS THE SEA? LIKE A BEACON?
IN MY MOVIES, ALL THE MONSTERS LIVE ON AN ISLAND OUT AT SEA AND THEY TRAVEL TO CITIES TO EAT FOOD AND DO BATTLE.
I HATE TO BRING IT UP, BUT IF THAT'S ALL TRUE, THEN LOGIC WOULD SUGGEST THAT THERE MAY BE MORE OF THEM COMING.
AND THAT MIGHT NOT BE GOOD NEWS.
4
BURP!

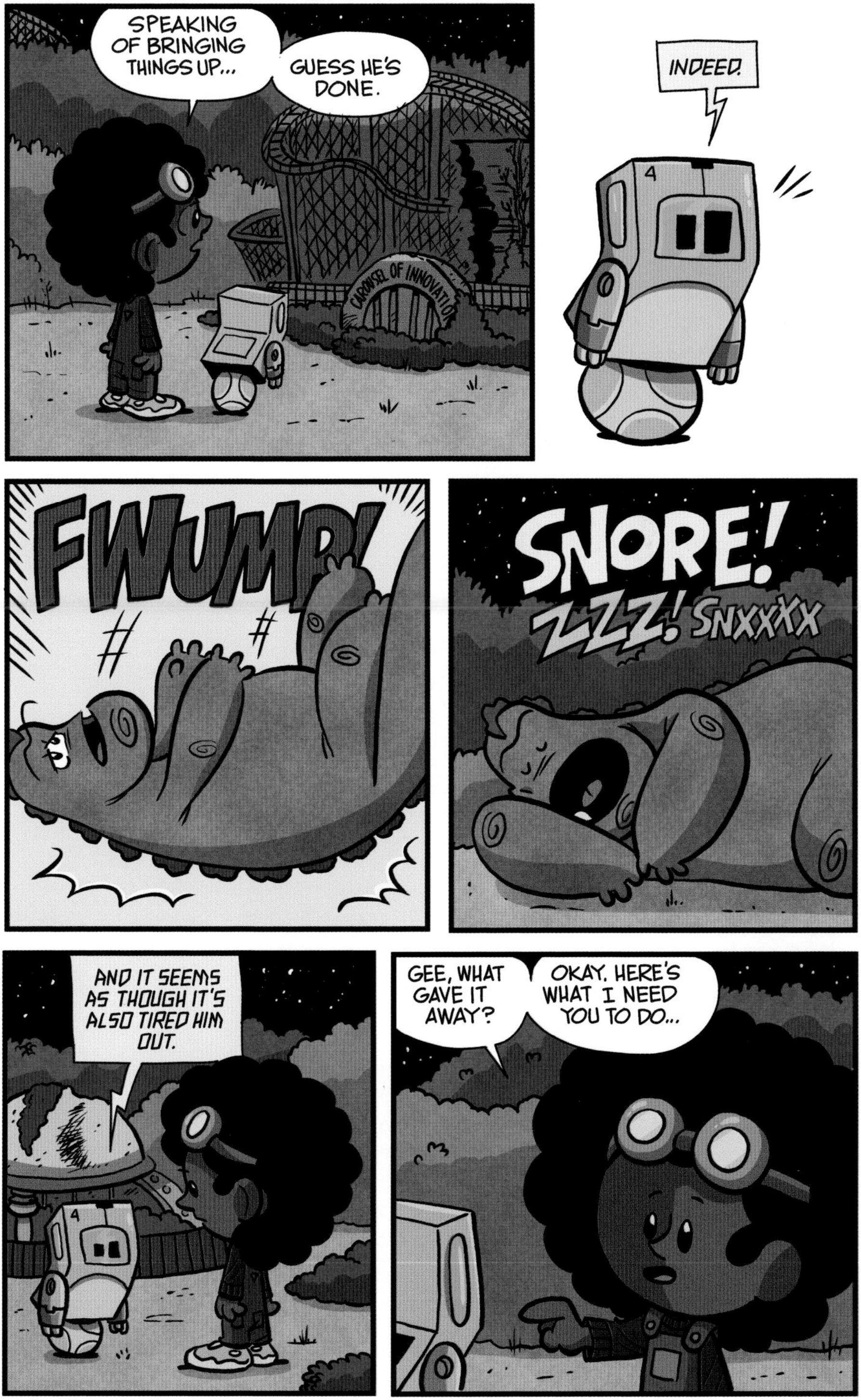
SPEAKING OF BRINGING THINGS UP...
GUESS HE'S DONE.
CAROUSEL OF INNOVATION
INDEED.
FWUMP!
SNORE!
ZZZ! SNXXXX
AND IT SEEMS AS THOUGH IT'S ALSO TIRED HIM OUT.
GEE, WHAT GAVE IT AWAY?
OKAY. HERE'S WHAT I NEED YOU TO DO...

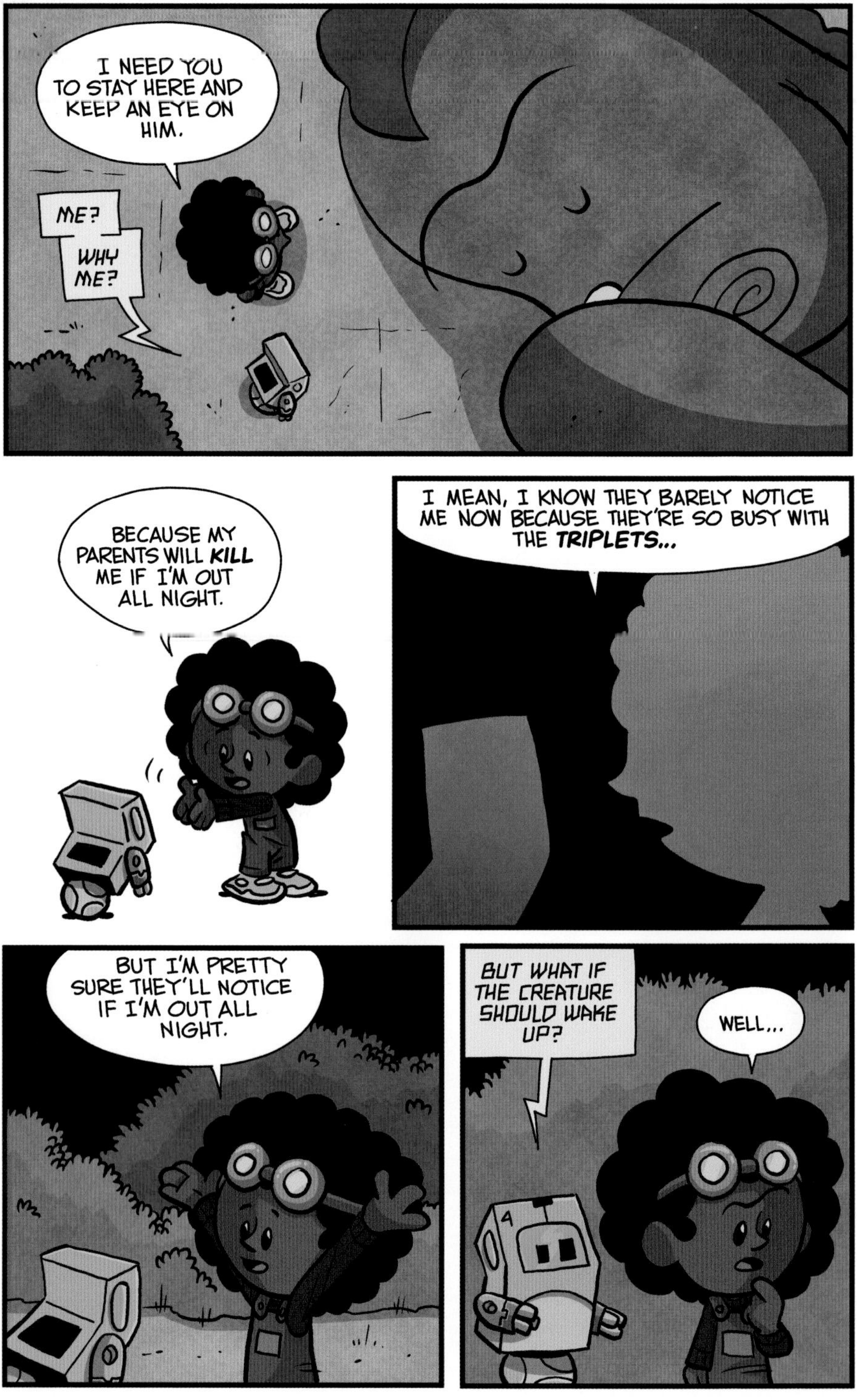
I NEED YOU TO STAY HERE AND KEEP AN EYE ON HIM.
ME?
WHY ME?
BECAUSE MY PARENTS WILL **KILL** ME IF I'M OUT ALL NIGHT.
I MEAN, I KNOW THEY BARELY NOTICE ME NOW BECAUSE THEY'RE SO BUSY WITH THE ***TRIPLETS...***
BUT I'M PRETTY SURE THEY'LL NOTICE IF I'M OUT ALL NIGHT.
BUT WHAT IF THE CREATURE SHOULD WAKE UP?
WELL...

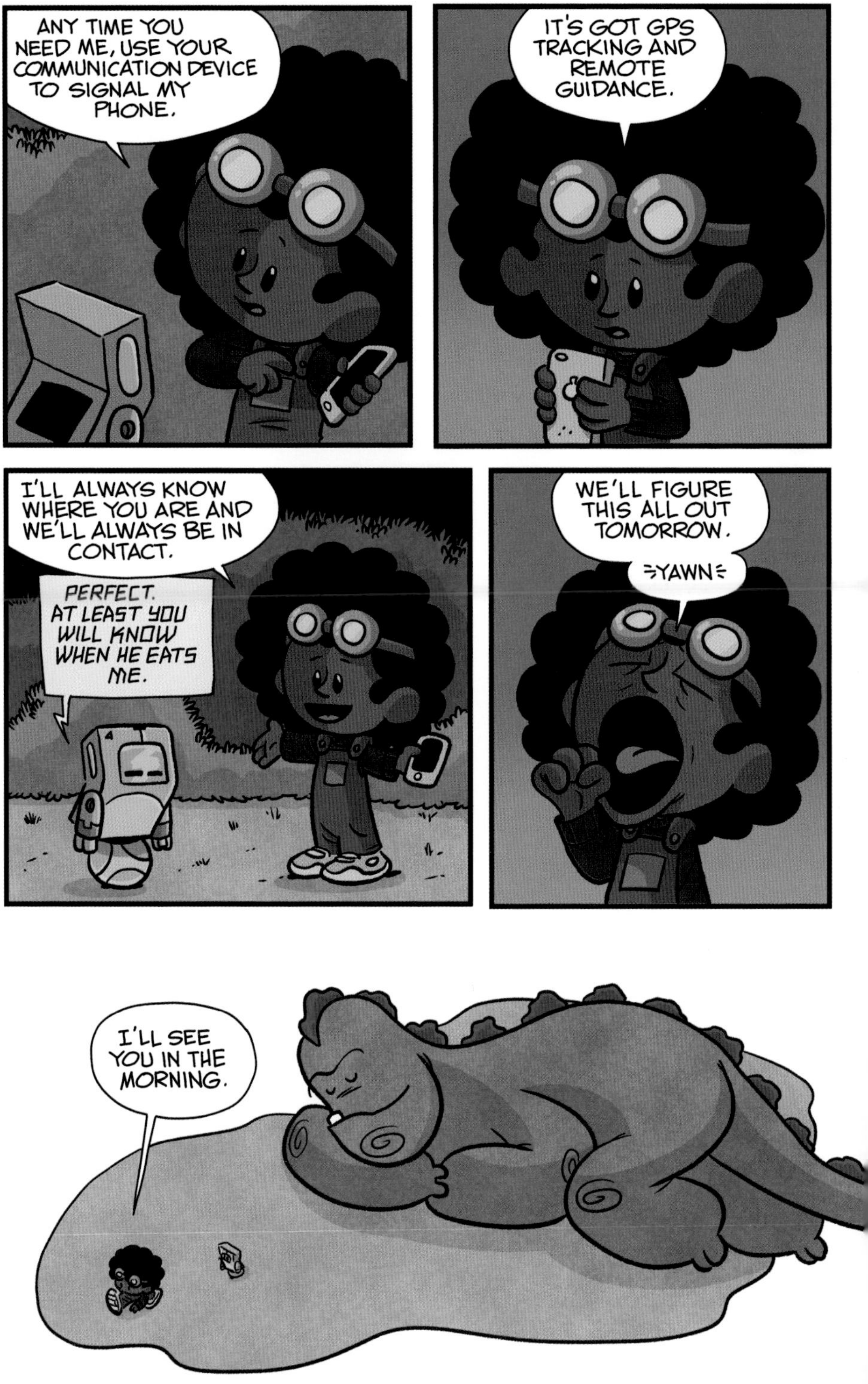
ANY TIME YOU NEED ME, USE YOUR COMMUNICATION DEVICE TO SIGNAL MY PHONE.
IT'S GOT GPS TRACKING AND REMOTE GUIDANCE.
I'LL ALWAYS KNOW WHERE YOU ARE AND WE'LL ALWAYS BE IN CONTACT.
PERFECT. AT LEAST YOU WILL KNOW WHEN HE EATS ME.
WE'LL FIGURE THIS ALL OUT TOMORROW.
YAWN
I'LL SEE YOU IN THE MORNING.

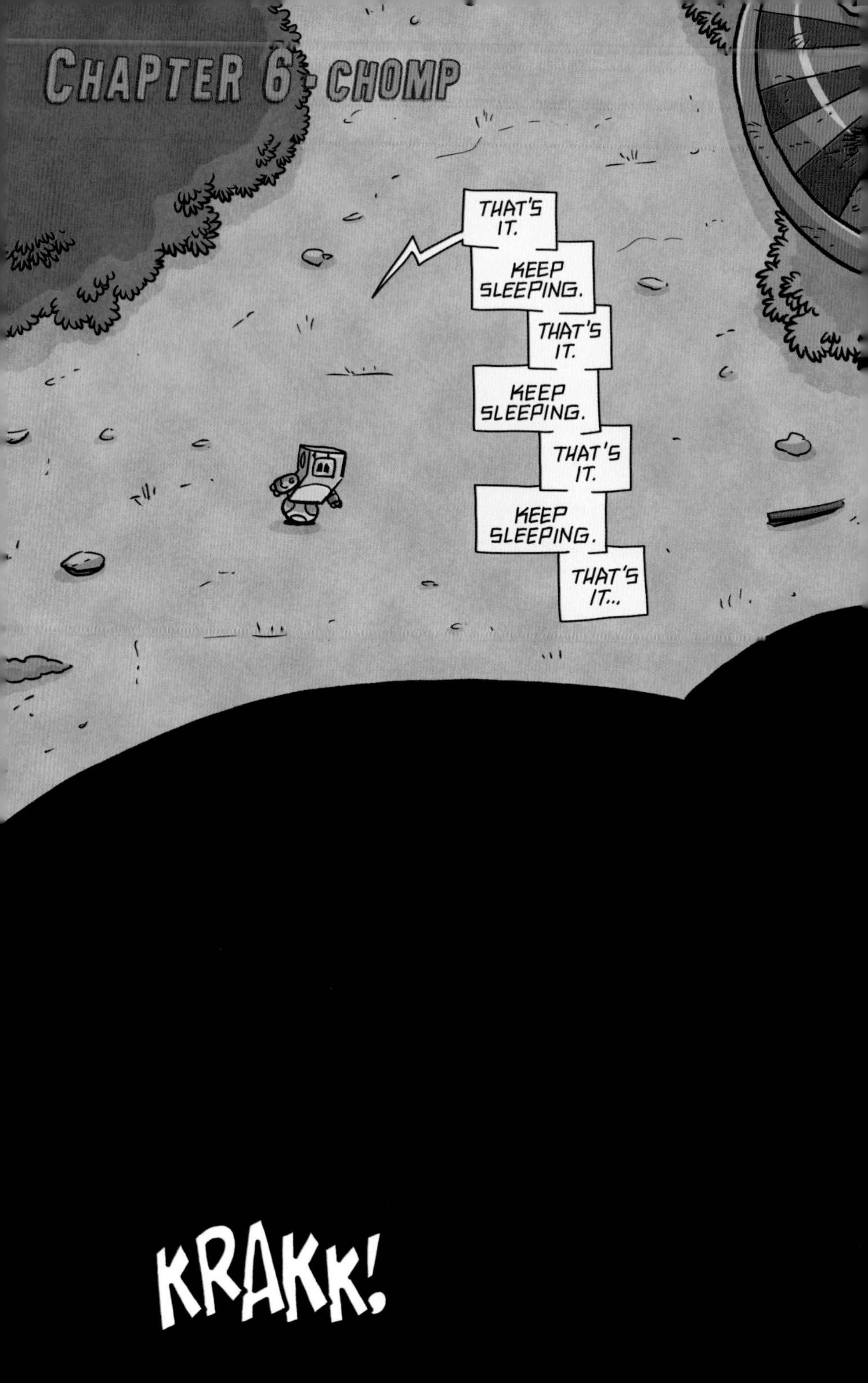
CHAPTER 6: CHOMP
THAT'S IT.
KEEP SLEEPING.
THAT'S IT.
KEEP SLEEPING.
THAT'S IT.
KEEP SLEEPING.
THAT'S IT...
KRAKK!

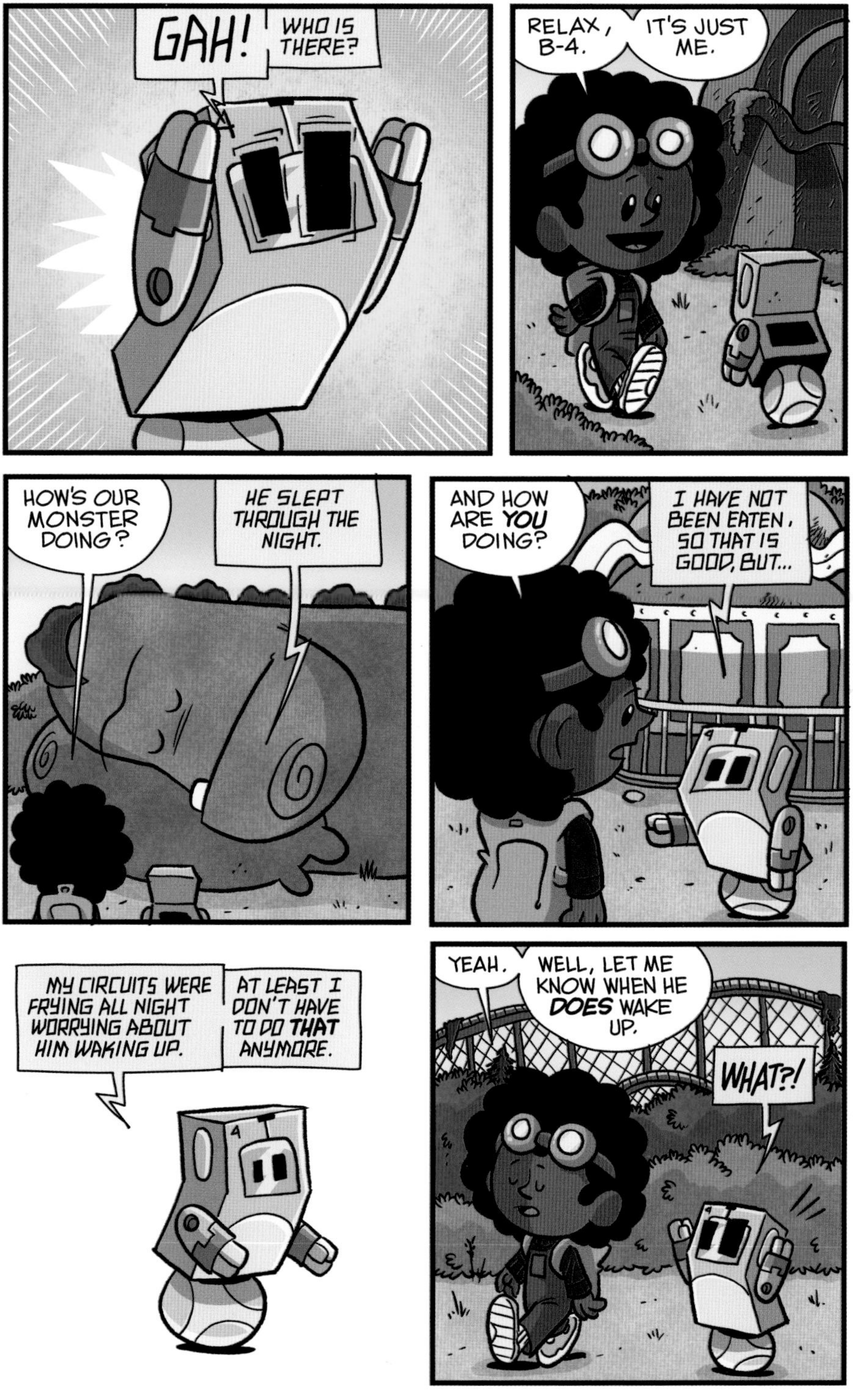
GAH! WHO IS THERE?
RELAX, B-4.
IT'S JUST ME.
HOW'S OUR MONSTER DOING?
HE SLEPT THROUGH THE NIGHT.
AND HOW ARE **YOU** DOING?
I HAVE NOT BEEN EATEN, SO THAT IS GOOD, BUT...
MY CIRCUITS WERE FRYING ALL NIGHT WORRYING ABOUT HIM WAKING UP.
AT LEAST I DON'T HAVE TO DO **THAT** ANYMORE.
YEAH.
WELL, LET ME KNOW WHEN HE **DOES** WAKE UP.
WHAT?!

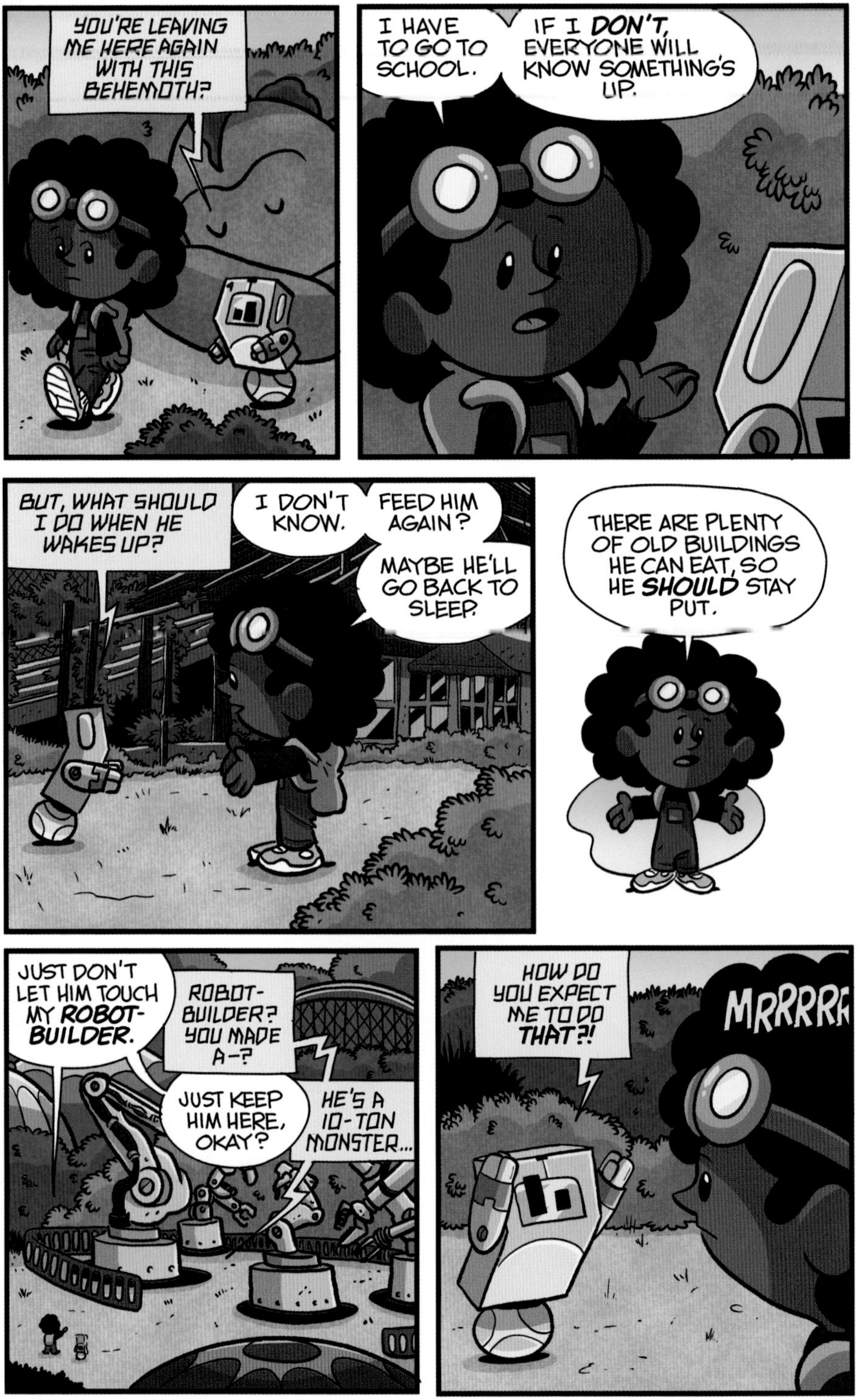
YOU'RE LEAVING ME HERE AGAIN WITH THIS BEHEMOTH?
I HAVE TO GO TO SCHOOL.
IF I DON'T, EVERYONE WILL KNOW SOMETHING'S UP.
BUT, WHAT SHOULD I DO WHEN HE WAKES UP?
I DON'T KNOW.
FEED HIM AGAIN?
MAYBE HE'LL GO BACK TO SLEEP.
THERE ARE PLENTY OF OLD BUILDINGS HE CAN EAT, SO HE SHOULD STAY PUT.
JUST DON'T LET HIM TOUCH MY ROBOT-BUILDER.
ROBOT-BUILDER? YOU MADE A–?
JUST KEEP HIM HERE, OKAY?
HE'S A 10-TON MONSTER...
HOW DO YOU EXPECT ME TO DO THAT?!
MRRRRR

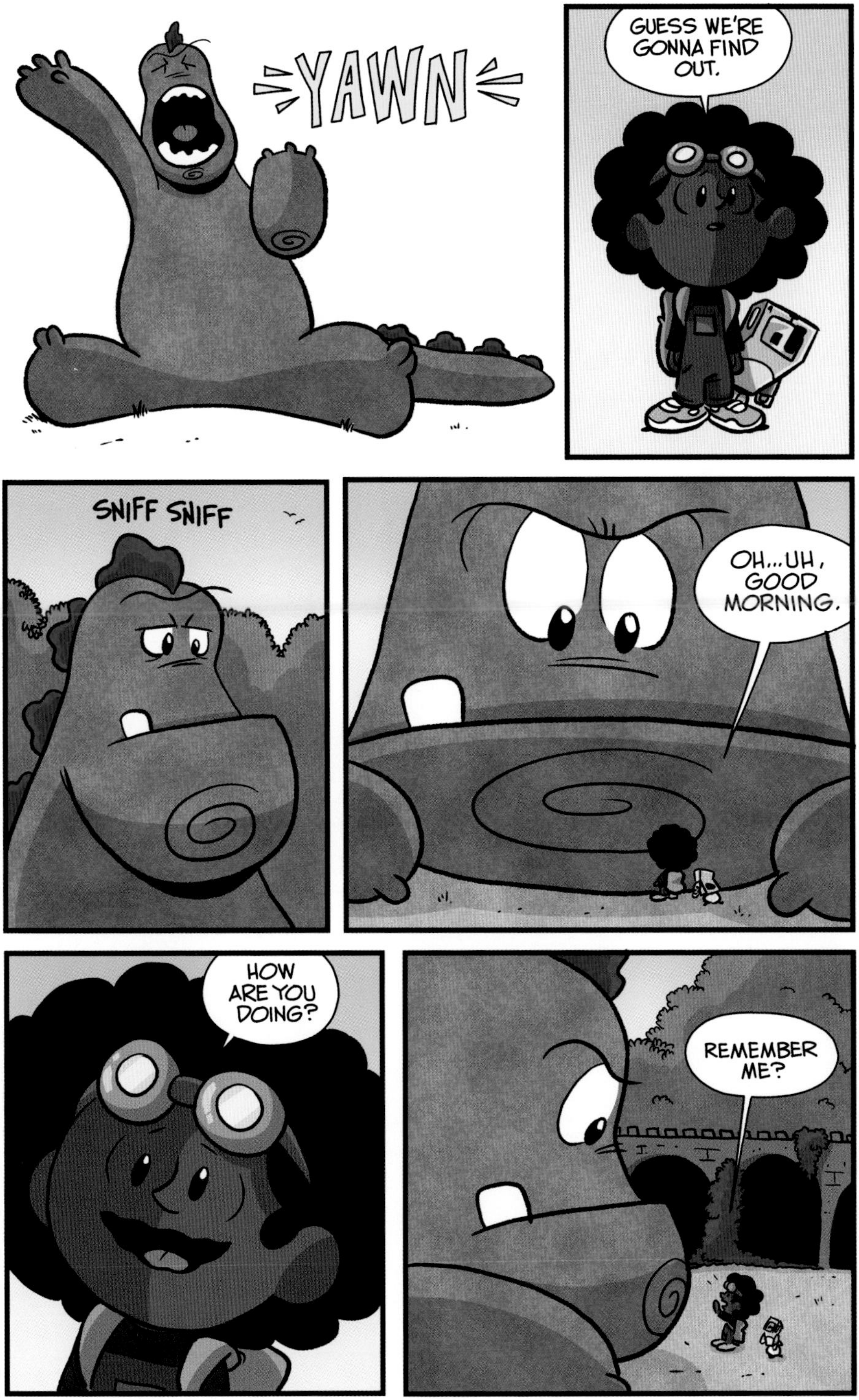
YAWN
GUESS WE'RE GONNA FIND OUT.
SNIFF SNIFF
OH...UH, GOOD MORNING.
HOW ARE YOU DOING?
REMEMBER ME?

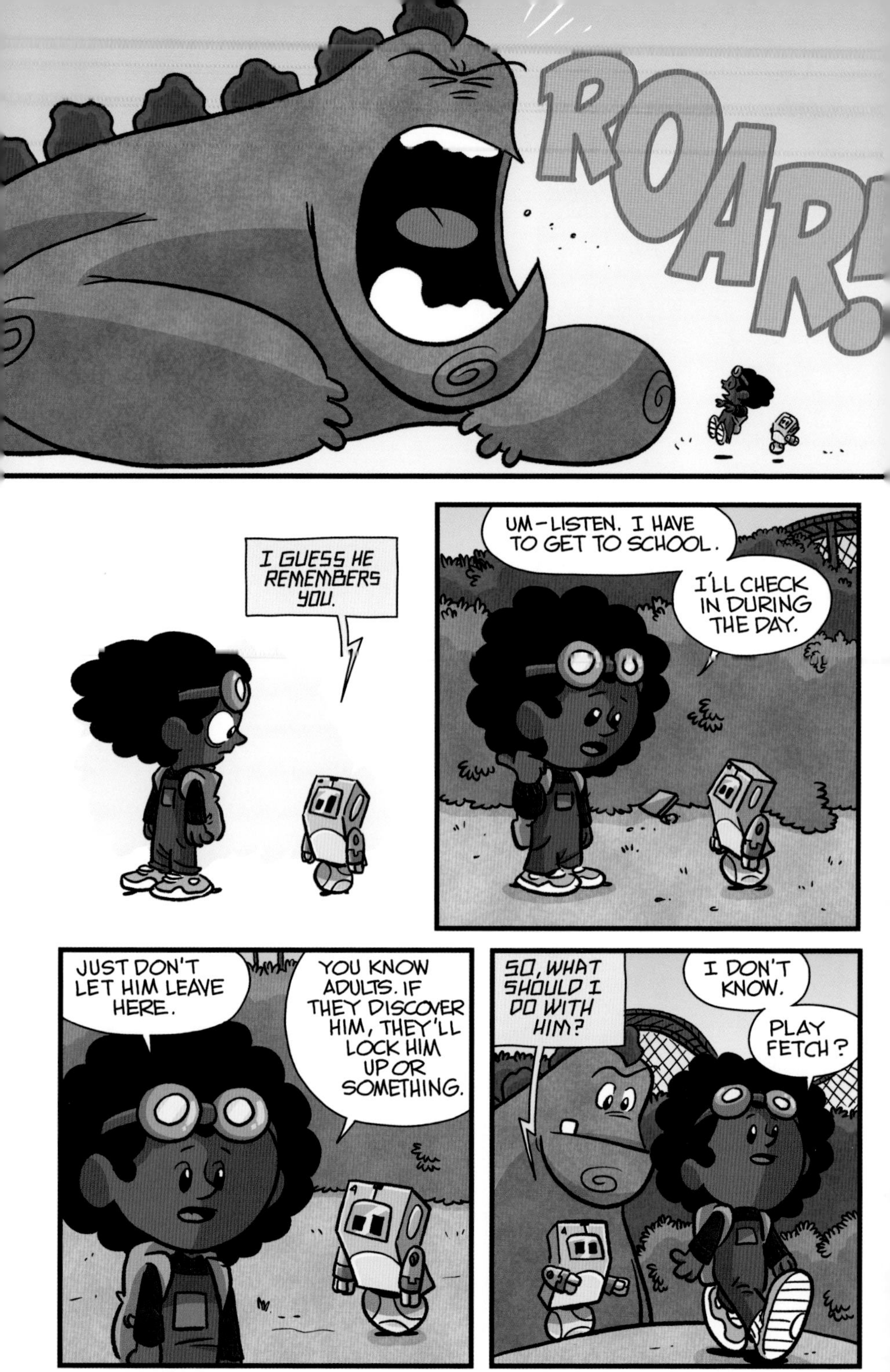
ROAR!
I GUESS HE REMEMBERS YOU.
UM-LISTEN. I HAVE TO GET TO SCHOOL.
I'LL CHECK IN DURING THE DAY.
JUST DON'T LET HIM LEAVE HERE.
YOU KNOW ADULTS. IF THEY DISCOVER HIM, THEY'LL LOCK HIM UP OR SOMETHING.
SO, WHAT SHOULD I DO WITH HIM?
I DON'T KNOW.
PLAY FETCH?

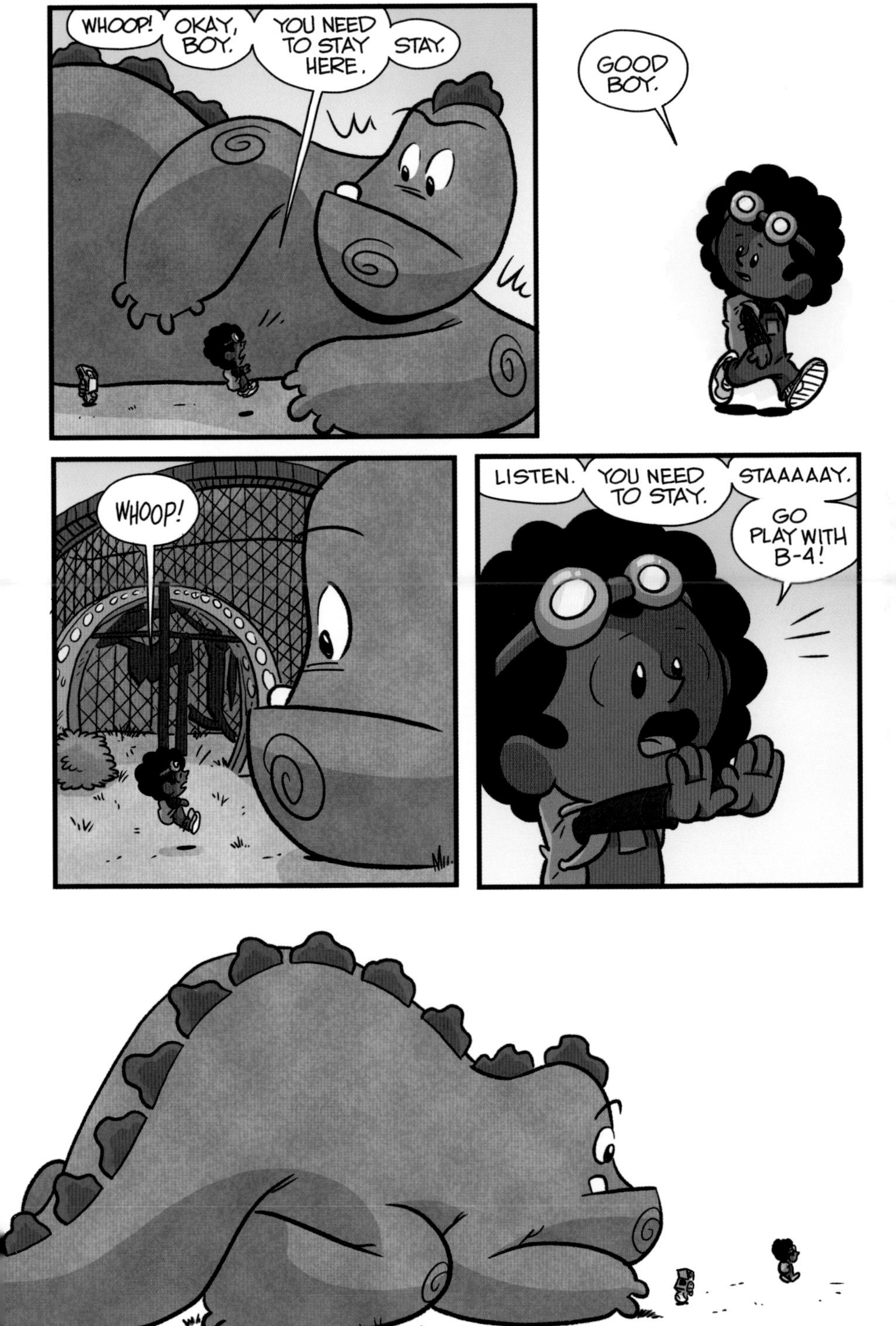
WHOOP!
OKAY, BOY.
YOU NEED TO STAY HERE.
STAY.
GOOD BOY.
WHOOP!
LISTEN.
YOU NEED TO STAY.
STAAAAAY.
GO PLAY WITH B-4!

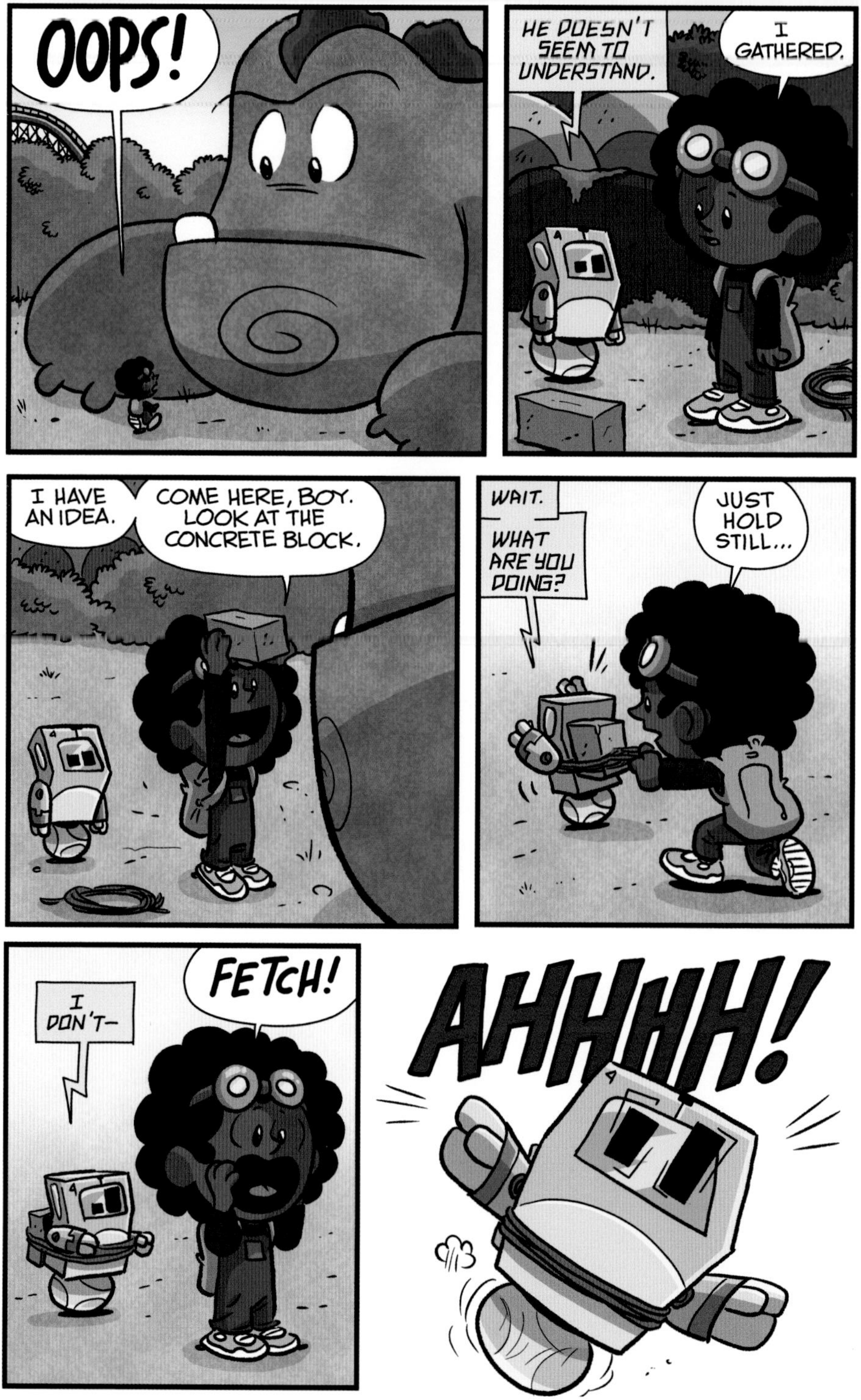
OOPS!
HE DOESN'T SEEM TO UNDERSTAND.
I GATHERED.
I HAVE AN IDEA.
COME HERE, BOY. LOOK AT THE CONCRETE BLOCK.
WAIT.
WHAT ARE YOU DOING?
JUST HOLD STILL...
I DON'T–
FETCH!
AHHHH!

SORRY, B-4!

I'M LATE!

MAN, I HOPE B-4 WILL BE OKAY.

AND, I HOPE THE MONSTER DOESN'T RUN OFF.

I WISH I COULD TALK TO HIM SO HE COULD UNDERSTAND ME AND I COULD UNDERSTAND HIM.

THAT GIVES ME AN IDEA.

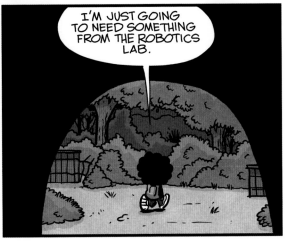

I'M JUST GOING TO NEED SOMETHING FROM THE ROBOTICS LAB.

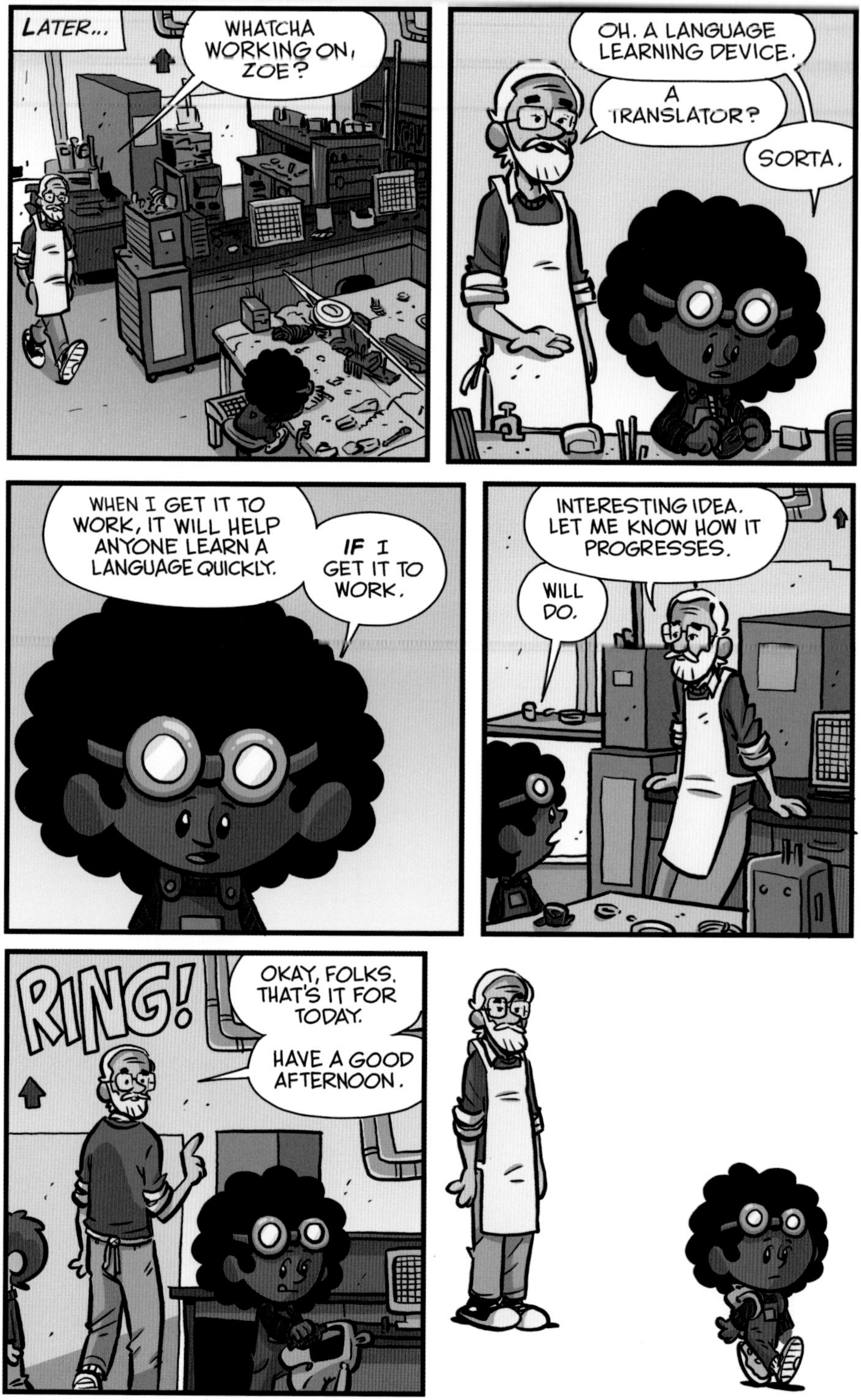
LATER...
WHATCHA WORKING ON, ZOE?
OH. A LANGUAGE LEARNING DEVICE.
A TRANSLATOR?
SORTA.
WHEN I GET IT TO WORK, IT WILL HELP ANYONE LEARN A LANGUAGE QUICKLY.
IF I GET IT TO WORK.
INTERESTING IDEA. LET ME KNOW HOW IT PROGRESSES.
WILL DO.
RING!
OKAY, FOLKS. THAT'S IT FOR TODAY.
HAVE A GOOD AFTERNOON.

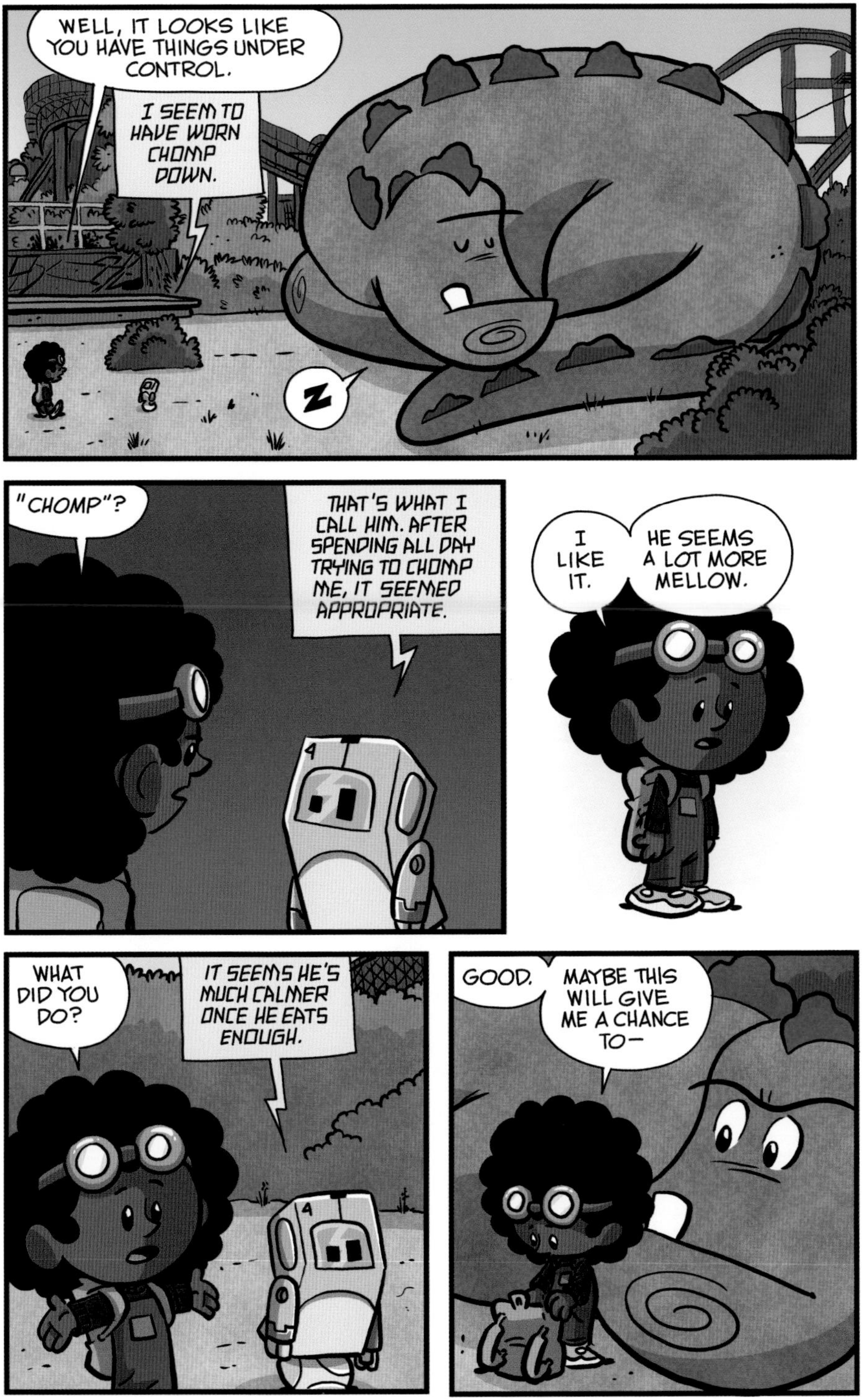
WELL, IT LOOKS LIKE YOU HAVE THINGS UNDER CONTROL.
I SEEM TO HAVE WORN CHOMP DOWN.
Z
"CHOMP"?
THAT'S WHAT I CALL HIM. AFTER SPENDING ALL DAY TRYING TO CHOMP ME, IT SEEMED APPROPRIATE.
I LIKE IT.
HE SEEMS A LOT MORE MELLOW.
WHAT DID YOU DO?
IT SEEMS HE'S MUCH CALMER ONCE HE EATS ENOUGH.
GOOD.
MAYBE THIS WILL GIVE ME A CHANCE TO—

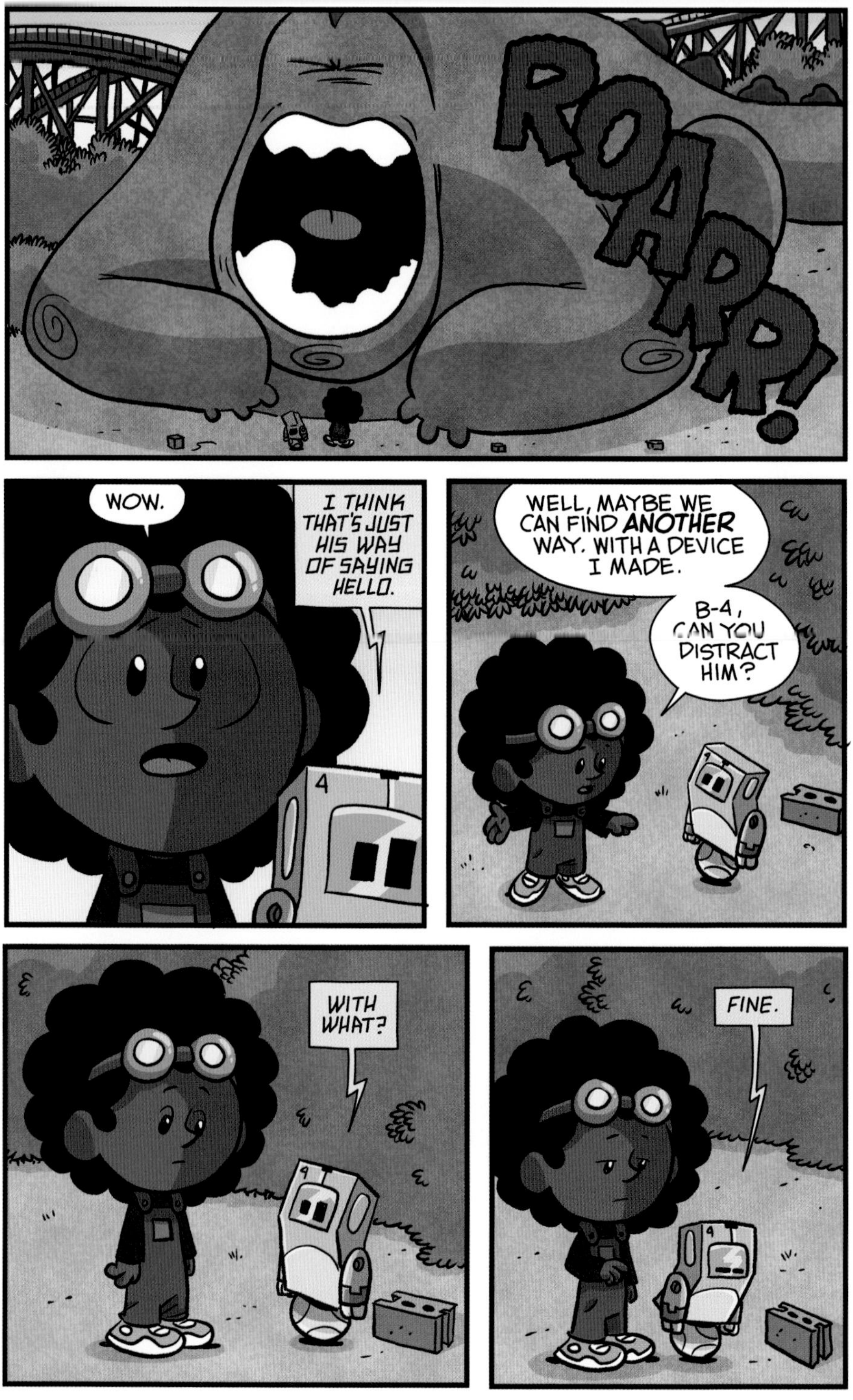
ROARR!
WOW.
I THINK THAT'S JUST HIS WAY OF SAYING HELLO.
WELL, MAYBE WE CAN FIND **ANOTHER** WAY. WITH A DEVICE I MADE.
B-4, CAN YOU DISTRACT HIM?
WITH WHAT?
FINE.

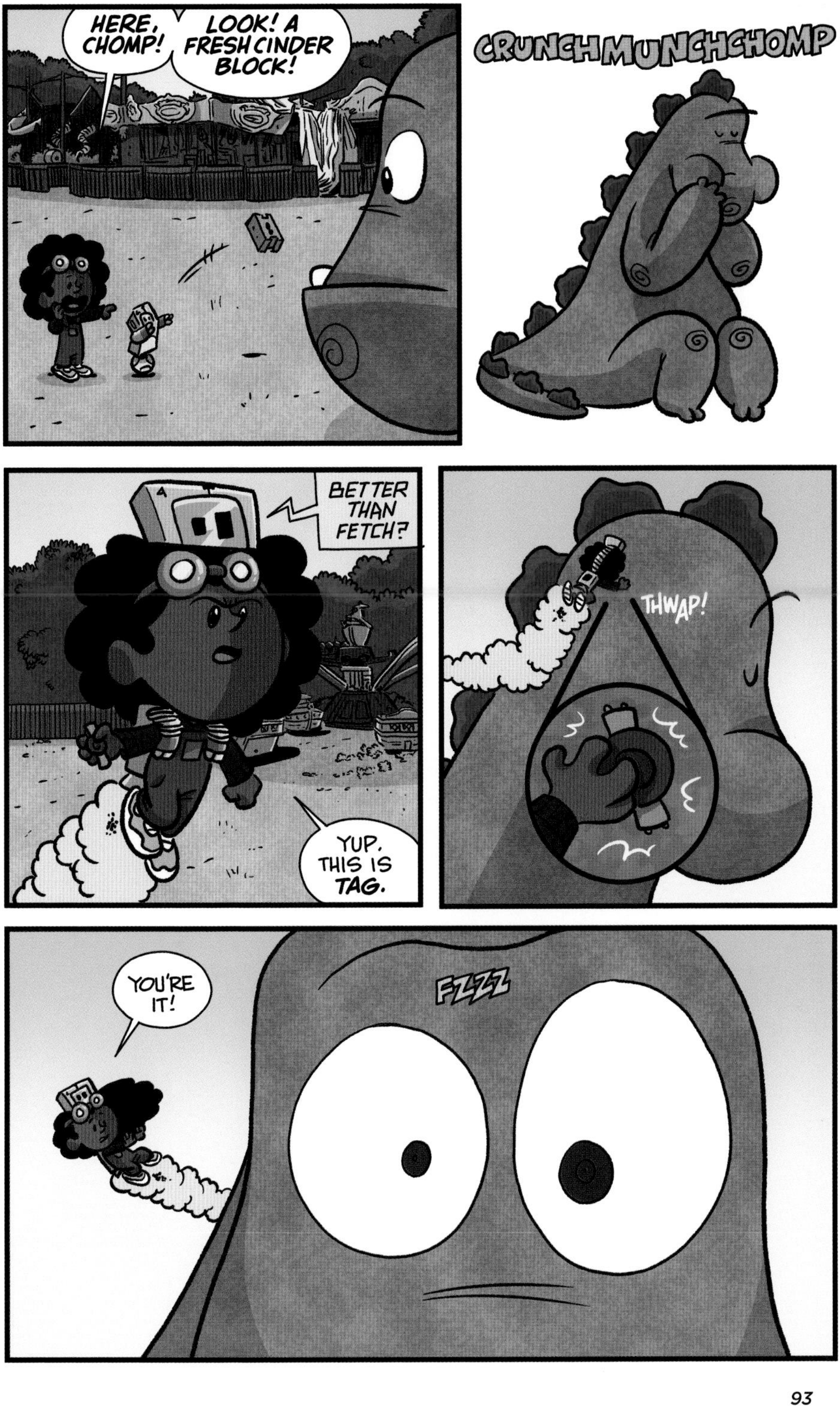
HERE, CHOMP!
LOOK! A FRESH CINDER BLOCK!
CRUNCHMUNCHCHOMP
BETTER THAN FETCH?
YUP. THIS IS TAG.
THWAP!
YOU'RE IT!
FZZZ

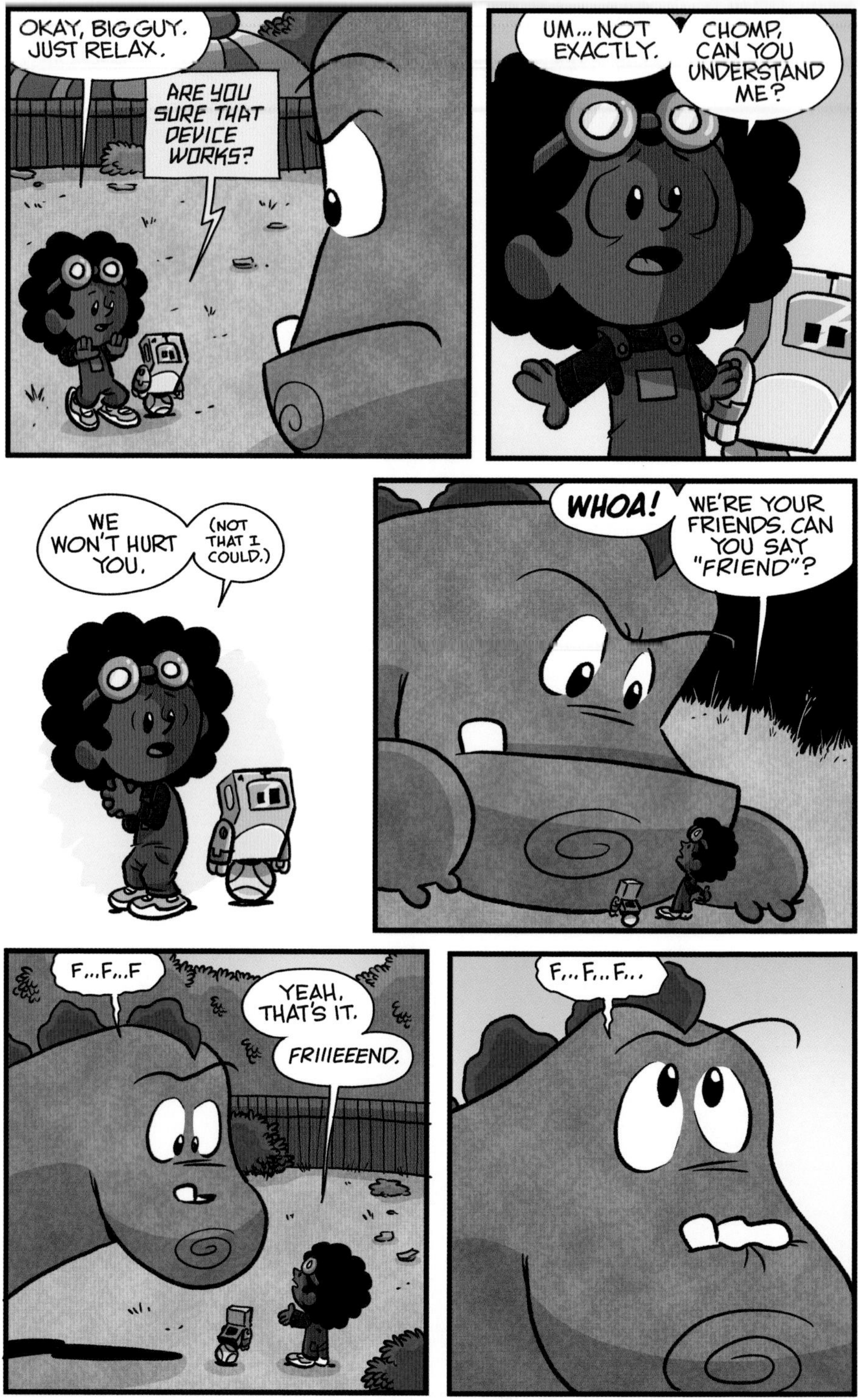
OKAY, BIG GUY. JUST RELAX.
ARE YOU SURE THAT DEVICE WORKS?
UM... NOT EXACTLY.
CHOMP, CAN YOU UNDERSTAND ME?
WE WON'T HURT YOU.
(NOT THAT I COULD.)
WHOA!
WE'RE YOUR FRIENDS. CAN YOU SAY "FRIEND"?
F...F...F
YEAH, THAT'S IT.
FRIIIEEEND.
F... F... F...

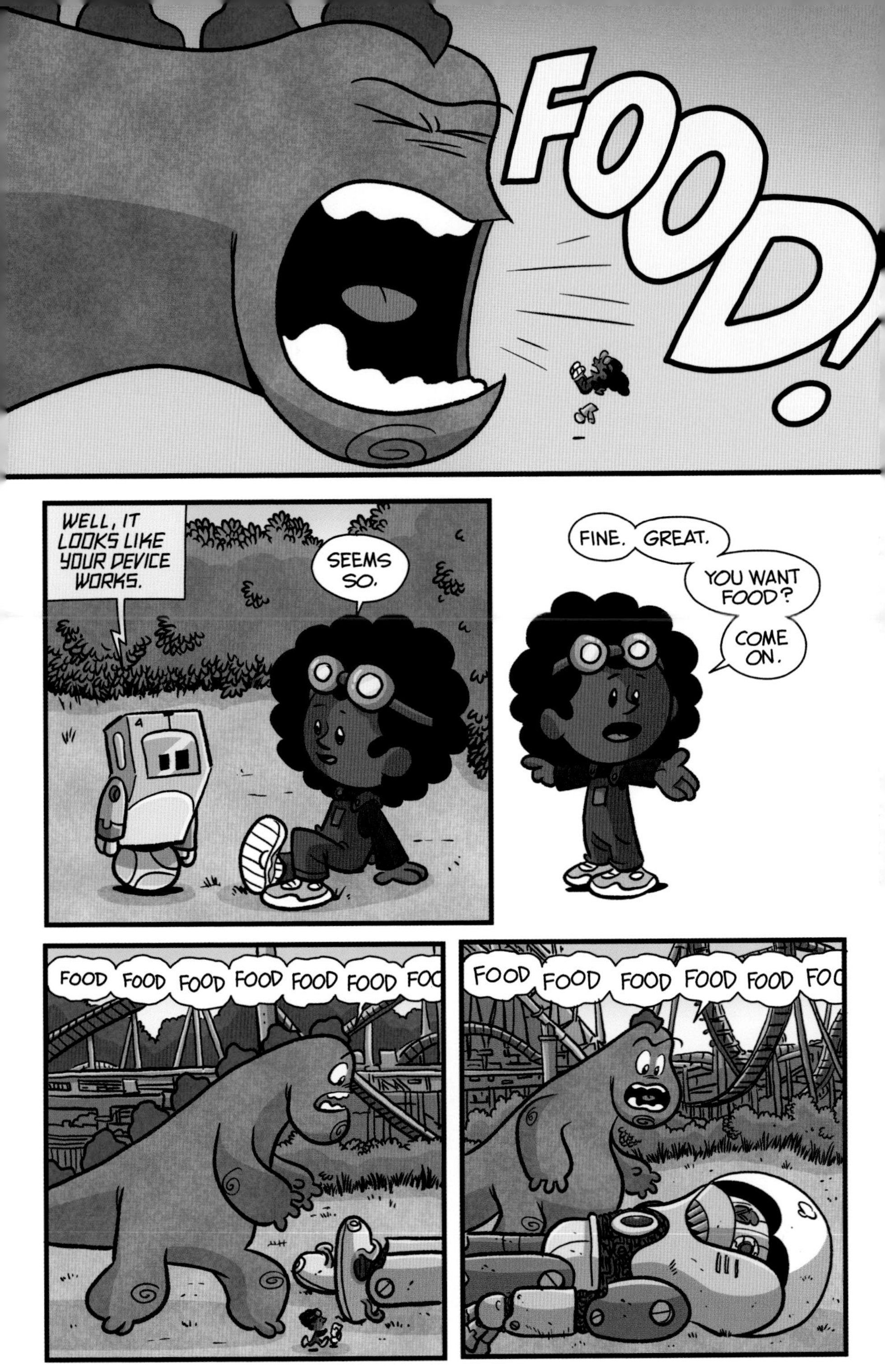

FOOD!!
WELL, IT LOOKS LIKE YOUR DEVICE WORKS.
SEEMS SO.
FINE. GREAT.
YOU WANT FOOD?
COME ON.
FOOD FOOD FOOD FOOD FOOD FOOD
FOOD FOOD FOOD FOOD FOOD

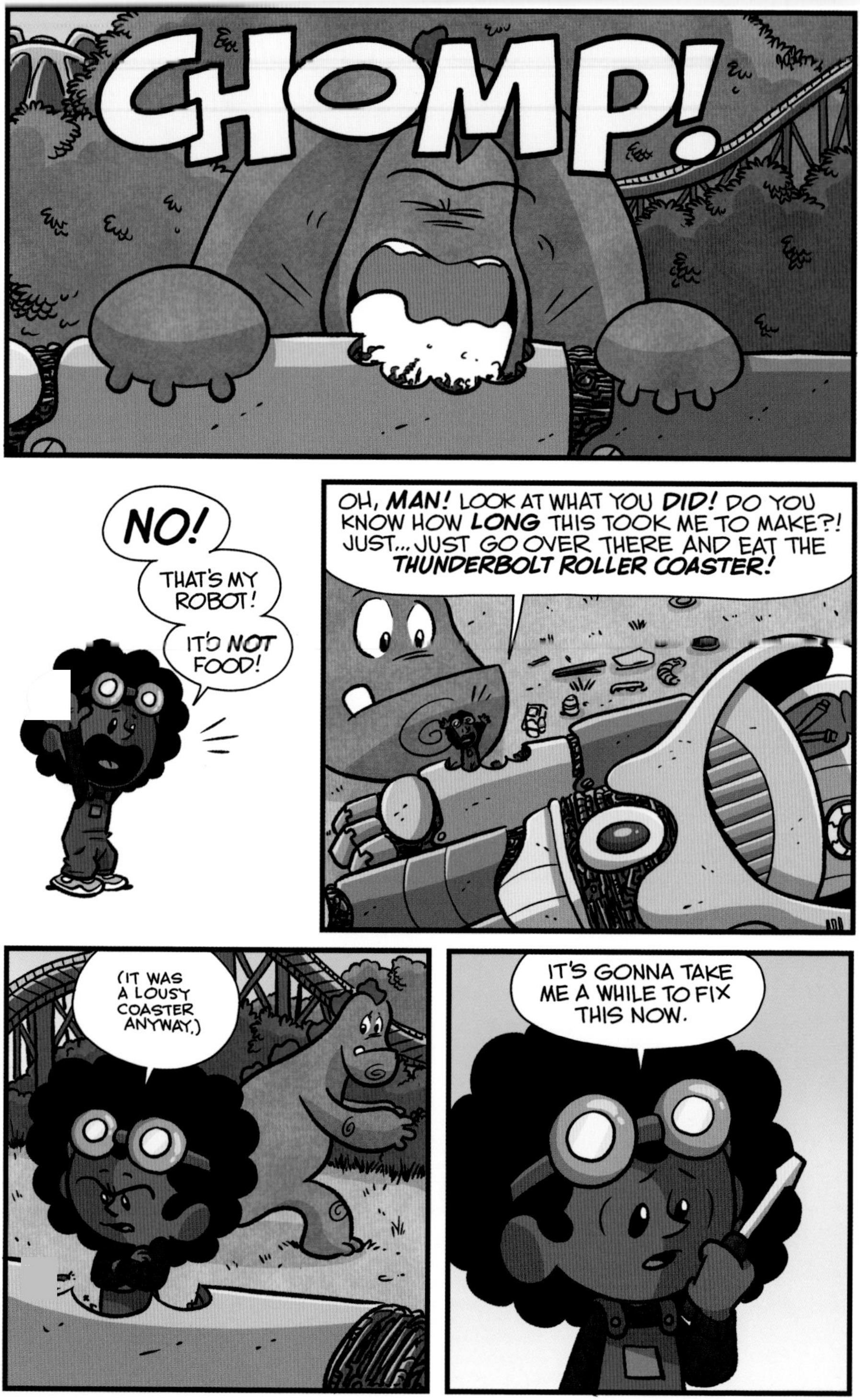
CHOMP!
NO!
THAT'S MY ROBOT!
IT'S NOT FOOD!
OH, MAN! LOOK AT WHAT YOU DID! DO YOU KNOW HOW LONG THIS TOOK ME TO MAKE?! JUST... JUST GO OVER THERE AND EAT THE THUNDERBOLT ROLLER COASTER!
(IT WAS A LOUSY COASTER ANYWAY.)
IT'S GONNA TAKE ME A WHILE TO FIX THIS NOW.

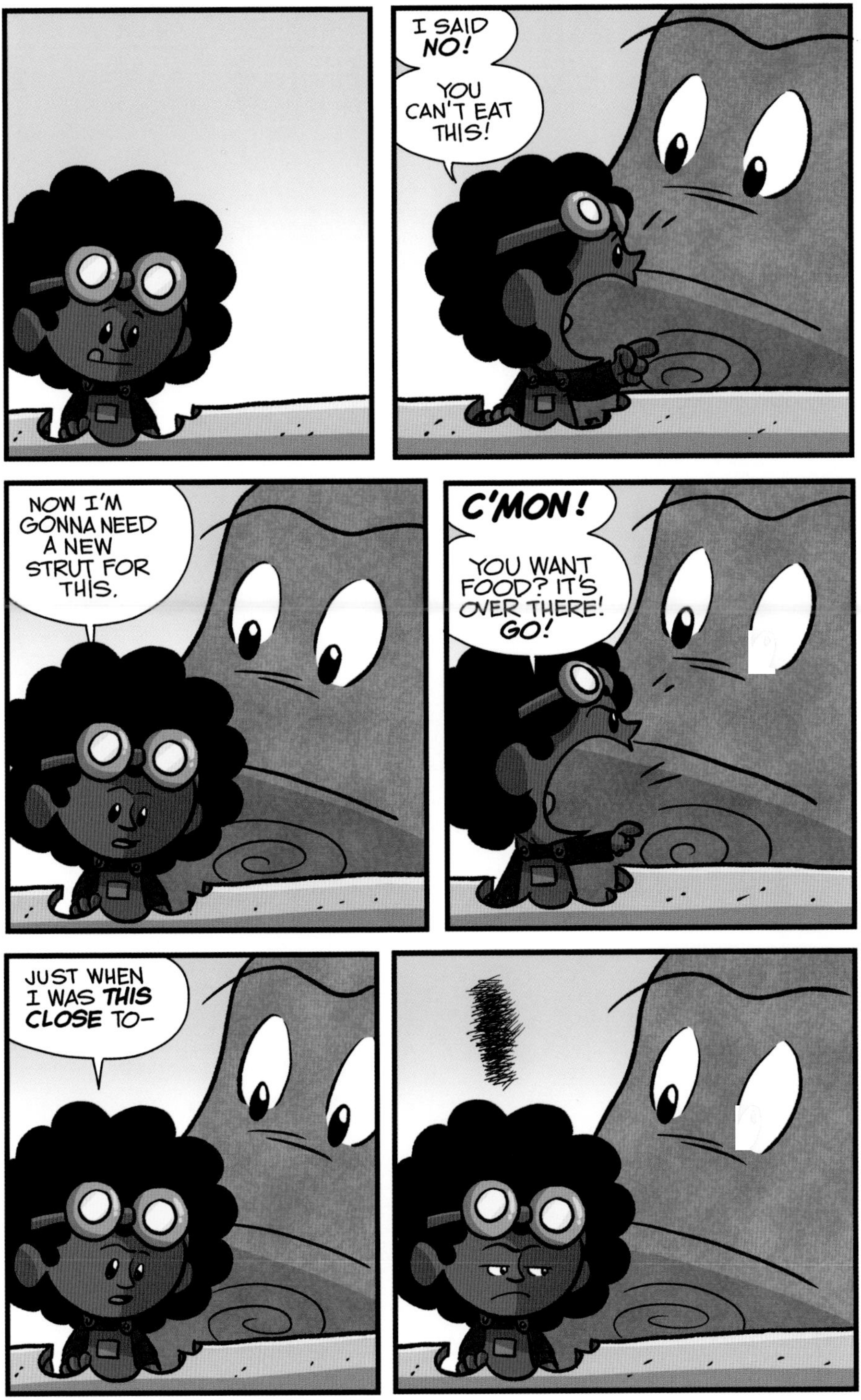
I SAID NO!
YOU CAN'T EAT THIS!
NOW I'M GONNA NEED A NEW STRUT FOR THIS.
C'MON!
YOU WANT FOOD? IT'S OVER THERE! GO!
JUST WHEN I WAS THIS CLOSE TO-

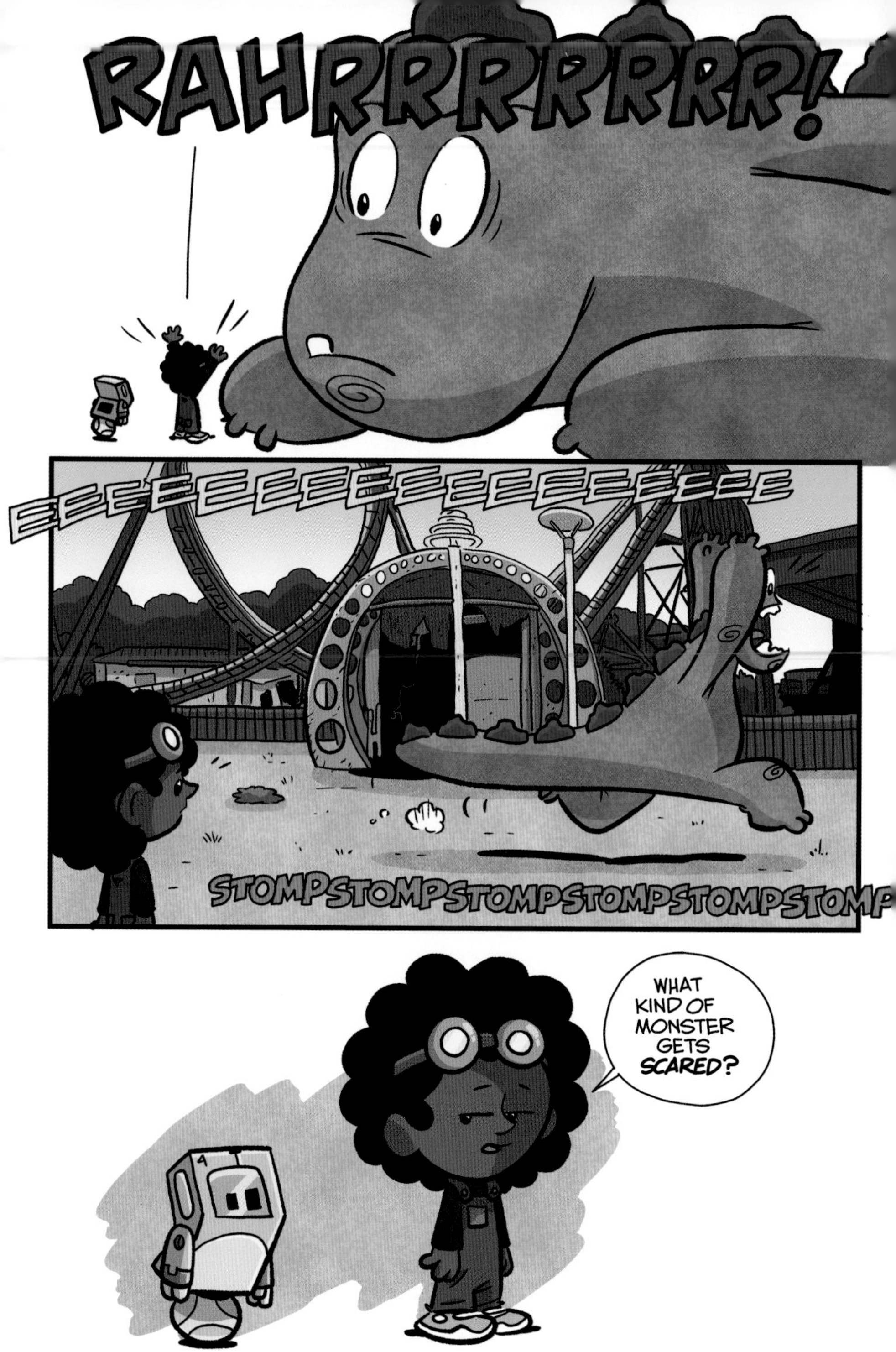
RAHRRRRRRRR!
EEEEEEEEEEEEEEEEEEE
STOMPSTOMPSTOMPSTOMPSTOMPSTOMPSTOMP
WHAT KIND OF MONSTER GETS SCARED?

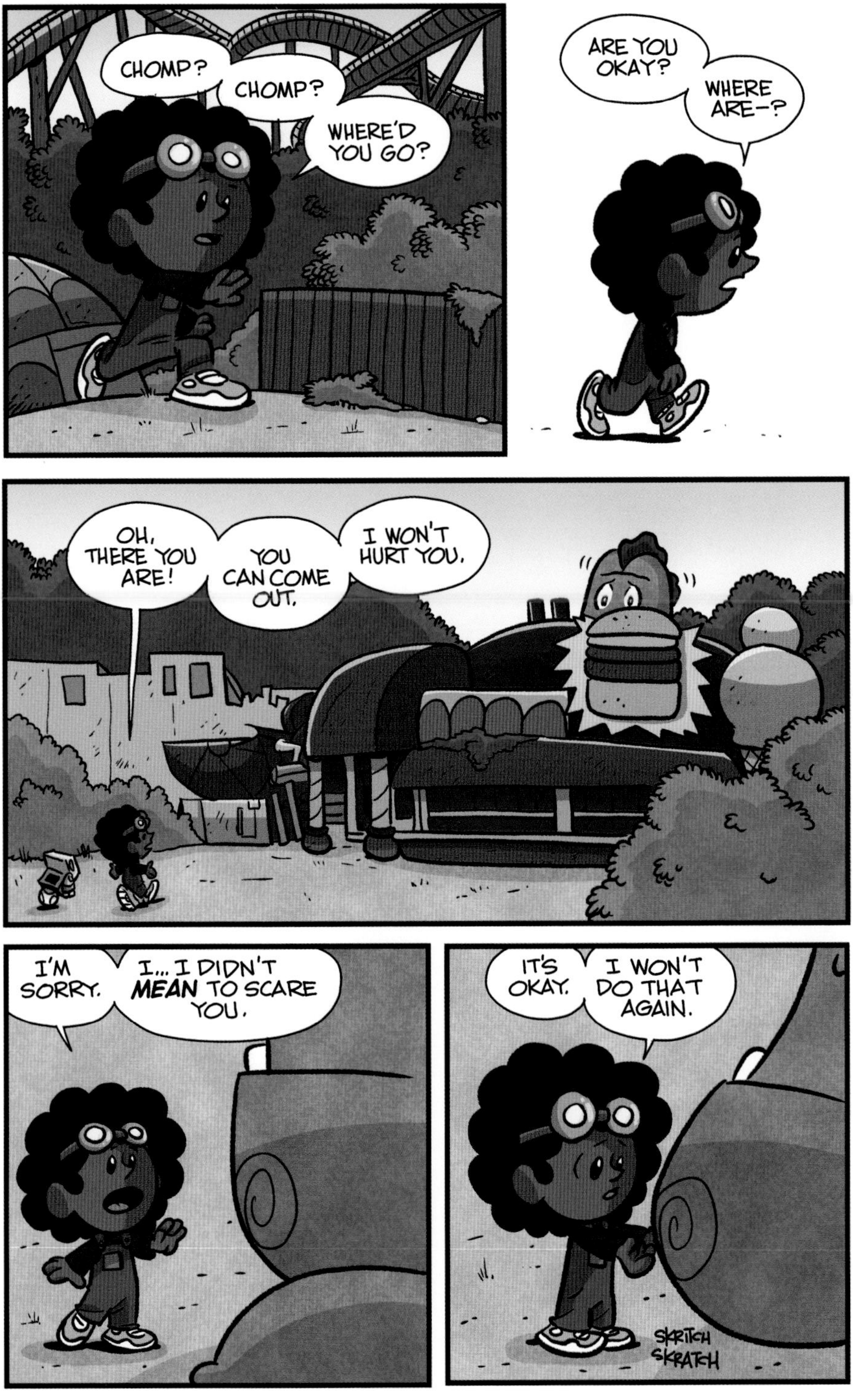
CHOMP?
CHOMP?
WHERE'D YOU GO?
ARE YOU OKAY?
WHERE ARE-?
OH, THERE YOU ARE!
YOU CAN COME OUT.
I WON'T HURT YOU.
I'M SORRY.
I... I DIDN'T MEAN TO SCARE YOU.
IT'S OKAY.
I WON'T DO THAT AGAIN.
SKRITCH SKRATCH

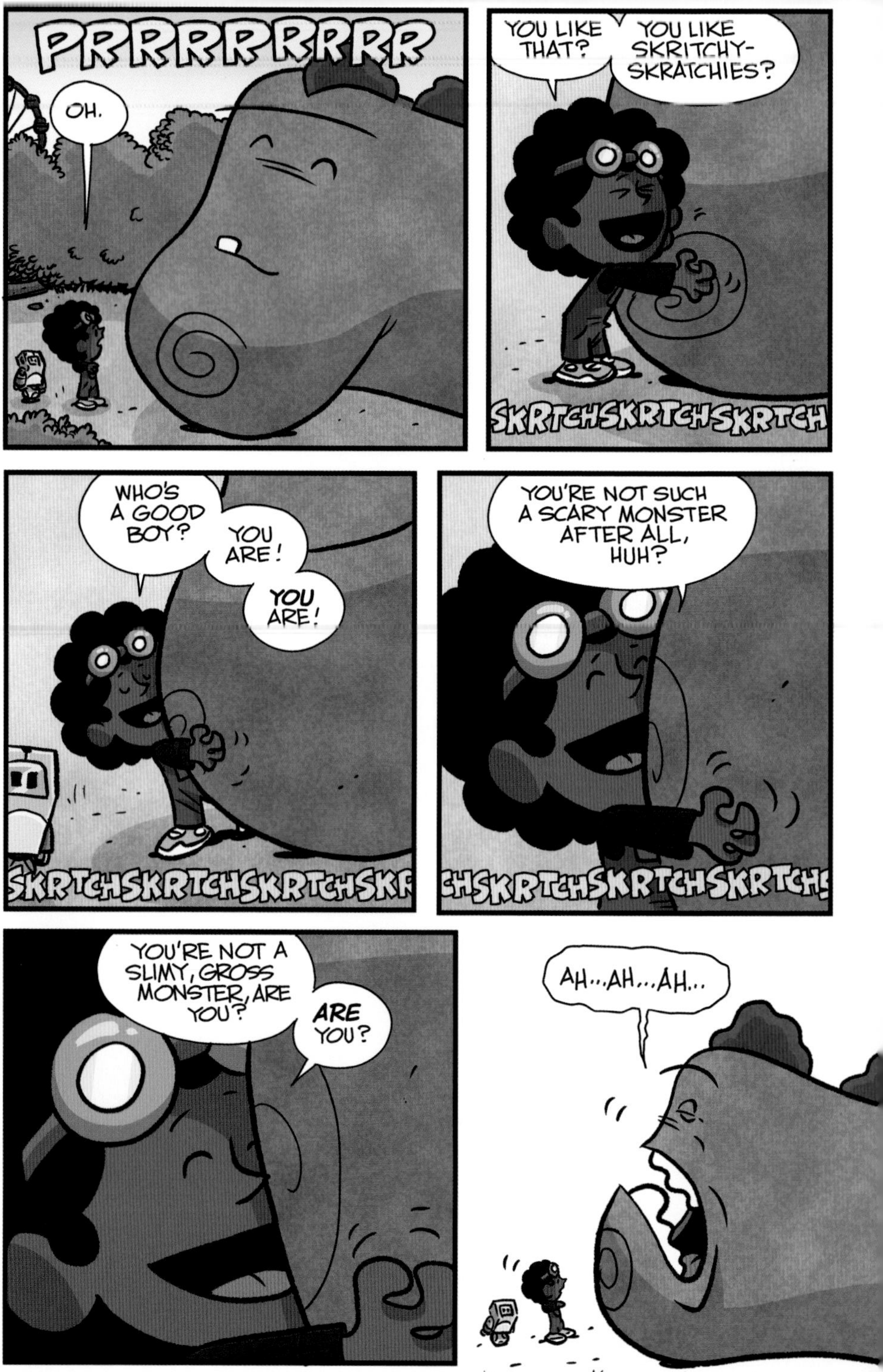
PRRRRRRRRR
OH.
YOU LIKE THAT?
YOU LIKE SKRITCHY-SKRATCHIES?
SKRTCHSKRTCHSKRTCH
WHO'S A GOOD BOY?
YOU ARE!
YOU ARE!
SKRTCHSKRTCHSKRTCHSKR
YOU'RE NOT SUCH A SCARY MONSTER AFTER ALL, HUH?
CHSKRTCHSKRTCHSKRTCH
YOU'RE NOT A SLIMY, GROSS MONSTER, ARE YOU?
ARE YOU?
AH...AH...AH...

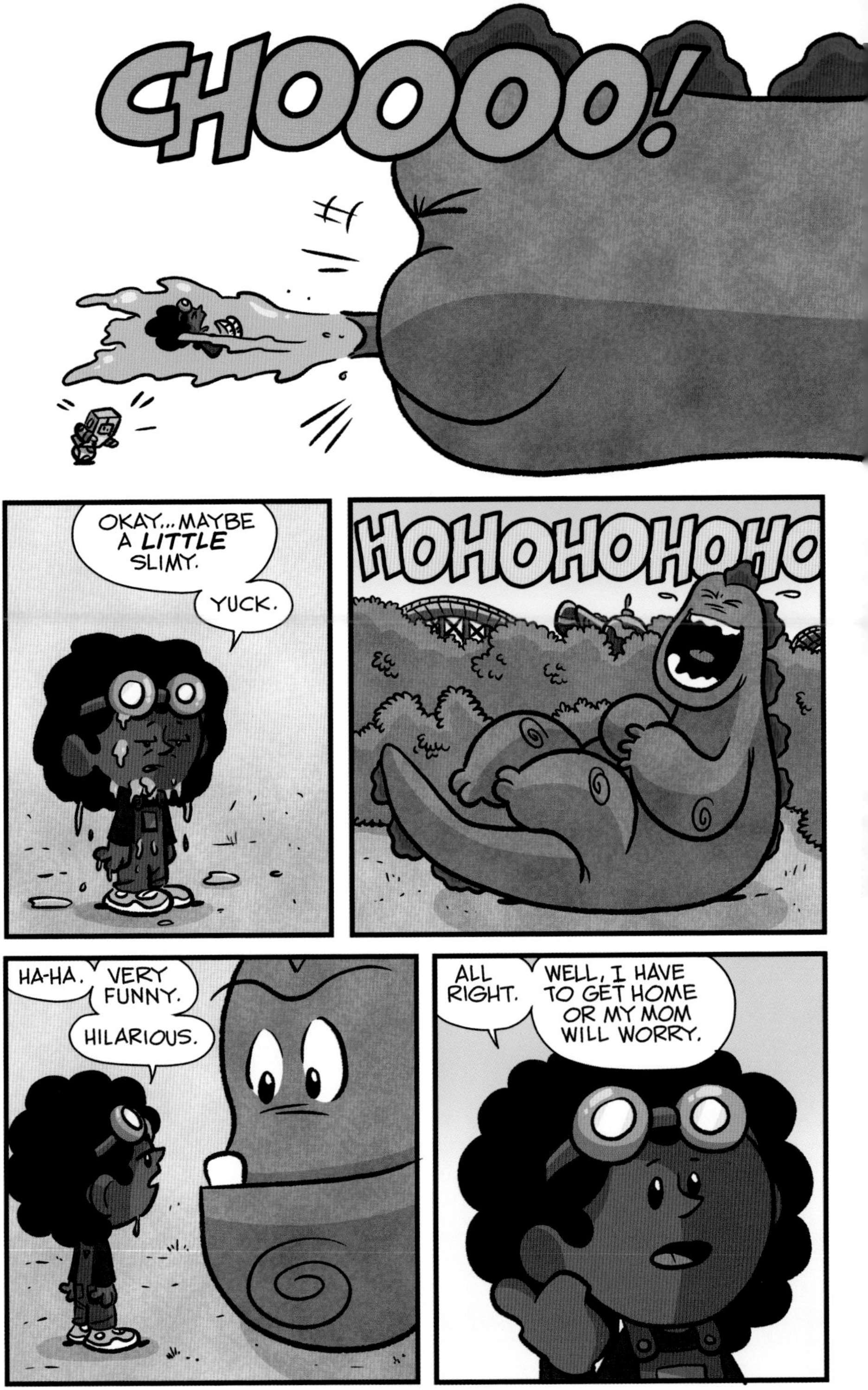
CHOOOO!
OKAY... MAYBE A LITTLE SLIMY.
YUCK.
HOHOHOHOHOHO
HA-HA.
VERY FUNNY.
HILARIOUS.
ALL RIGHT.
WELL, I HAVE TO GET HOME OR MY MOM WILL WORRY.

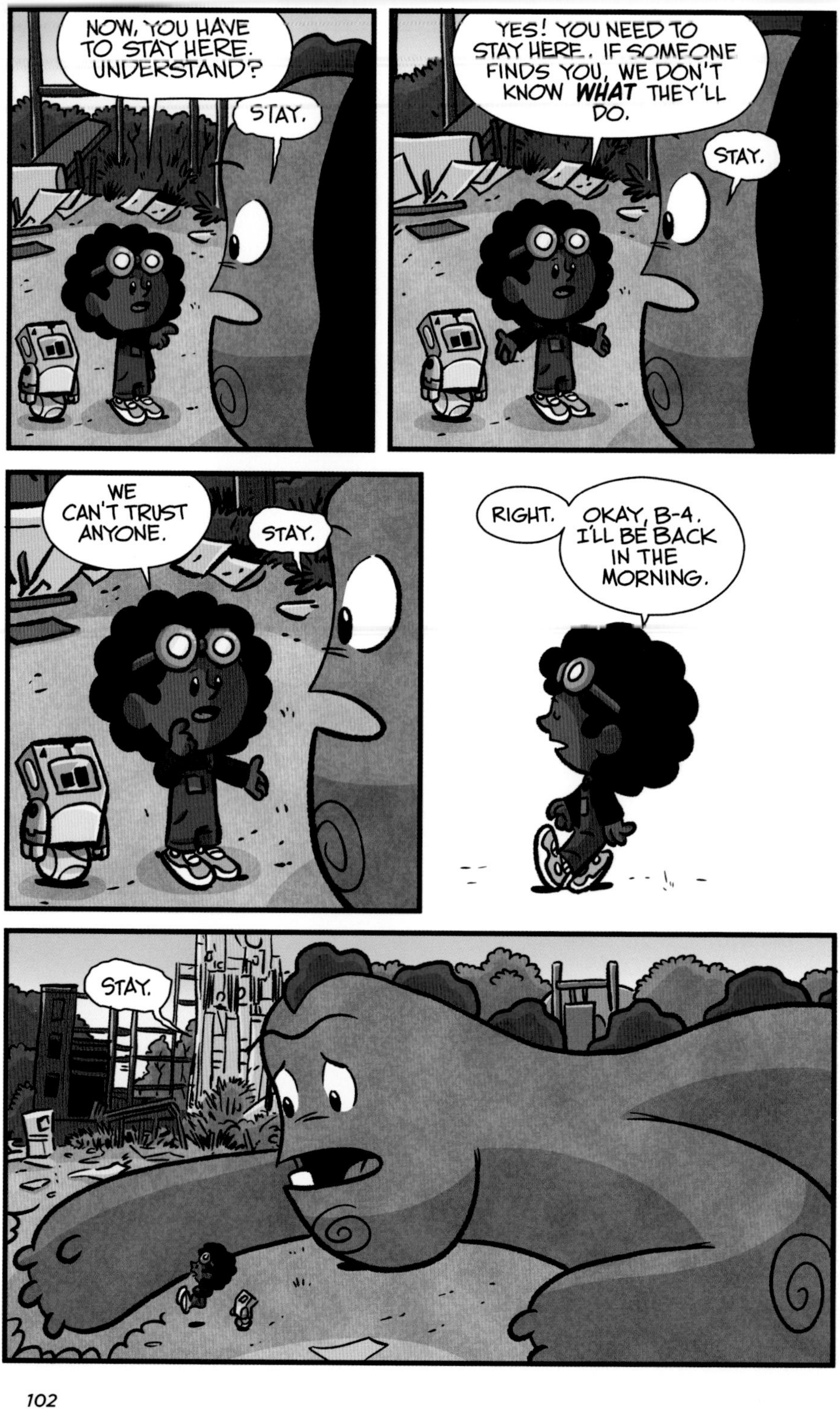
NOW, YOU HAVE TO STAY HERE. UNDERSTAND?
STAY.
YES! YOU NEED TO STAY HERE. IF SOMEONE FINDS YOU, WE DON'T KNOW **WHAT** THEY'LL DO.
STAY.
WE CAN'T TRUST ANYONE.
STAY.
RIGHT.
OKAY, B-4. I'LL BE BACK IN THE MORNING.
STAY.

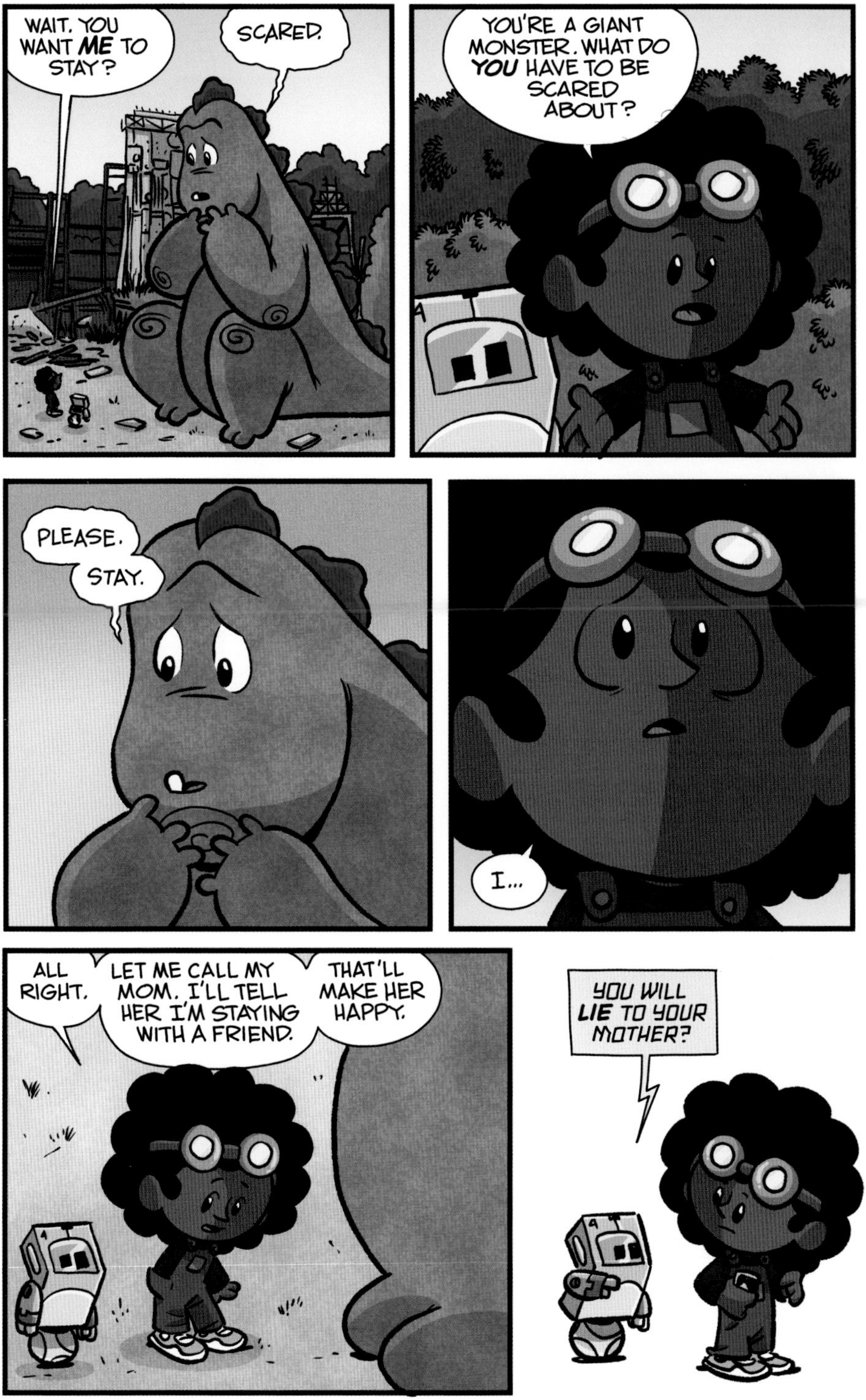
WAIT. YOU WANT **ME** TO STAY?
SCARED.
YOU'RE A GIANT MONSTER. WHAT DO **YOU** HAVE TO BE SCARED ABOUT?
PLEASE.
STAY.
I...
ALL RIGHT.
LET ME CALL MY MOM. I'LL TELL HER I'M STAYING WITH A FRIEND.
THAT'LL MAKE HER HAPPY.
YOU WILL **LIE** TO YOUR MOTHER?

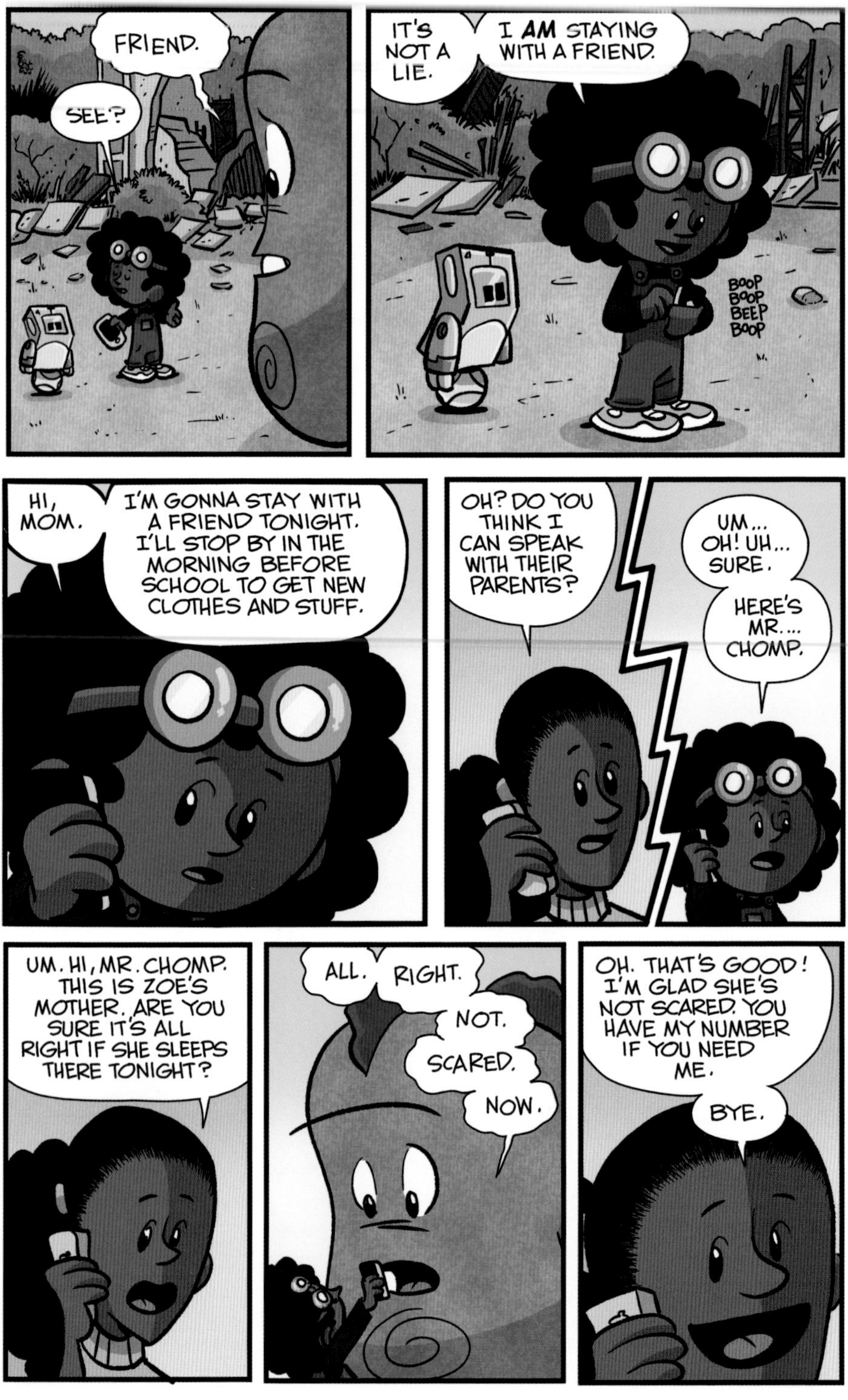

FRIEND.
SEE?
IT'S NOT A LIE.
I **AM** STAYING WITH A FRIEND.
BOOP BOOP BEEP BOOP
HI, MOM.
I'M GONNA STAY WITH A FRIEND TONIGHT. I'LL STOP BY IN THE MORNING BEFORE SCHOOL TO GET NEW CLOTHES AND STUFF.
OH? DO YOU THINK I CAN SPEAK WITH THEIR PARENTS?
UM... OH! UH... SURE.
HERE'S MR.... CHOMP.
UM. HI, MR. CHOMP. THIS IS ZOE'S MOTHER. ARE YOU SURE IT'S ALL RIGHT IF SHE SLEEPS THERE TONIGHT?
ALL.
RIGHT.
NOT.
SCARED.
NOW.
OH. THAT'S GOOD! I'M GLAD SHE'S NOT SCARED. YOU HAVE MY NUMBER IF YOU NEED ME.
BYE.

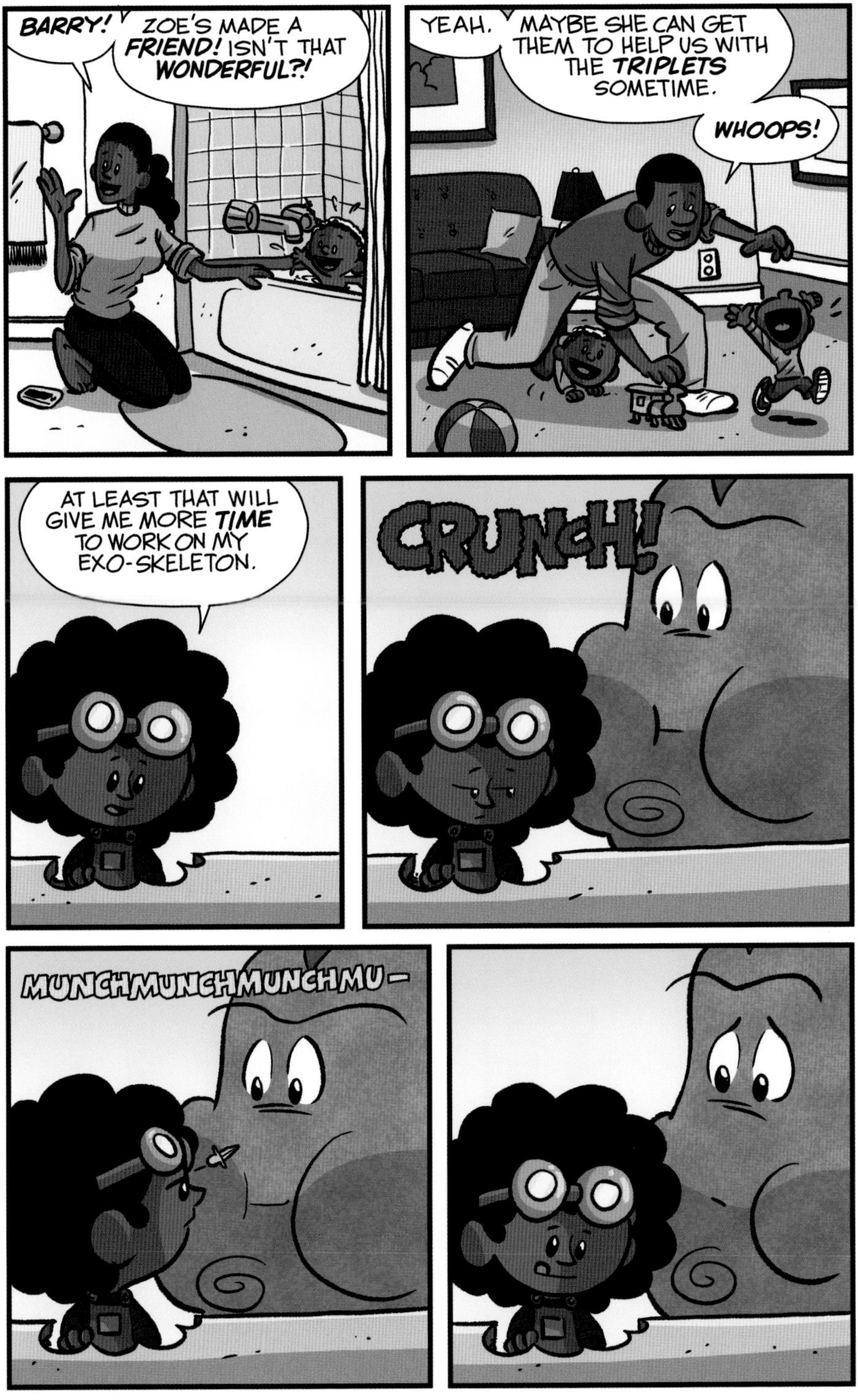
BARRY!
ZOE'S MADE A FRIEND! ISN'T THAT WONDERFUL?!
YEAH.
MAYBE SHE CAN GET THEM TO HELP US WITH THE TRIPLETS SOMETIME.
WHOOPS!
AT LEAST THAT WILL GIVE ME MORE TIME TO WORK ON MY EXO-SKELETON.
CRUNCH!
MUNCHMUNCHMUNCHMU—

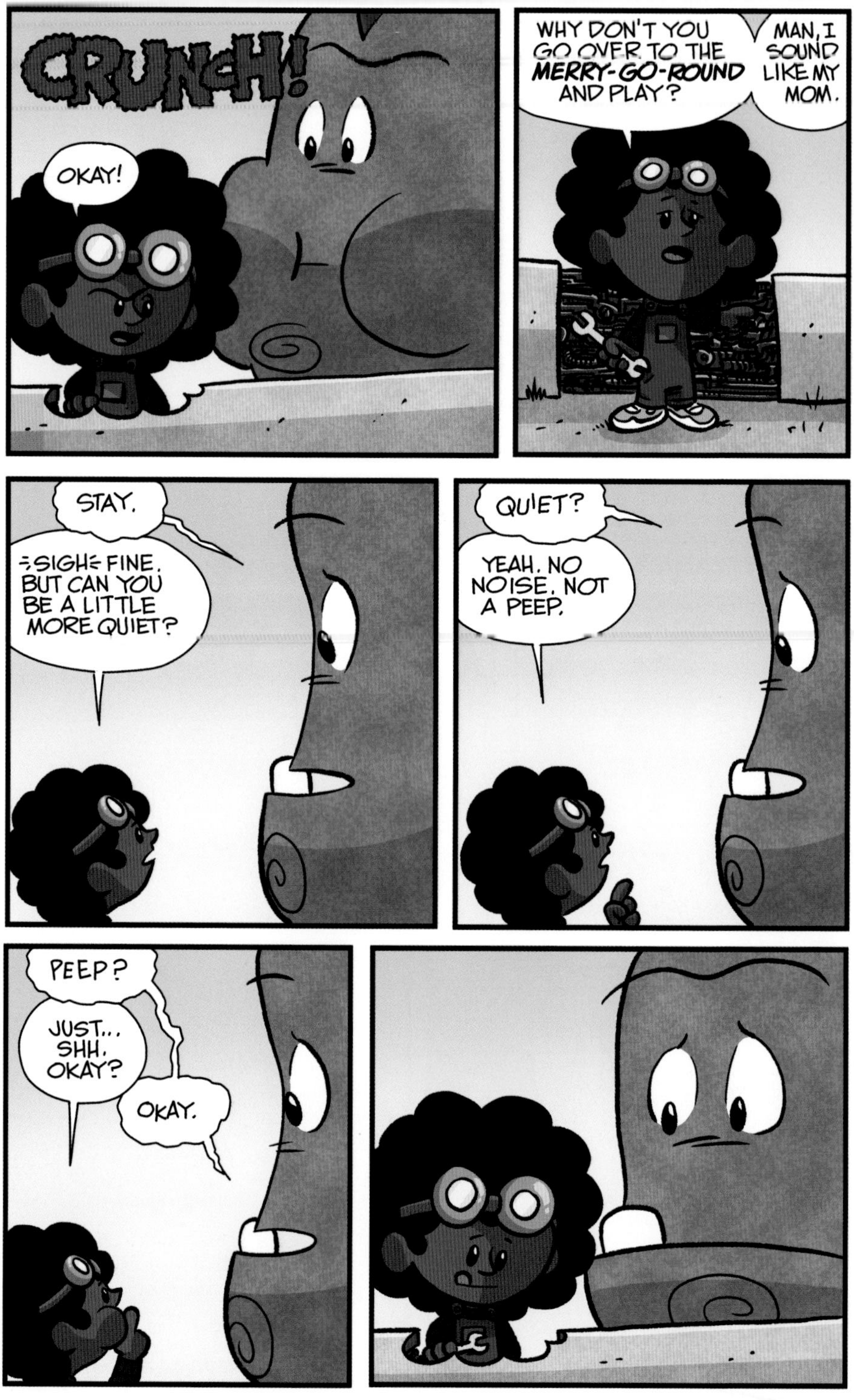
CRUNCH!
OKAY!
WHY DON'T YOU GO OVER TO THE **MERRY-GO-ROUND** AND PLAY?
MAN, I SOUND LIKE MY MOM.
STAY.
=SIGH= FINE. BUT CAN YOU BE A LITTLE MORE QUIET?
QUIET?
YEAH. NO NOISE. NOT A PEEP.
PEEP?
JUST... SHH. OKAY?
OKAY.

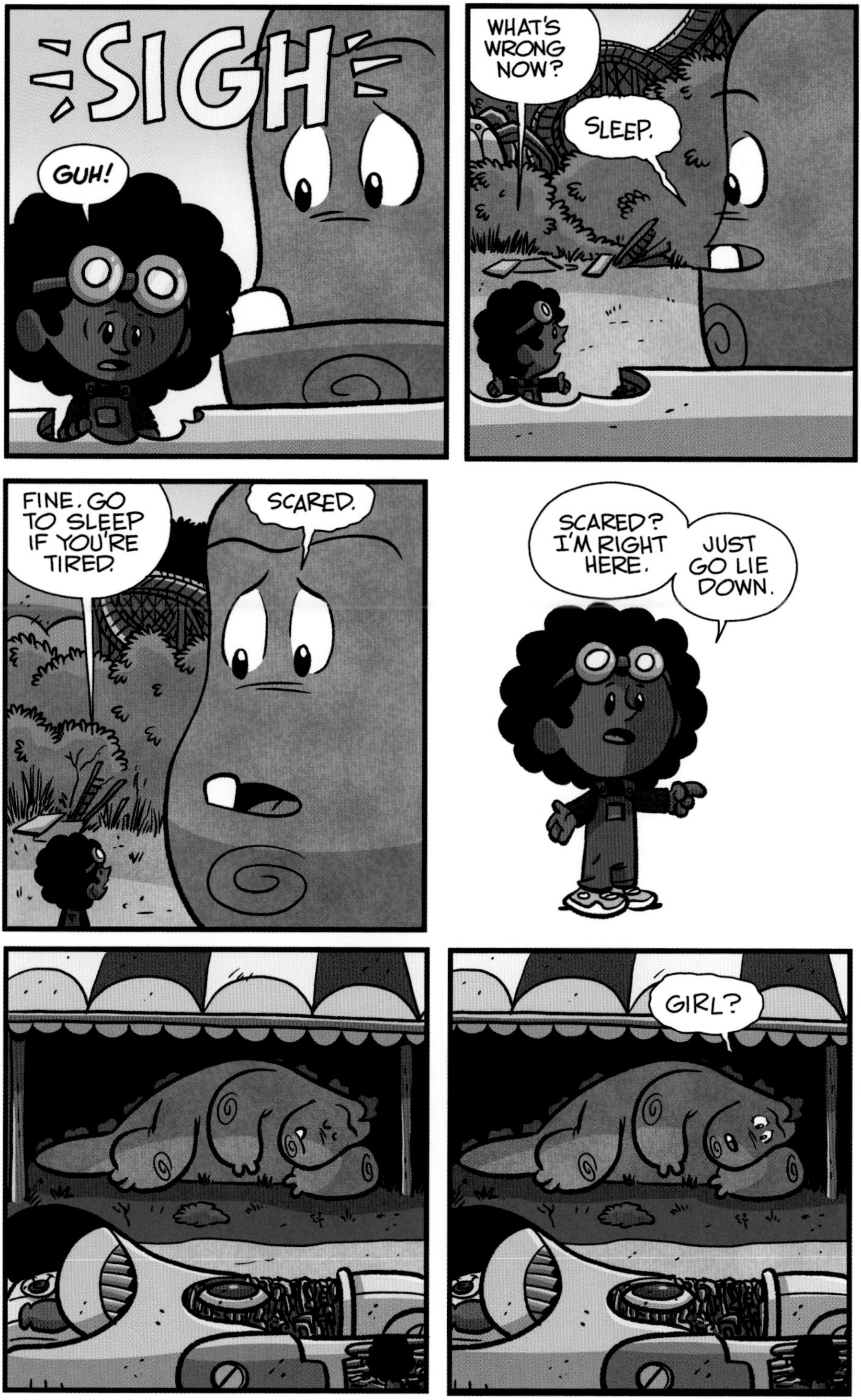
SIGH
GUH!
WHAT'S WRONG NOW?
SLEEP.
FINE. GO TO SLEEP IF YOU'RE TIRED.
SCARED.
SCARED? I'M RIGHT HERE.
JUST GO LIE DOWN.
GIRL?

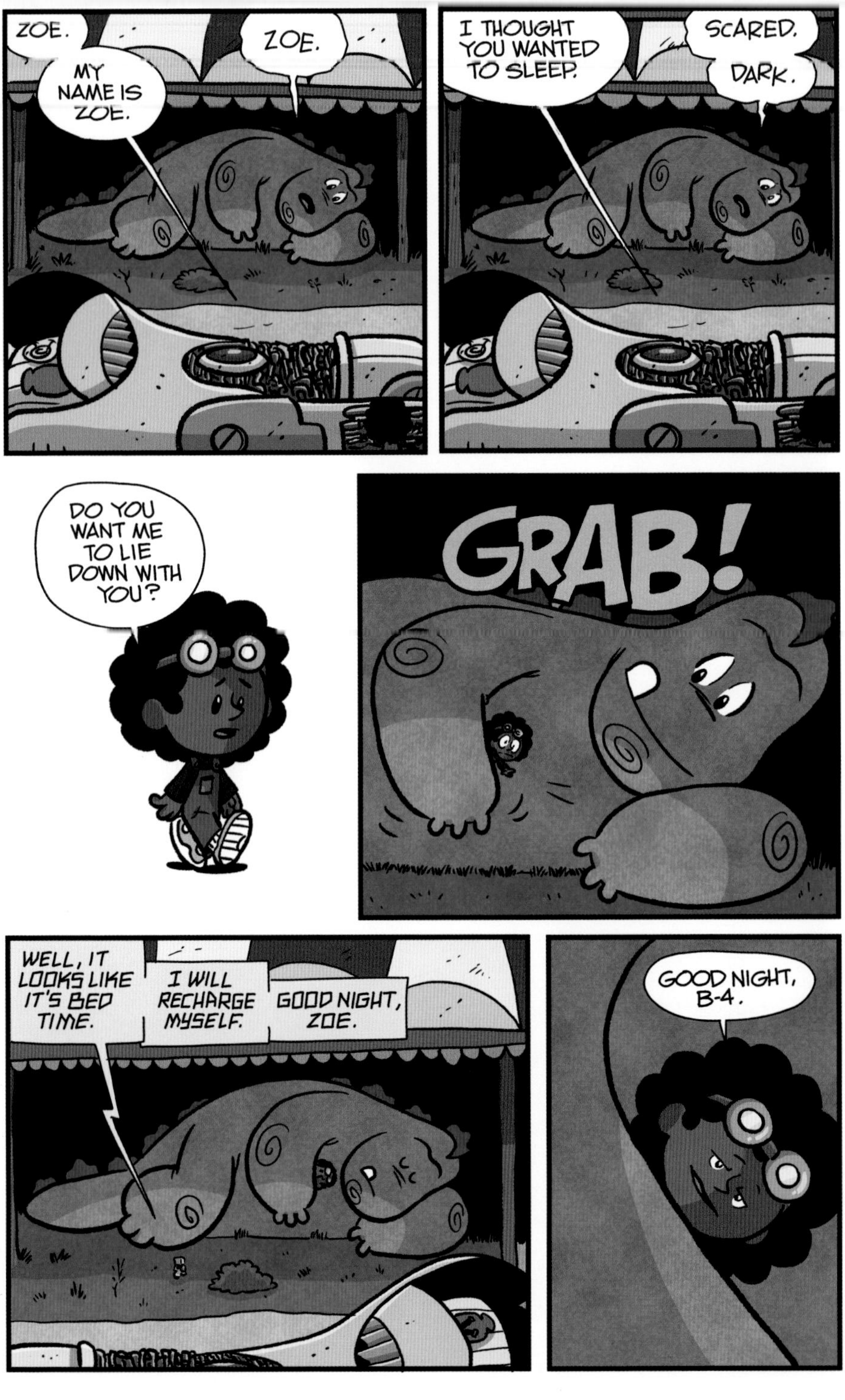

ZOE.
MY NAME IS ZOE.
ZOE.
I THOUGHT YOU WANTED TO SLEEP.
SCARED.
DARK.
DO YOU WANT ME TO LIE DOWN WITH YOU?
GRAB!
WELL, IT LOOKS LIKE IT'S BED TIME.
I WILL RECHARGE MYSELF.
GOOD NIGHT, ZOE.
GOOD NIGHT, B-4.

CHAPTER 7 - MORE MONSTERS

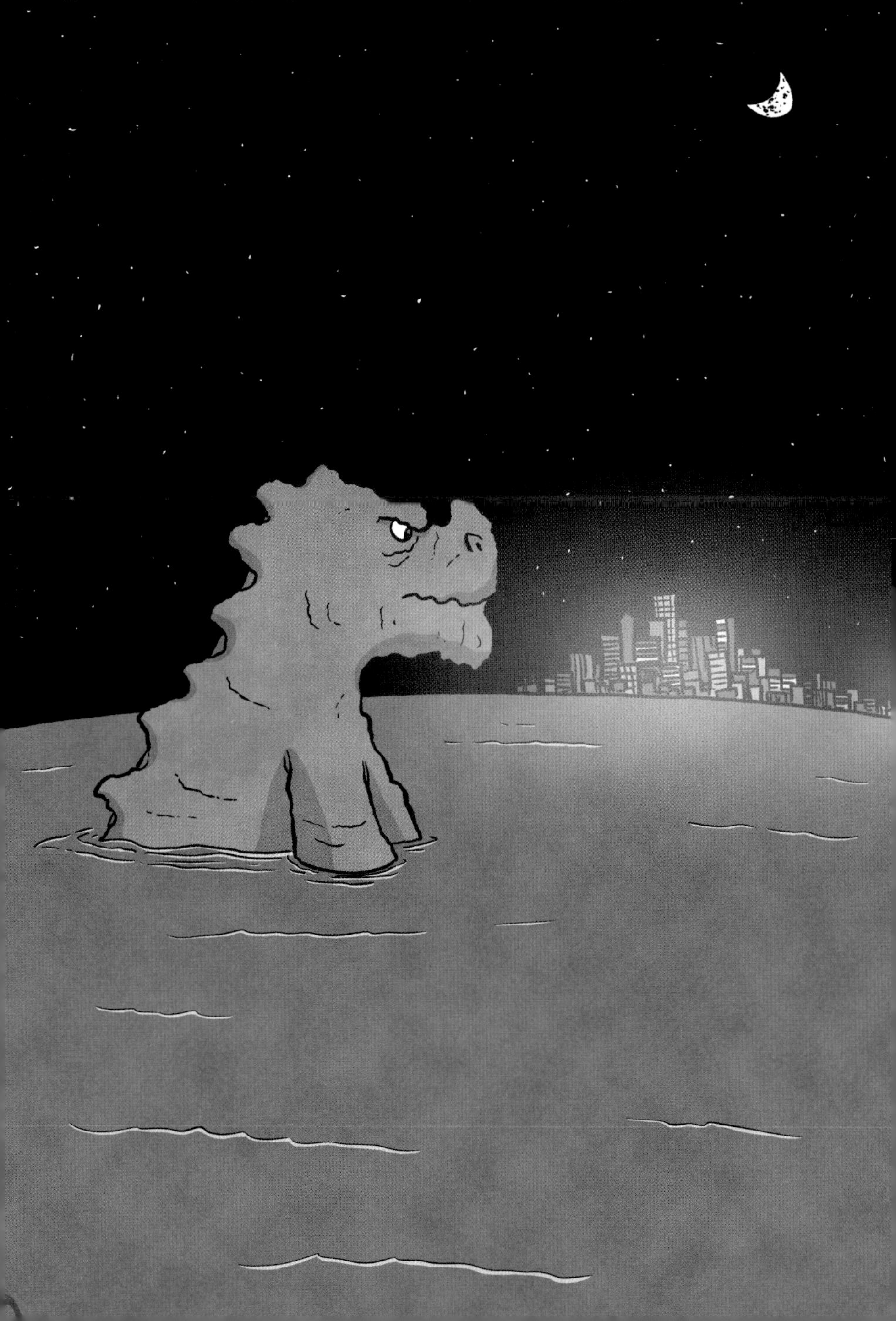

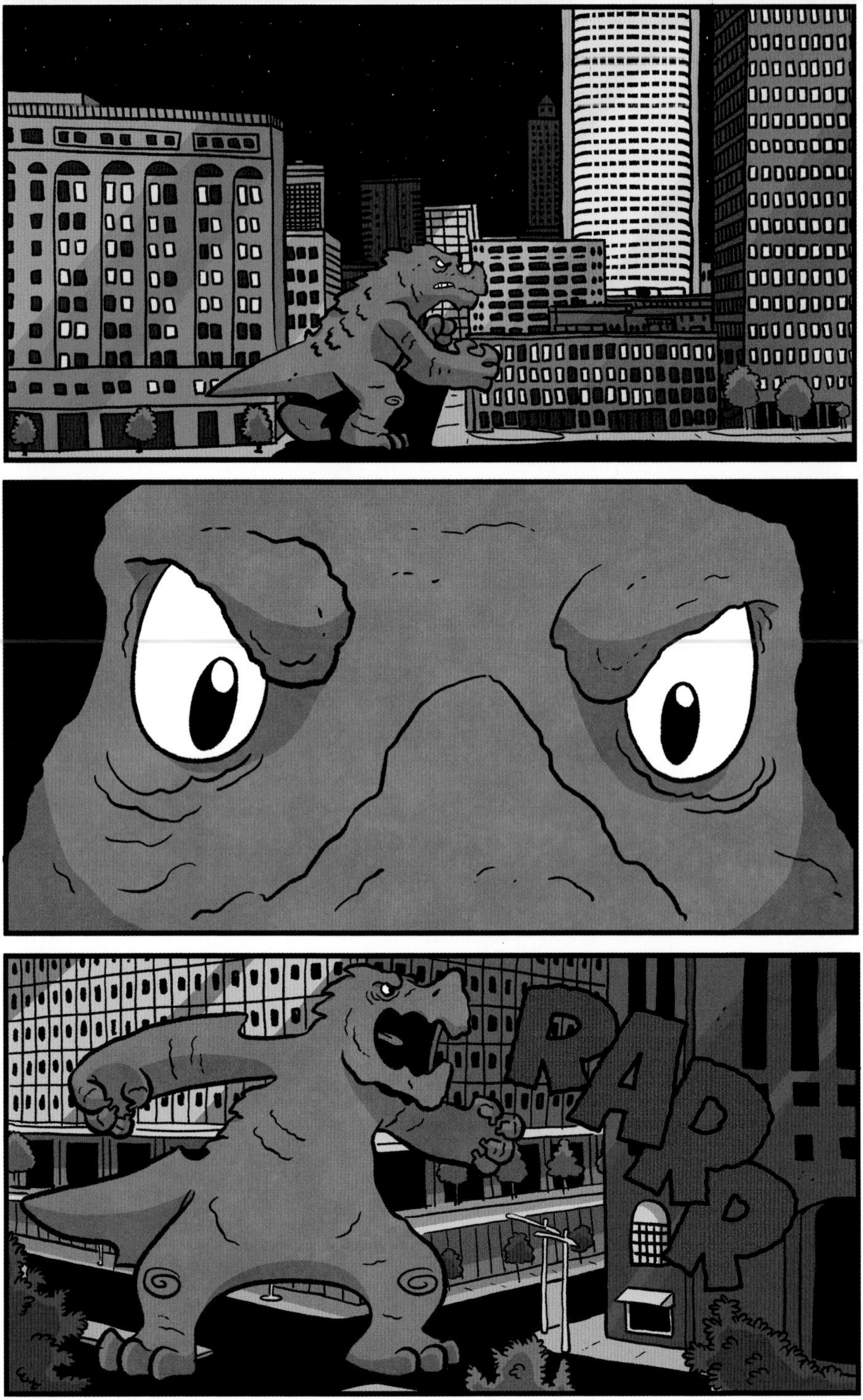
RAPP

Chapter 8 · Once Bitten

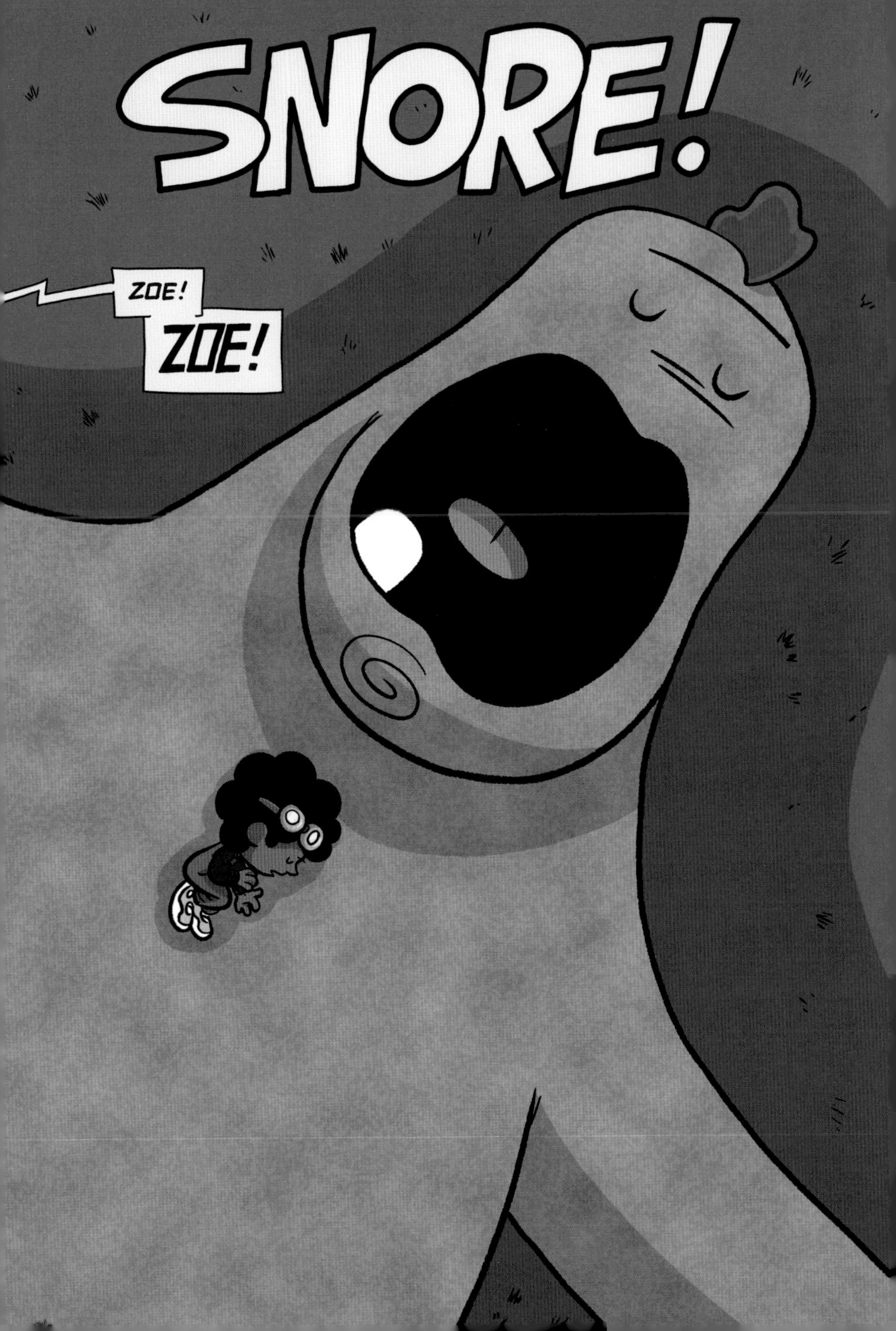
SNORE!
ZOE!
ZOE!

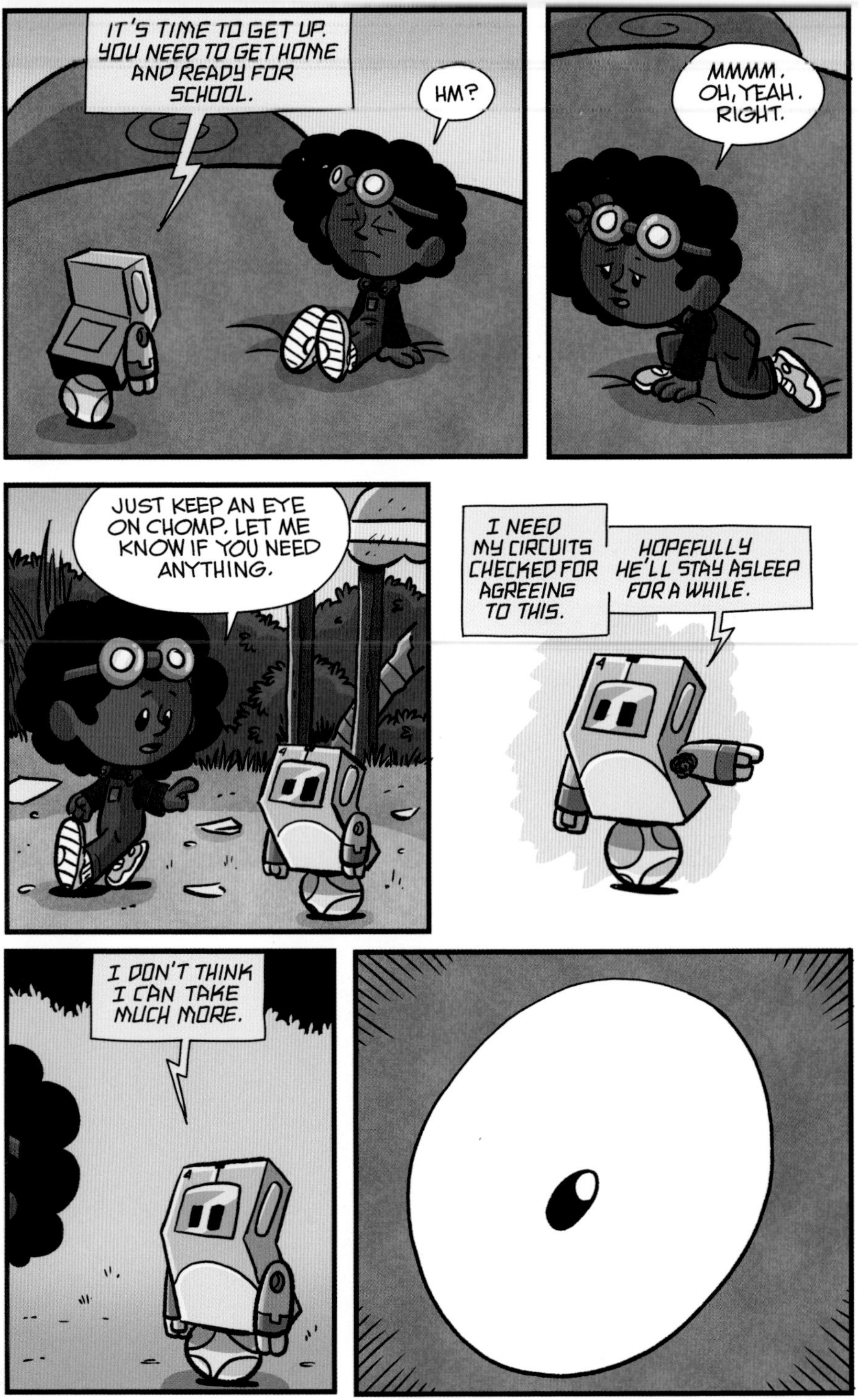
IT'S TIME TO GET UP. YOU NEED TO GET HOME AND READY FOR SCHOOL.
HM?
MMMM. OH, YEAH. RIGHT.
JUST KEEP AN EYE ON CHOMP. LET ME KNOW IF YOU NEED ANYTHING.
I NEED MY CIRCUITS CHECKED FOR AGREEING TO THIS.
HOPEFULLY HE'LL STAY ASLEEP FOR A WHILE.
I DON'T THINK I CAN TAKE MUCH MORE.

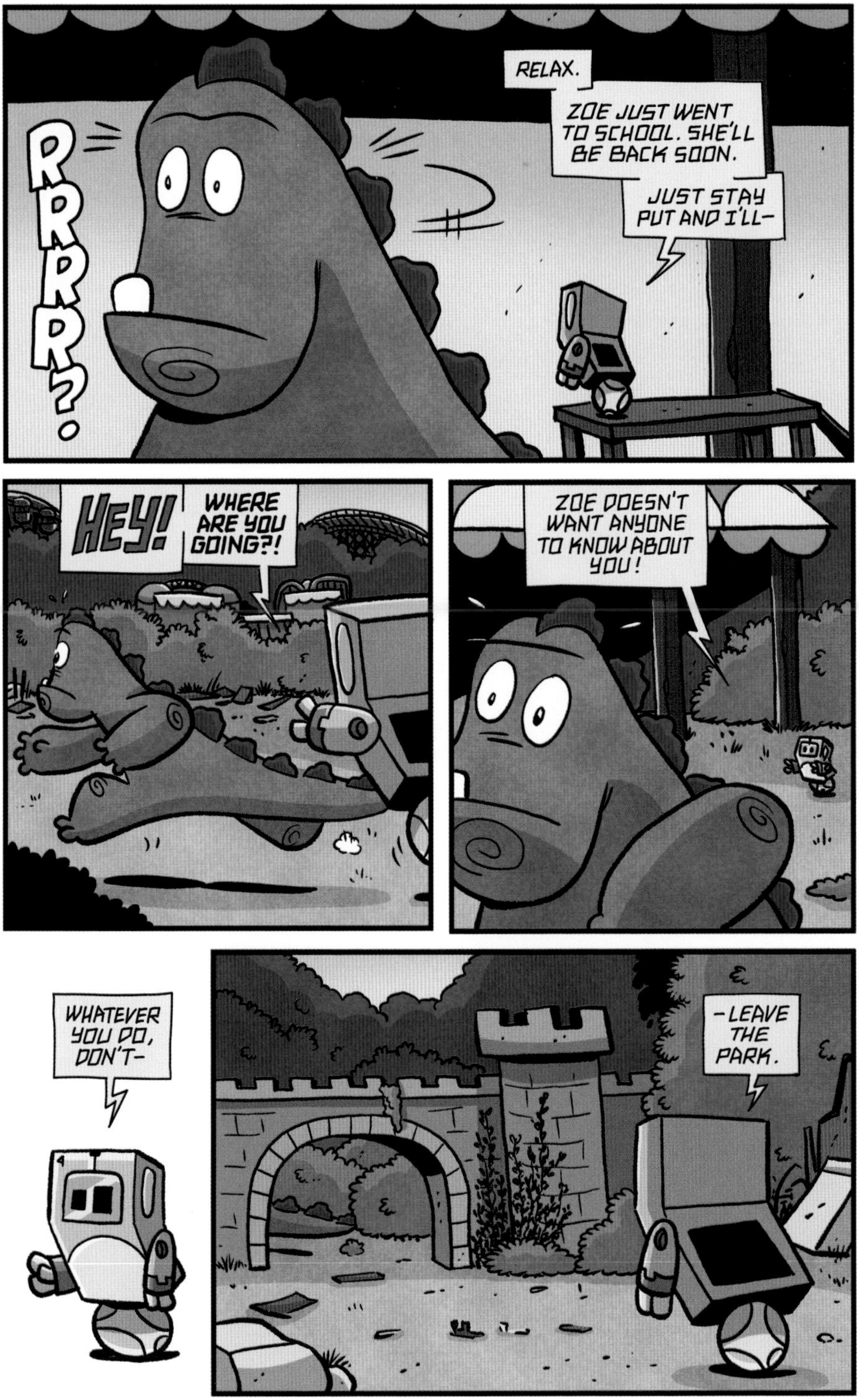
RRRRR?
RELAX.
ZOE JUST WENT TO SCHOOL. SHE'LL BE BACK SOON.
JUST STAY PUT AND I'LL–
HEY!
WHERE ARE YOU GOING?!
ZOE DOESN'T WANT ANYONE TO KNOW ABOUT YOU!
WHATEVER YOU DO, DON'T–
–LEAVE THE PARK.

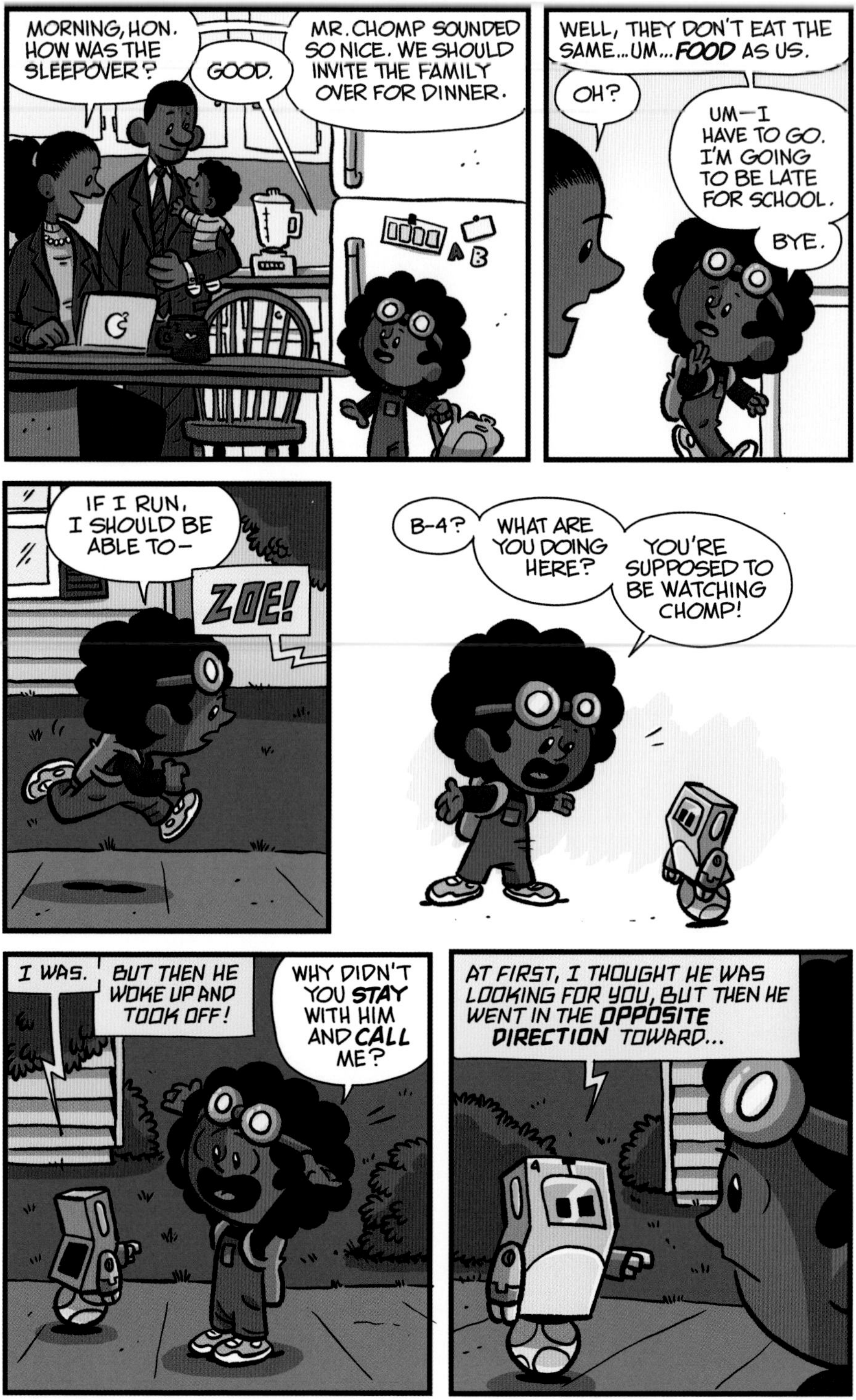
MORNING, HON. HOW WAS THE SLEEPOVER?
GOOD.
MR. CHOMP SOUNDED SO NICE. WE SHOULD INVITE THE FAMILY OVER FOR DINNER.
WELL, THEY DON'T EAT THE SAME...UM...FOOD AS US.
OH?
UM—I HAVE TO GO. I'M GOING TO BE LATE FOR SCHOOL.
BYE.
IF I RUN, I SHOULD BE ABLE TO—
ZOE!
B-4?
WHAT ARE YOU DOING HERE?
YOU'RE SUPPOSED TO BE WATCHING CHOMP!
I WAS.
BUT THEN HE WOKE UP AND TOOK OFF!
WHY DIDN'T YOU STAY WITH HIM AND CALL ME?
AT FIRST, I THOUGHT HE WAS LOOKING FOR YOU, BUT THEN HE WENT IN THE OPPOSITE DIRECTION TOWARD...

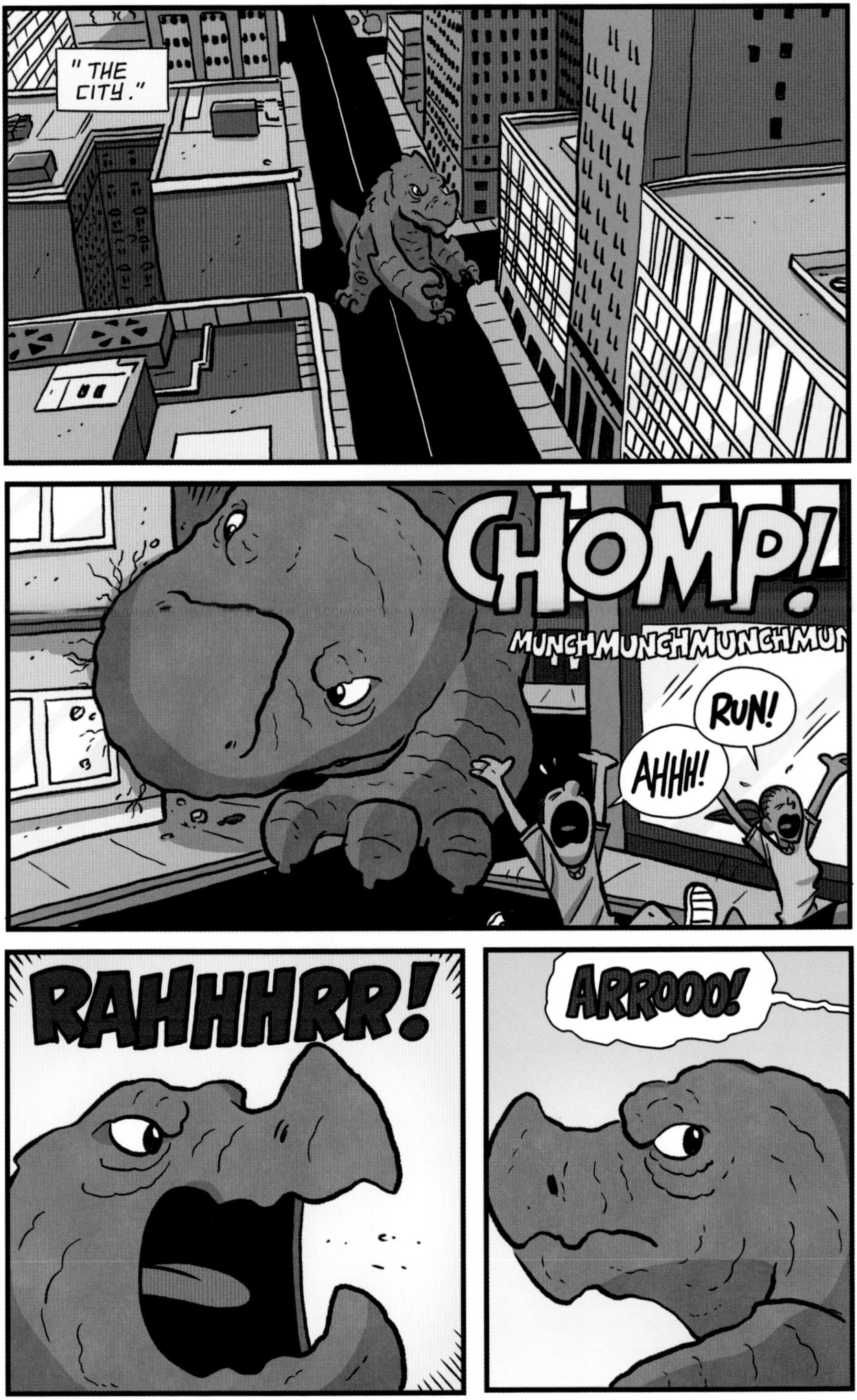
"THE CITY."
CHOMP!
MUNCHMUNCHMUNCHMUN
RUN!
AHHH!
RAHHHRR!
ARROOO!

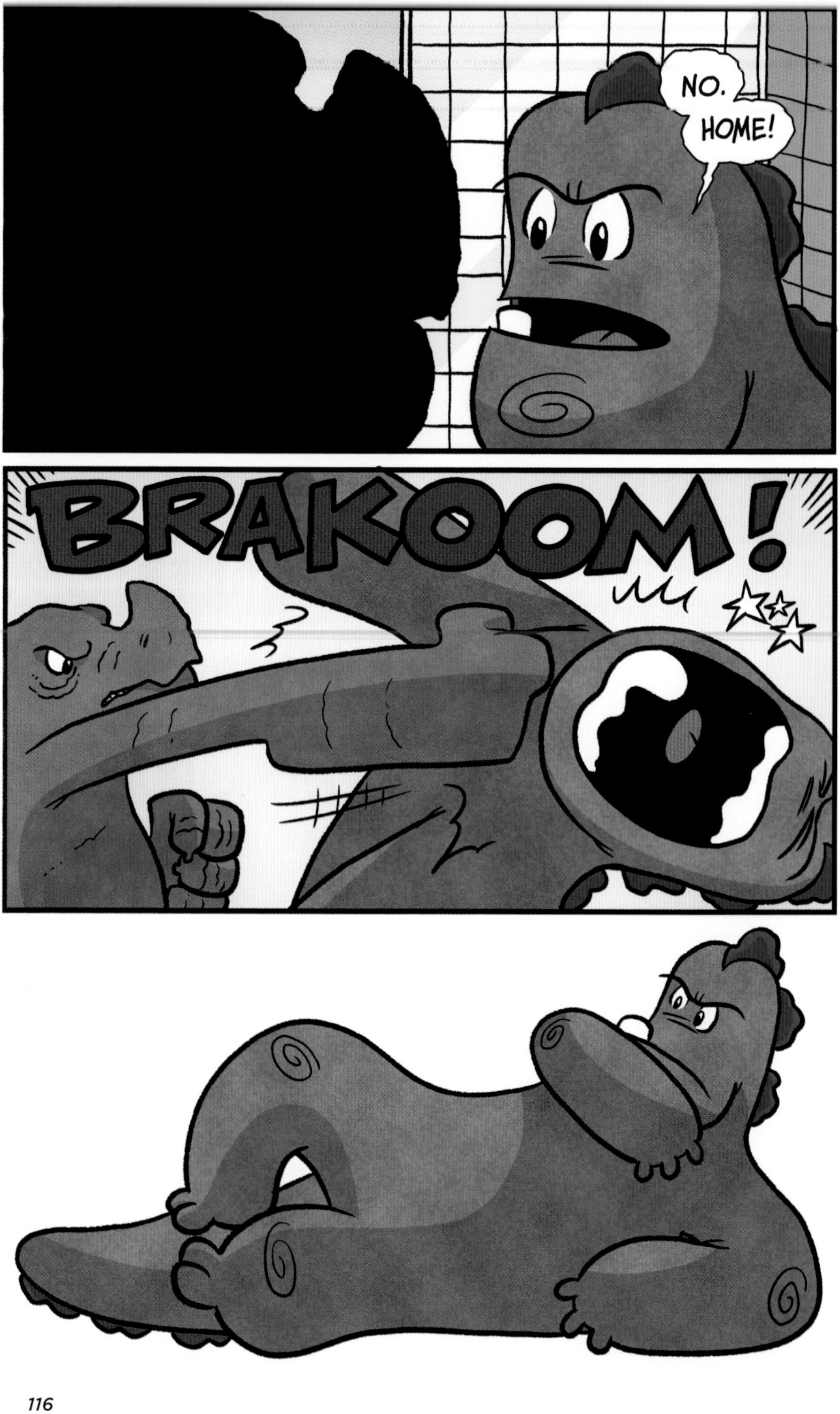
NO.
HOME!
BRAKOOM!

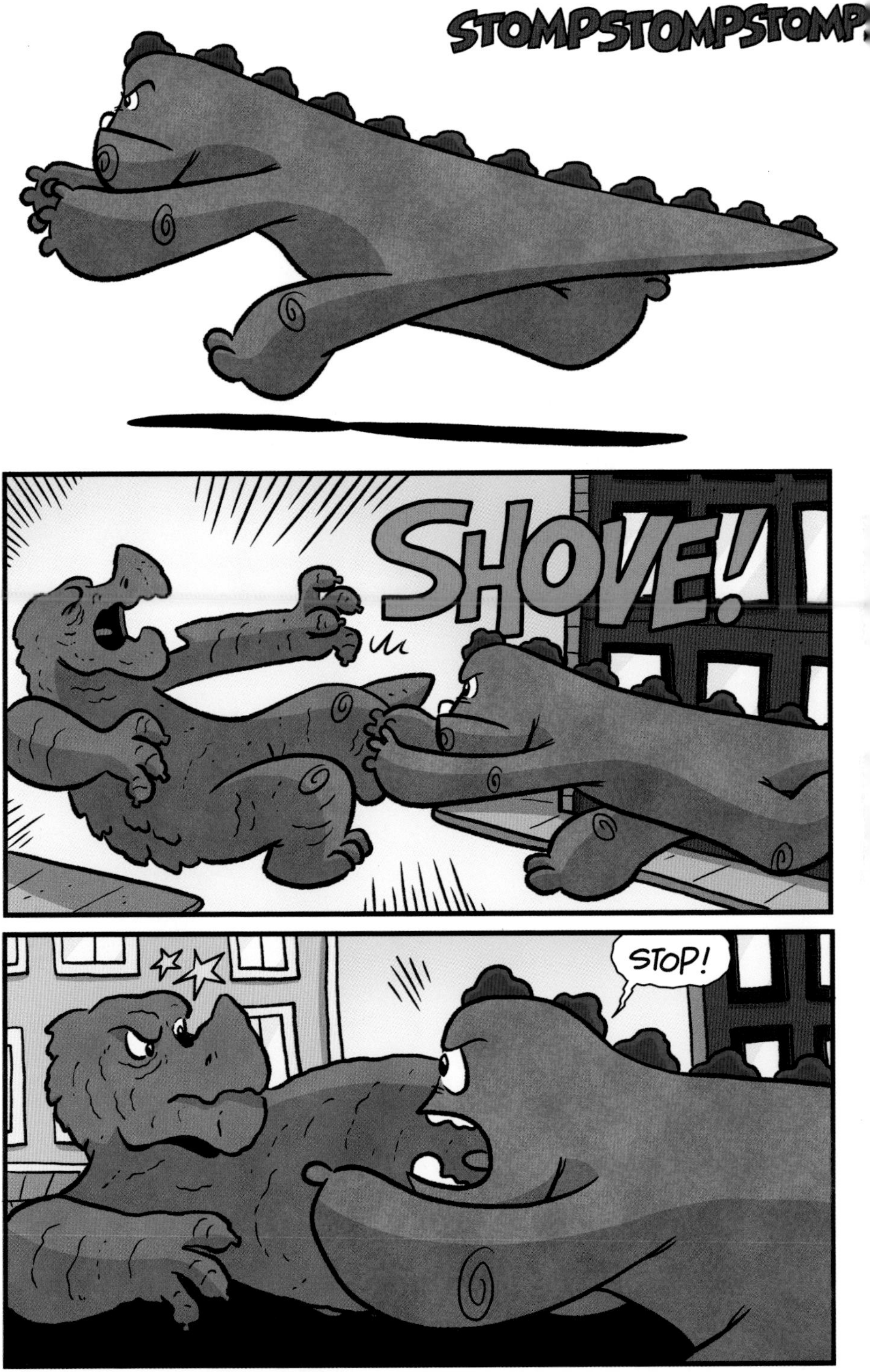
STOMPSTOMPSTOMP
SHOVE!
STOP!

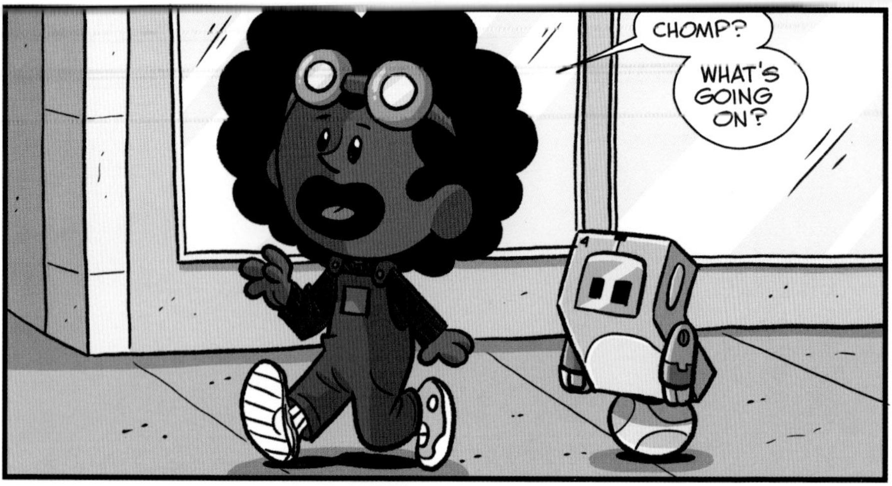
CHOMP?
WHAT'S GOING ON?

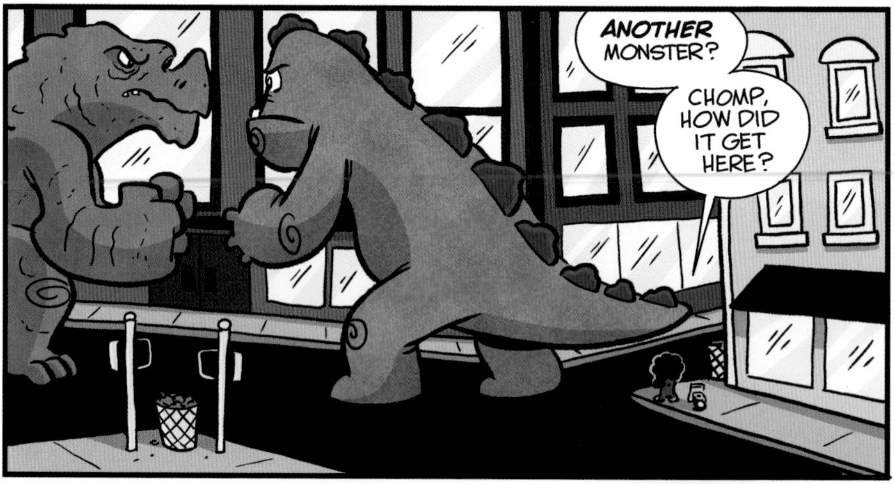
ANOTHER MONSTER?
CHOMP, HOW DID IT GET HERE?

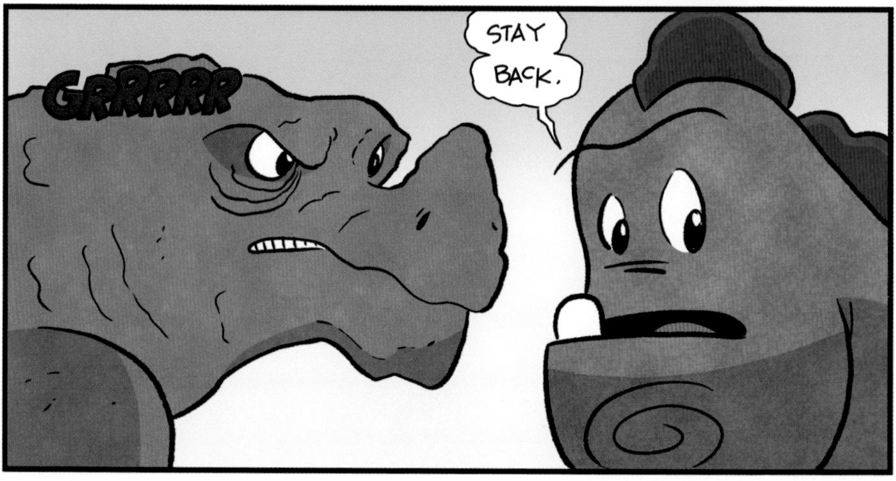
GRRRRR
STAY BACK.

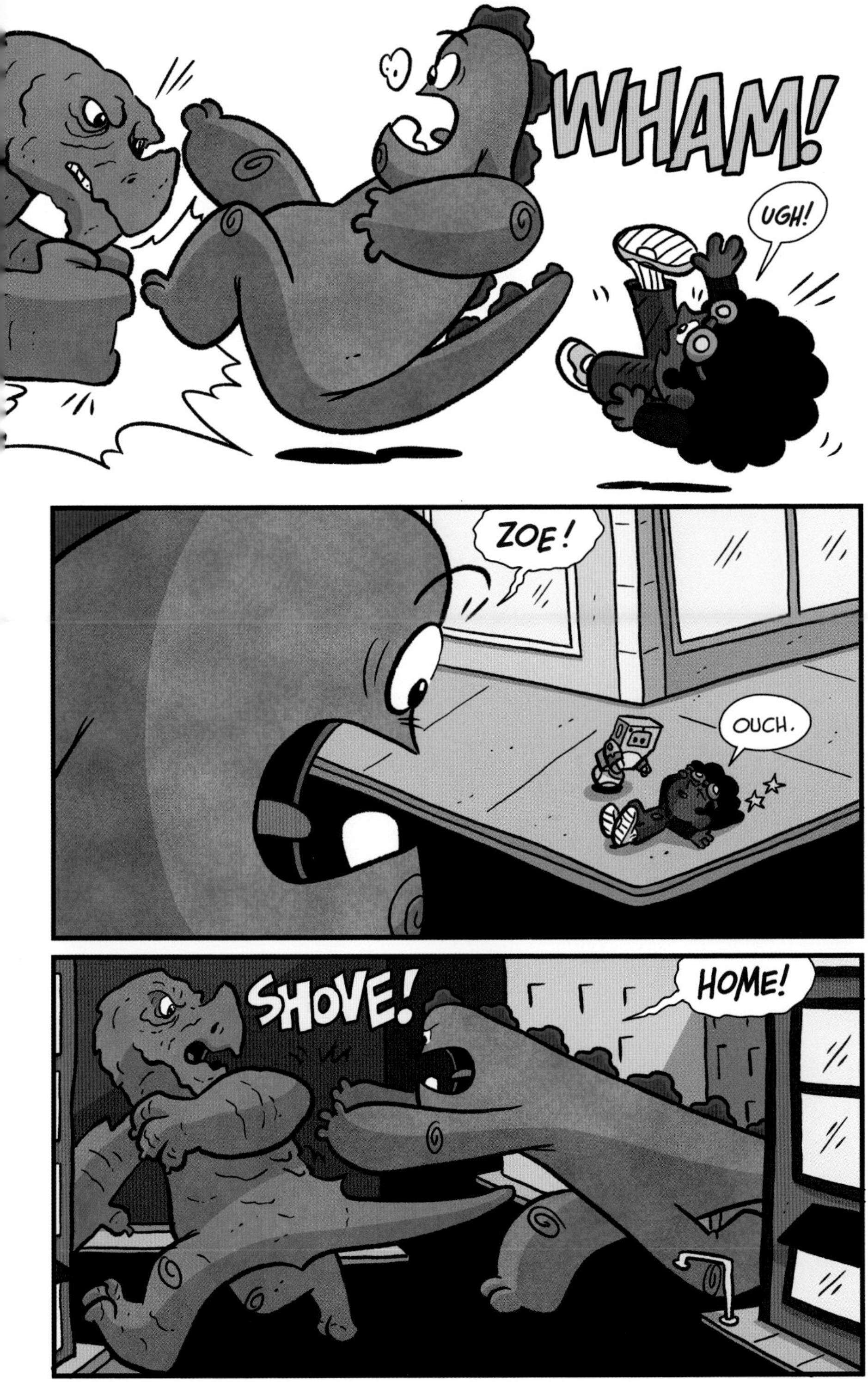
WHAM!
UGH!
ZOE!
OUCH.
SHOVE!
HOME!

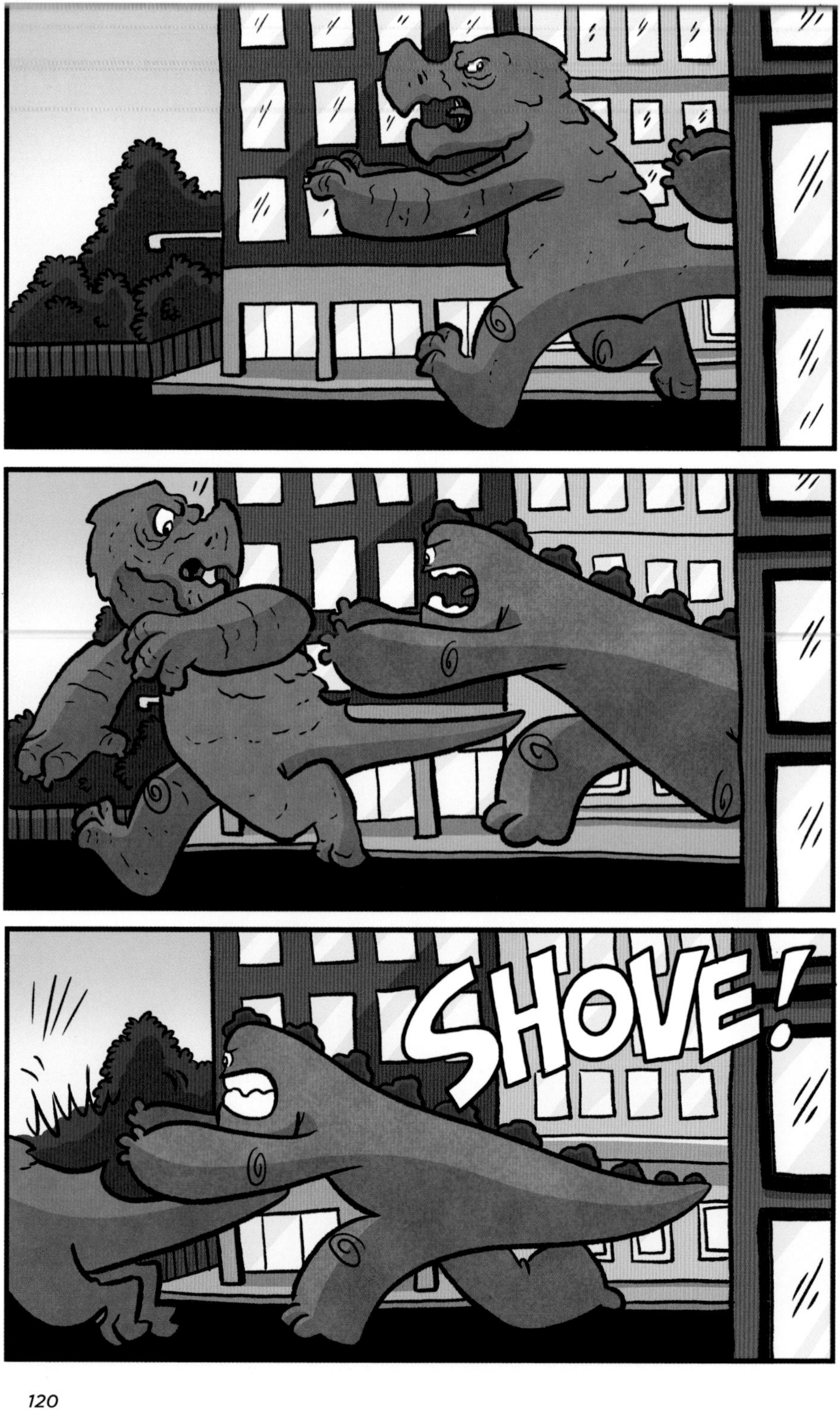
SHOVE!

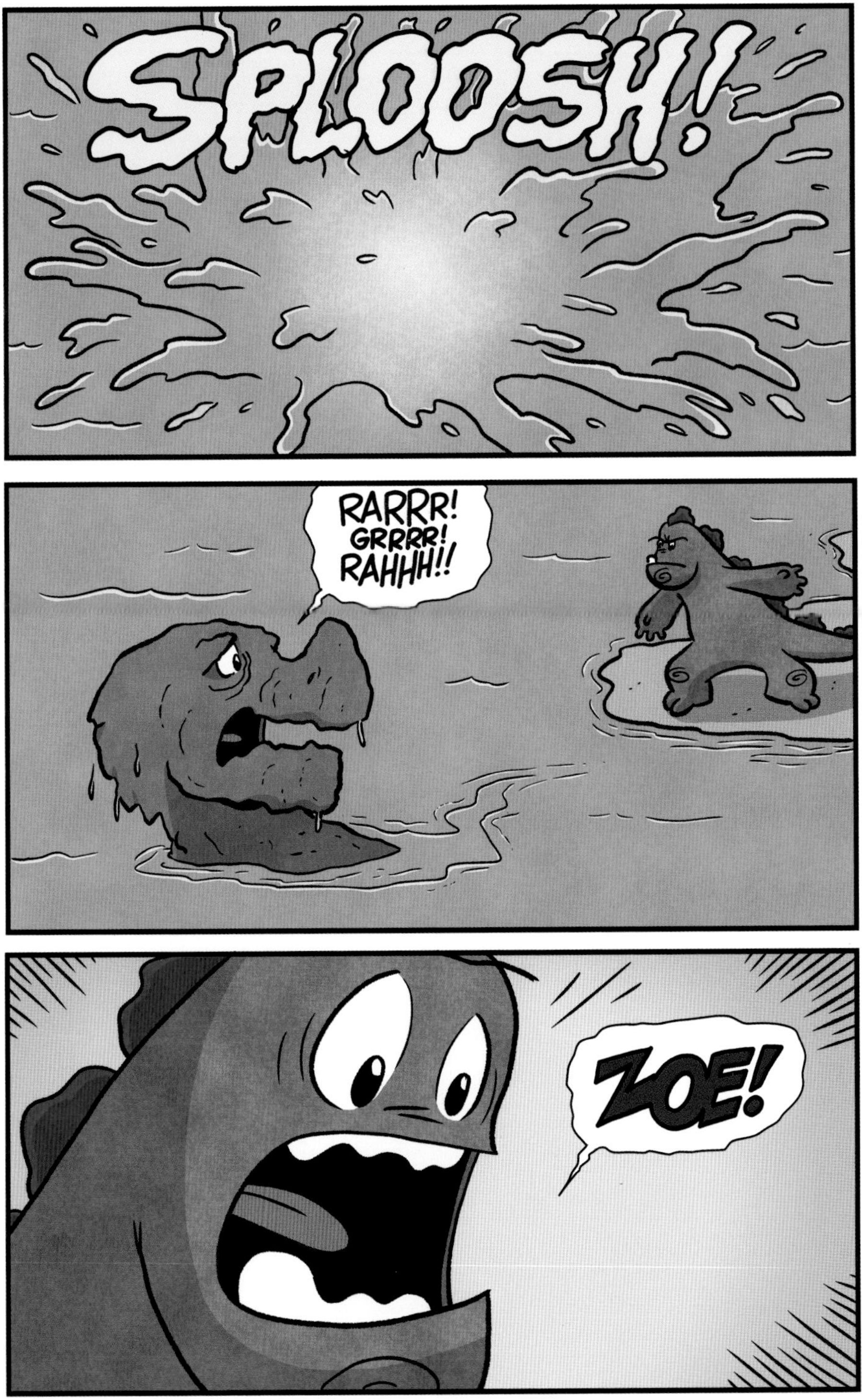
SPLOOSH!
RARRR! GRRRR! RAHHH!!
ZOE!

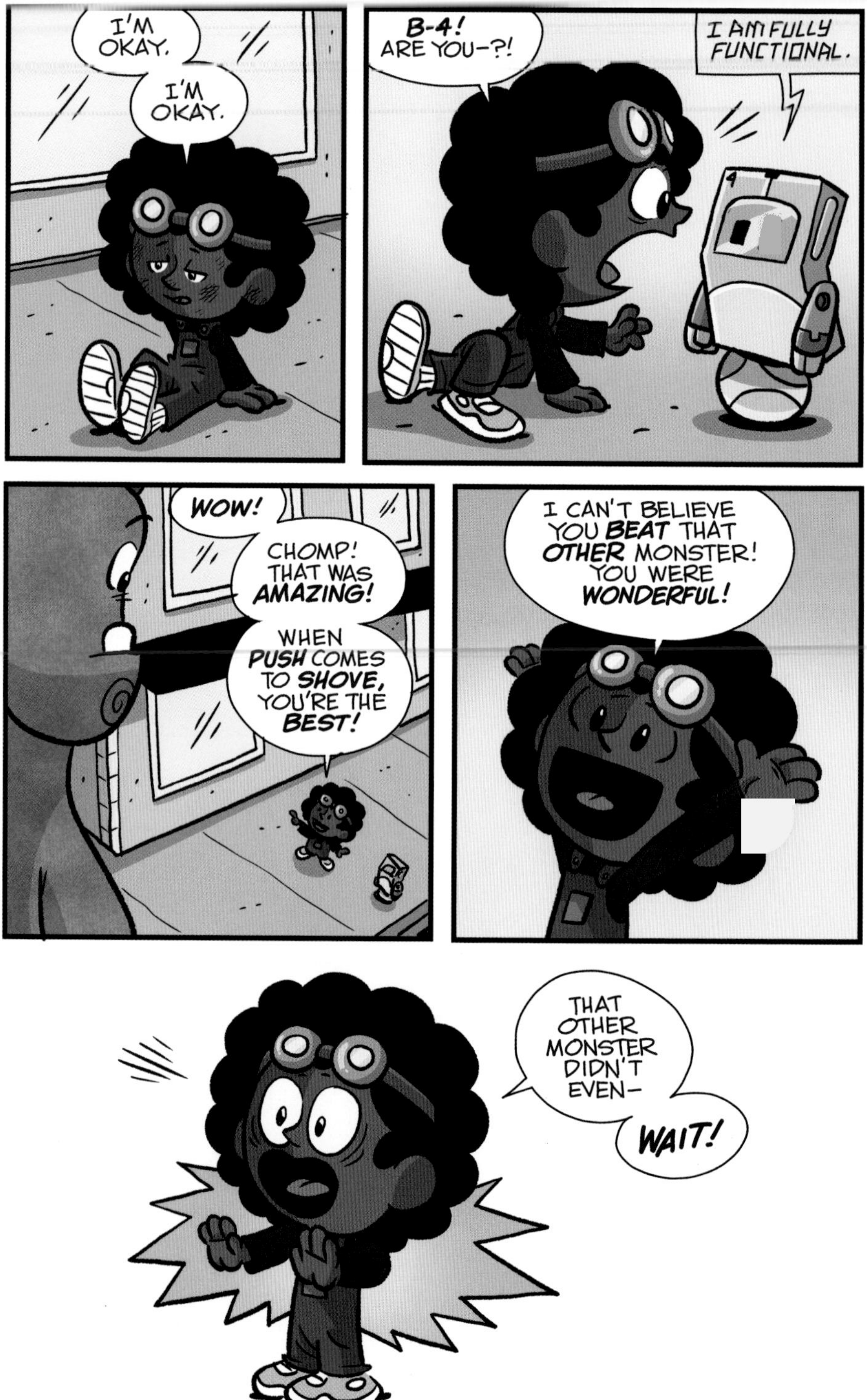
I'M OKAY.
I'M OKAY.
B-4! ARE YOU-?!
I AM FULLY FUNCTIONAL.
WOW!
CHOMP! THAT WAS AMAZING!
WHEN PUSH COMES TO SHOVE, YOU'RE THE BEST!
I CAN'T BELIEVE YOU BEAT THAT OTHER MONSTER! YOU WERE WONDERFUL!
THAT OTHER MONSTER DIDN'T EVEN-
WAIT!

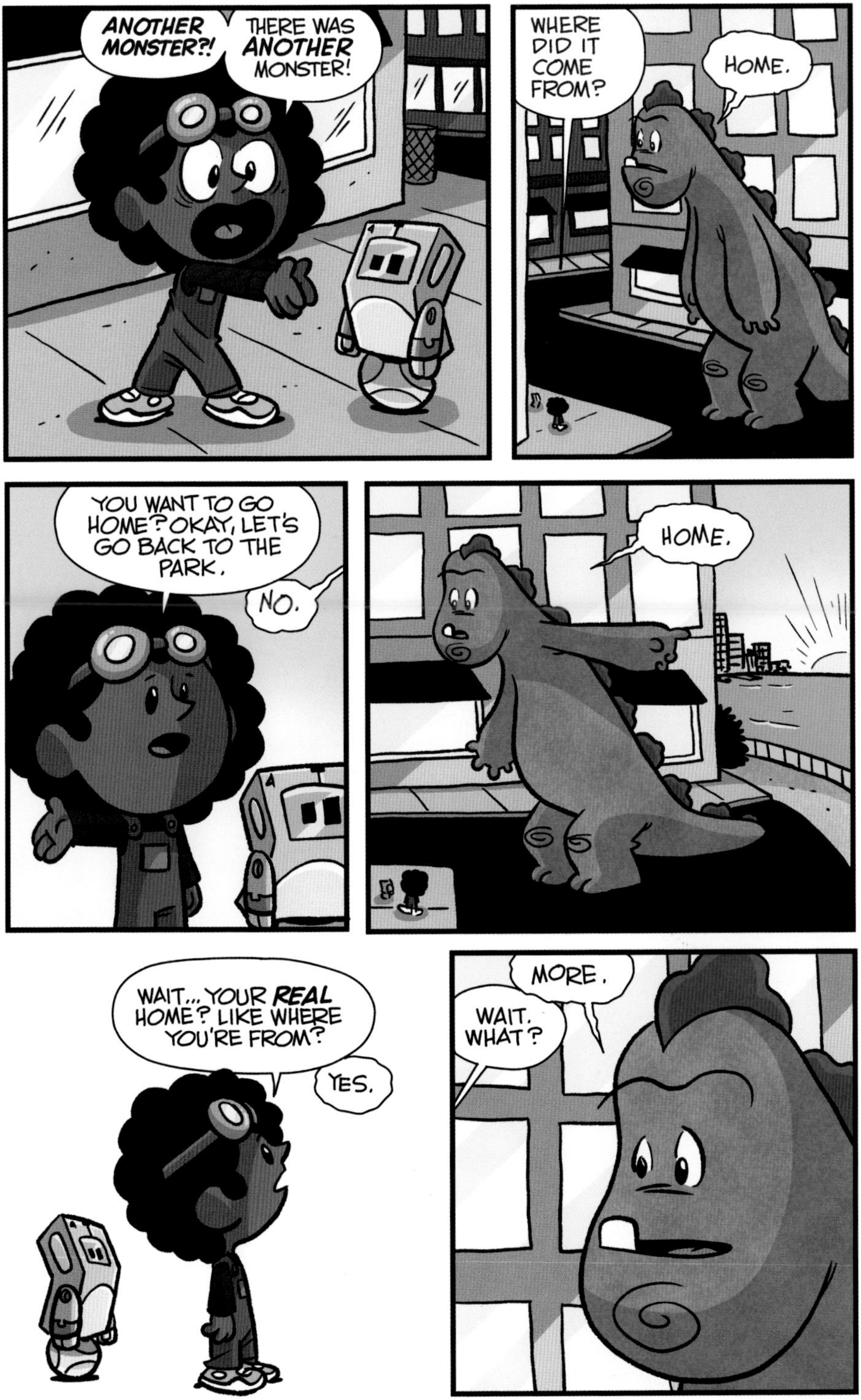

ANOTHER MONSTER?!
THERE WAS ANOTHER MONSTER!
WHERE DID IT COME FROM?
HOME.
YOU WANT TO GO HOME? OKAY, LET'S GO BACK TO THE PARK.
NO.
HOME.
WAIT... YOUR REAL HOME? LIKE WHERE YOU'RE FROM?
YES.
WAIT. WHAT?
MORE.

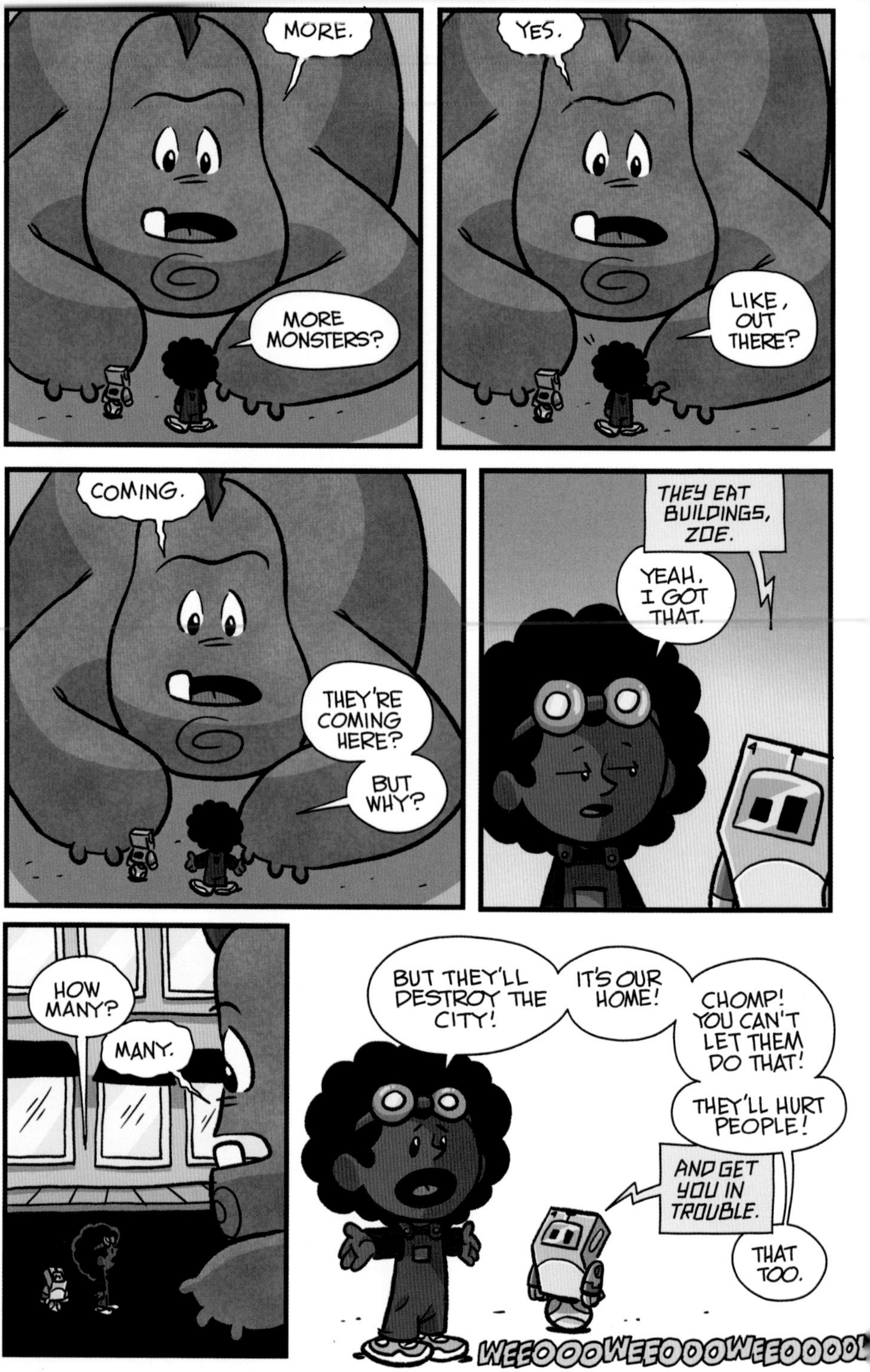
MORE.
MORE MONSTERS?
YES.
LIKE, OUT THERE?
COMING.
THEY'RE COMING HERE?
BUT WHY?
THEY EAT BUILDINGS, ZOE.
YEAH, I GOT THAT.
HOW MANY?
MANY.
BUT THEY'LL DESTROY THE CITY!
IT'S OUR HOME!
CHOMP! YOU CAN'T LET THEM DO THAT!
THEY'LL HURT PEOPLE!
AND GET YOU IN TROUBLE.
THAT TOO.
WEEOOOWEEOOOWEEOOOO

WEEOOOWEEOOOWEEOOC

OH, NO! THE *POLICE* ARE COMING!

WE HAVE TO GET YOU OUT OF HERE— THEY'LL THINK *YOU* DID THIS!

OR YOU.

EVEN WORSE!

IEEOOOWEEOOOWEEOOOWEEOOC

WEEOOOWEEOOOWEEOOOWEEC

POLICE

OOWEEOOOWEEOOOWEEOOC

BASE, THIS IS CAR 810.

ARRIVED ON THE SCENE.

WHAT'S THE STATUS?

SCENE IS CLEAR, BUT YOU'RE GONNA THINK I'M *CRAZY.*

PAT, I'VE BEEN ON THIS JOB LONG ENOUGH SO THAT *NOTHING* WOULD MAKE ME THINK YOU'RE CRAZY.

UM...SOMETHING TOOK A *BITE* OUT OF A BUILDING.

YOU'RE *CRAZY.*

125

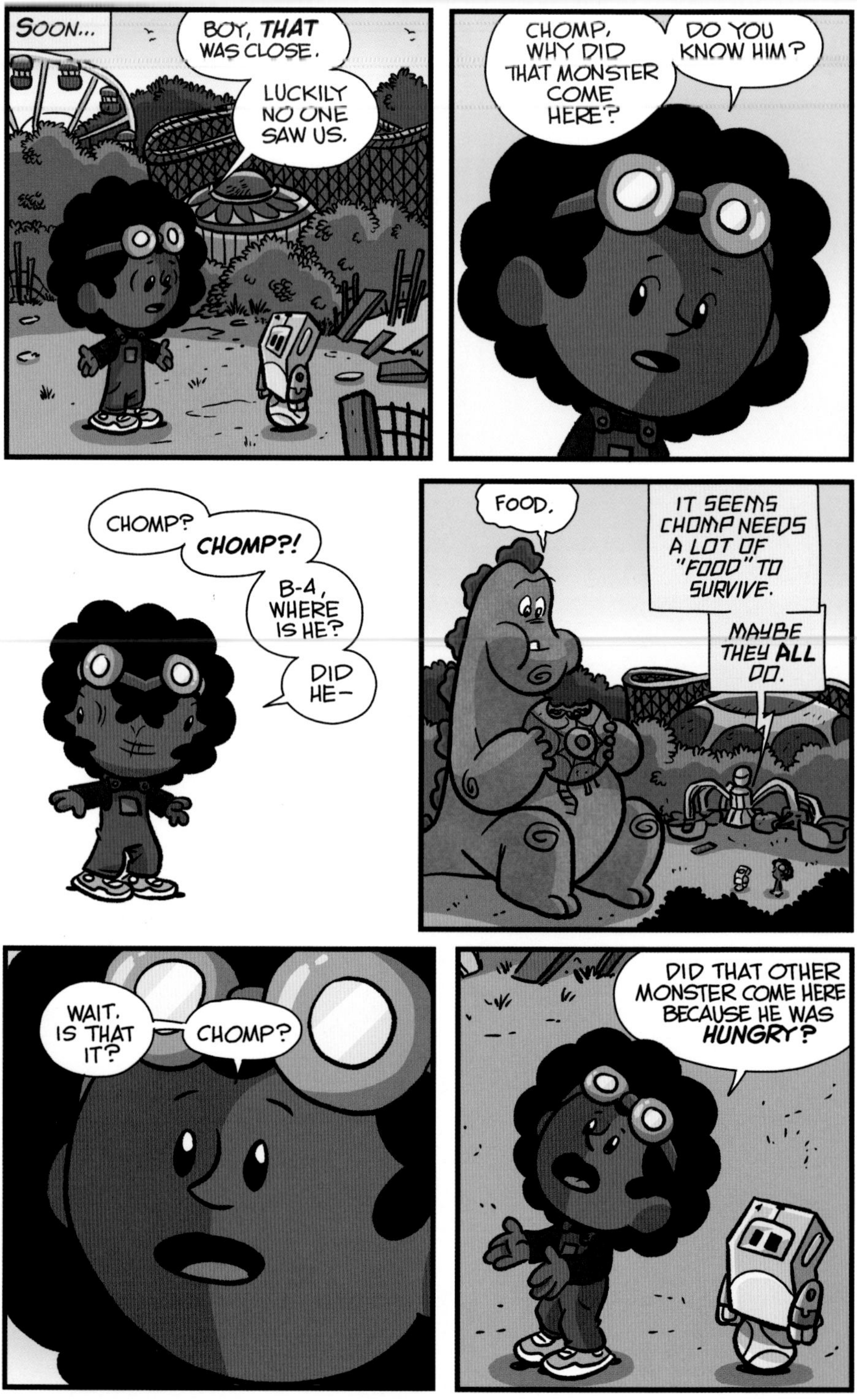
SOON...
BOY, THAT WAS CLOSE.
LUCKILY NO ONE SAW US.
CHOMP, WHY DID THAT MONSTER COME HERE?
DO YOU KNOW HIM?
CHOMP? CHOMP?!
B-4, WHERE IS HE?
DID HE–
FOOD.
IT SEEMS CHOMP NEEDS A LOT OF "FOOD" TO SURVIVE.
MAYBE THEY ALL DO.
WAIT. IS THAT IT?
CHOMP?
DID THAT OTHER MONSTER COME HERE BECAUSE HE WAS HUNGRY?

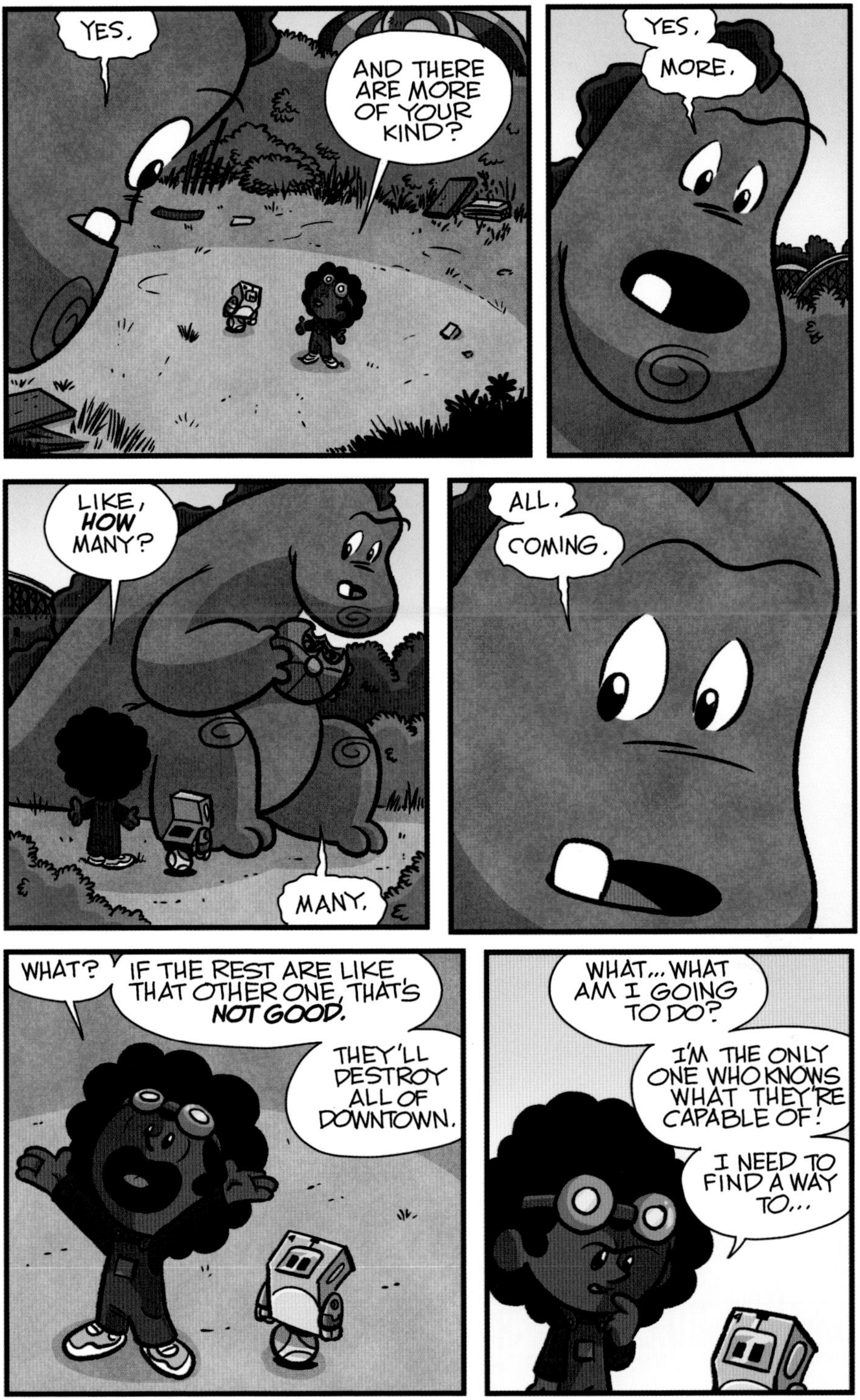
YES.
AND THERE ARE MORE OF YOUR KIND?
YES,
MORE.
LIKE, *HOW* MANY?
MANY.
ALL,
COMING.
WHAT?
IF THE REST ARE LIKE THAT OTHER ONE, THAT'S **NOT GOOD.**
THEY'LL DESTROY ALL OF DOWNTOWN.
WHAT... WHAT AM I GOING TO DO?
I'M THE ONLY ONE WHO KNOWS WHAT THEY'RE CAPABLE OF!
I NEED TO FIND A WAY TO...

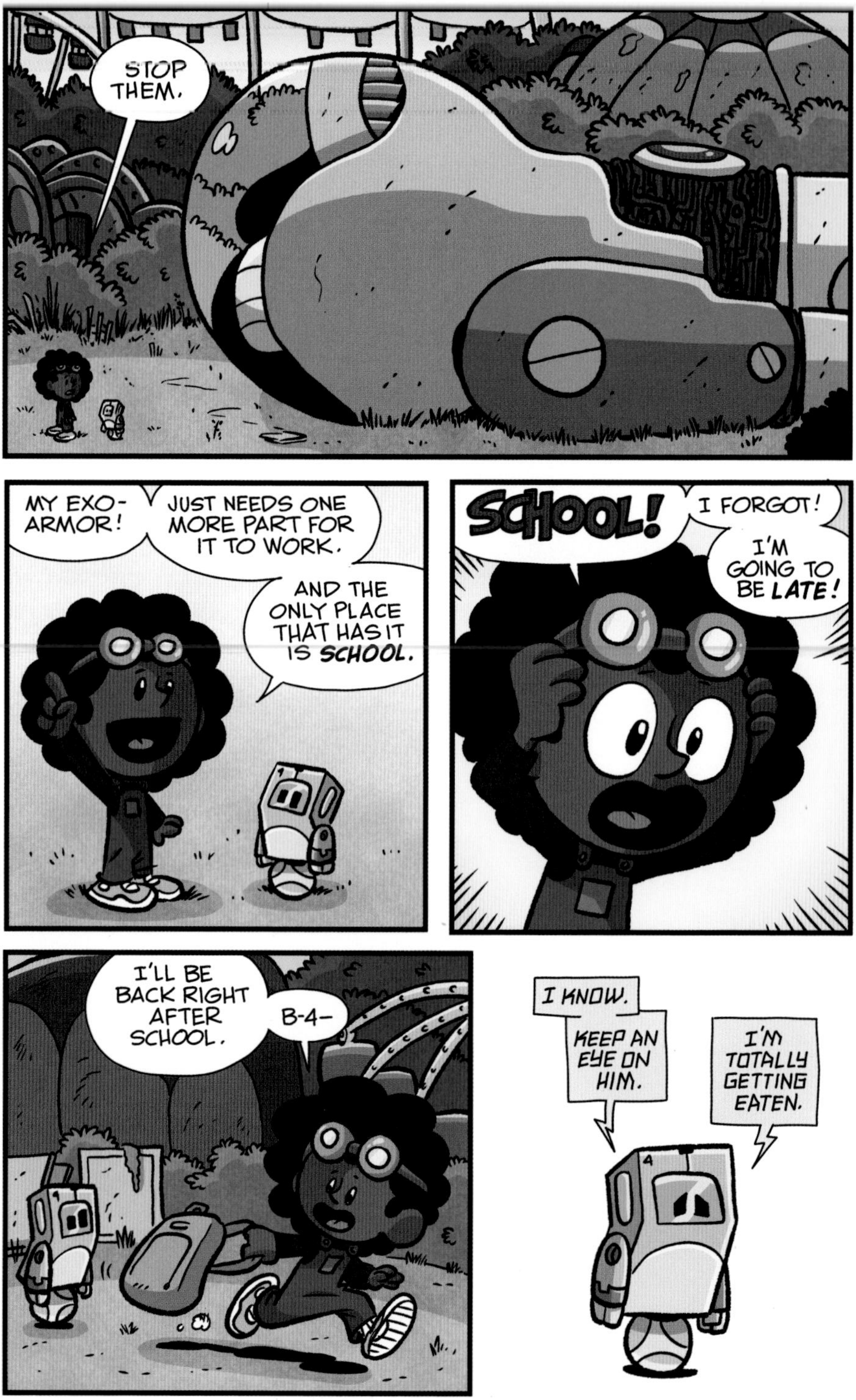
STOP THEM.
MY EXO-ARMOR!
JUST NEEDS ONE MORE PART FOR IT TO WORK.
AND THE ONLY PLACE THAT HAS IT IS SCHOOL.
SCHOOL!
I FORGOT!
I'M GOING TO BE LATE!
I'LL BE BACK RIGHT AFTER SCHOOL.
B-4–
I KNOW.
KEEP AN EYE ON HIM.
I'M TOTALLY GETTING EATEN.

CHAPTER 9 - GATHERING STORM

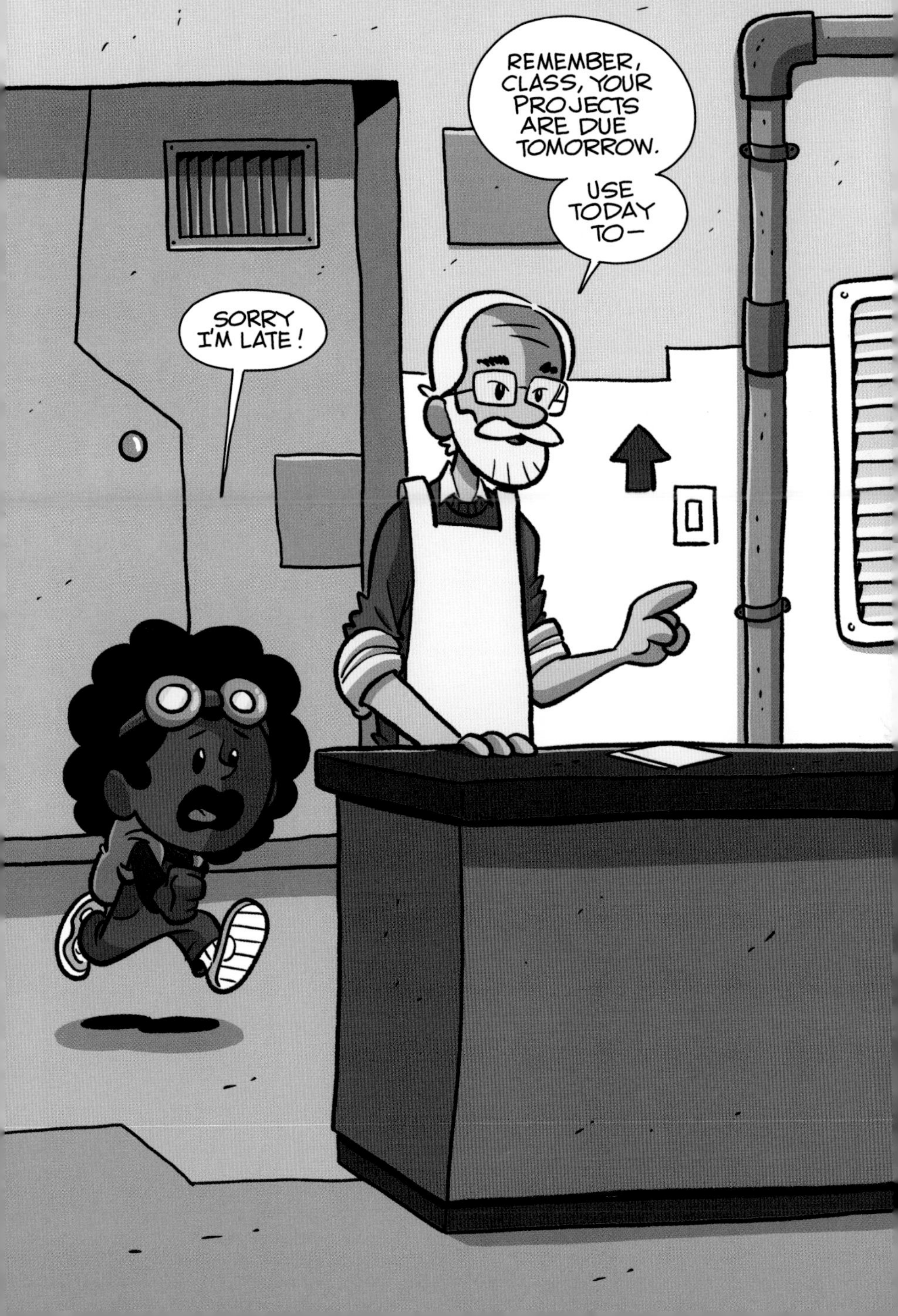
REMEMBER, CLASS, YOUR PROJECTS ARE DUE TOMORROW.
USE TODAY TO—
SORRY I'M LATE!

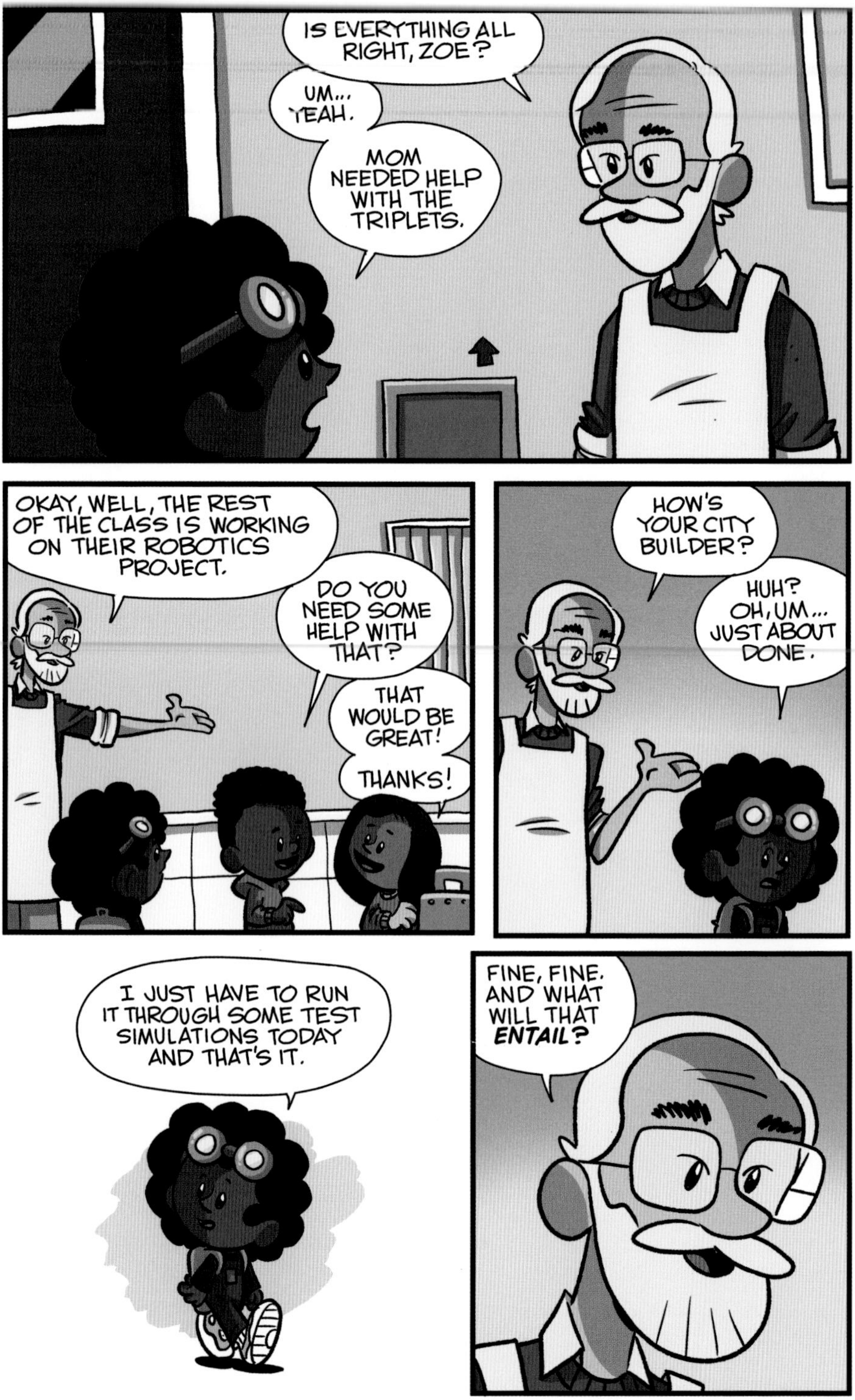
IS EVERYTHING ALL RIGHT, ZOE?
UM... YEAH.
MOM NEEDED HELP WITH THE TRIPLETS.
OKAY, WELL, THE REST OF THE CLASS IS WORKING ON THEIR ROBOTICS PROJECT.
DO YOU NEED SOME HELP WITH THAT?
THAT WOULD BE GREAT!
THANKS!
HOW'S YOUR CITY BUILDER?
HUH? OH, UM... JUST ABOUT DONE.
I JUST HAVE TO RUN IT THROUGH SOME TEST SIMULATIONS TODAY AND THAT'S IT.
FINE, FINE. AND WHAT WILL THAT ***ENTAIL?***

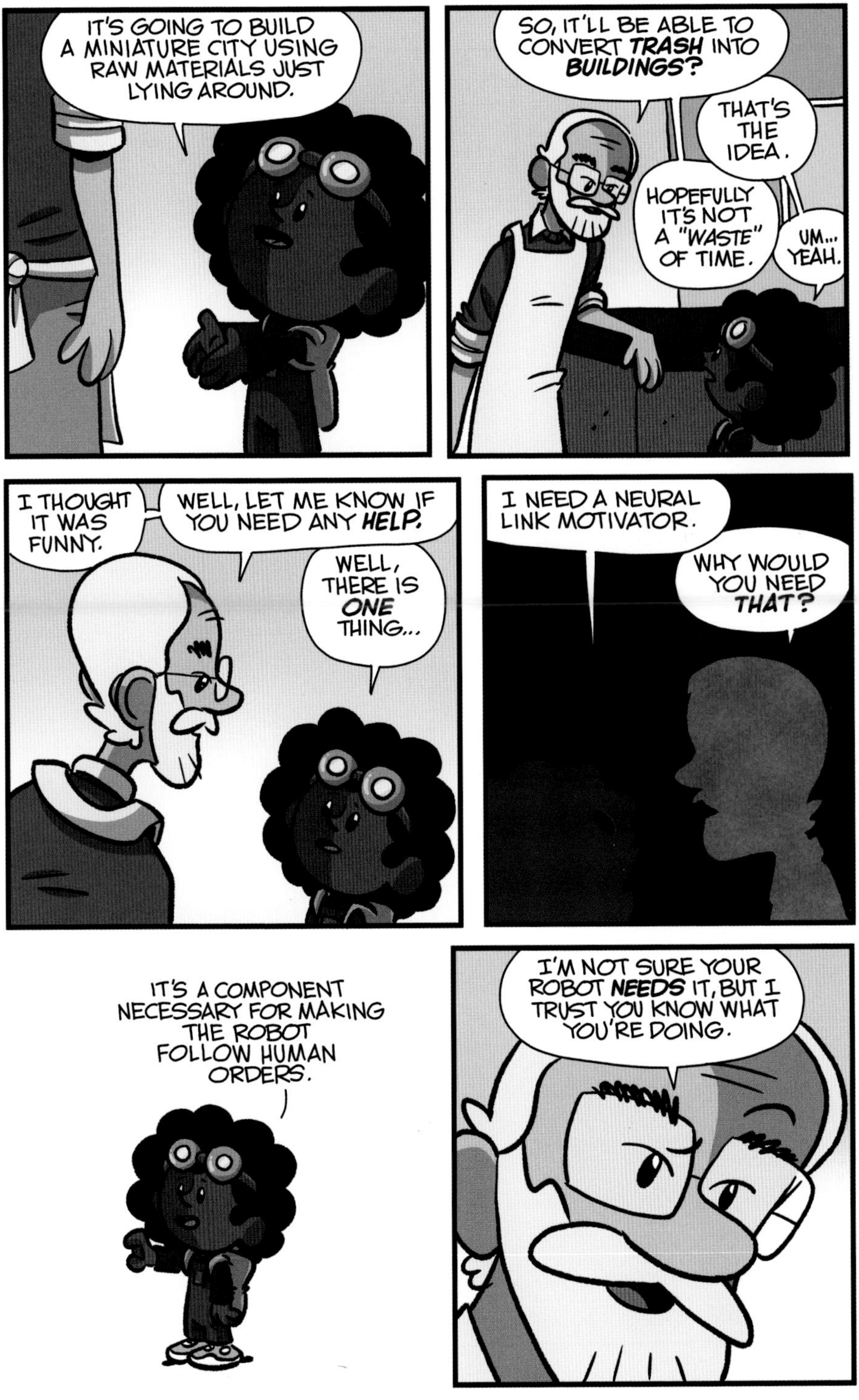
IT'S GOING TO BUILD A MINIATURE CITY USING RAW MATERIALS JUST LYING AROUND.
SO, IT'LL BE ABLE TO CONVERT TRASH INTO BUILDINGS?
THAT'S THE IDEA.
HOPEFULLY IT'S NOT A "WASTE" OF TIME.
UM... YEAH.
I THOUGHT IT WAS FUNNY.
WELL, LET ME KNOW IF YOU NEED ANY HELP.
WELL, THERE IS ONE THING...
I NEED A NEURAL LINK MOTIVATOR.
WHY WOULD YOU NEED THAT?
IT'S A COMPONENT NECESSARY FOR MAKING THE ROBOT FOLLOW HUMAN ORDERS.
I'M NOT SURE YOUR ROBOT NEEDS IT, BUT I TRUST YOU KNOW WHAT YOU'RE DOING.

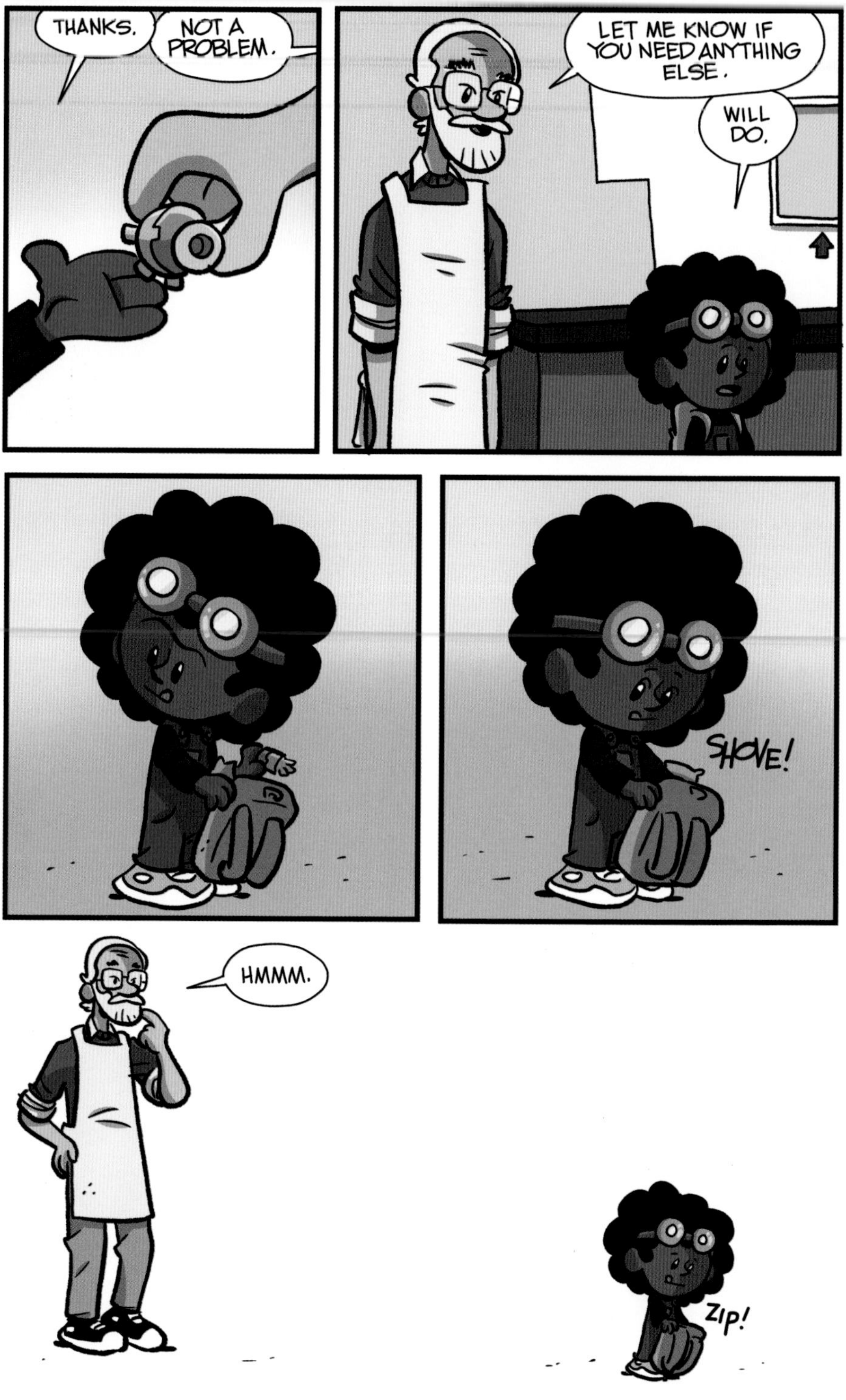
THANKS.
NOT A PROBLEM.
LET ME KNOW IF YOU NEED ANYTHING ELSE.
WILL DO.
SHOVE!
HMMM.
ZIP!

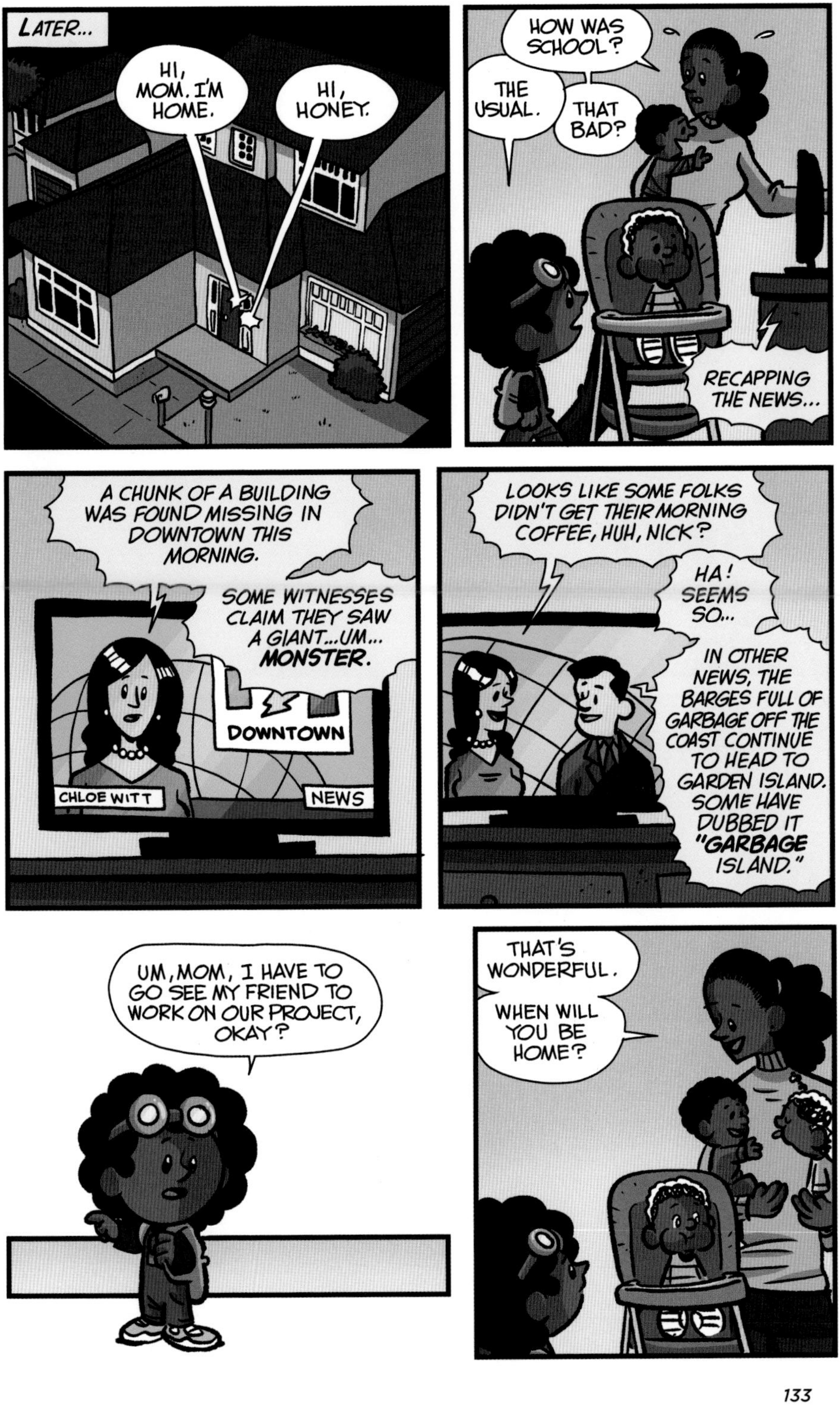
LATER...
HI, MOM. I'M HOME.
HI, HONEY.
HOW WAS SCHOOL?
THE USUAL.
THAT BAD?
RECAPPING THE NEWS...
A CHUNK OF A BUILDING WAS FOUND MISSING IN DOWNTOWN THIS MORNING.
SOME WITNESSES CLAIM THEY SAW A GIANT...UM... MONSTER.
DOWNTOWN
CHLOE WITT
NEWS
LOOKS LIKE SOME FOLKS DIDN'T GET THEIR MORNING COFFEE, HUH, NICK?
HA! SEEMS SO...
IN OTHER NEWS, THE BARGES FULL OF GARBAGE OFF THE COAST CONTINUE TO HEAD TO GARDEN ISLAND. SOME HAVE DUBBED IT "GARBAGE ISLAND."
UM, MOM, I HAVE TO GO SEE MY FRIEND TO WORK ON OUR PROJECT, OKAY?
THAT'S WONDERFUL.
WHEN WILL YOU BE HOME?

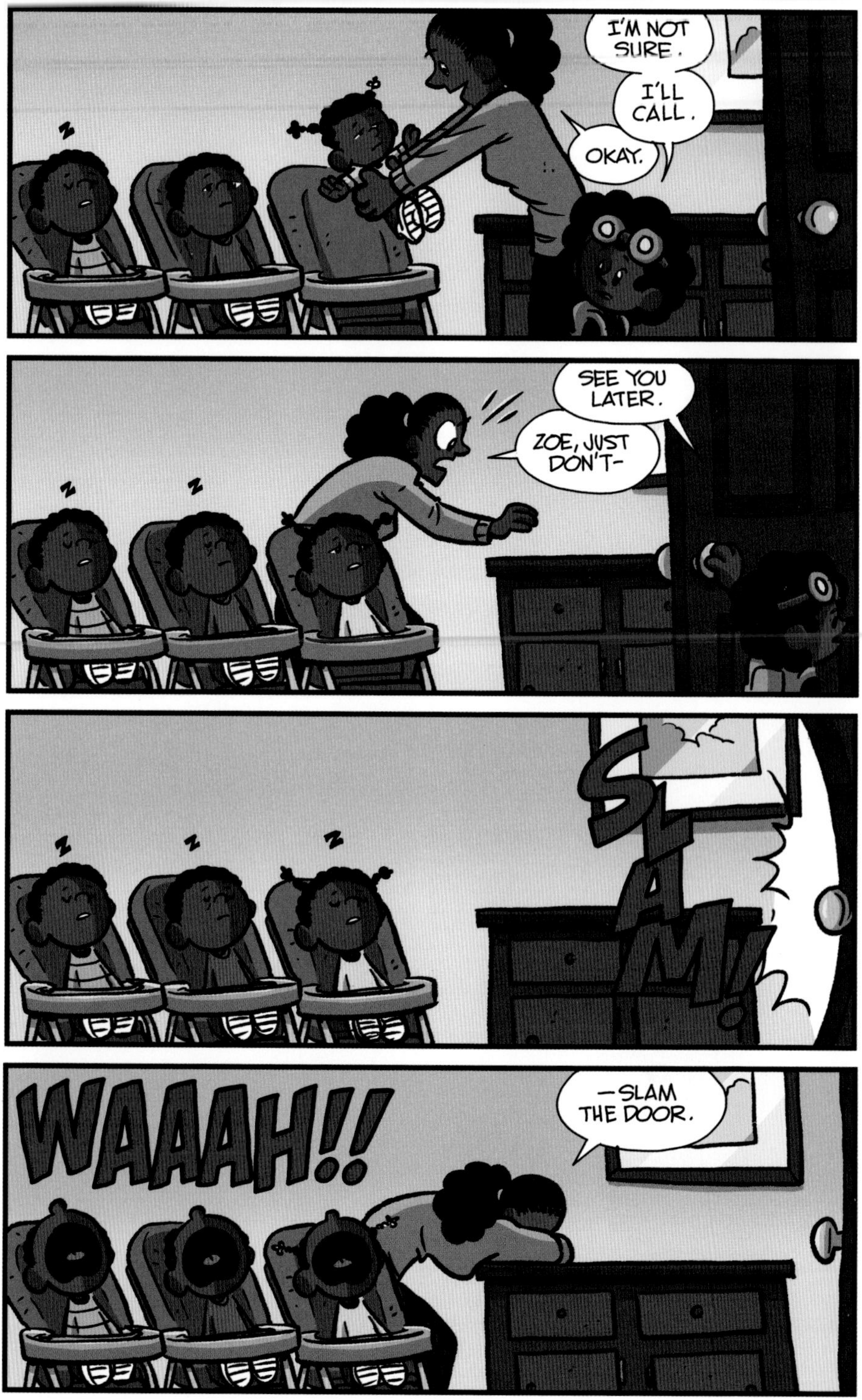
I'M NOT SURE.
I'LL CALL.
OKAY.
SEE YOU LATER.
ZOE, JUST DON'T-
SLAM!
WAAAH!!
—SLAM THE DOOR.

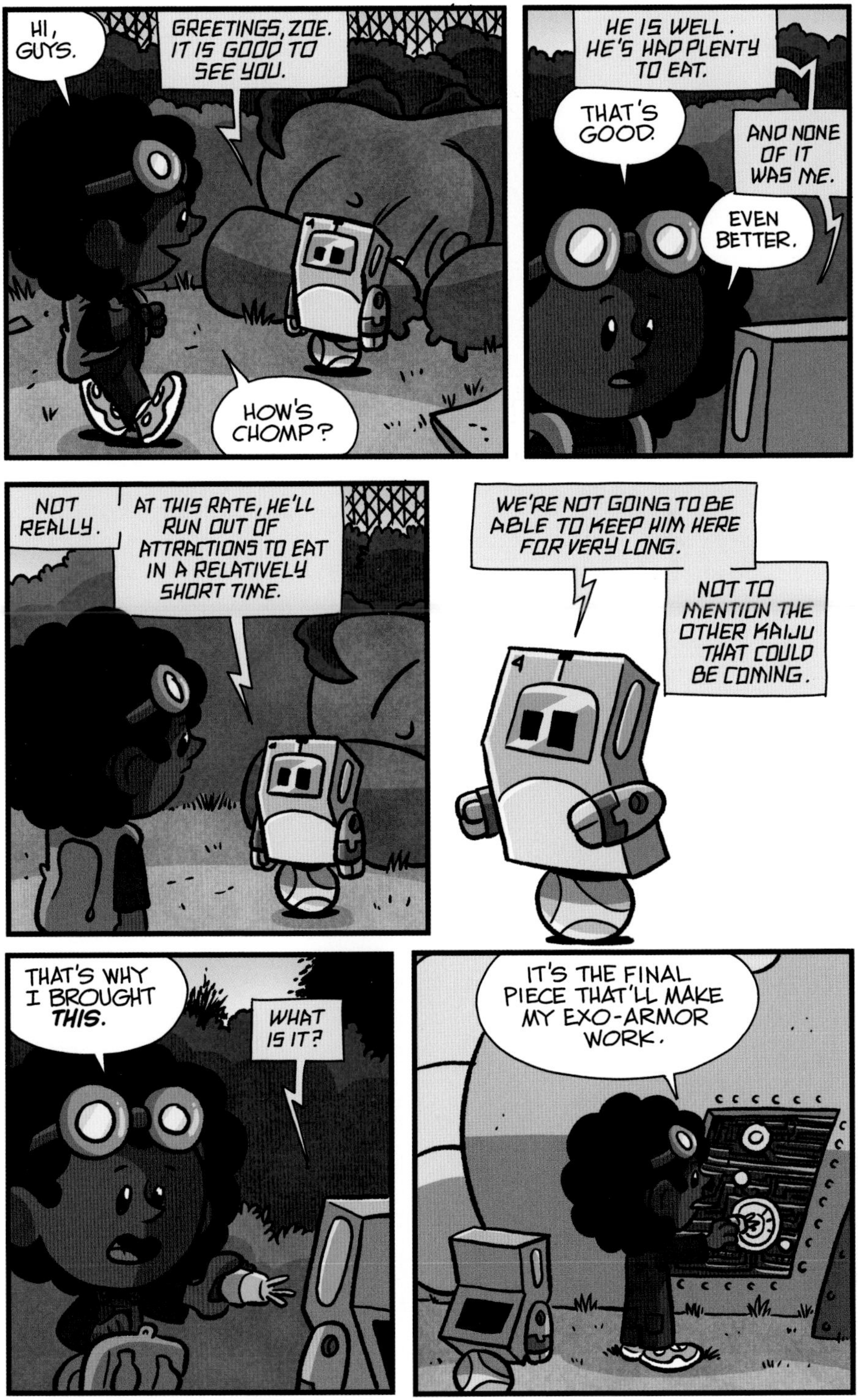

HI, GUYS.
GREETINGS, ZOE. IT IS GOOD TO SEE YOU.
HOW'S CHOMP?
HE IS WELL. HE'S HAD PLENTY TO EAT.
THAT'S GOOD.
AND NONE OF IT WAS ME.
EVEN BETTER.
NOT REALLY.
AT THIS RATE, HE'LL RUN OUT OF ATTRACTIONS TO EAT IN A RELATIVELY SHORT TIME.
WE'RE NOT GOING TO BE ABLE TO KEEP HIM HERE FOR VERY LONG.
NOT TO MENTION THE OTHER KAIJU THAT COULD BE COMING.
THAT'S WHY I BROUGHT **THIS**.
WHAT IS IT?
IT'S THE FINAL PIECE THAT'LL MAKE MY EXO-ARMOR WORK.

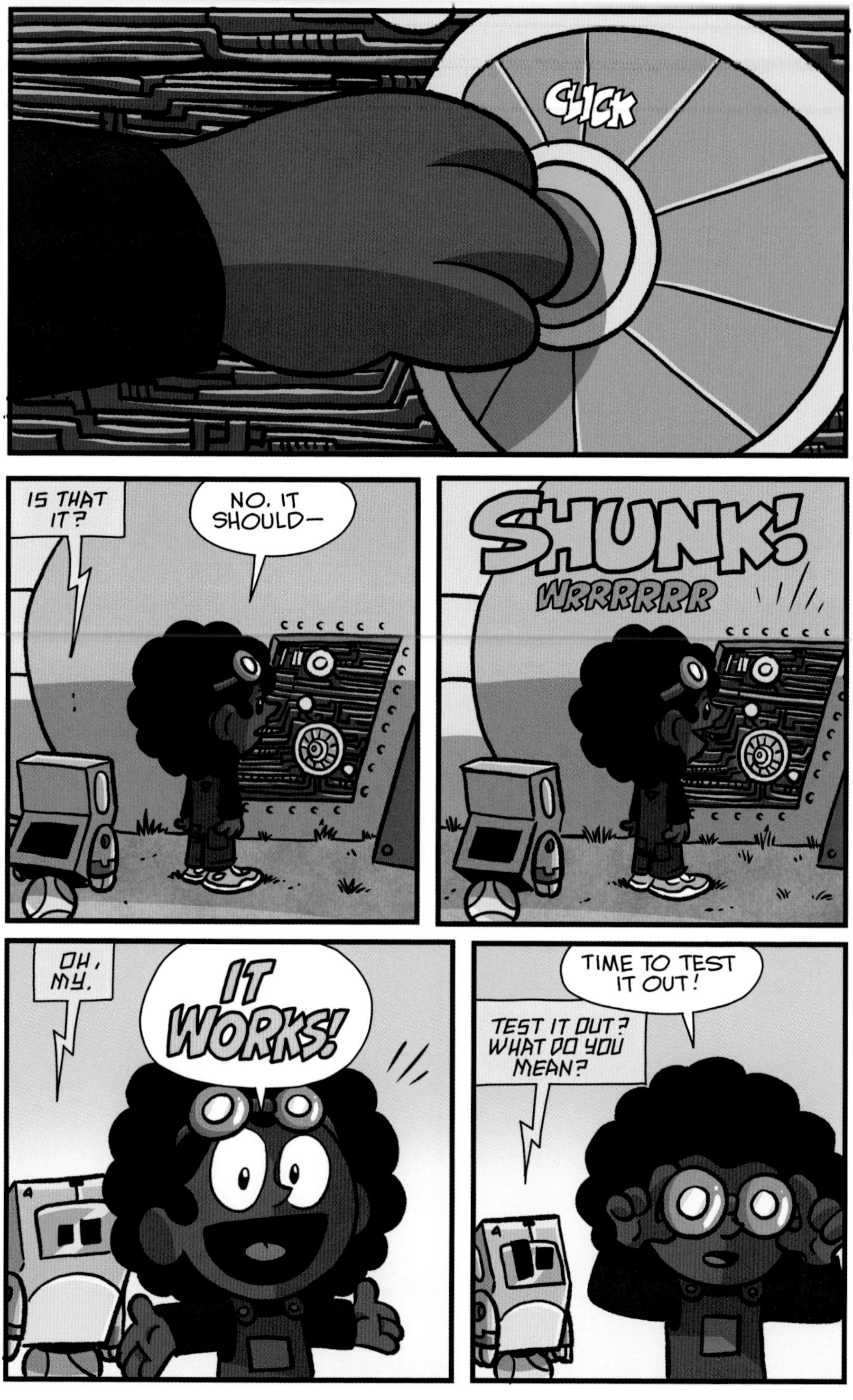
CLICK
IS THAT IT?
NO. IT SHOULD—
SHUNK!
WRRRRRR
OH, MY.
IT WORKS!
TIME TO TEST IT OUT!
TEST IT OUT? WHAT DO YOU MEAN?

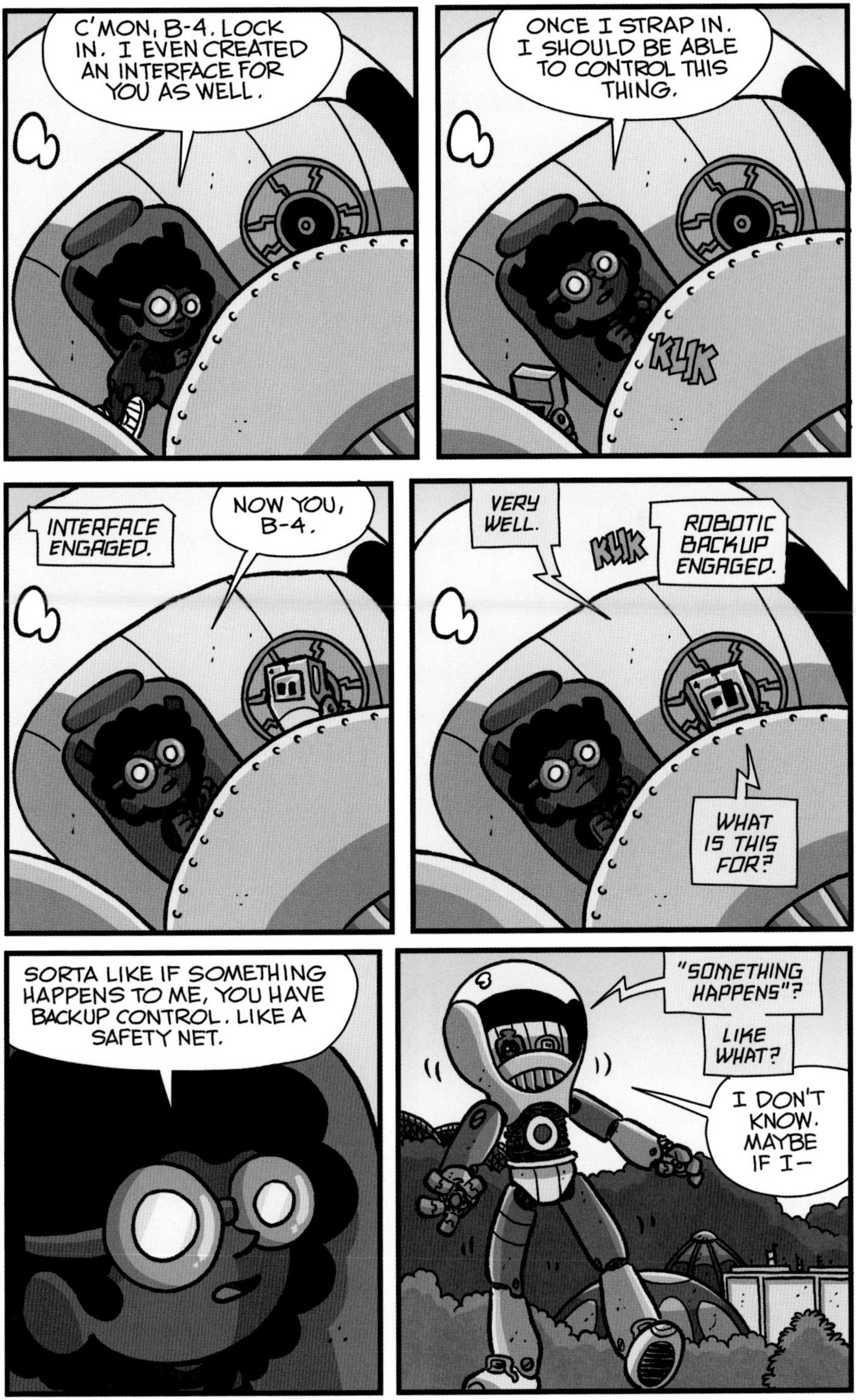
C'MON, B-4. LOCK IN. I EVEN CREATED AN INTERFACE FOR YOU AS WELL.
ONCE I STRAP IN. I SHOULD BE ABLE TO CONTROL THIS THING.
KLIK
INTERFACE ENGAGED.
NOW YOU, B-4.
VERY WELL.
KLIK
ROBOTIC BACKUP ENGAGED.
WHAT IS THIS FOR?
SORTA LIKE IF SOMETHING HAPPENS TO ME, YOU HAVE BACKUP CONTROL. LIKE A SAFETY NET.
"SOMETHING HAPPENS"?
LIKE WHAT?
I DON'T KNOW. MAYBE IF I–

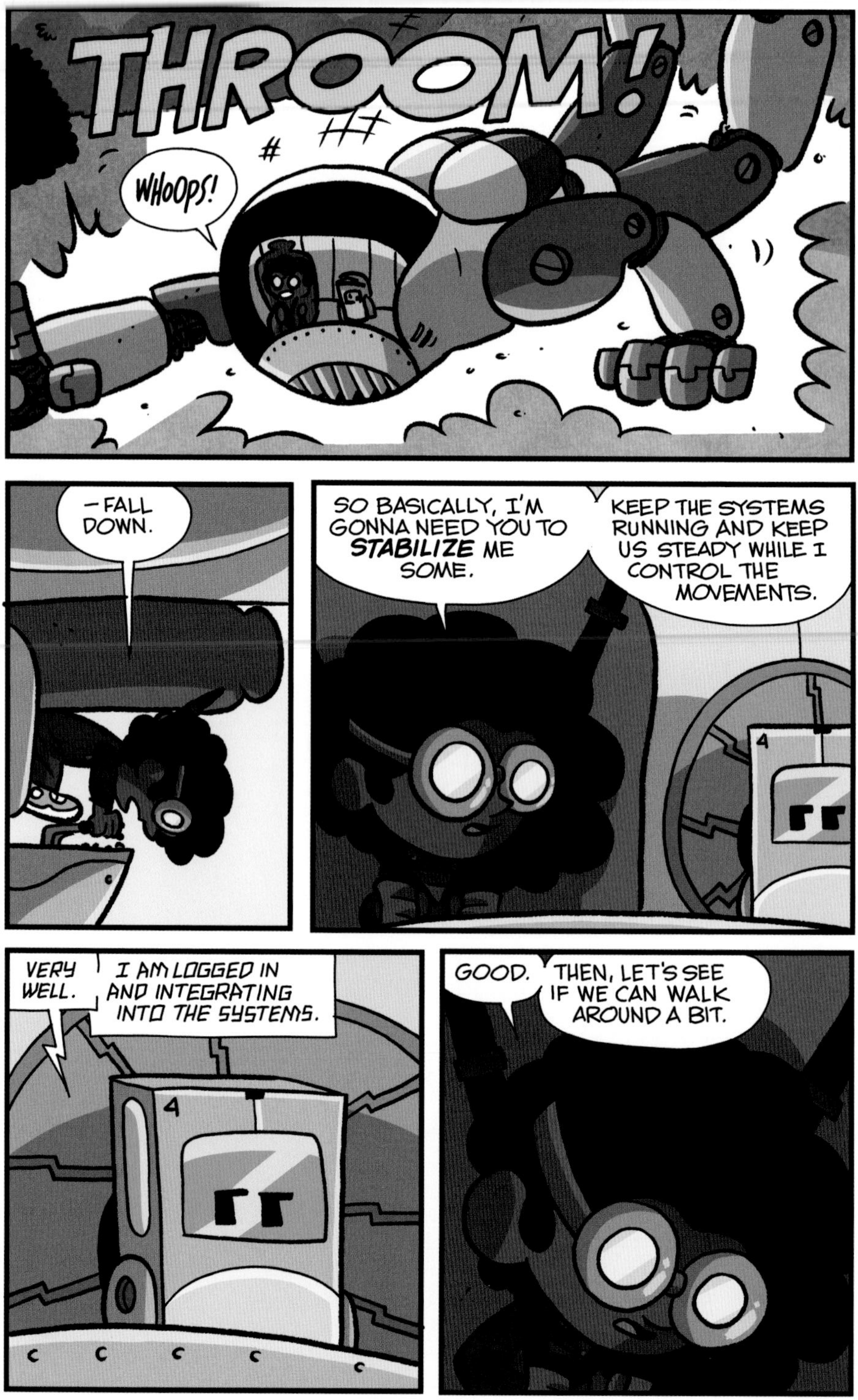

THROOM!
WHOOPS!
—FALL DOWN.
SO BASICALLY, I'M GONNA NEED YOU TO STABILIZE ME SOME.
KEEP THE SYSTEMS RUNNING AND KEEP US STEADY WHILE I CONTROL THE MOVEMENTS.
VERY WELL.
I AM LOGGED IN AND INTEGRATING INTO THE SYSTEMS.
GOOD.
THEN, LET'S SEE IF WE CAN WALK AROUND A BIT.
4

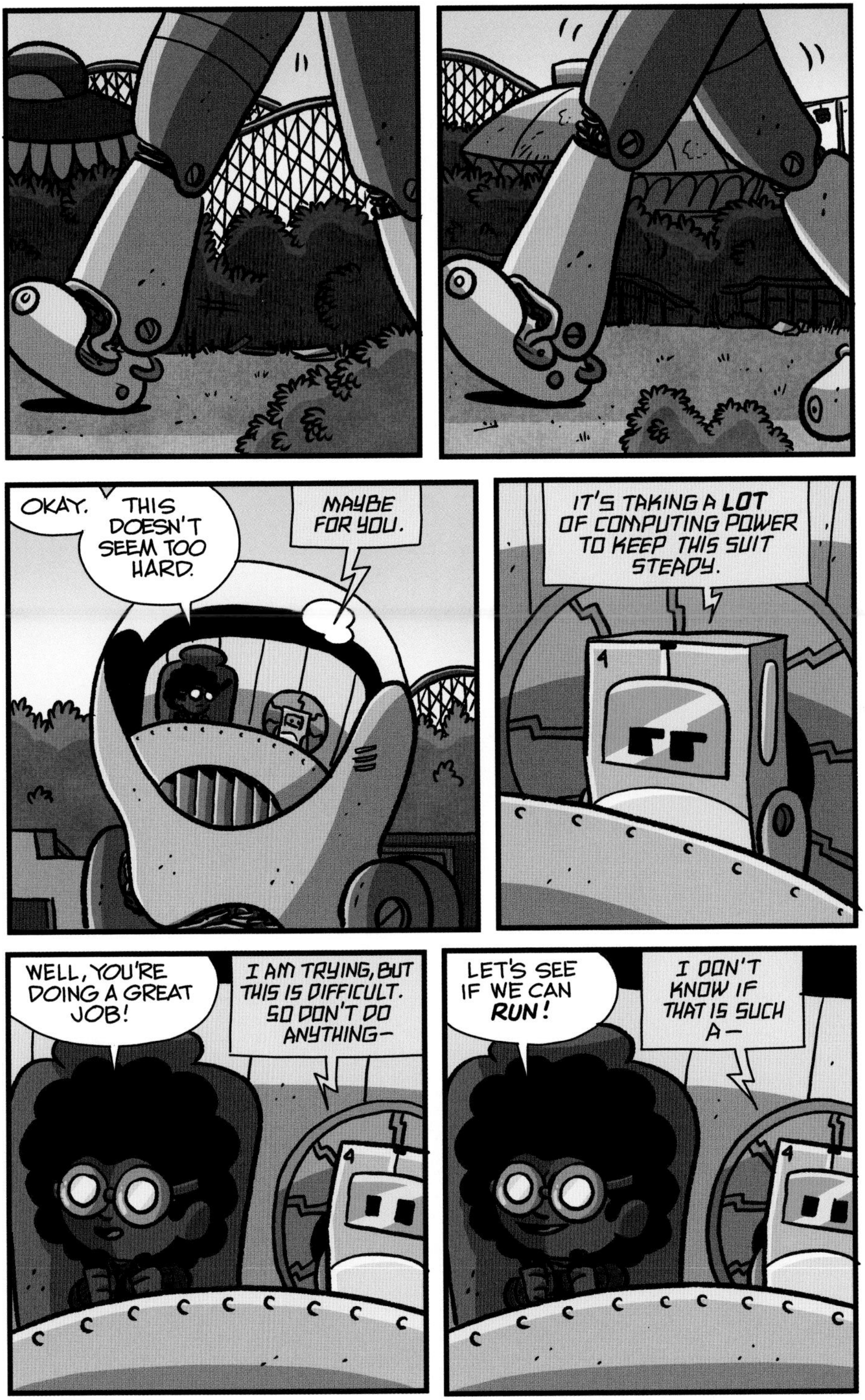
OKAY.
THIS DOESN'T SEEM TOO HARD.
MAYBE FOR YOU.
IT'S TAKING A LOT OF COMPUTING POWER TO KEEP THIS SUIT STEADY.
WELL, YOU'RE DOING A GREAT JOB!
I AM TRYING, BUT THIS IS DIFFICULT. SO DON'T DO ANYTHING—
LET'S SEE IF WE CAN RUN!
I DON'T KNOW IF THAT IS SUCH A—

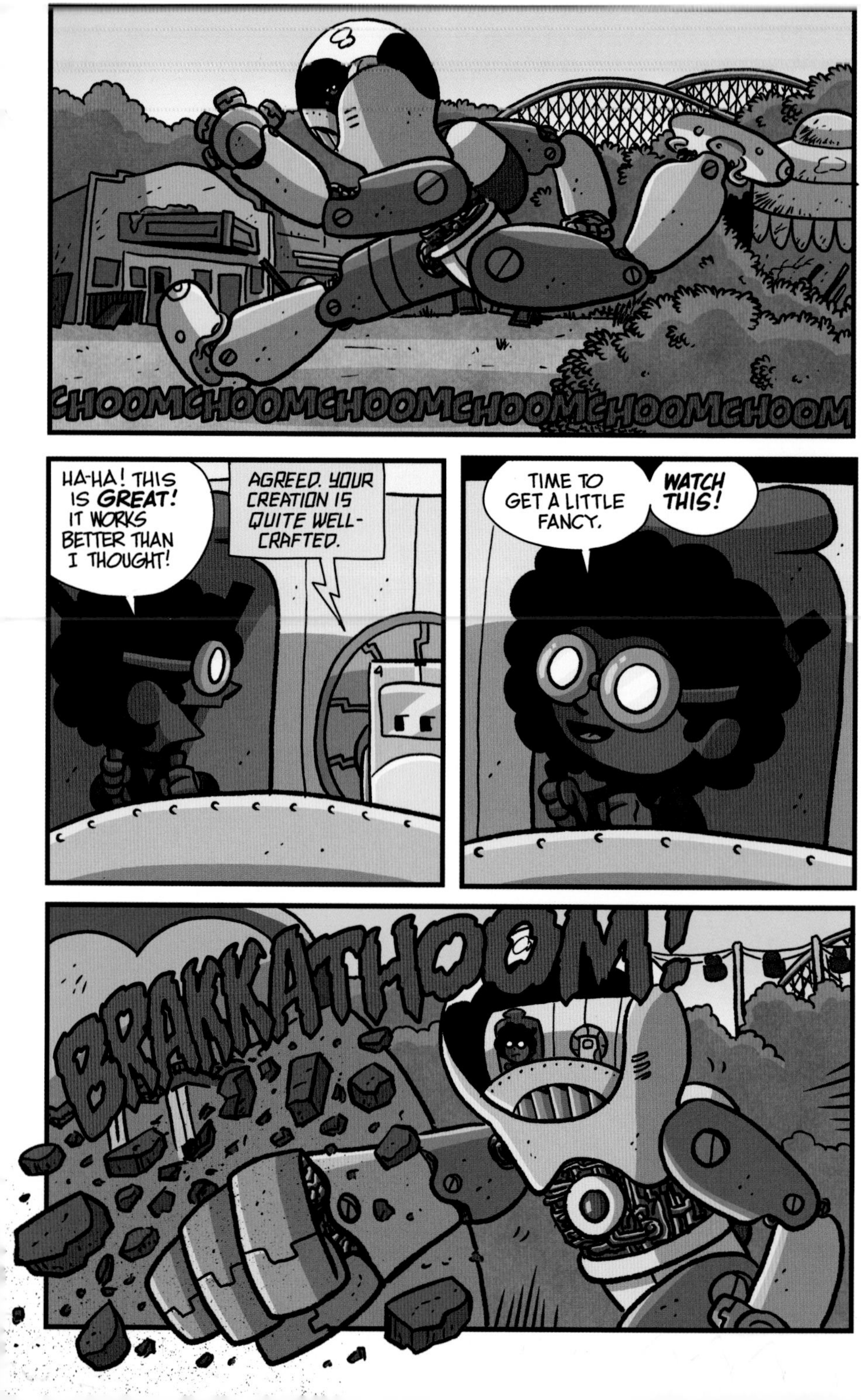
CHOOMCHOOMCHOOMCHOOMCHOOMCHOOM
HA-HA! THIS IS **GREAT!** IT WORKS BETTER THAN I THOUGHT!
AGREED. YOUR CREATION IS QUITE WELL-CRAFTED.
TIME TO GET A LITTLE FANCY.
WATCH THIS!
BRAKKATHOOM!

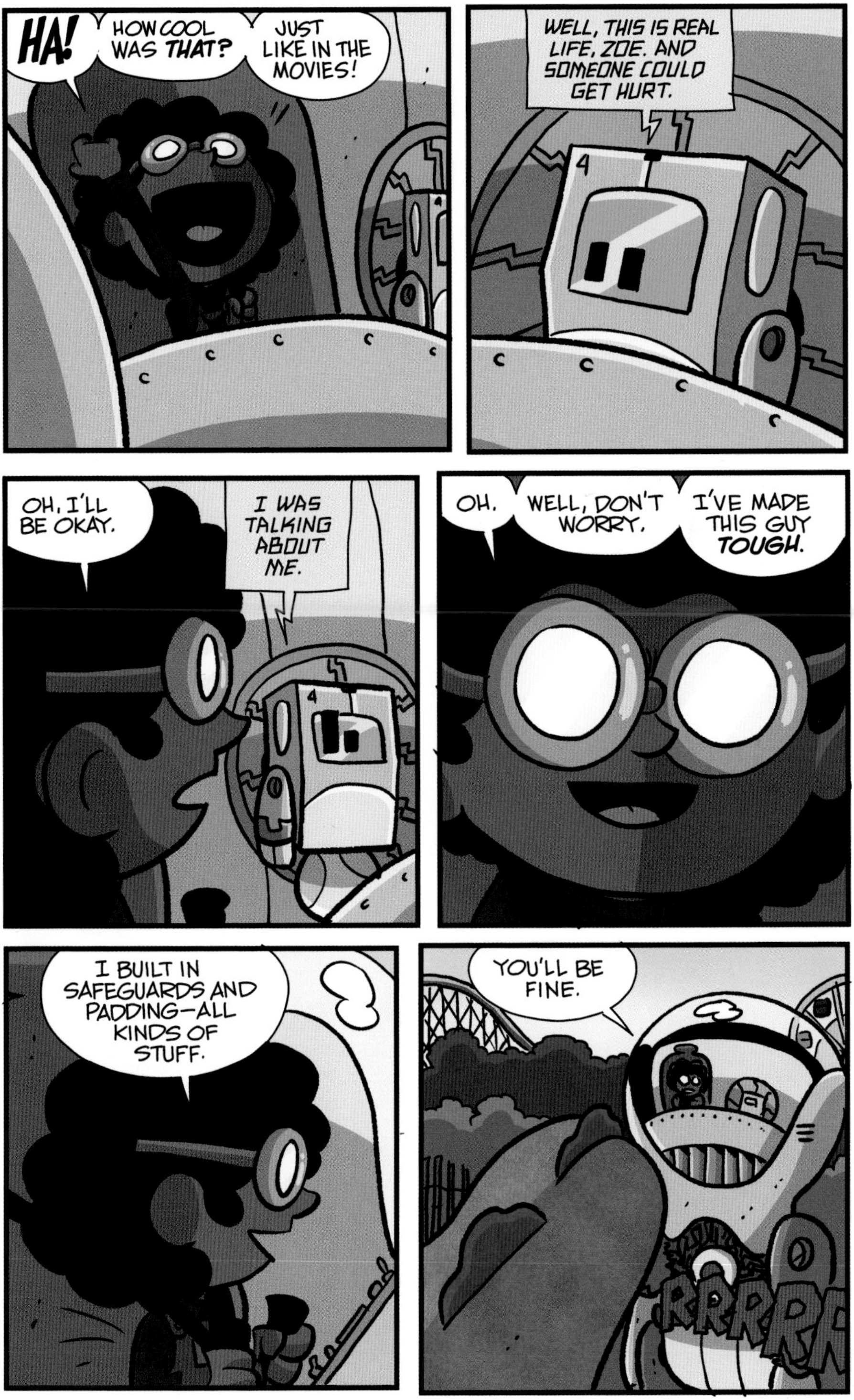
HA!
HOW COOL WAS THAT?
JUST LIKE IN THE MOVIES!
WELL, THIS IS REAL LIFE, ZOE. AND SOMEONE COULD GET HURT.
OH, I'LL BE OKAY.
I WAS TALKING ABOUT ME.
OH.
WELL, DON'T WORRY.
I'VE MADE THIS GUY TOUGH.
I BUILT IN SAFEGUARDS AND PADDING—ALL KINDS OF STUFF.
YOU'LL BE FINE.
RRRRR

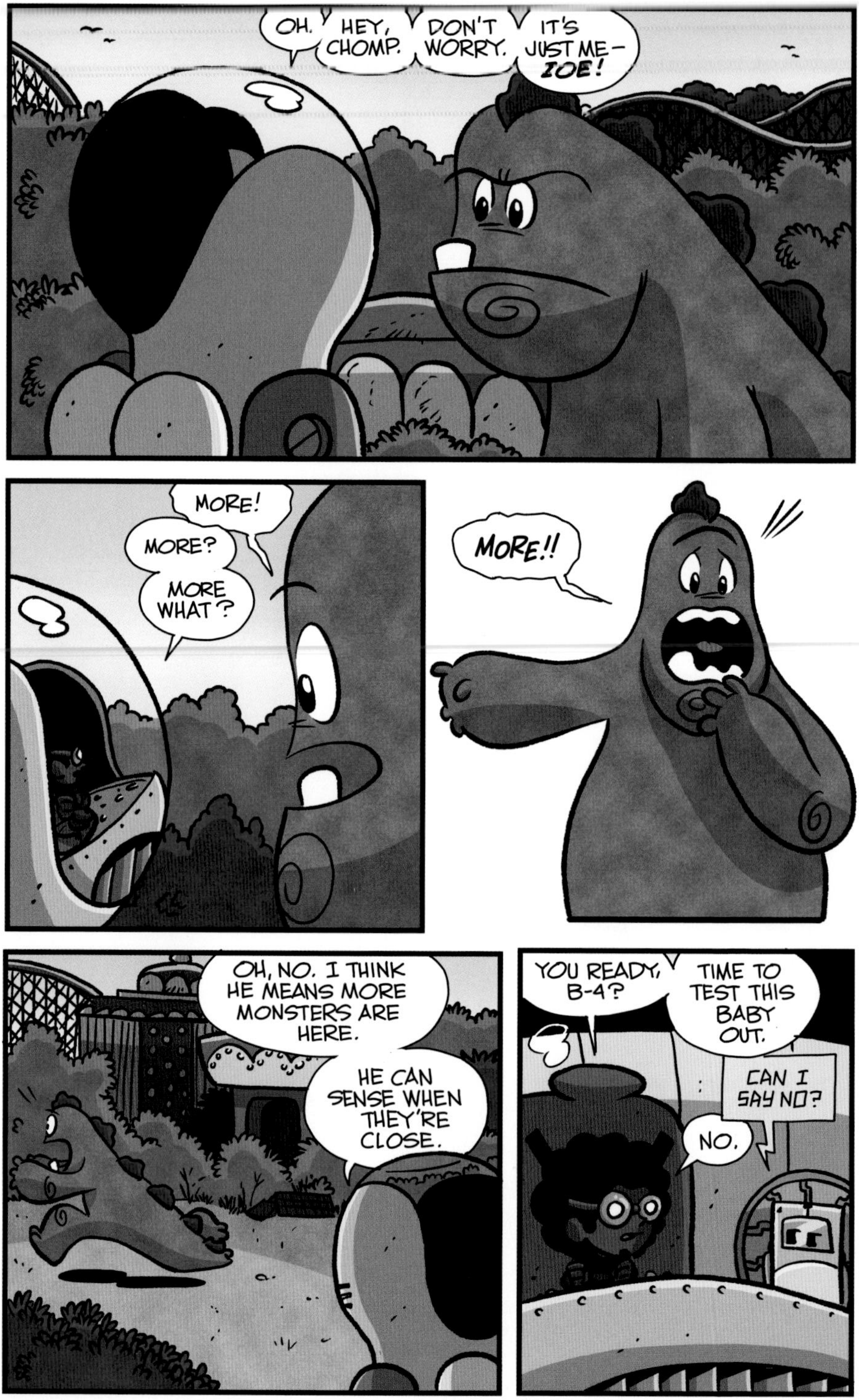
OH.
HEY, CHOMP.
DON'T WORRY.
IT'S JUST ME—JOE!
MORE!
MORE?
MORE WHAT?
MORE!!
OH, NO. I THINK HE MEANS MORE MONSTERS ARE HERE.
HE CAN SENSE WHEN THEY'RE CLOSE.
YOU READY, B-4?
TIME TO TEST THIS BABY OUT.
CAN I SAY NO?
NO.

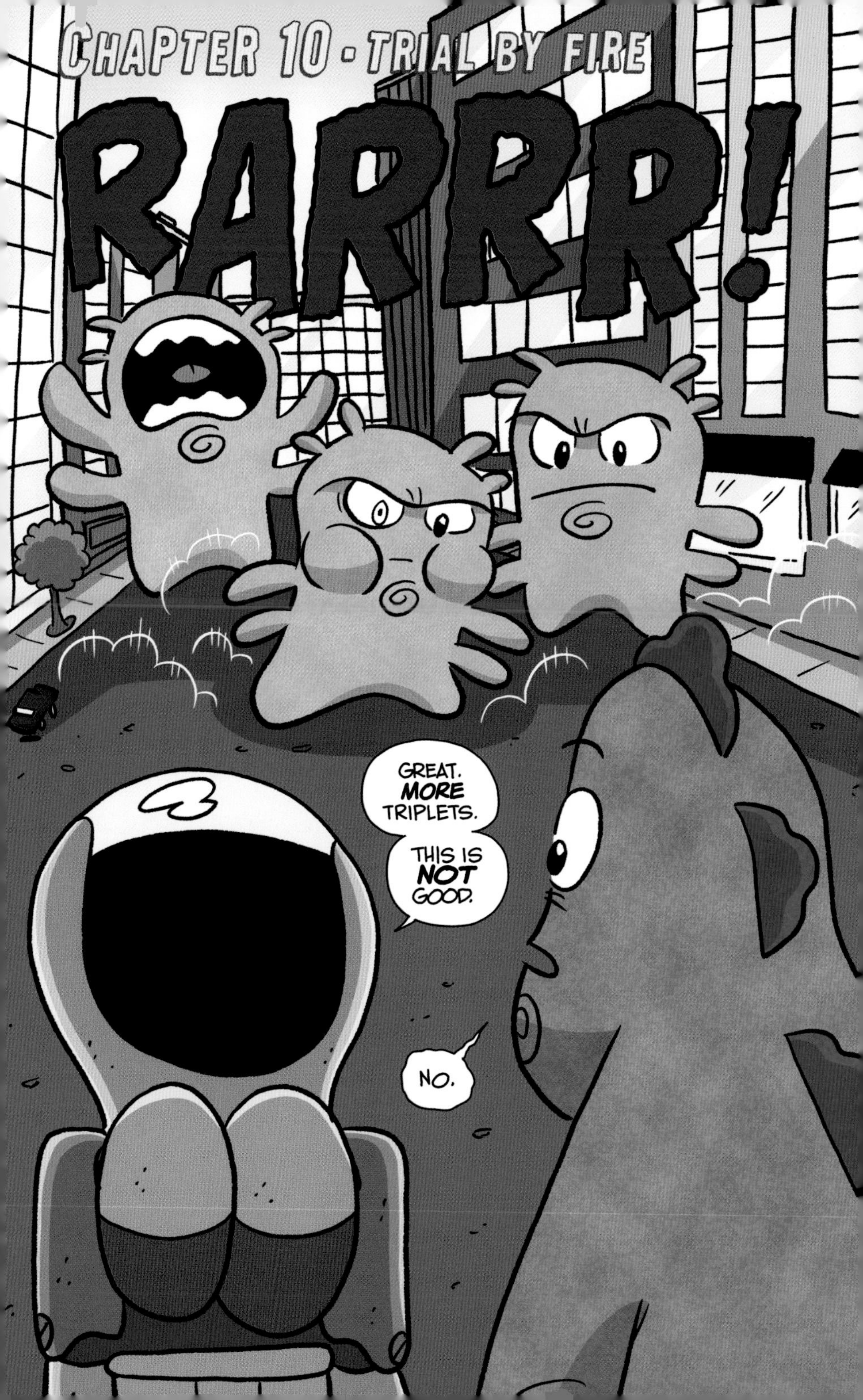
CHAPTER 10 - TRIAL BY FIRE
RARRR!
GREAT. MORE TRIPLETS.
THIS IS NOT GOOD.
NO.

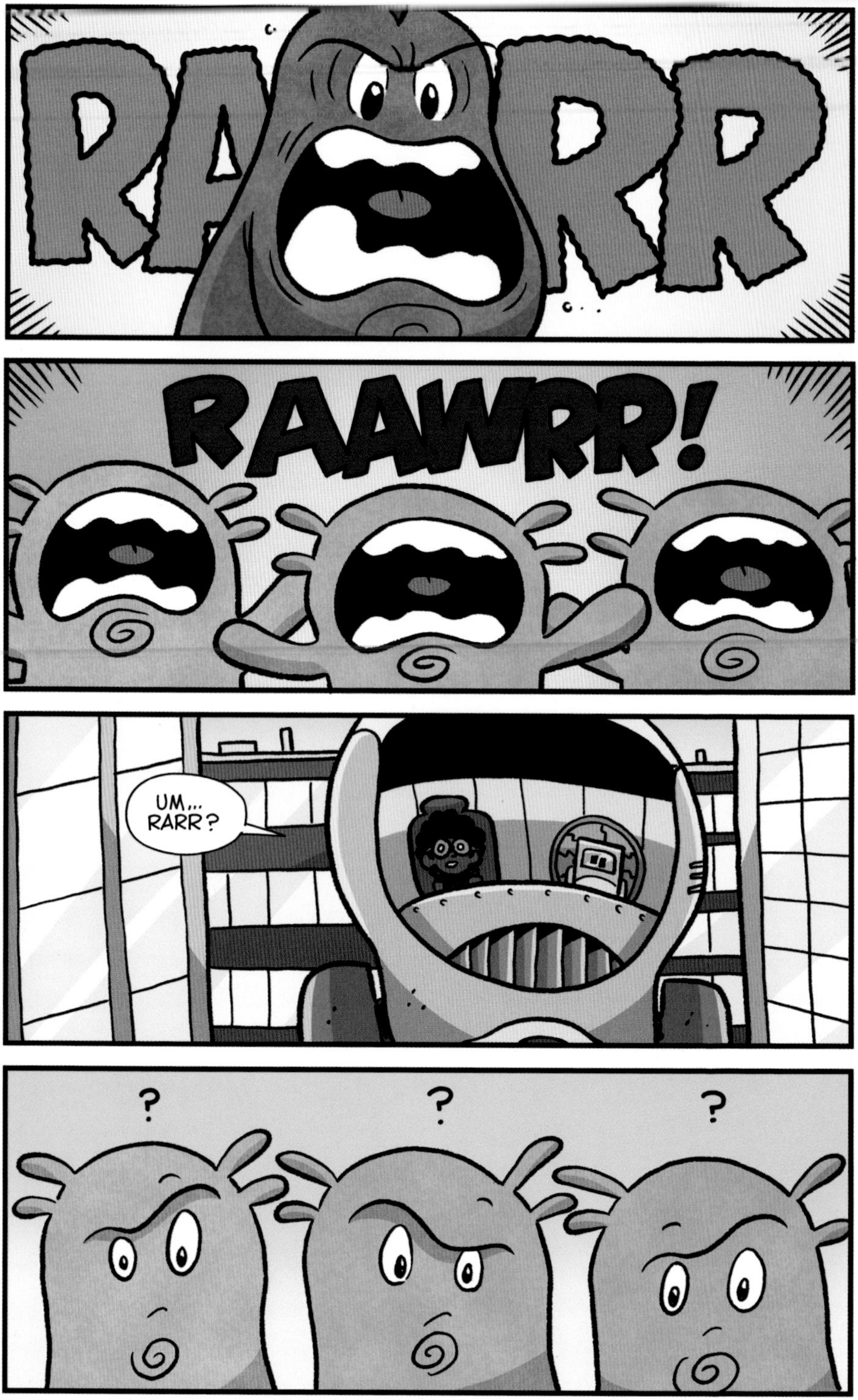
RAWRR
RAAWRR!
UM... RARR?
?
?
?

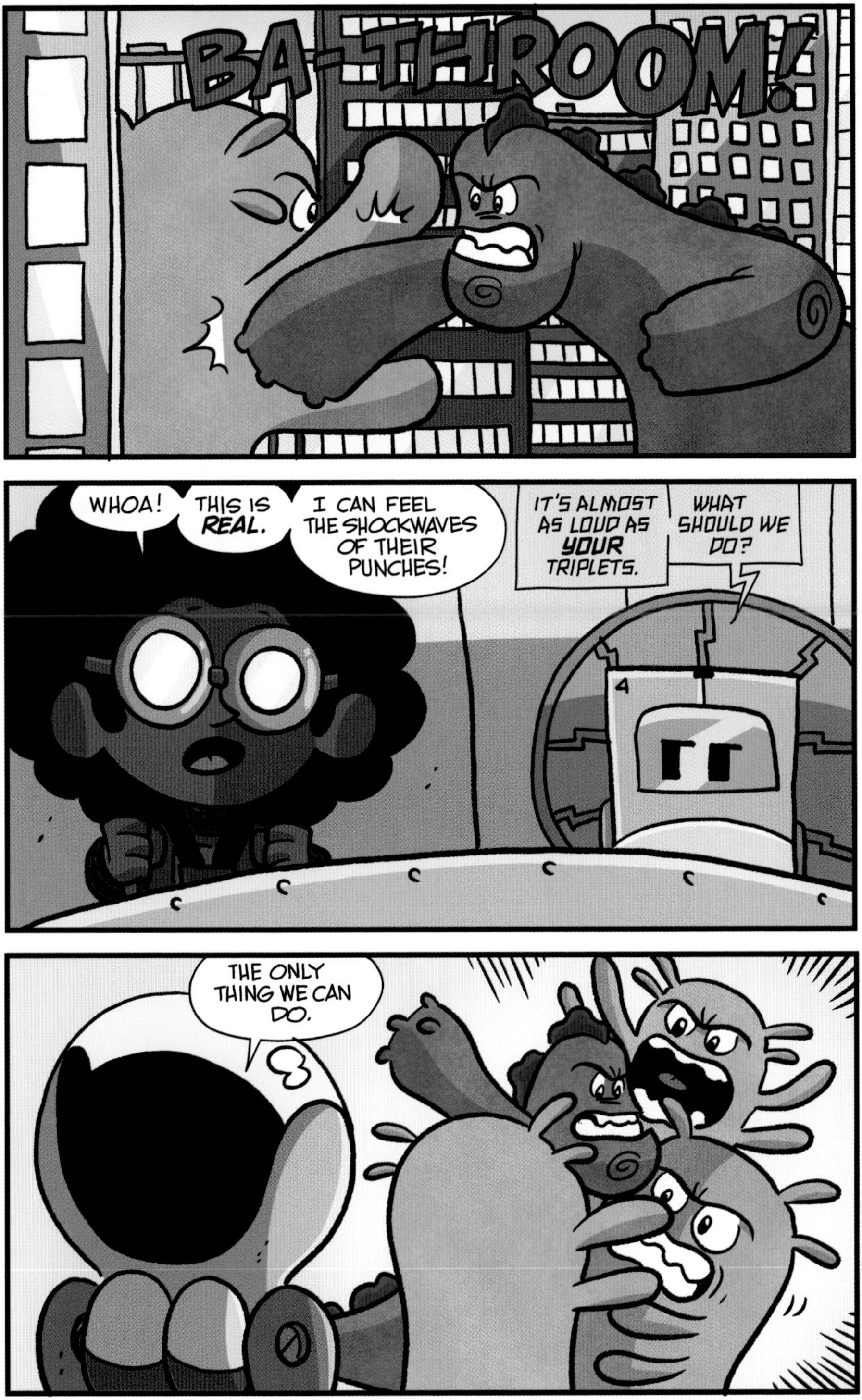
BA-THROOM!
WHOA!
THIS IS REAL.
I CAN FEEL THE SHOCKWAVES OF THEIR PUNCHES!
IT'S ALMOST AS LOUD AS YOUR TRIPLETS.
WHAT SHOULD WE DO?
4
THE ONLY THING WE CAN DO.

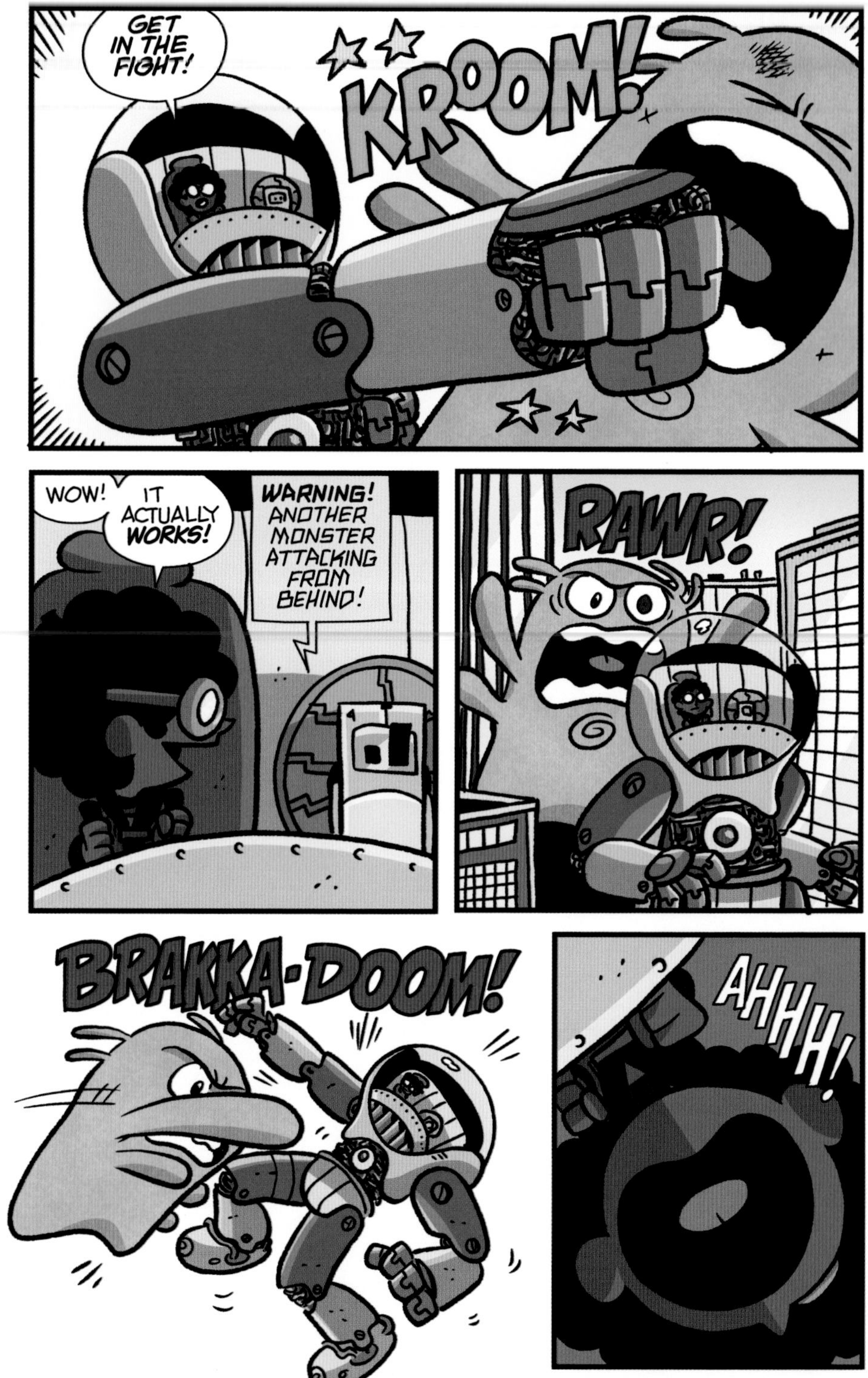
GET IN THE FIGHT!
KROOM!
WOW!
IT ACTUALLY WORKS!
WARNING! ANOTHER MONSTER ATTACKING FROM BEHIND!
RAWR!
BRAKKA-DOOM!
AHHHH!

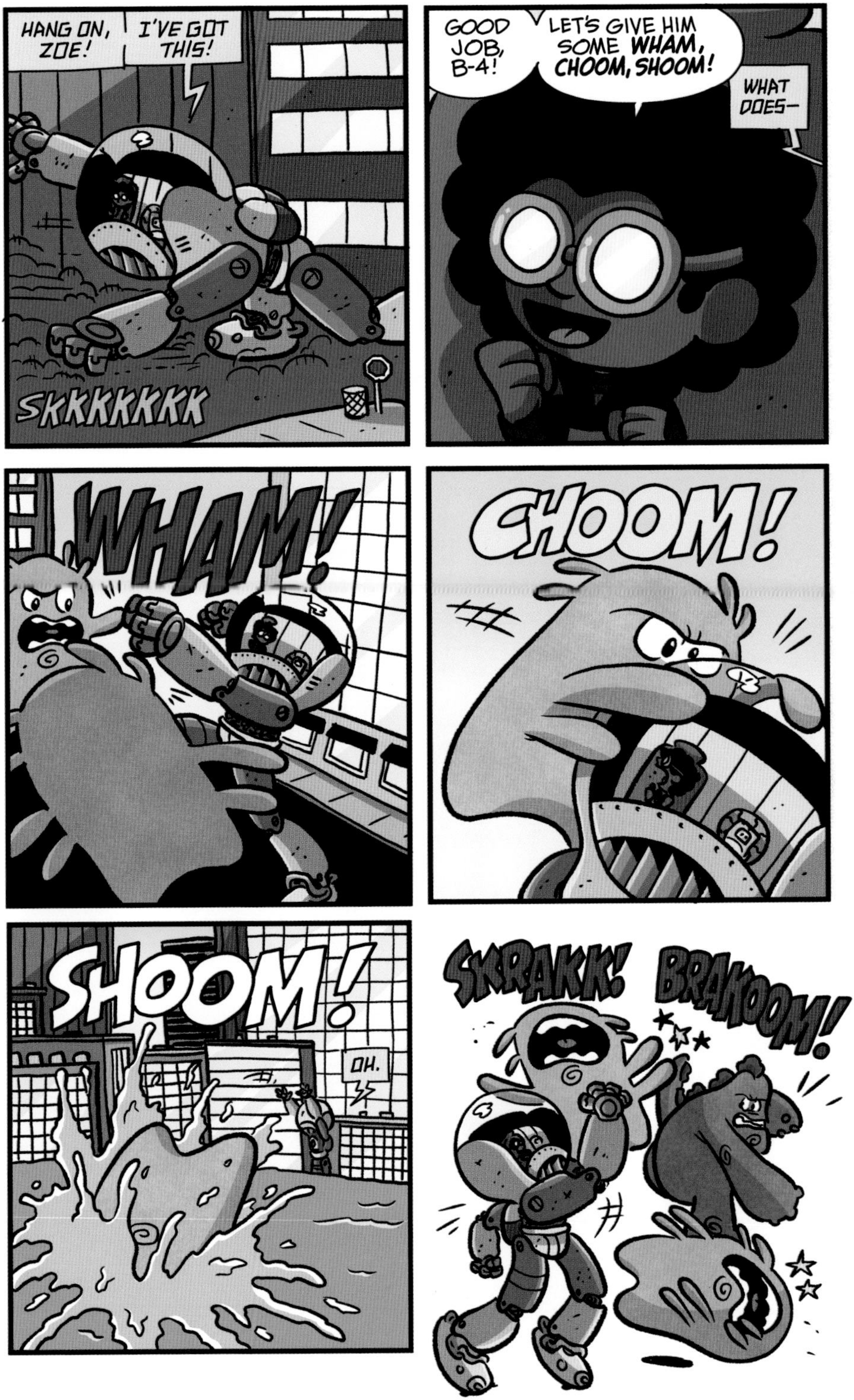
HANG ON, ZOE!
I'VE GOT THIS!
SKKKKKKK
GOOD JOB, B-4!
LET'S GIVE HIM SOME WHAM, CHOOM, SHOOM!
WHAT DOES—
WHAM!
CHOOM!
SHOOM!
OH.
SKRAKK! BRAKOOM!

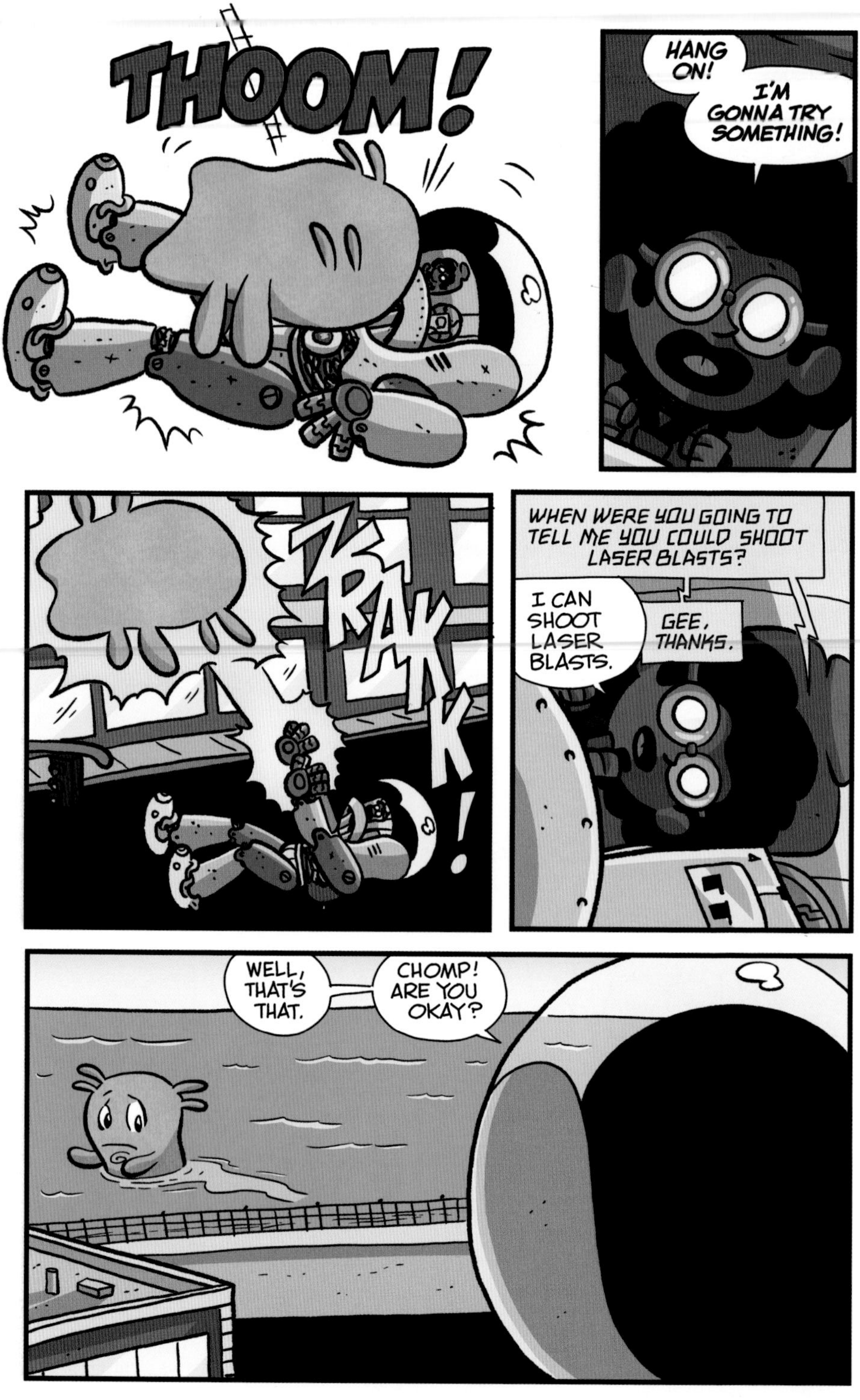
THOOM!
HANG ON!
I'M GONNA TRY SOMETHING!
ZZRAKK!
WHEN WERE YOU GOING TO TELL ME YOU COULD SHOOT LASER BLASTS?
I CAN SHOOT LASER BLASTS.
GEE, THANKS.
WELL, THAT'S THAT.
CHOMP! ARE YOU OKAY?

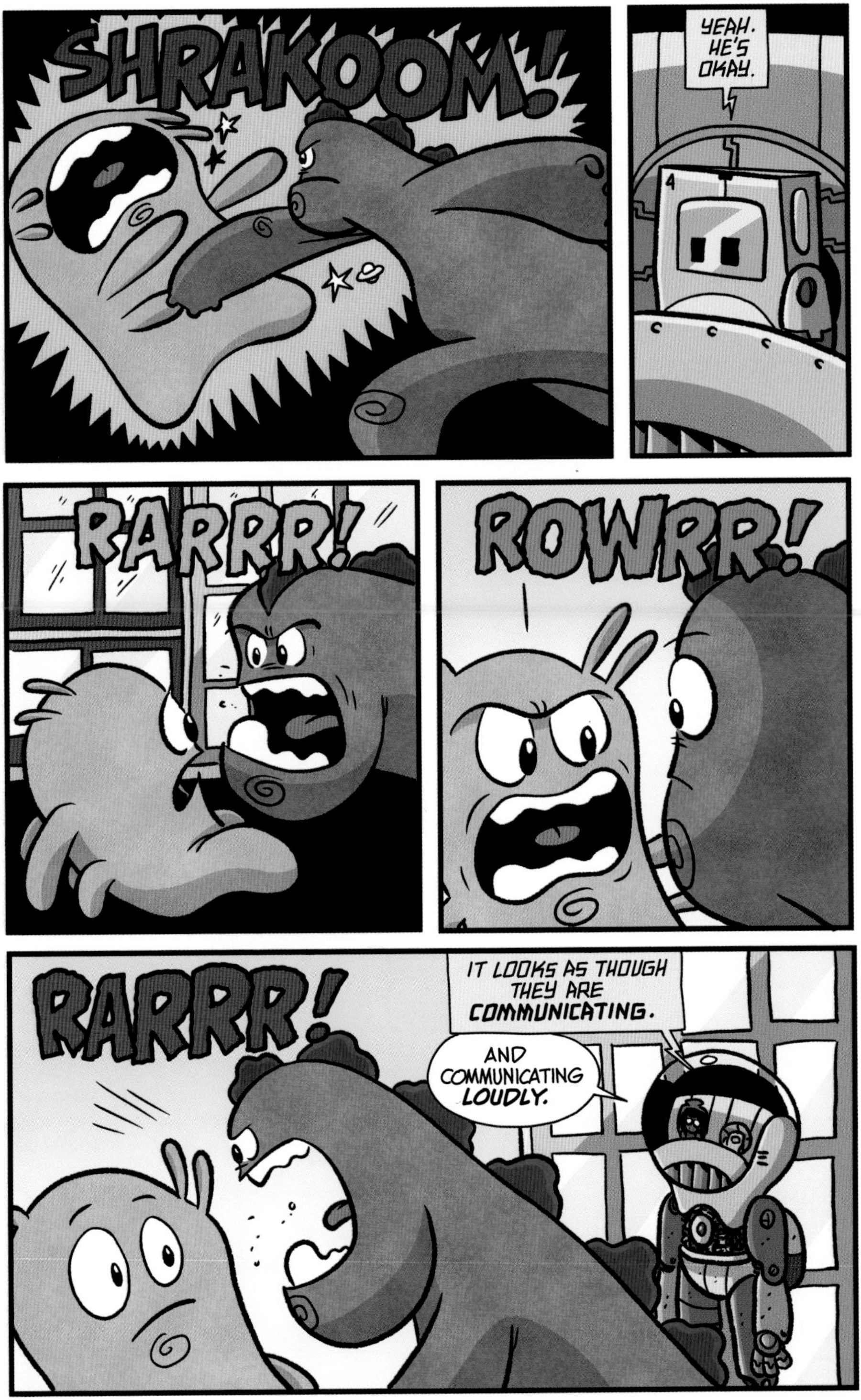
SHRAKOOM!
YEAH. HE'S OKAY.
RARRR!
ROWRR!
RARRR!
IT LOOKS AS THOUGH THEY ARE COMMUNICATING.
AND COMMUNICATING LOUDLY.

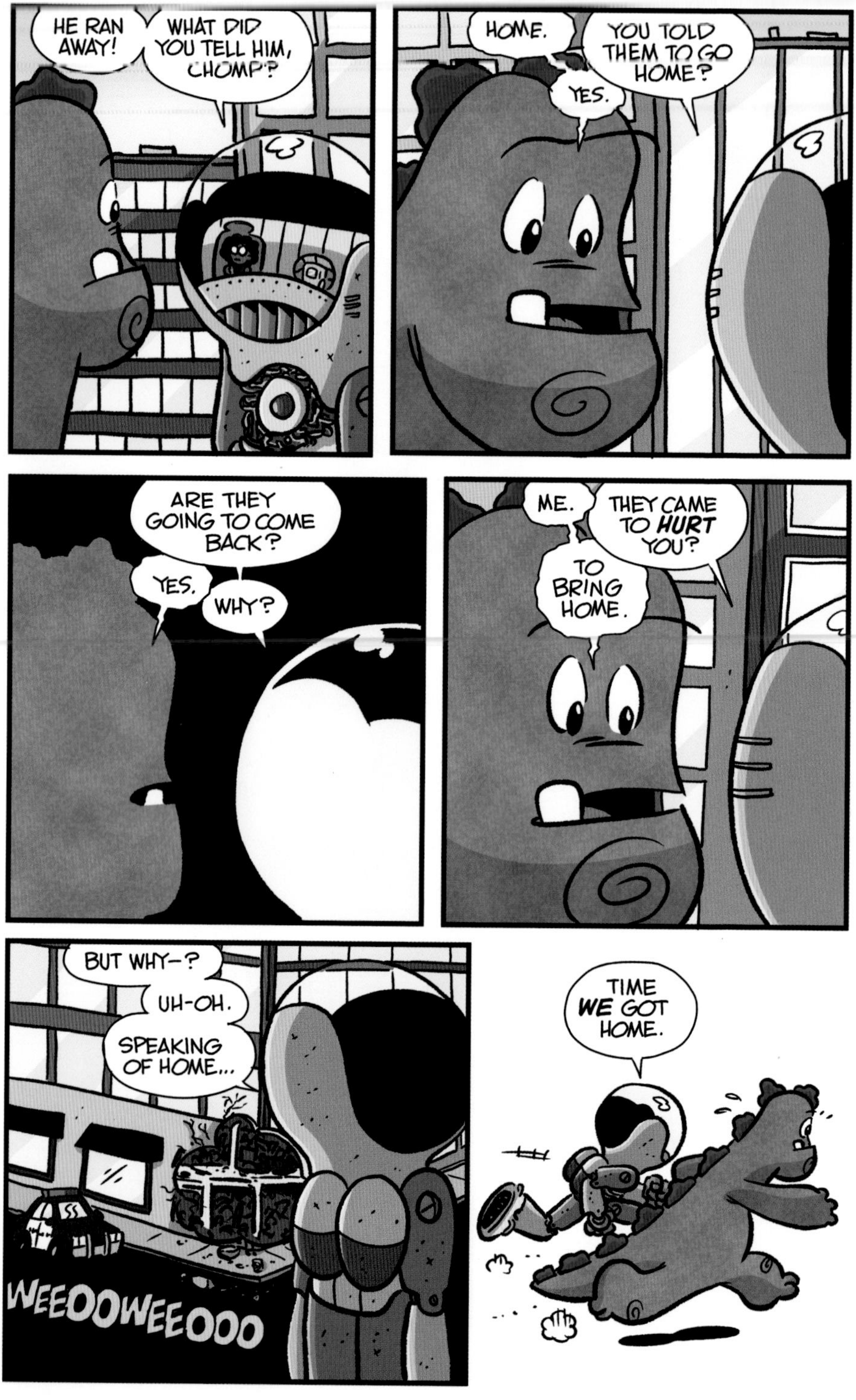
HE RAN AWAY!
WHAT DID YOU TELL HIM, CHOMP?
HOME.
YES.
YOU TOLD THEM TO GO HOME?
ARE THEY GOING TO COME BACK?
YES.
WHY?
ME.
TO BRING HOME.
THEY CAME TO HURT YOU?
BUT WHY-?
UH-OH.
SPEAKING OF HOME...
WEEOOWEEOOO
TIME WE GOT HOME.

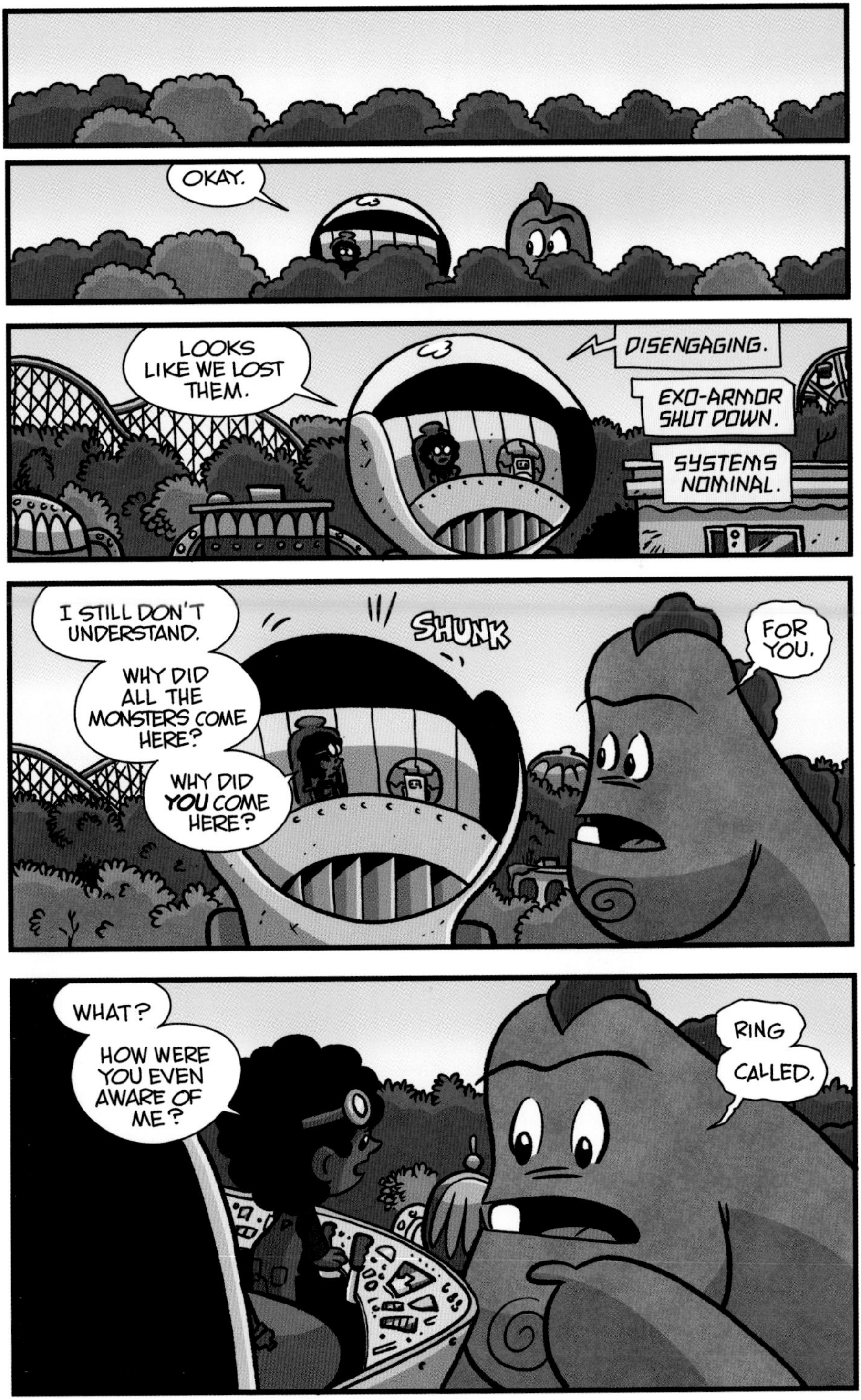
OKAY.
LOOKS LIKE WE LOST THEM.
DISENGAGING.
EXO-ARMOR SHUT DOWN.
SYSTEMS NOMINAL.
I STILL DON'T UNDERSTAND.
WHY DID ALL THE MONSTERS COME HERE?
WHY DID *YOU* COME HERE?
SHUNK
FOR YOU.
WHAT?
HOW WERE YOU EVEN AWARE OF ME?
RING
CALLED.

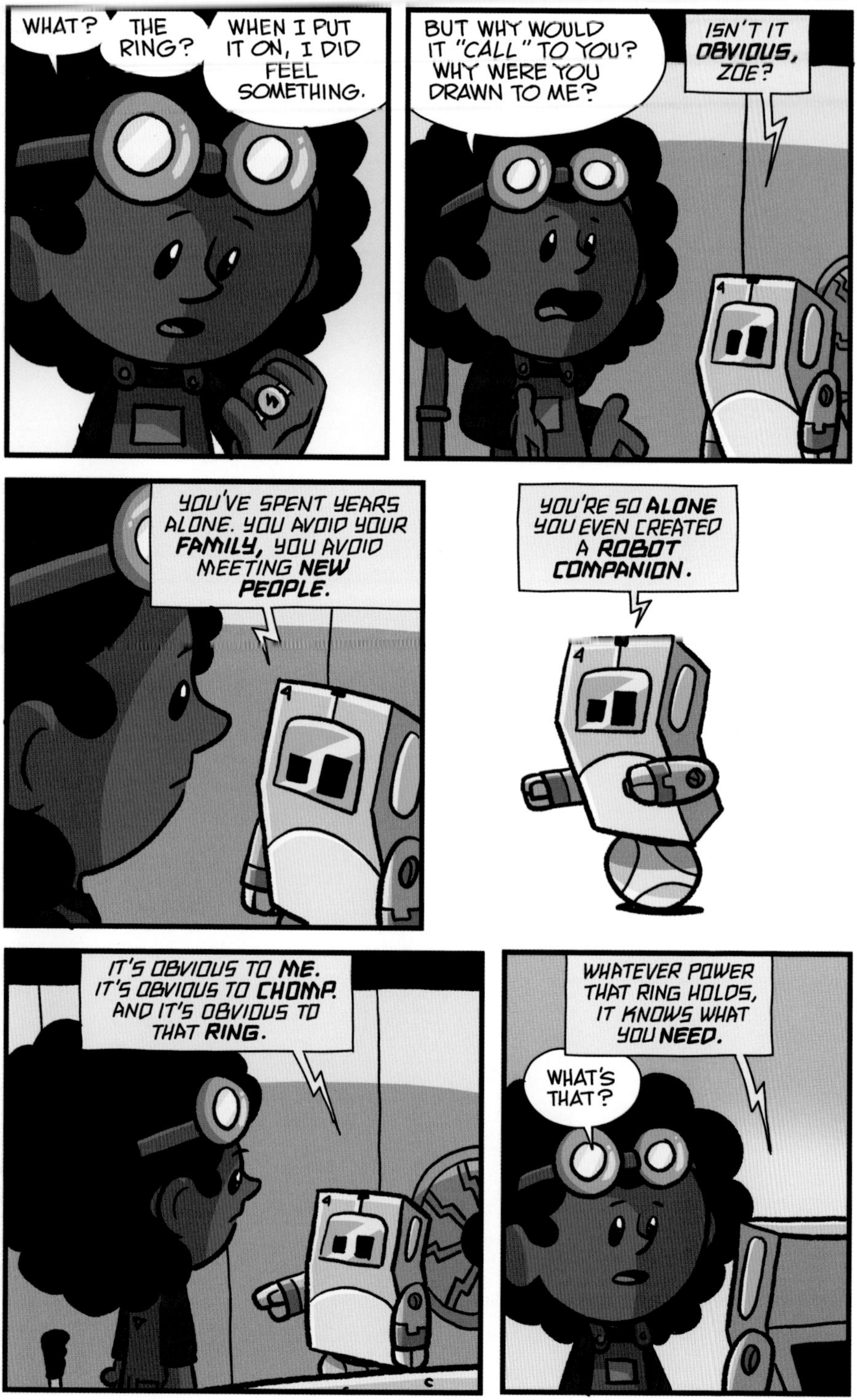
WHAT?
THE RING?
WHEN I PUT IT ON, I DID FEEL SOMETHING.
BUT WHY WOULD IT "CALL" TO YOU? WHY WERE YOU DRAWN TO ME?
ISN'T IT OBVIOUS, ZOE?
YOU'VE SPENT YEARS ALONE. YOU AVOID YOUR FAMILY, YOU AVOID MEETING NEW PEOPLE.
YOU'RE SO ALONE YOU EVEN CREATED A ROBOT COMPANION.
IT'S OBVIOUS TO ME. IT'S OBVIOUS TO CHOMP. AND IT'S OBVIOUS TO THAT RING.
WHATEVER POWER THAT RING HOLDS, IT KNOWS WHAT YOU NEED.
WHAT'S THAT?

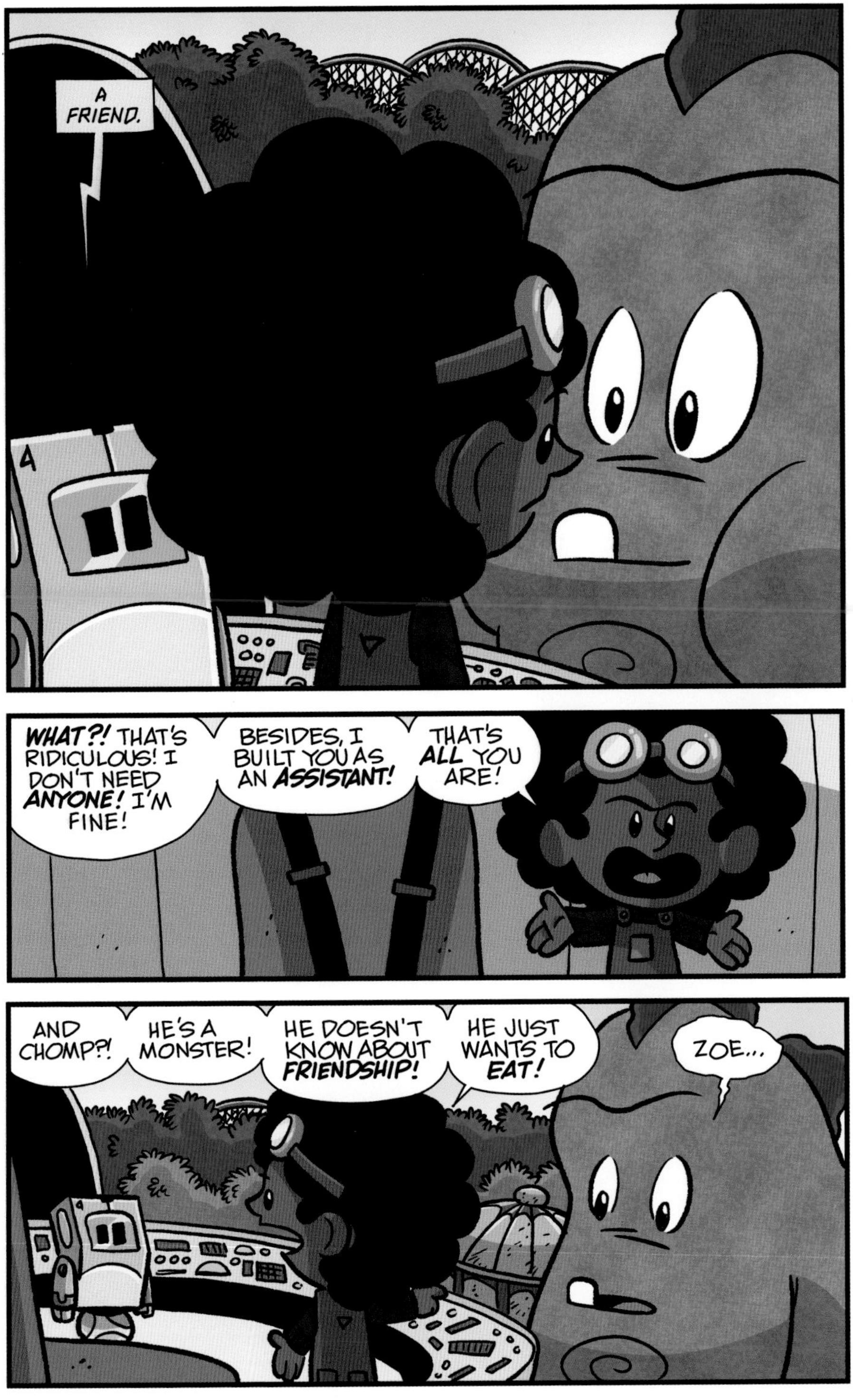
A FRIEND.
WHAT?! THAT'S RIDICULOUS! I DON'T NEED ANYONE! I'M FINE!
BESIDES, I BUILT YOU AS AN ASSISTANT!
THAT'S ALL YOU ARE!
AND CHOMP?!
HE'S A MONSTER!
HE DOESN'T KNOW ABOUT FRIENDSHIP!
HE JUST WANTS TO EAT!
ZOE...

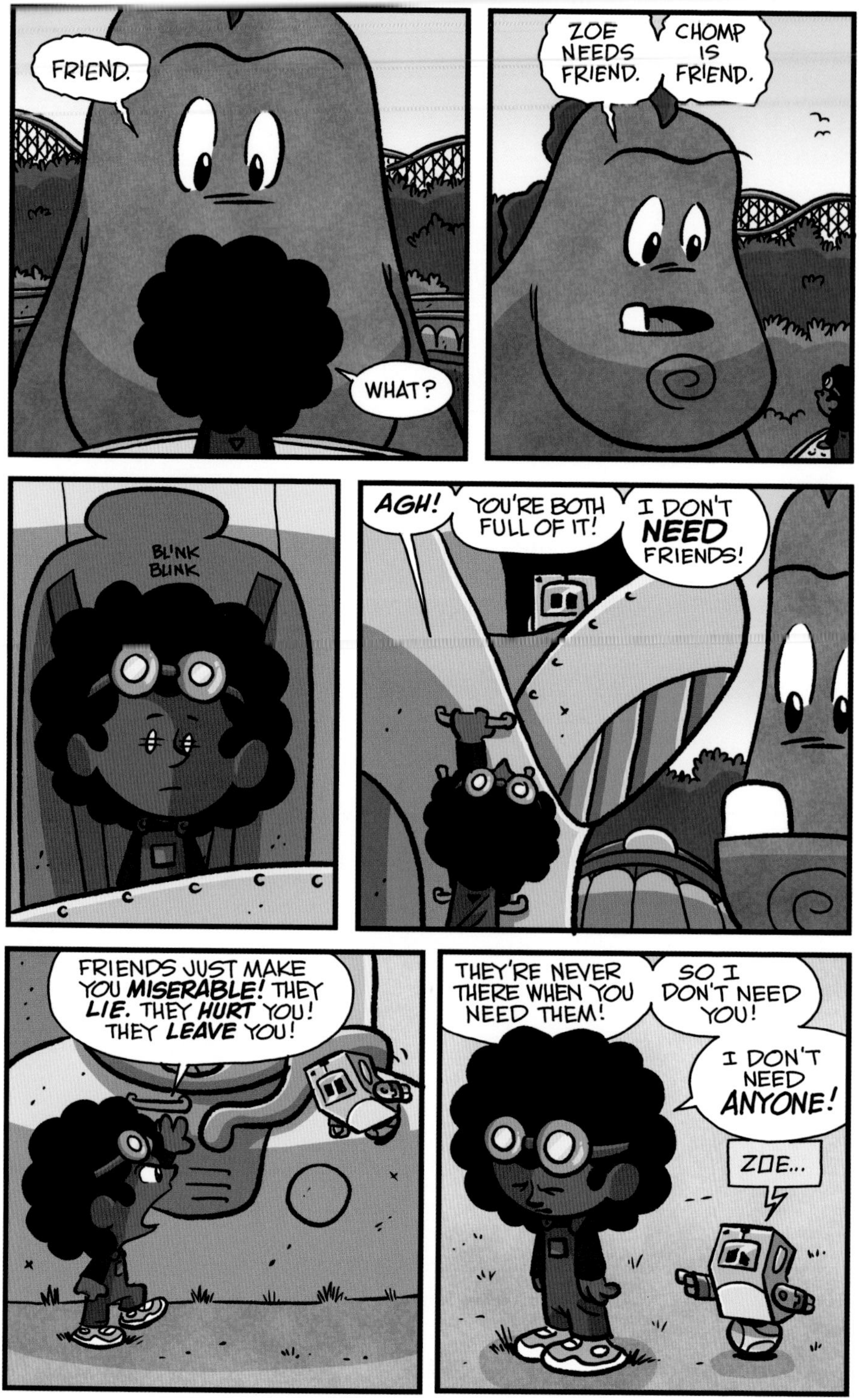
FRIEND.
WHAT?
ZOE NEEDS FRIEND.
CHOMP IS FRIEND.
BLINK BLINK
AGH!
YOU'RE BOTH FULL OF IT!
I DON'T NEED FRIENDS!
FRIENDS JUST MAKE YOU MISERABLE! THEY LIE. THEY HURT YOU! THEY LEAVE YOU!
THEY'RE NEVER THERE WHEN YOU NEED THEM!
SO I DON'T NEED YOU!
I DON'T NEED ANYONE!
ZOE...

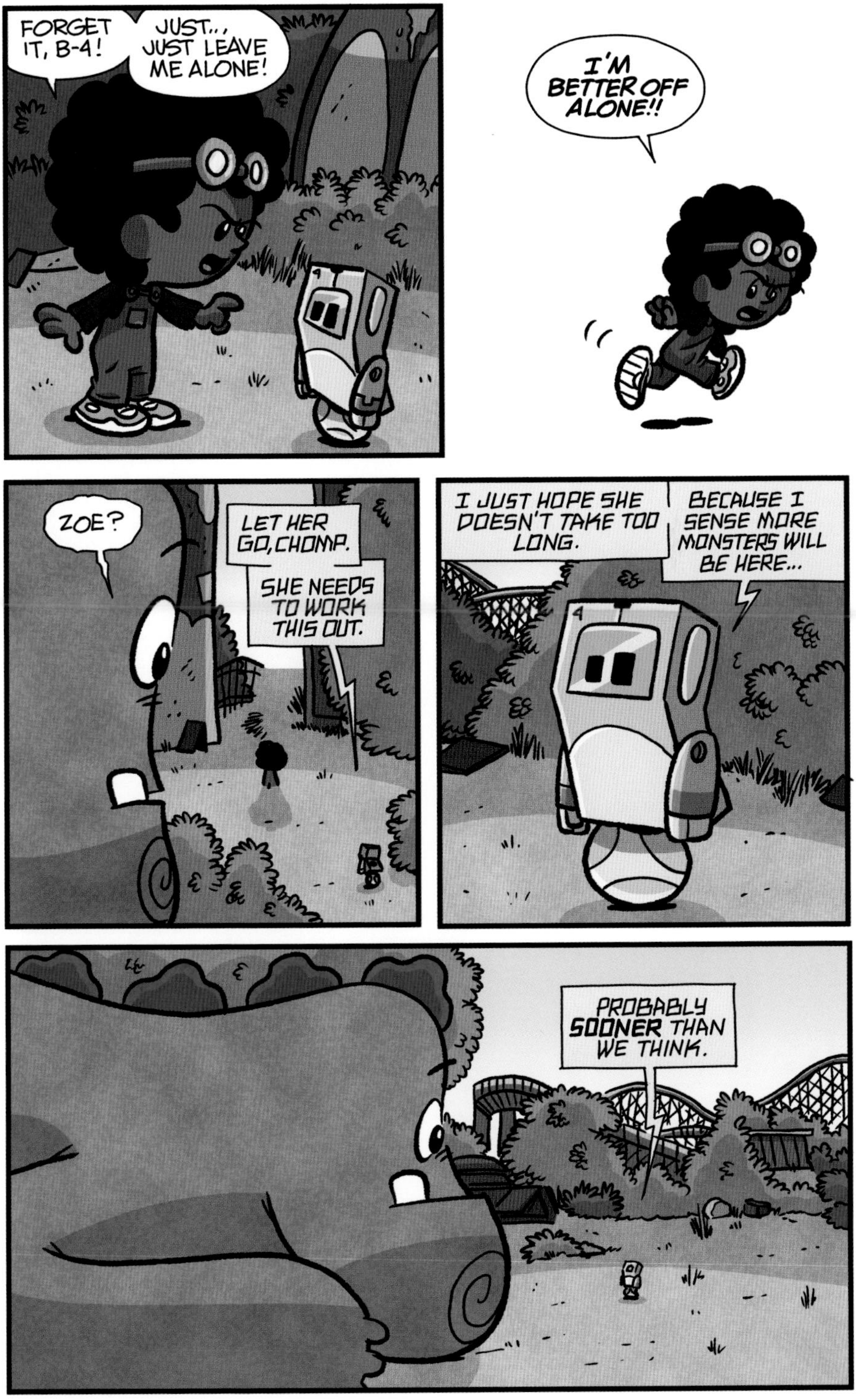
FORGET IT, B-4!
JUST..., JUST LEAVE ME ALONE!
I'M BETTER OFF ALONE!!
ZOE?
LET HER GO, CHOMP.
SHE NEEDS TO WORK THIS OUT.
I JUST HOPE SHE DOESN'T TAKE TOO LONG.
BECAUSE I SENSE MORE MONSTERS WILL BE HERE...
PROBABLY **SOONER** THAN WE THINK.

Chapter 11 - With Friends Like These

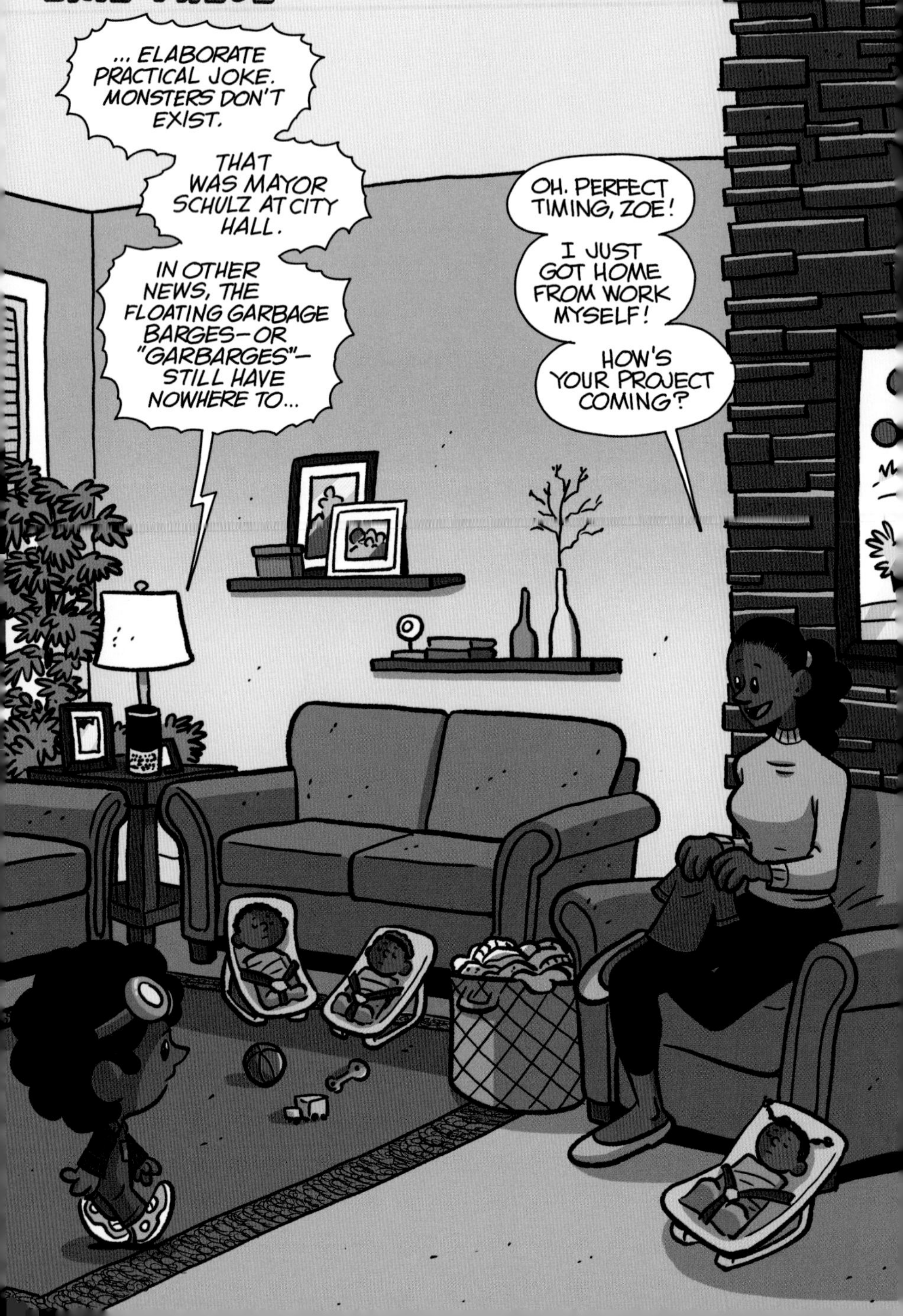

... ELABORATE PRACTICAL JOKE. MONSTERS DON'T EXIST.
THAT WAS MAYOR SCHULZ AT CITY HALL.
IN OTHER NEWS, THE FLOATING GARBAGE BARGES—OR "GARBARGES"— STILL HAVE NOWHERE TO...
OH. PERFECT TIMING, ZOE!
I JUST GOT HOME FROM WORK MYSELF!
HOW'S YOUR PROJECT COMING?

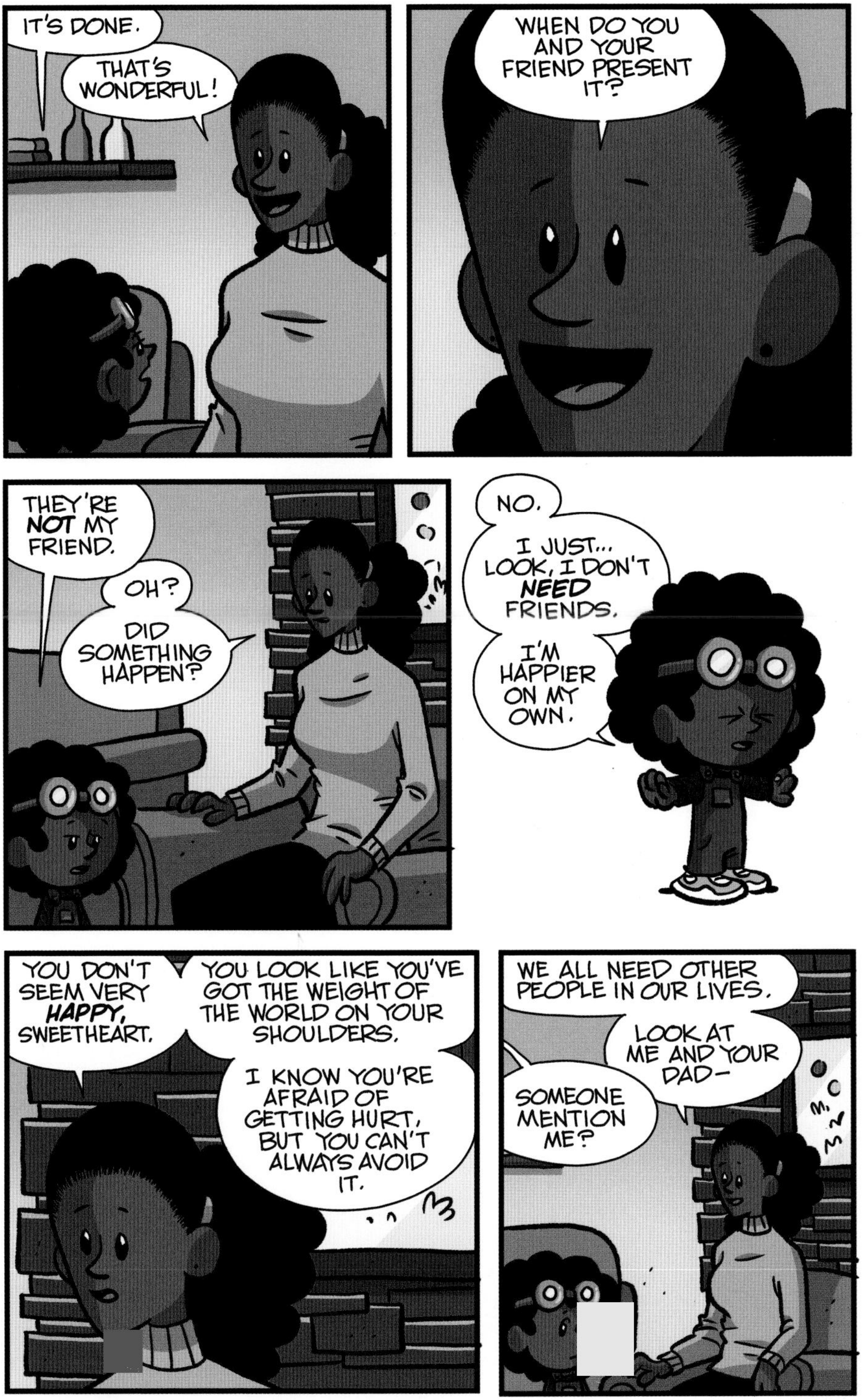
IT'S DONE.
THAT'S WONDERFUL!
WHEN DO YOU AND YOUR FRIEND PRESENT IT?
THEY'RE **NOT** MY FRIEND.
OH?
DID SOMETHING HAPPEN?
NO.
I JUST... LOOK, I DON'T **NEED** FRIENDS.
I'M HAPPIER ON MY OWN.
YOU DON'T SEEM VERY **HAPPY,** SWEETHEART.
YOU LOOK LIKE YOU'VE GOT THE WEIGHT OF THE WORLD ON YOUR SHOULDERS.
I KNOW YOU'RE AFRAID OF GETTING HURT, BUT YOU CAN'T ALWAYS AVOID IT.
WE ALL NEED OTHER PEOPLE IN OUR LIVES.
LOOK AT ME AND YOUR DAD–
SOMEONE MENTION ME?

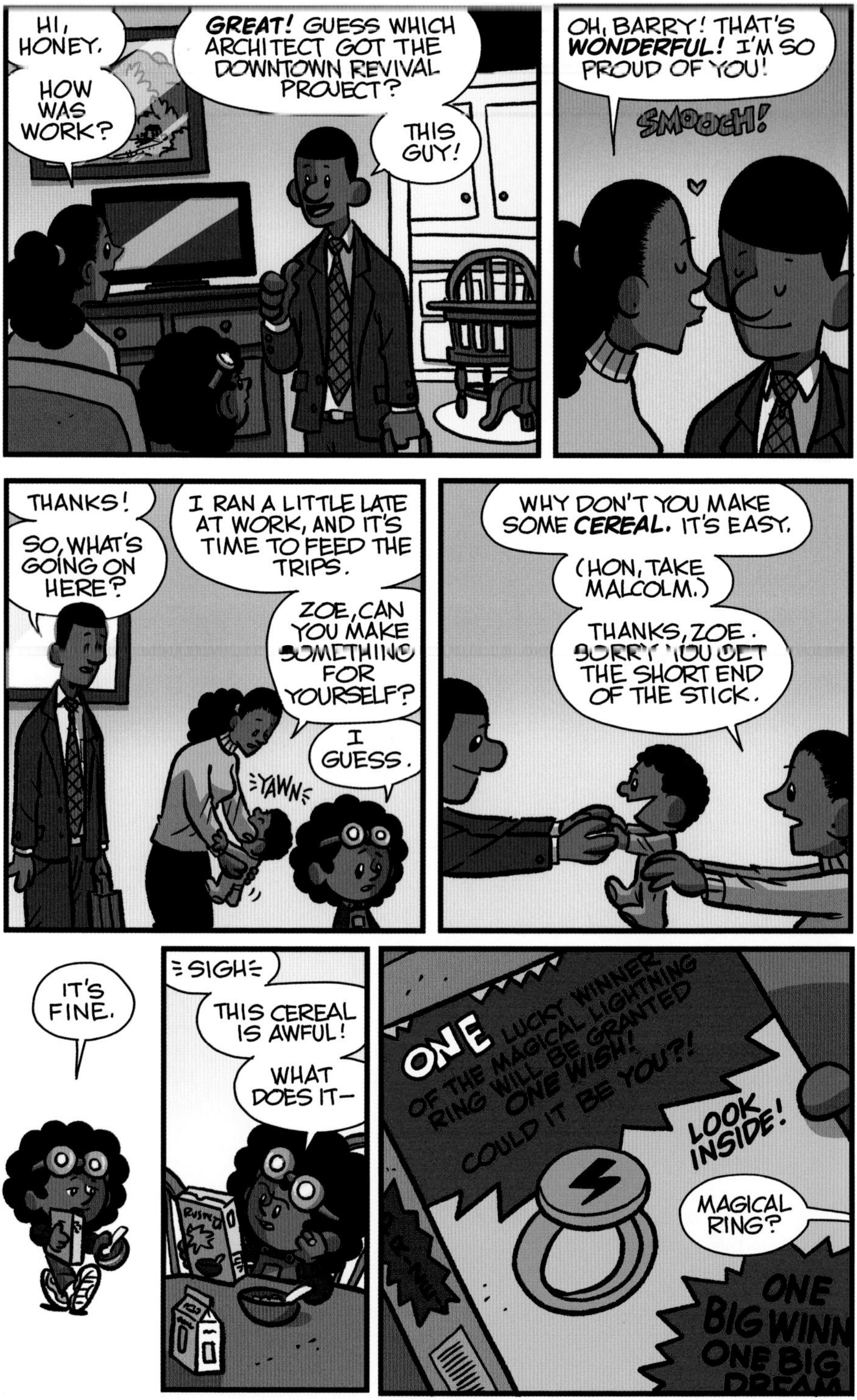
HI, HONEY.
HOW WAS WORK?
GREAT! GUESS WHICH ARCHITECT GOT THE DOWNTOWN REVIVAL PROJECT?
THIS GUY!
OH, BARRY! THAT'S WONDERFUL! I'M SO PROUD OF YOU!
SMOOCH!
THANKS!
SO, WHAT'S GOING ON HERE?
I RAN A LITTLE LATE AT WORK, AND IT'S TIME TO FEED THE TRIPS.
ZOE, CAN YOU MAKE SOMETHING FOR YOURSELF?
YAWN
I GUESS.
WHY DON'T YOU MAKE SOME CEREAL. IT'S EASY.
(HON, TAKE MALCOLM.)
THANKS, ZOE. SORRY YOU GET THE SHORT END OF THE STICK.
IT'S FINE.
SIGH
THIS CEREAL IS AWFUL!
WHAT DOES IT—
ONE LUCKY WINNER OF THE MAGICAL LIGHTNING RING WILL BE GRANTED ONE WISH! COULD IT BE YOU?!
LOOK INSIDE!
MAGICAL RING?
ONE BIG WINN
ONE BIG

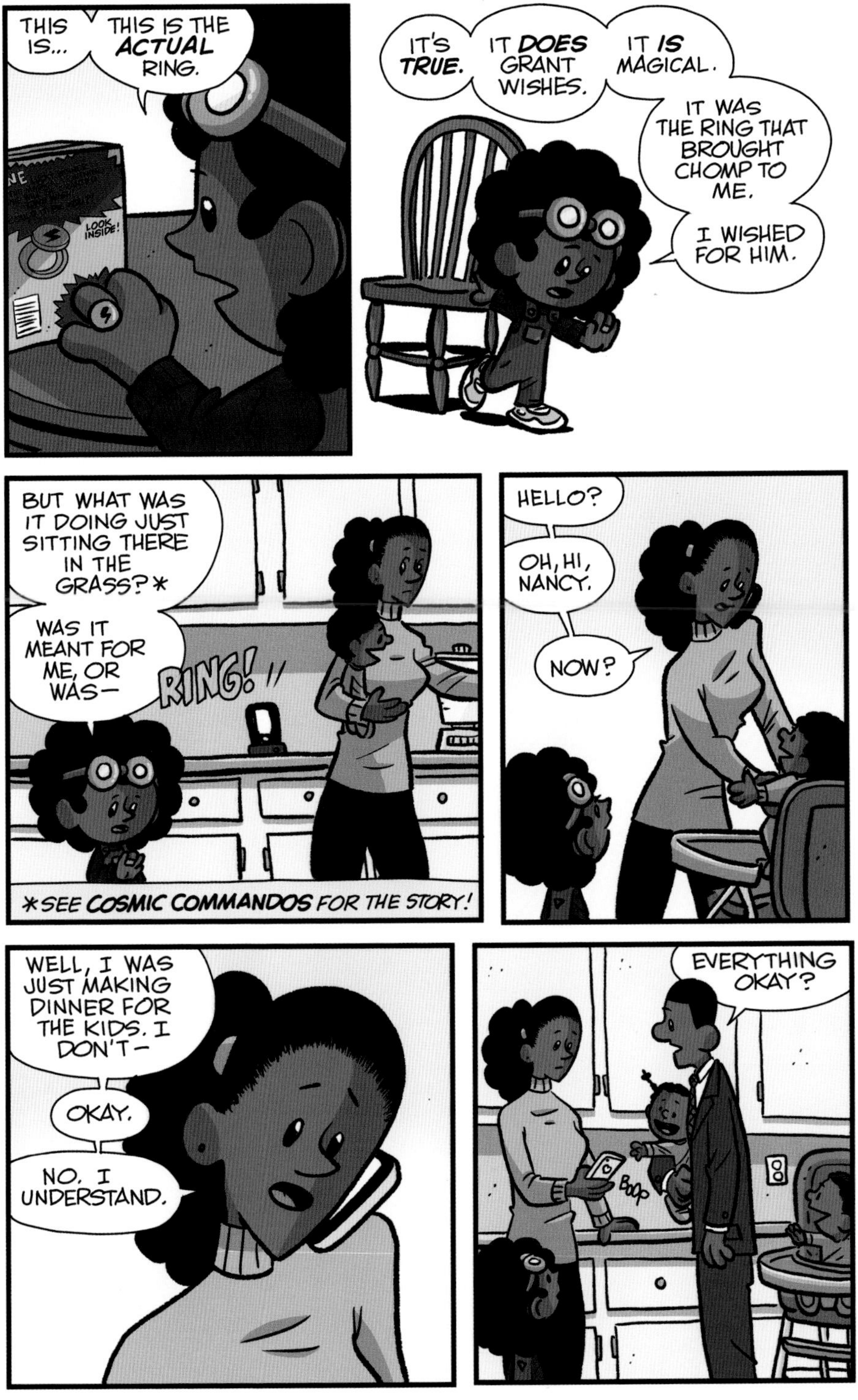
THIS IS...
THIS IS THE ACTUAL RING.
LOOK INSIDE!
IT'S TRUE.
IT DOES GRANT WISHES.
IT IS MAGICAL.
IT WAS THE RING THAT BROUGHT CHOMP TO ME.
I WISHED FOR HIM.
BUT WHAT WAS IT DOING JUST SITTING THERE IN THE GRASS?*
WAS IT MEANT FOR ME, OR WAS—
RING!
*SEE COSMIC COMMANDOS FOR THE STORY!
HELLO?
OH, HI, NANCY.
NOW?
WELL, I WAS JUST MAKING DINNER FOR THE KIDS. I DON'T—
OKAY.
NO. I UNDERSTAND.
EVERYTHING OKAY?
BOOP

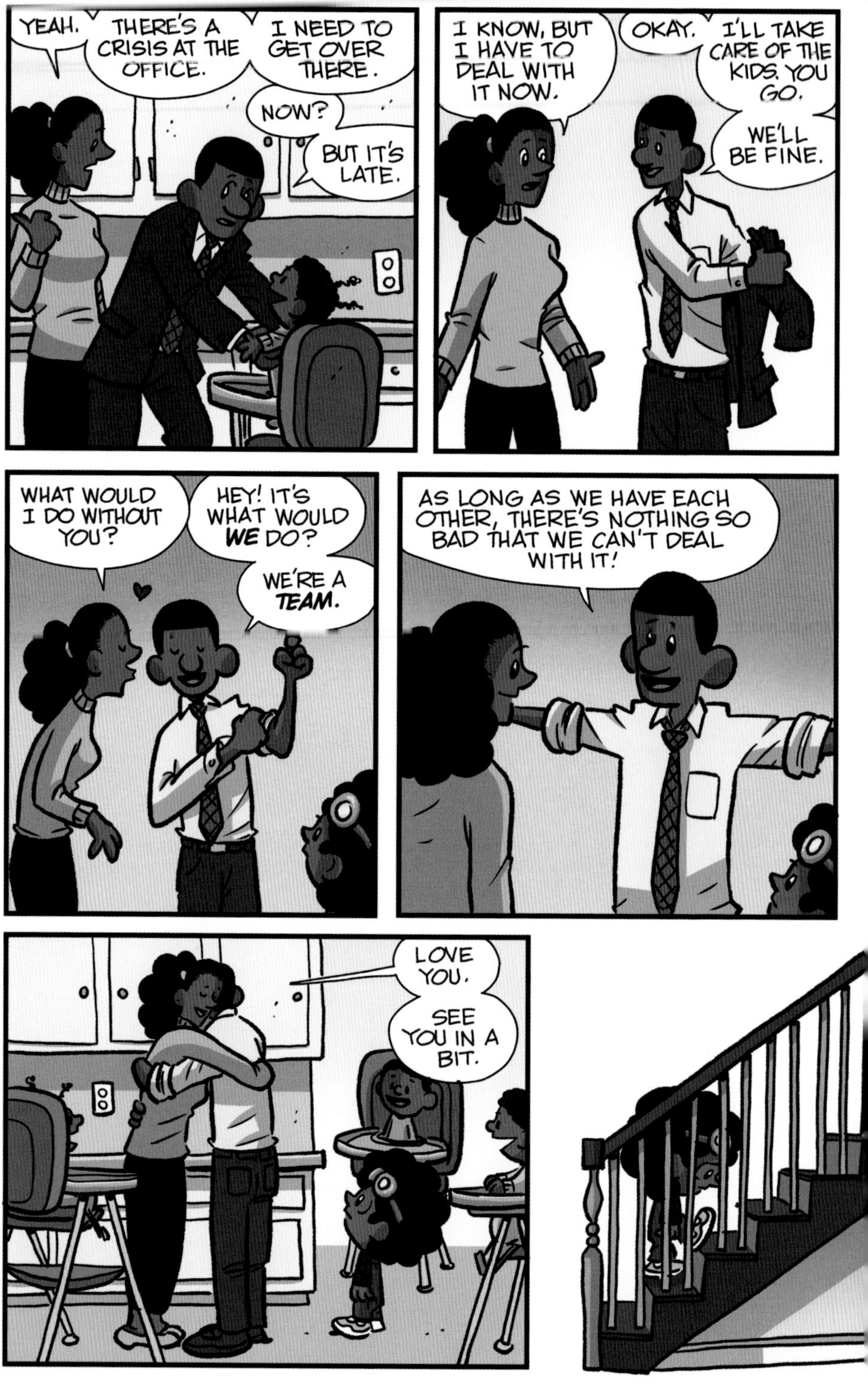
YEAH.
THERE'S A CRISIS AT THE OFFICE.
I NEED TO GET OVER THERE.
NOW?
BUT IT'S LATE.
I KNOW, BUT I HAVE TO DEAL WITH IT NOW.
OKAY.
I'LL TAKE CARE OF THE KIDS. YOU GO.
WE'LL BE FINE.
WHAT WOULD I DO WITHOUT YOU?
HEY! IT'S WHAT WOULD WE DO?
WE'RE A TEAM.
AS LONG AS WE HAVE EACH OTHER, THERE'S NOTHING SO BAD THAT WE CAN'T DEAL WITH IT!
LOVE YOU.
SEE YOU IN A BIT.

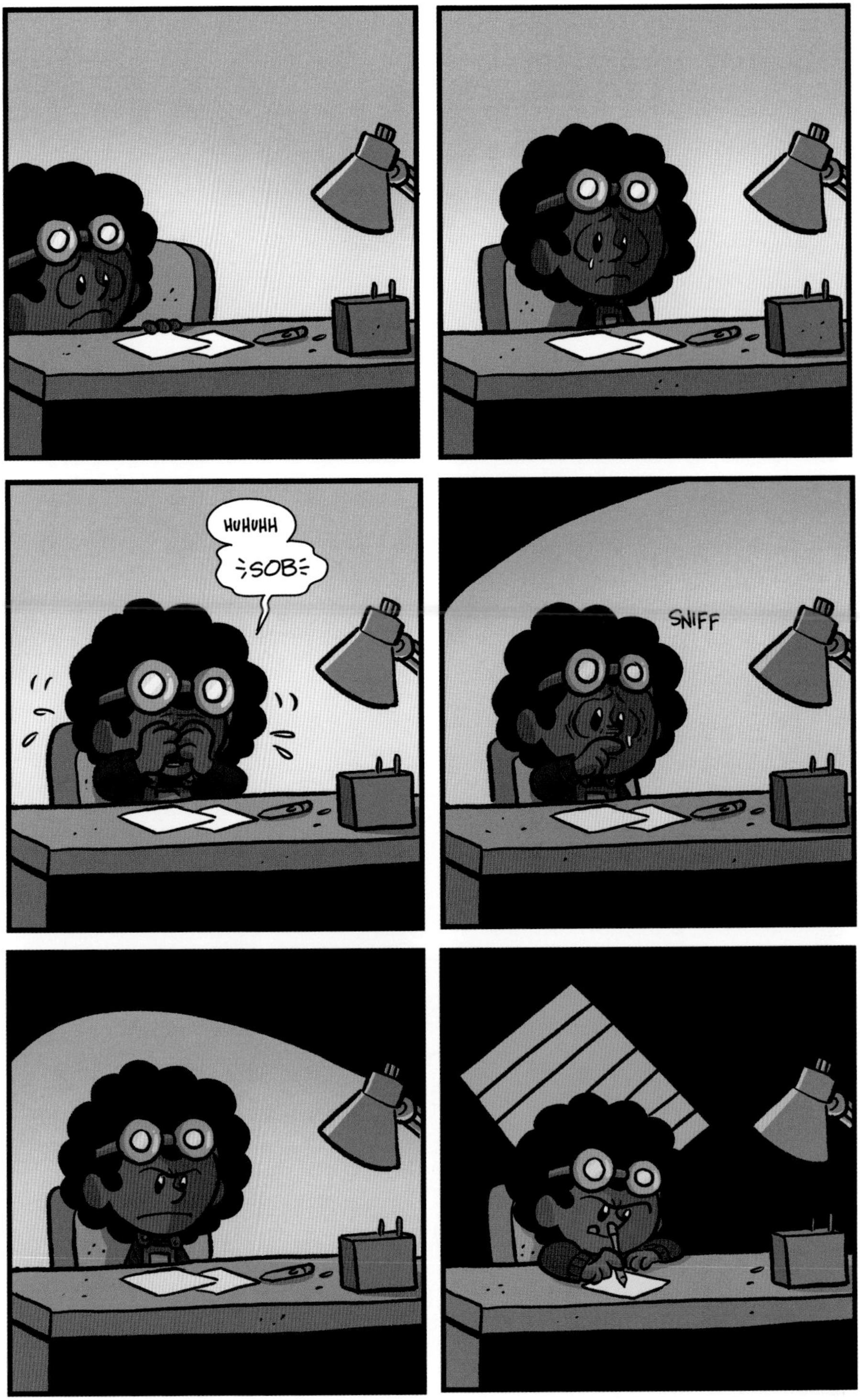
HUHUHH
SOB
SNIFF

Chapter 12 • A Little Help from My Friends

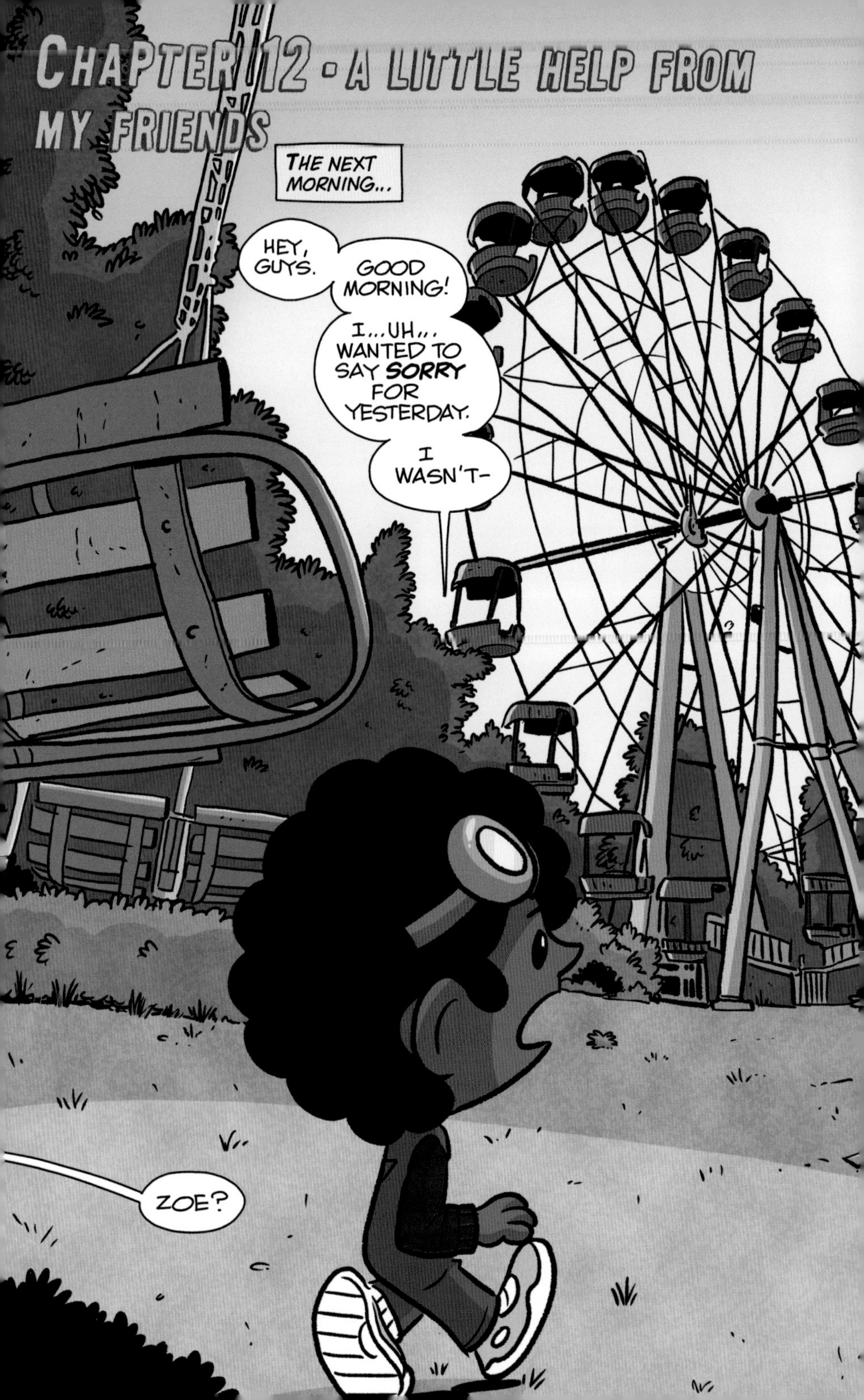
THE NEXT MORNING...
HEY, GUYS.
GOOD MORNING!
I...UH... WANTED TO SAY SORRY FOR YESTERDAY.
I WASN'T-
ZOE?

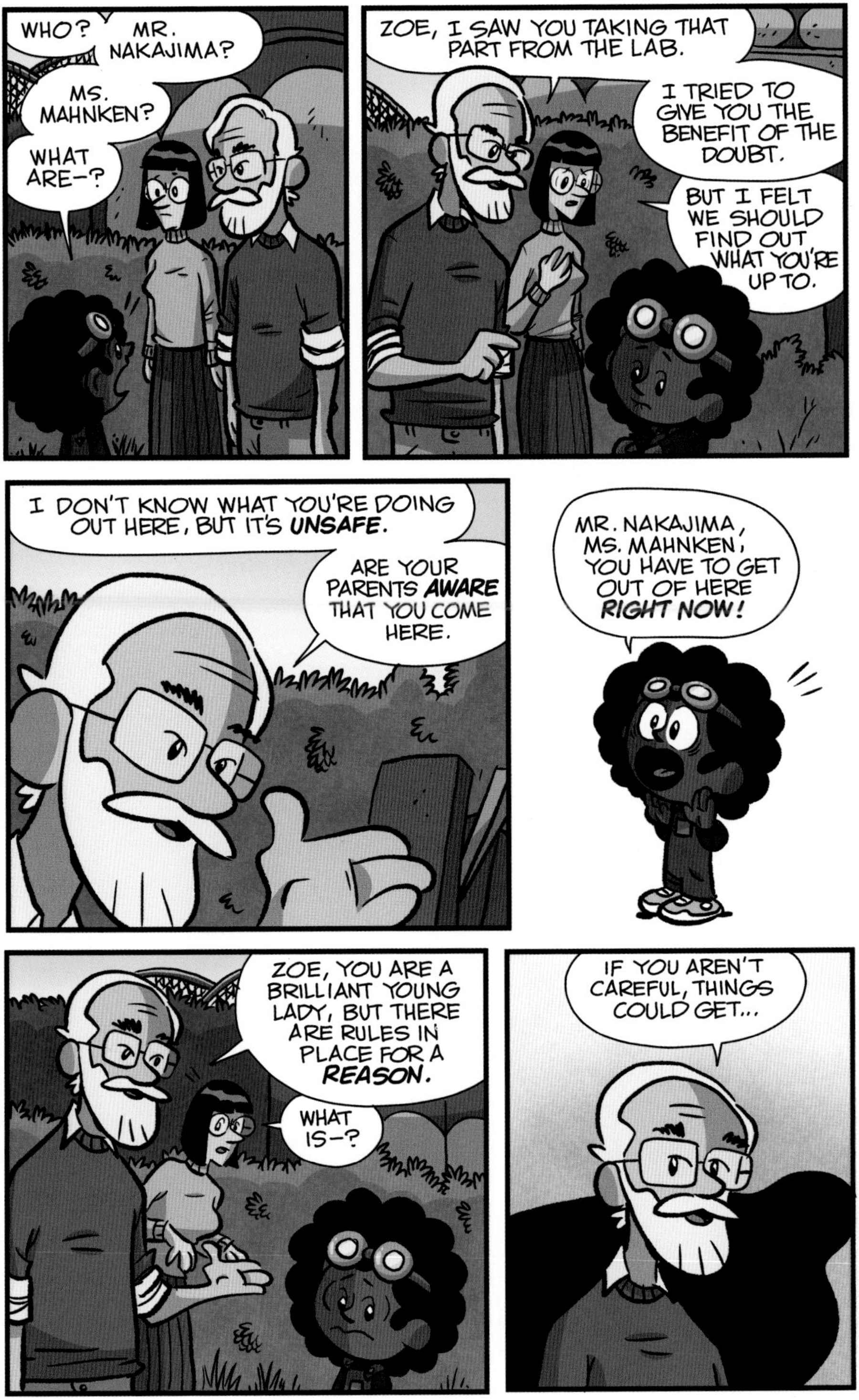
WHO?
MR. NAKAJIMA?
MS. MAHNKEN?
WHAT ARE–?
ZOE, I SAW YOU TAKING THAT PART FROM THE LAB.
I TRIED TO GIVE YOU THE BENEFIT OF THE DOUBT.
BUT I FELT WE SHOULD FIND OUT WHAT YOU'RE UP TO.
I DON'T KNOW WHAT YOU'RE DOING OUT HERE, BUT IT'S UNSAFE.
ARE YOUR PARENTS AWARE THAT YOU COME HERE.
MR. NAKAJIMA, MS. MAHNKEN, YOU HAVE TO GET OUT OF HERE RIGHT NOW!
ZOE, YOU ARE A BRILLIANT YOUNG LADY, BUT THERE ARE RULES IN PLACE FOR A REASON.
WHAT IS–?
IF YOU AREN'T CAREFUL, THINGS COULD GET...

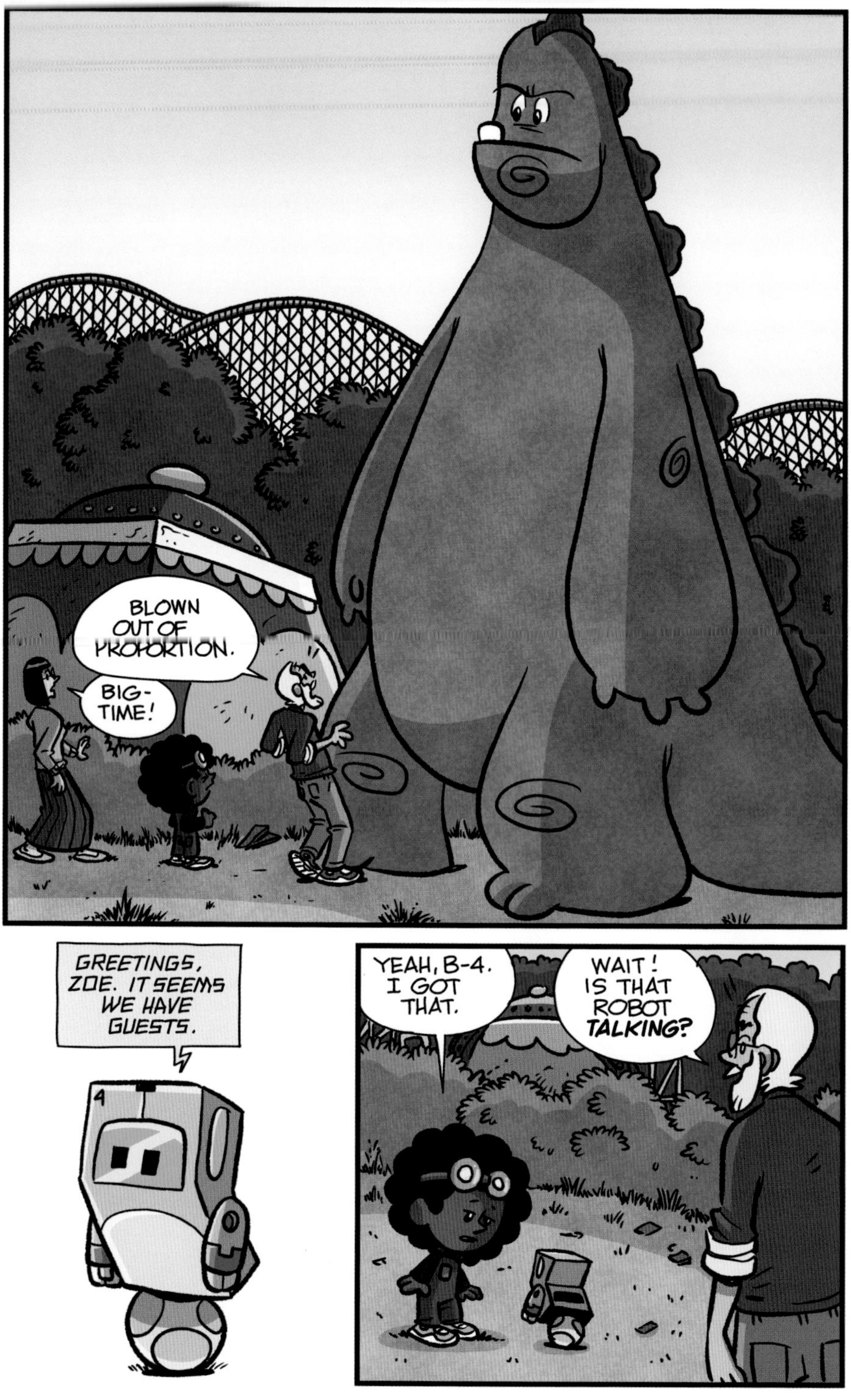
BLOWN OUT OF PROPORTION.
BIG-TIME!
GREETINGS, ZOE. IT SEEMS WE HAVE GUESTS.
4
YEAH, B-4. I GOT THAT.
WAIT! IS THAT ROBOT *TALKING?*

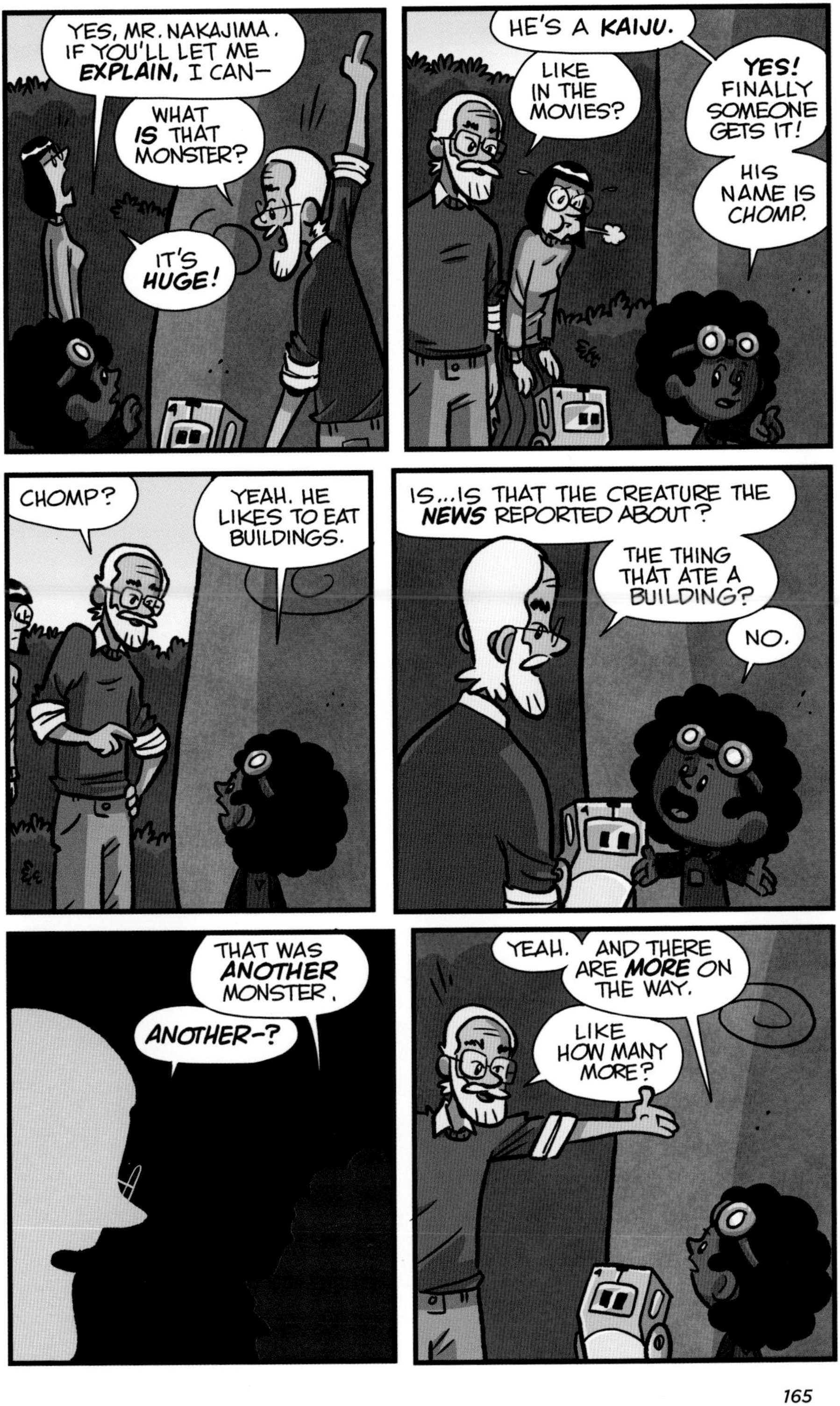
YES, MR. NAKAJIMA. IF YOU'LL LET ME EXPLAIN, I CAN—
WHAT IS THAT MONSTER?
IT'S HUGE!
HE'S A KAIJU.
LIKE IN THE MOVIES?
YES! FINALLY SOMEONE GETS IT!
HIS NAME IS CHOMP.
CHOMP?
YEAH. HE LIKES TO EAT BUILDINGS.
IS...IS THAT THE CREATURE THE NEWS REPORTED ABOUT?
THE THING THAT ATE A BUILDING?
NO.
THAT WAS ANOTHER MONSTER.
ANOTHER-?
YEAH.
AND THERE ARE MORE ON THE WAY.
LIKE HOW MANY MORE?

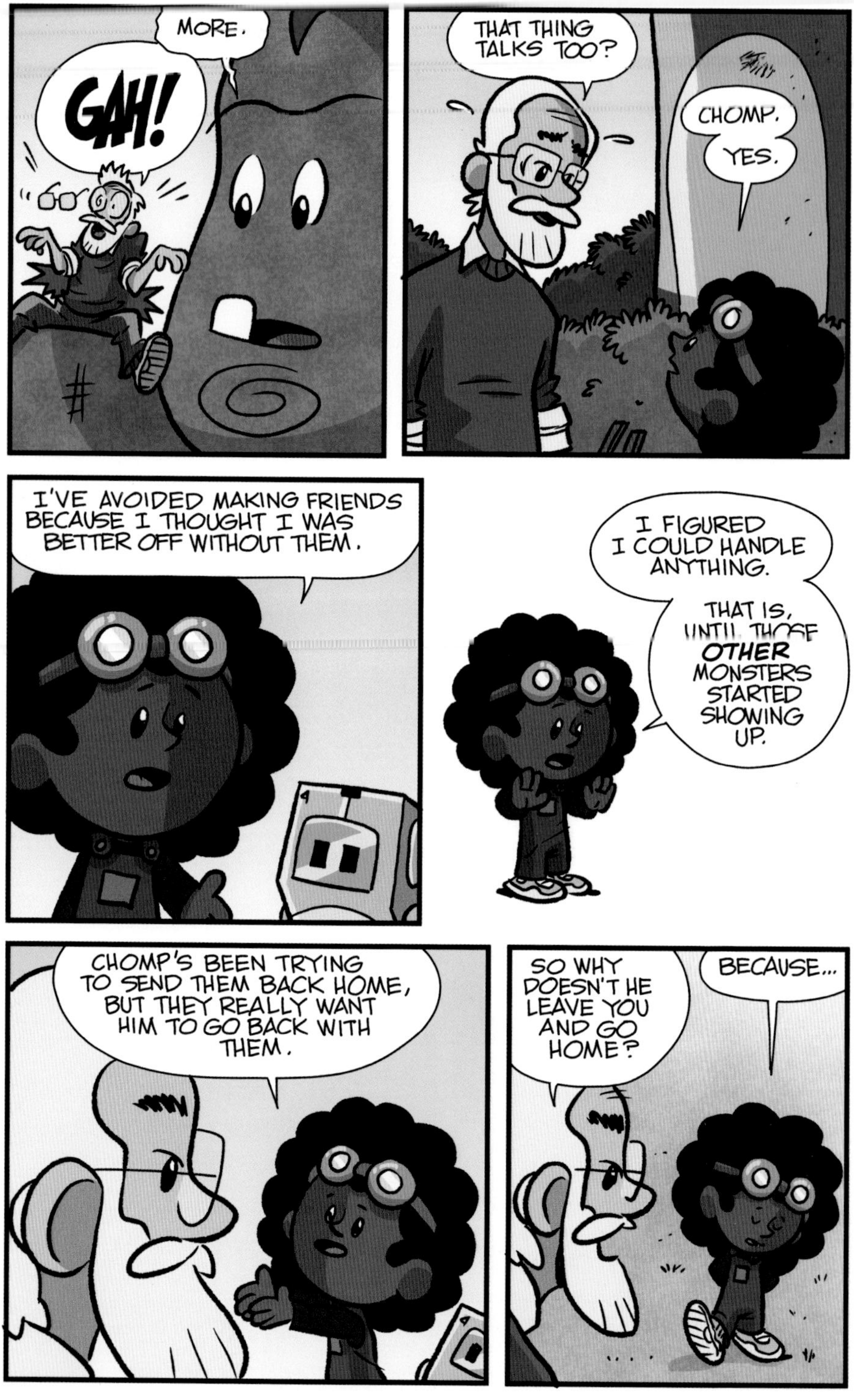
MORE.
GAH!
THAT THING TALKS TOO?
CHOMP.
YES.
I'VE AVOIDED MAKING FRIENDS BECAUSE I THOUGHT I WAS BETTER OFF WITHOUT THEM.
I FIGURED I COULD HANDLE ANYTHING.
THAT IS, UNTIL THOSE *OTHER* MONSTERS STARTED SHOWING UP.
CHOMP'S BEEN TRYING TO SEND THEM BACK HOME, BUT THEY REALLY WANT HIM TO GO BACK WITH THEM.
SO WHY DOESN'T HE LEAVE YOU AND GO HOME?
BECAUSE...

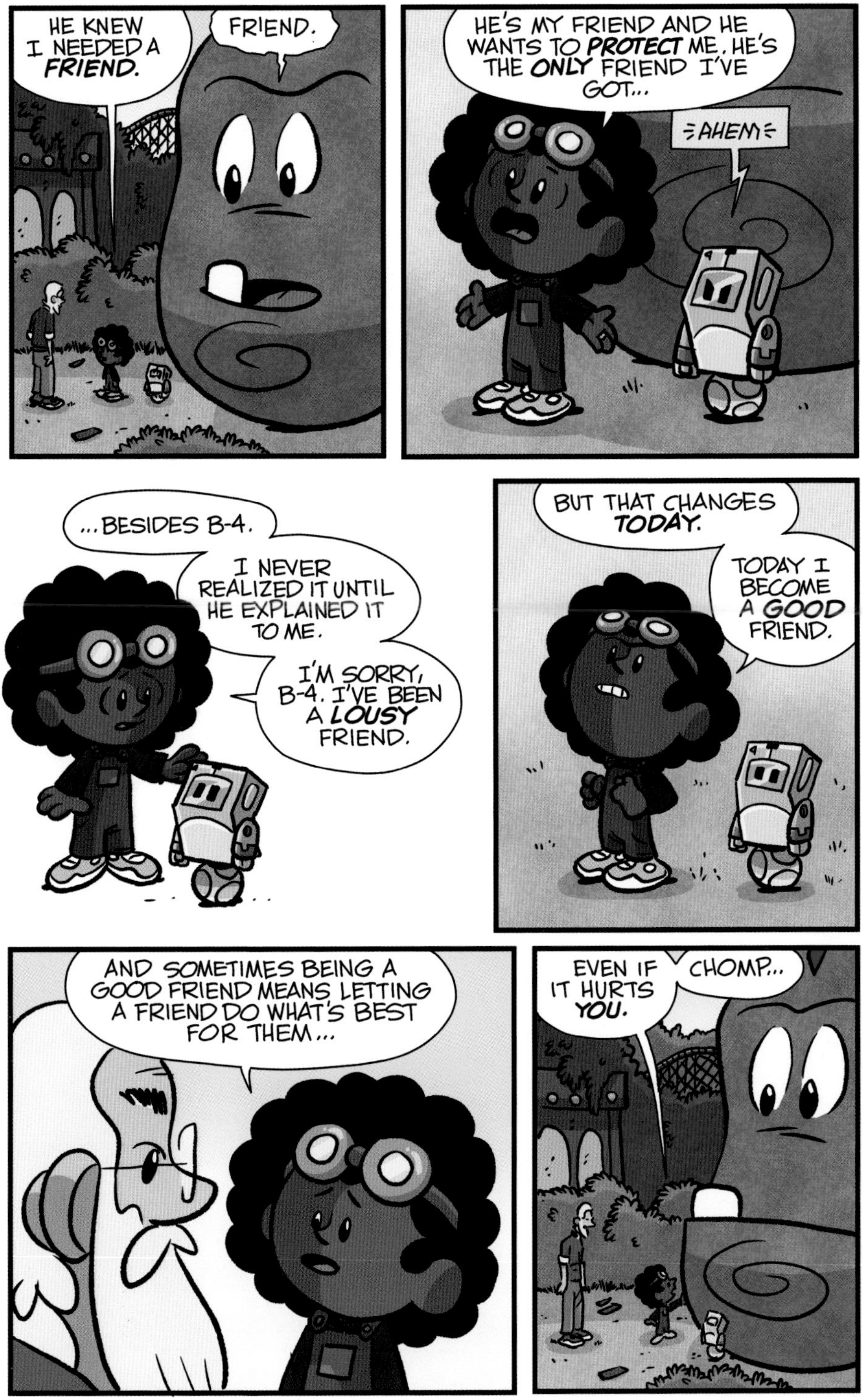
HE KNEW I NEEDED A FRIEND.
FRIEND.
HE'S MY FRIEND AND HE WANTS TO PROTECT ME. HE'S THE ONLY FRIEND I'VE GOT...
AHEM
...BESIDES B-4.
I NEVER REALIZED IT UNTIL HE EXPLAINED IT TO ME.
I'M SORRY, B-4. I'VE BEEN A LOUSY FRIEND.
BUT THAT CHANGES TODAY.
TODAY I BECOME A GOOD FRIEND.
AND SOMETIMES BEING A GOOD FRIEND MEANS LETTING A FRIEND DO WHAT'S BEST FOR THEM...
EVEN IF IT HURTS YOU.
CHOMP...

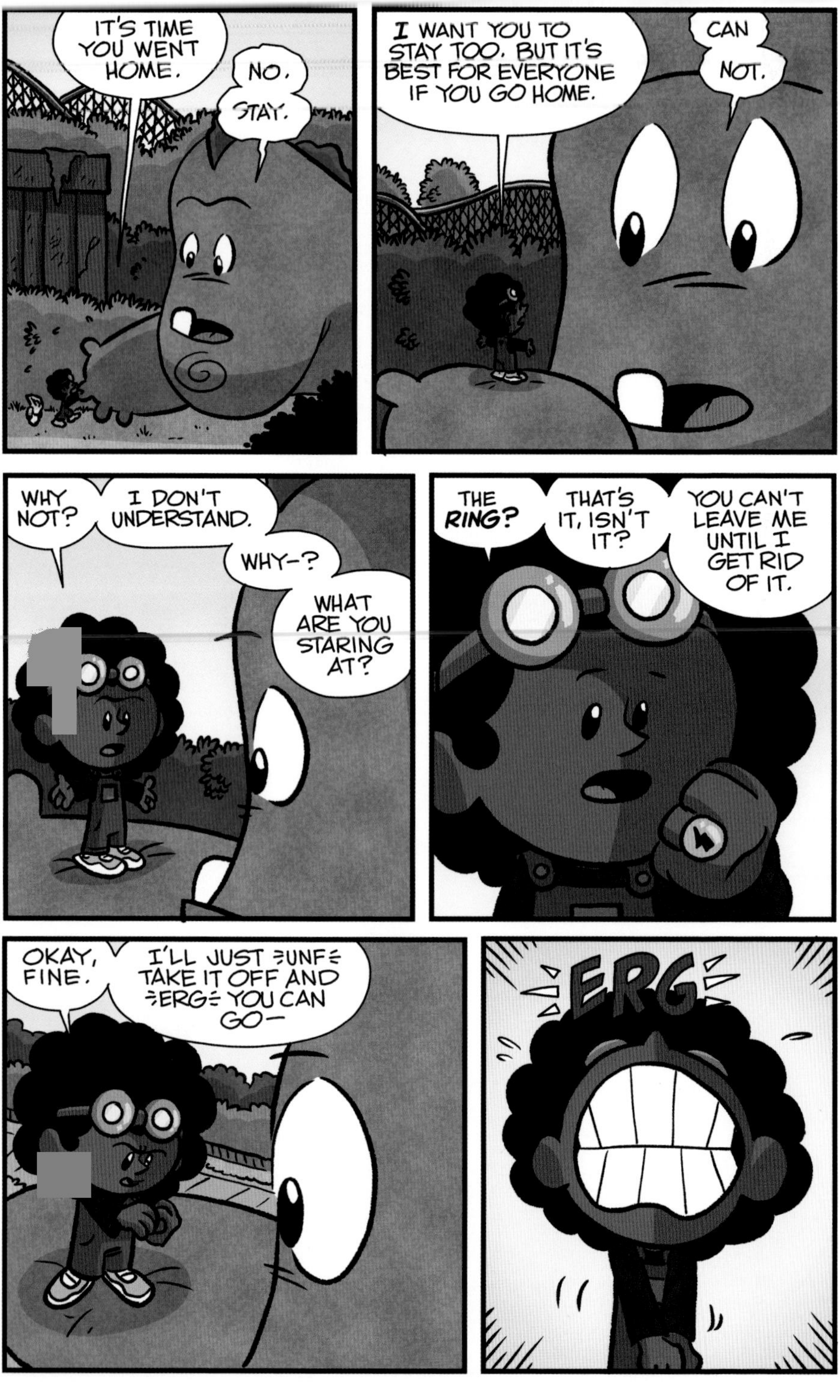
IT'S TIME YOU WENT HOME.
NO.
STAY.
I WANT YOU TO STAY TOO. BUT IT'S BEST FOR EVERYONE IF YOU GO HOME.
CAN
NOT.
WHY NOT?
I DON'T UNDERSTAND.
WHY-?
WHAT ARE YOU STARING AT?
THE RING?
THAT'S IT, ISN'T IT?
YOU CAN'T LEAVE ME UNTIL I GET RID OF IT.
OKAY, FINE.
I'LL JUST UNF TAKE IT OFF AND ERG YOU CAN GO—
ERG

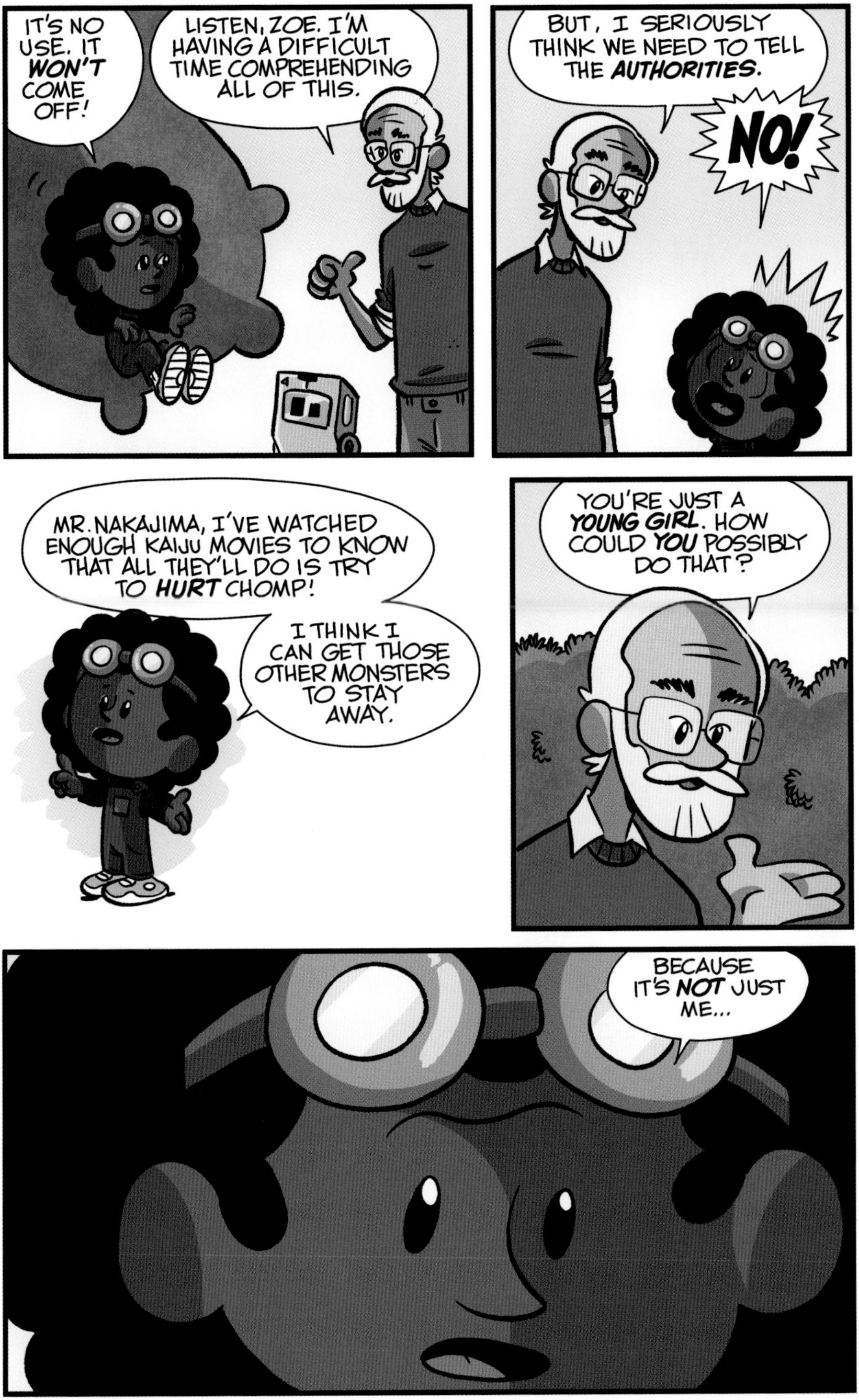

IT'S NO USE. IT WON'T COME OFF!
LISTEN, ZOE. I'M HAVING A DIFFICULT TIME COMPREHENDING ALL OF THIS.
BUT, I SERIOUSLY THINK WE NEED TO TELL THE AUTHORITIES.
NO!
MR. NAKAJIMA, I'VE WATCHED ENOUGH KAIJU MOVIES TO KNOW THAT ALL THEY'LL DO IS TRY TO HURT CHOMP!
I THINK I CAN GET THOSE OTHER MONSTERS TO STAY AWAY.
YOU'RE JUST A YOUNG GIRL. HOW COULD YOU POSSIBLY DO THAT?
BECAUSE IT'S NOT JUST ME...

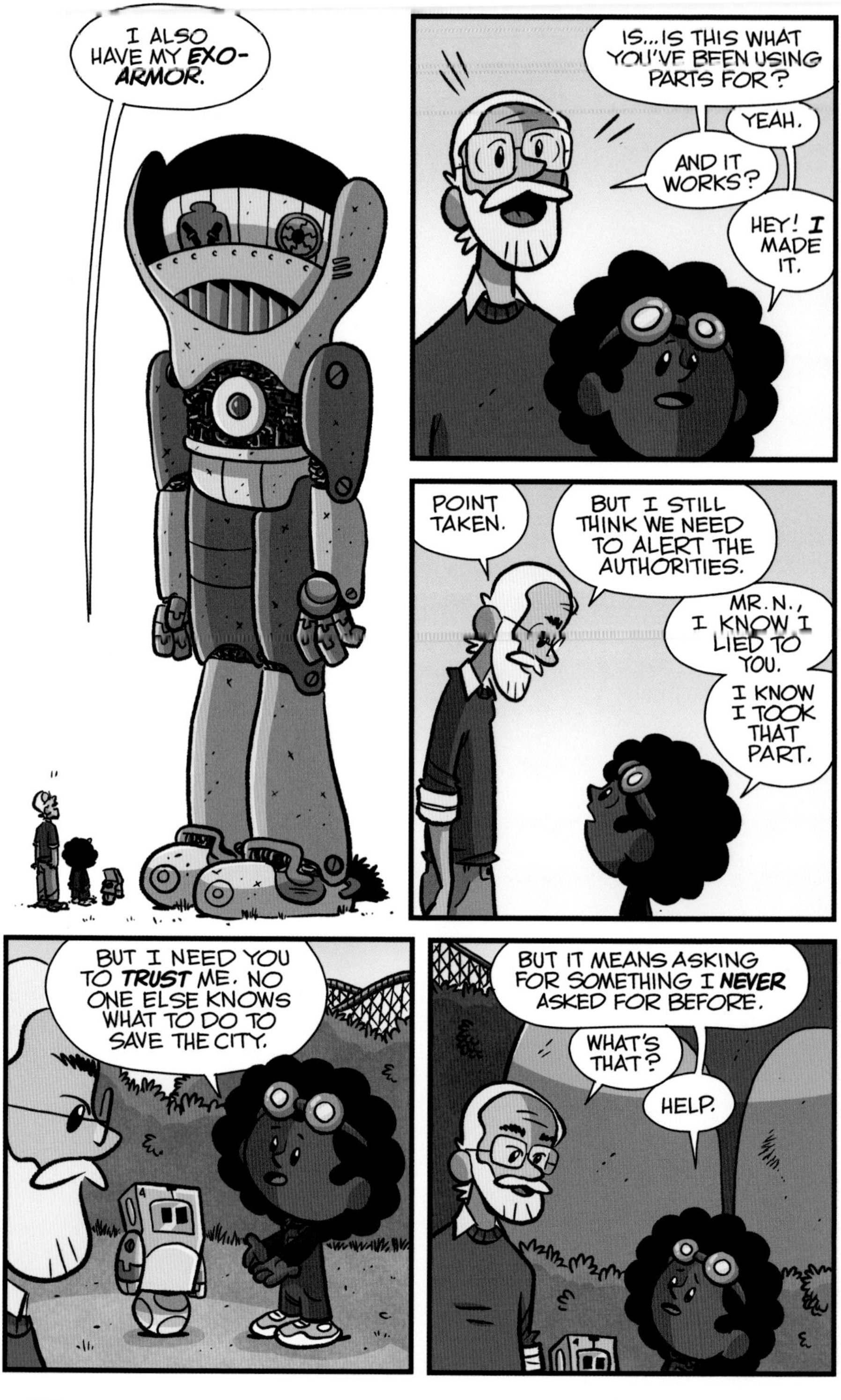
I ALSO HAVE MY **EXO-ARMOR**.
IS...IS THIS WHAT YOU'VE BEEN USING PARTS FOR?
YEAH.
AND IT WORKS?
HEY! **I** MADE IT.
POINT TAKEN.
BUT I STILL THINK WE NEED TO ALERT THE AUTHORITIES.
MR. N., I KNOW I LIED TO YOU.
I KNOW I TOOK THAT PART.
BUT I NEED YOU TO **TRUST** ME. NO ONE ELSE KNOWS WHAT TO DO TO SAVE THE CITY.
BUT IT MEANS ASKING FOR SOMETHING I **NEVER** ASKED FOR BEFORE.
WHAT'S THAT?
HELP.

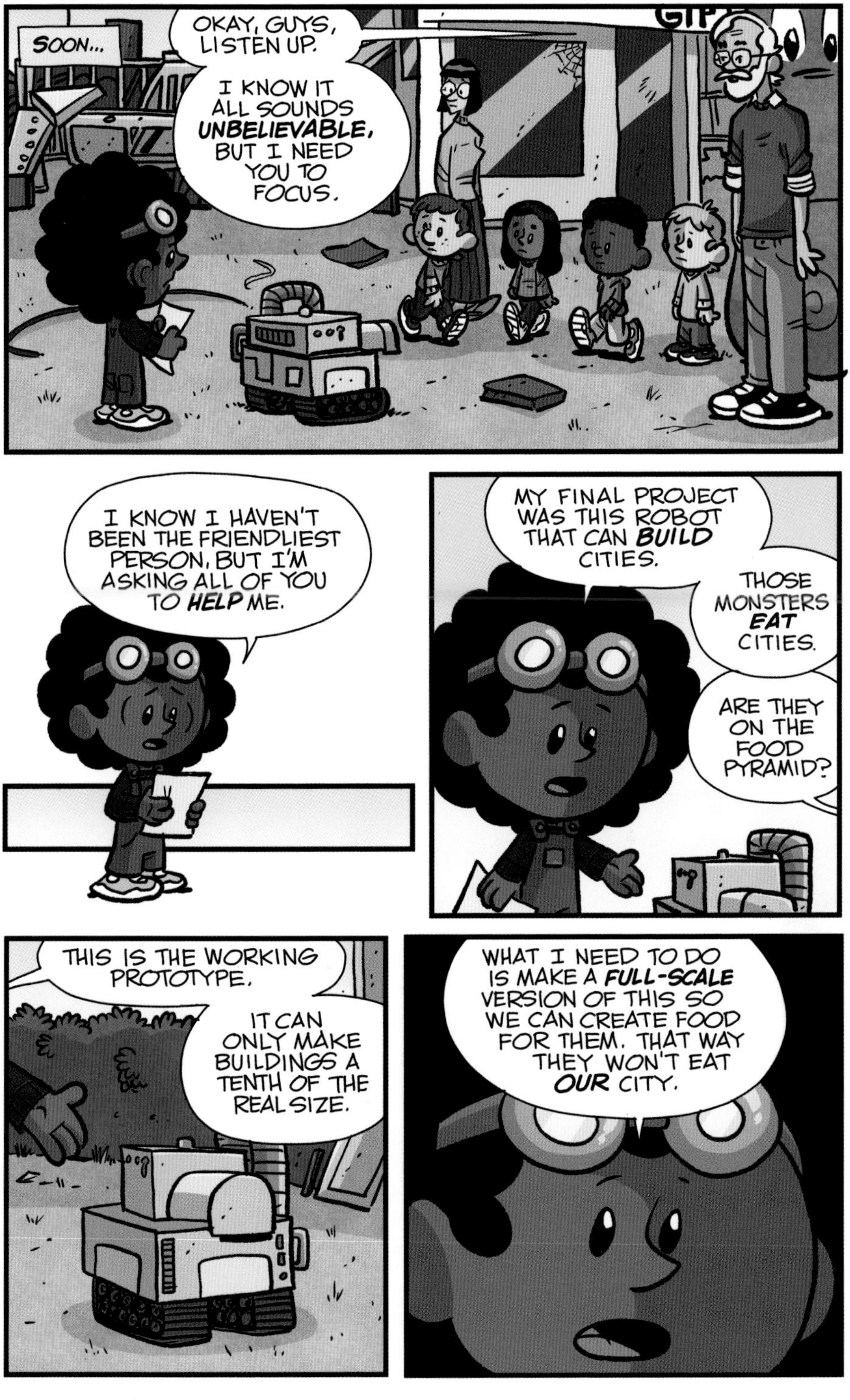
SOON...
OKAY, GUYS, LISTEN UP.
I KNOW IT ALL SOUNDS UNBELIEVABLE, BUT I NEED YOU TO FOCUS.
I KNOW I HAVEN'T BEEN THE FRIENDLIEST PERSON, BUT I'M ASKING ALL OF YOU TO HELP ME.
MY FINAL PROJECT WAS THIS ROBOT THAT CAN BUILD CITIES.
THOSE MONSTERS EAT CITIES.
ARE THEY ON THE FOOD PYRAMID?
THIS IS THE WORKING PROTOTYPE.
IT CAN ONLY MAKE BUILDINGS A TENTH OF THE REAL SIZE.
WHAT I NEED TO DO IS MAKE A FULL-SCALE VERSION OF THIS SO WE CAN CREATE FOOD FOR THEM. THAT WAY THEY WON'T EAT OUR CITY.

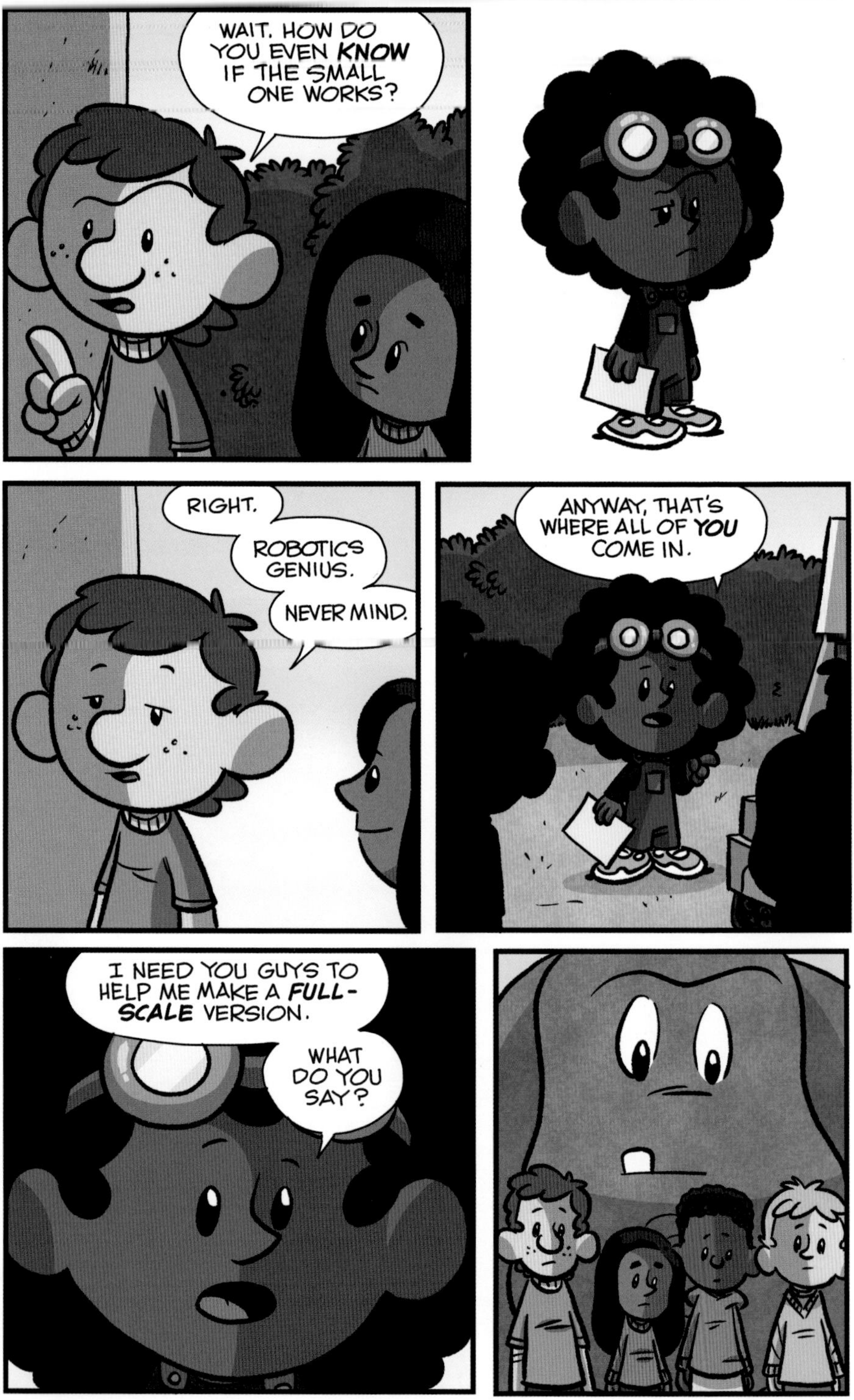
WAIT. HOW DO YOU EVEN KNOW IF THE SMALL ONE WORKS?
RIGHT.
ROBOTICS GENIUS.
NEVER MIND.
ANYWAY, THAT'S WHERE ALL OF YOU COME IN.
I NEED YOU GUYS TO HELP ME MAKE A FULL-SCALE VERSION.
WHAT DO YOU SAY?

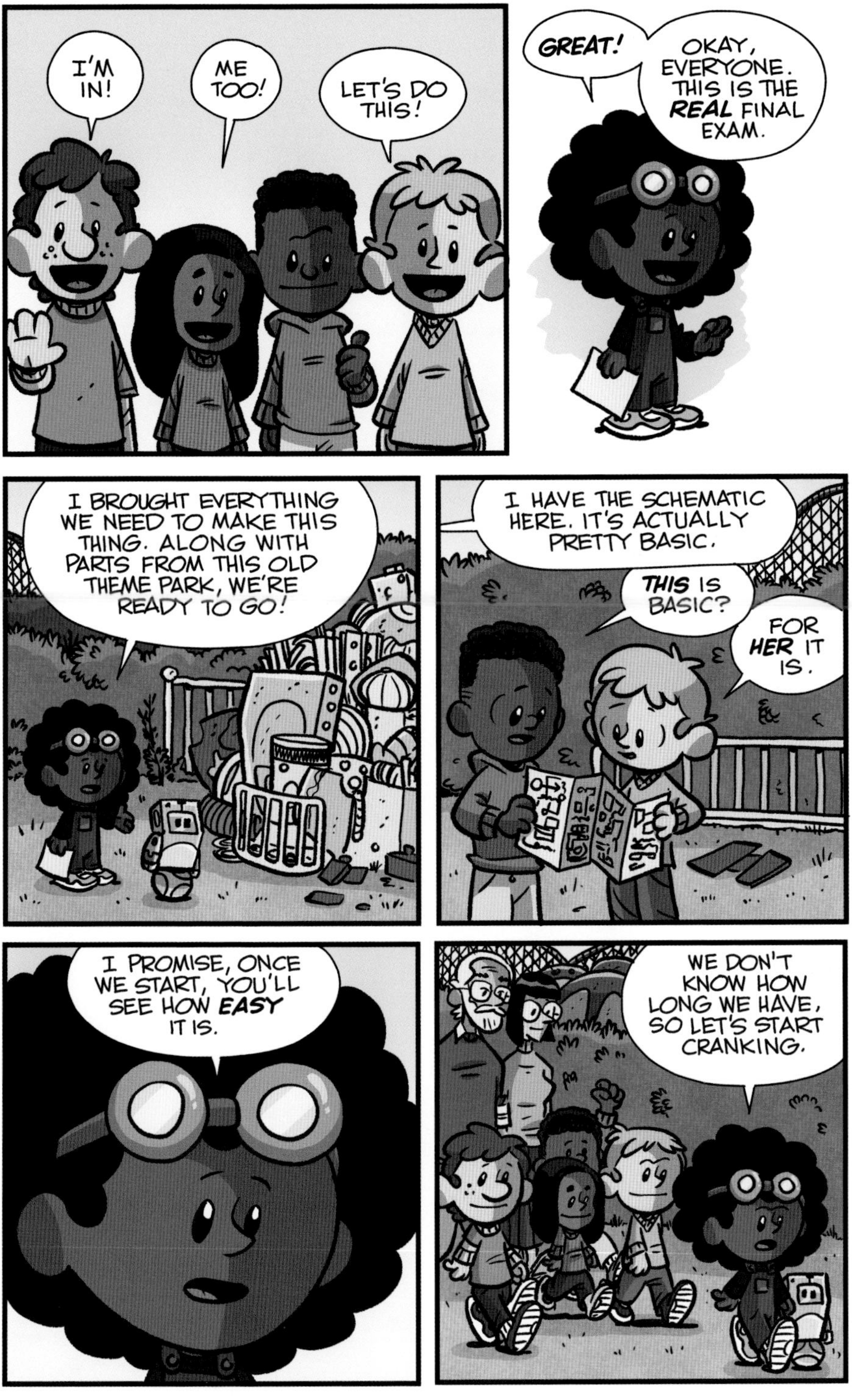
I'M IN!
ME TOO!
LET'S DO THIS!
GREAT!
OKAY, EVERYONE. THIS IS THE REAL FINAL EXAM.
I BROUGHT EVERYTHING WE NEED TO MAKE THIS THING. ALONG WITH PARTS FROM THIS OLD THEME PARK, WE'RE READY TO GO!
I HAVE THE SCHEMATIC HERE. IT'S ACTUALLY PRETTY BASIC.
THIS IS BASIC?
FOR HER IT IS.
I PROMISE, ONCE WE START, YOU'LL SEE HOW EASY IT IS.
WE DON'T KNOW HOW LONG WE HAVE, SO LET'S START CRANKING.

CHAPTER 13 - BEFORE THE STORM

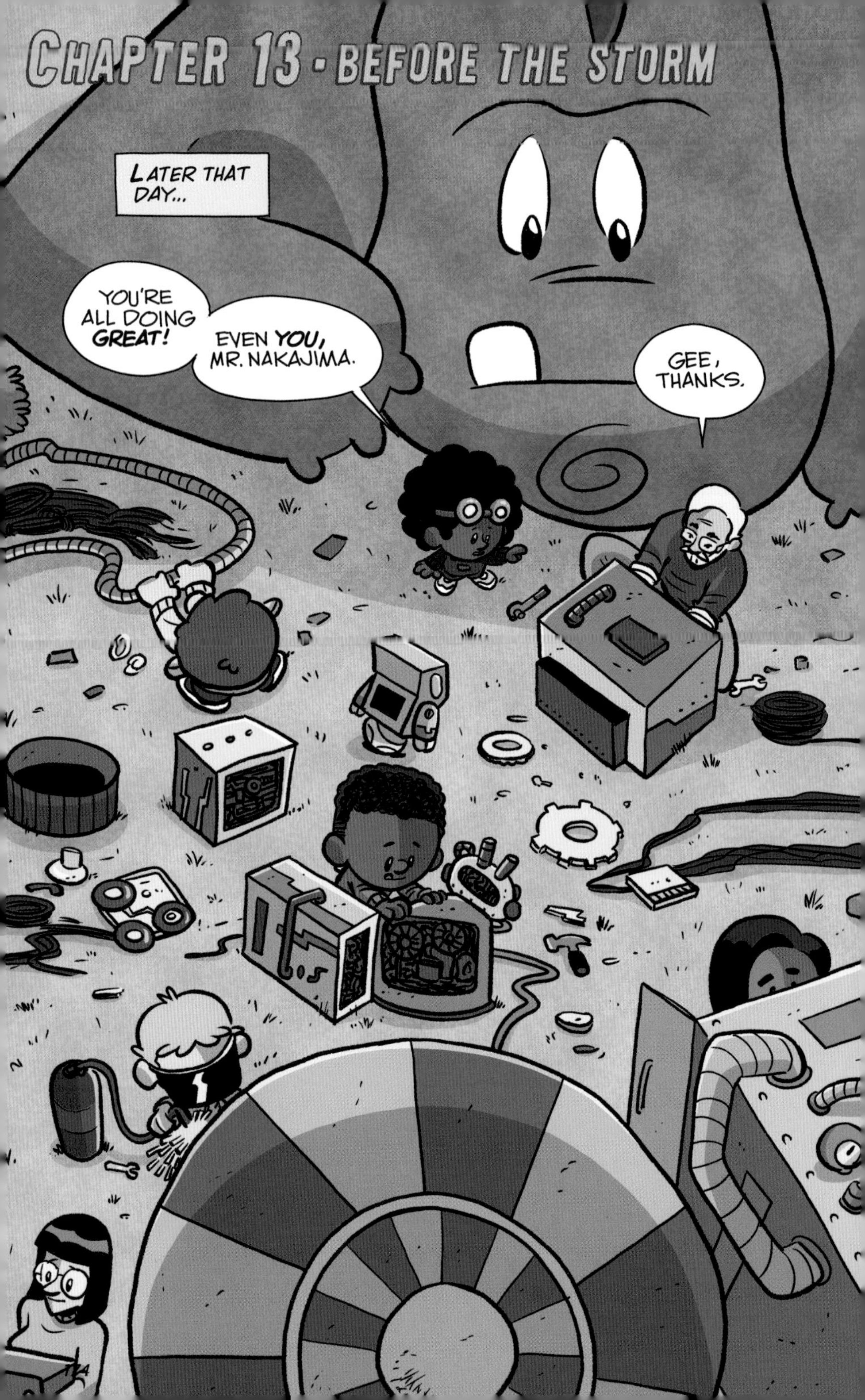
LATER THAT DAY...
YOU'RE ALL DOING GREAT!
EVEN YOU, MR. NAKAJIMA.
GEE, THANKS.

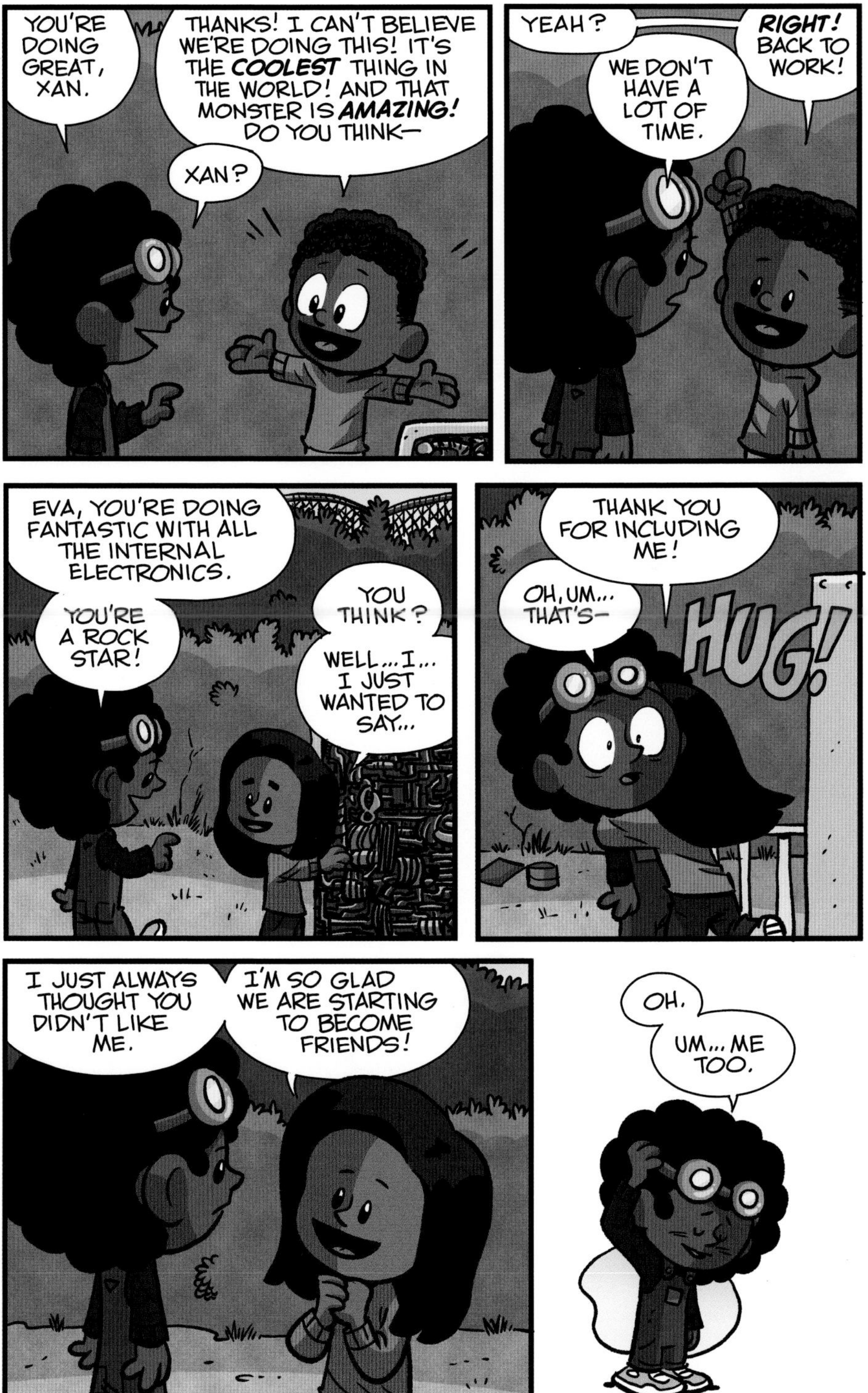
YOU'RE DOING GREAT, XAN.
THANKS! I CAN'T BELIEVE WE'RE DOING THIS! IT'S THE **COOLEST** THING IN THE WORLD! AND THAT MONSTER IS **AMAZING!** DO YOU THINK—
XAN?
YEAH?
WE DON'T HAVE A LOT OF TIME.
RIGHT! BACK TO WORK!
EVA, YOU'RE DOING FANTASTIC WITH ALL THE INTERNAL ELECTRONICS.
YOU'RE A ROCK STAR!
YOU THINK?
WELL... I... I JUST WANTED TO SAY...
THANK YOU FOR INCLUDING ME!
OH, UM... THAT'S—
HUG!
I JUST ALWAYS THOUGHT YOU DIDN'T LIKE ME.
I'M SO GLAD WE ARE STARTING TO BECOME FRIENDS!
OH.
UM... ME TOO.

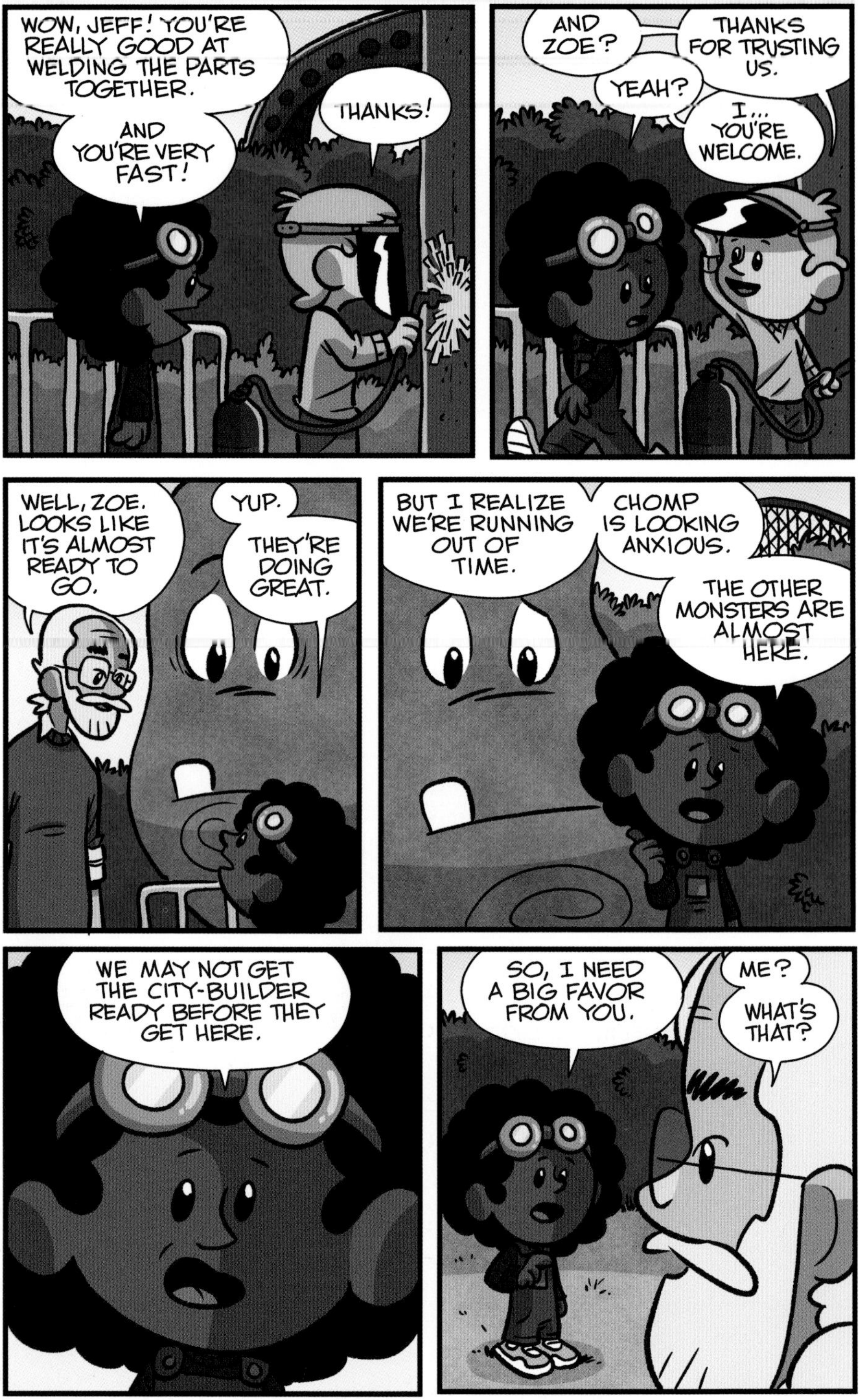
WOW, JEFF! YOU'RE REALLY GOOD AT WELDING THE PARTS TOGETHER.
AND YOU'RE VERY FAST!
THANKS!
AND ZOE?
THANKS FOR TRUSTING US.
YEAH?
I... YOU'RE WELCOME.
WELL, ZOE. LOOKS LIKE IT'S ALMOST READY TO GO.
YUP.
THEY'RE DOING GREAT.
BUT I REALIZE WE'RE RUNNING OUT OF TIME.
CHOMP IS LOOKING ANXIOUS.
THE OTHER MONSTERS ARE ALMOST HERE.
WE MAY NOT GET THE CITY-BUILDER READY BEFORE THEY GET HERE.
SO, I NEED A BIG FAVOR FROM YOU.
ME?
WHAT'S THAT?

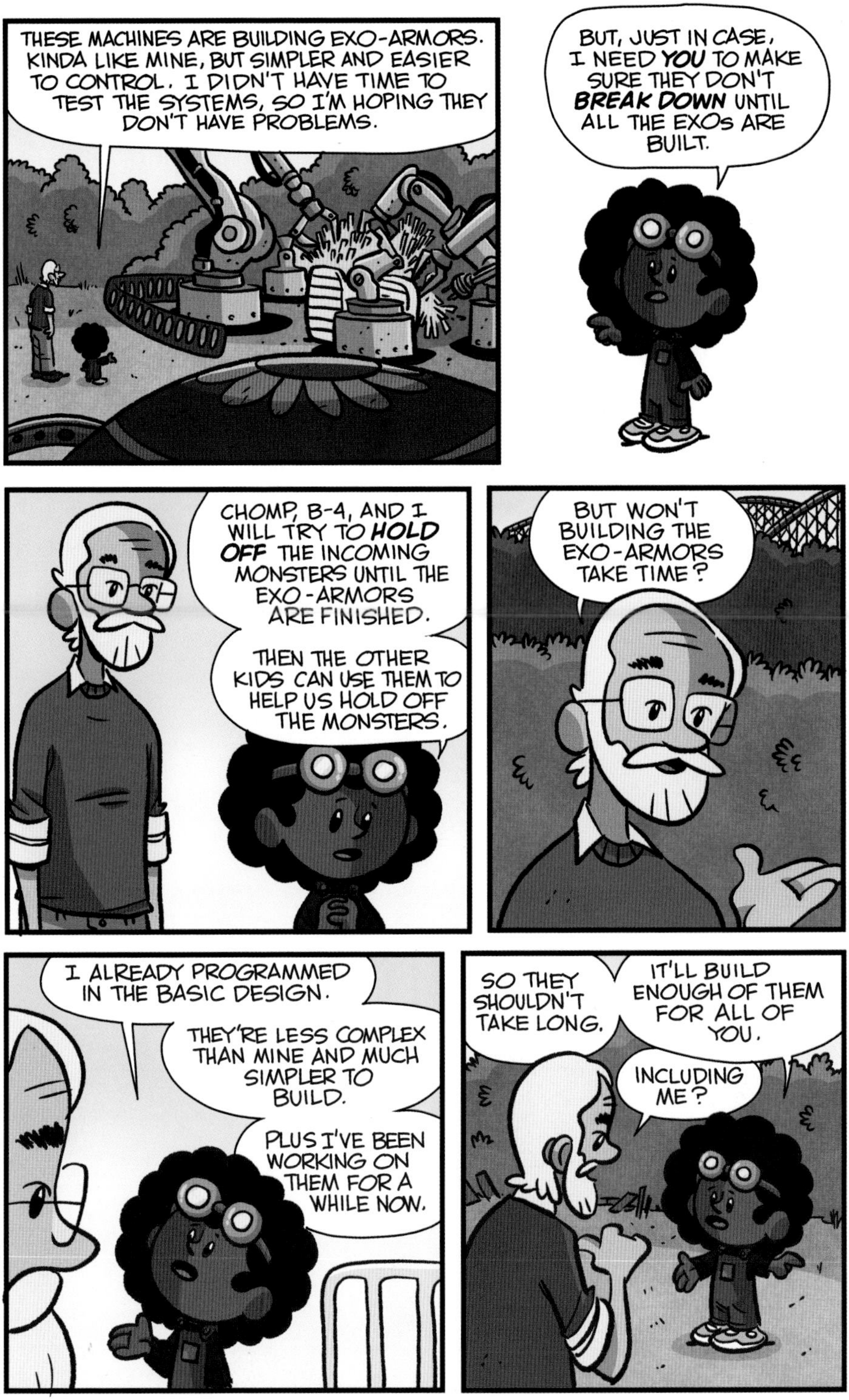
THESE MACHINES ARE BUILDING EXO-ARMORS. KINDA LIKE MINE, BUT SIMPLER AND EASIER TO CONTROL. I DIDN'T HAVE TIME TO TEST THE SYSTEMS, SO I'M HOPING THEY DON'T HAVE PROBLEMS.
BUT, JUST IN CASE, I NEED **YOU** TO MAKE SURE THEY DON'T **BREAK DOWN** UNTIL ALL THE EXOs ARE BUILT.
CHOMP, B-4, AND I WILL TRY TO **HOLD OFF** THE INCOMING MONSTERS UNTIL THE EXO-ARMORS ARE FINISHED.
THEN THE OTHER KIDS CAN USE THEM TO HELP US HOLD OFF THE MONSTERS.
BUT WON'T BUILDING THE EXO-ARMORS TAKE TIME?
I ALREADY PROGRAMMED IN THE BASIC DESIGN.
THEY'RE LESS COMPLEX THAN MINE AND MUCH SIMPLER TO BUILD.
PLUS I'VE BEEN WORKING ON THEM FOR A WHILE NOW.
SO THEY SHOULDN'T TAKE LONG.
IT'LL BUILD ENOUGH OF THEM FOR ALL OF YOU.
INCLUDING ME?

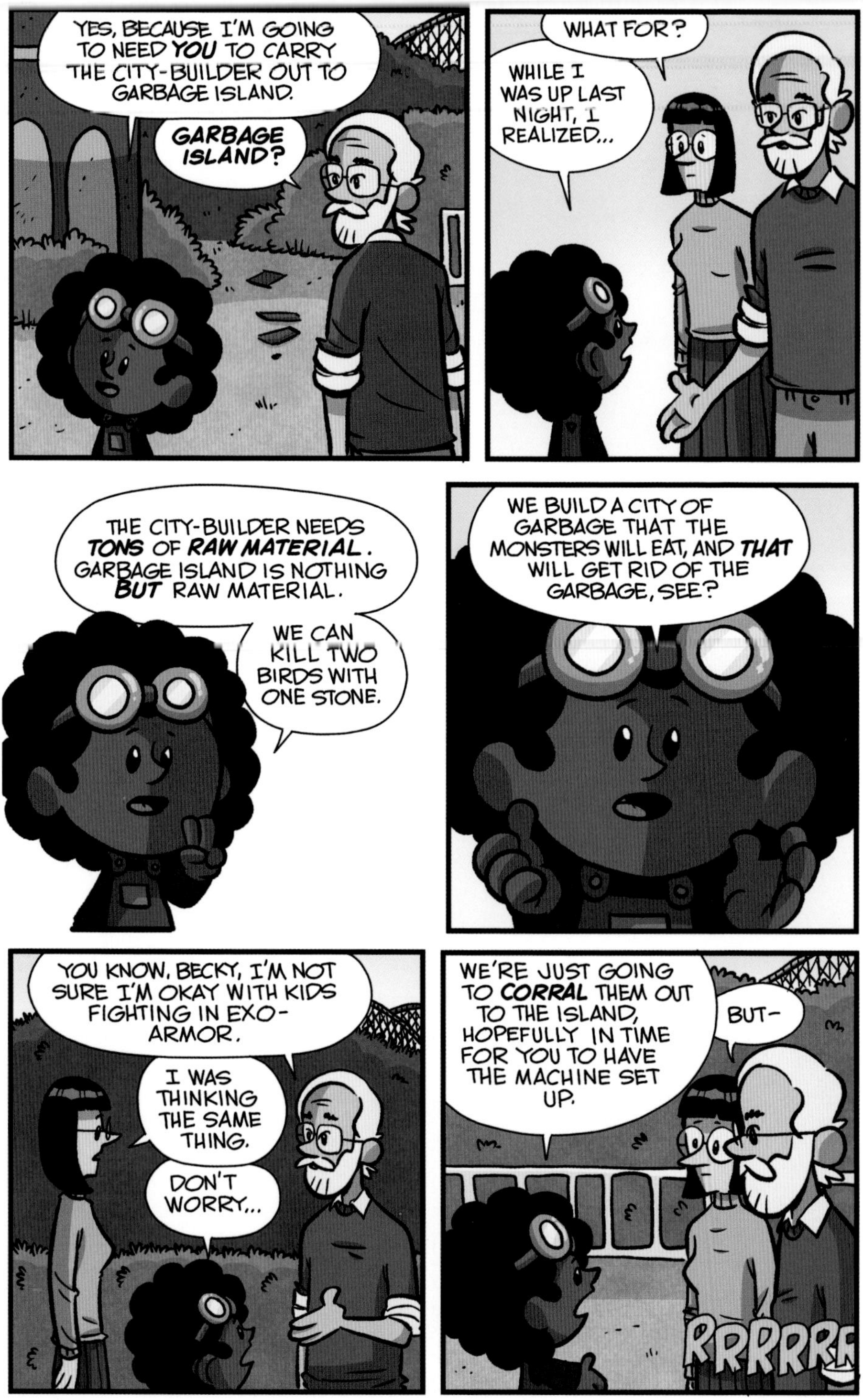
YES, BECAUSE I'M GOING TO NEED YOU TO CARRY THE CITY-BUILDER OUT TO GARBAGE ISLAND.
GARBAGE ISLAND?
WHAT FOR?
WHILE I WAS UP LAST NIGHT, I REALIZED...
THE CITY-BUILDER NEEDS TONS OF RAW MATERIAL. GARBAGE ISLAND IS NOTHING BUT RAW MATERIAL.
WE CAN KILL TWO BIRDS WITH ONE STONE.
WE BUILD A CITY OF GARBAGE THAT THE MONSTERS WILL EAT, AND THAT WILL GET RID OF THE GARBAGE, SEE?
YOU KNOW, BECKY, I'M NOT SURE I'M OKAY WITH KIDS FIGHTING IN EXO-ARMOR.
I WAS THINKING THE SAME THING.
DON'T WORRY...
WE'RE JUST GOING TO CORRAL THEM OUT TO THE ISLAND, HOPEFULLY IN TIME FOR YOU TO HAVE THE MACHINE SET UP.
BUT-
RRRRRR

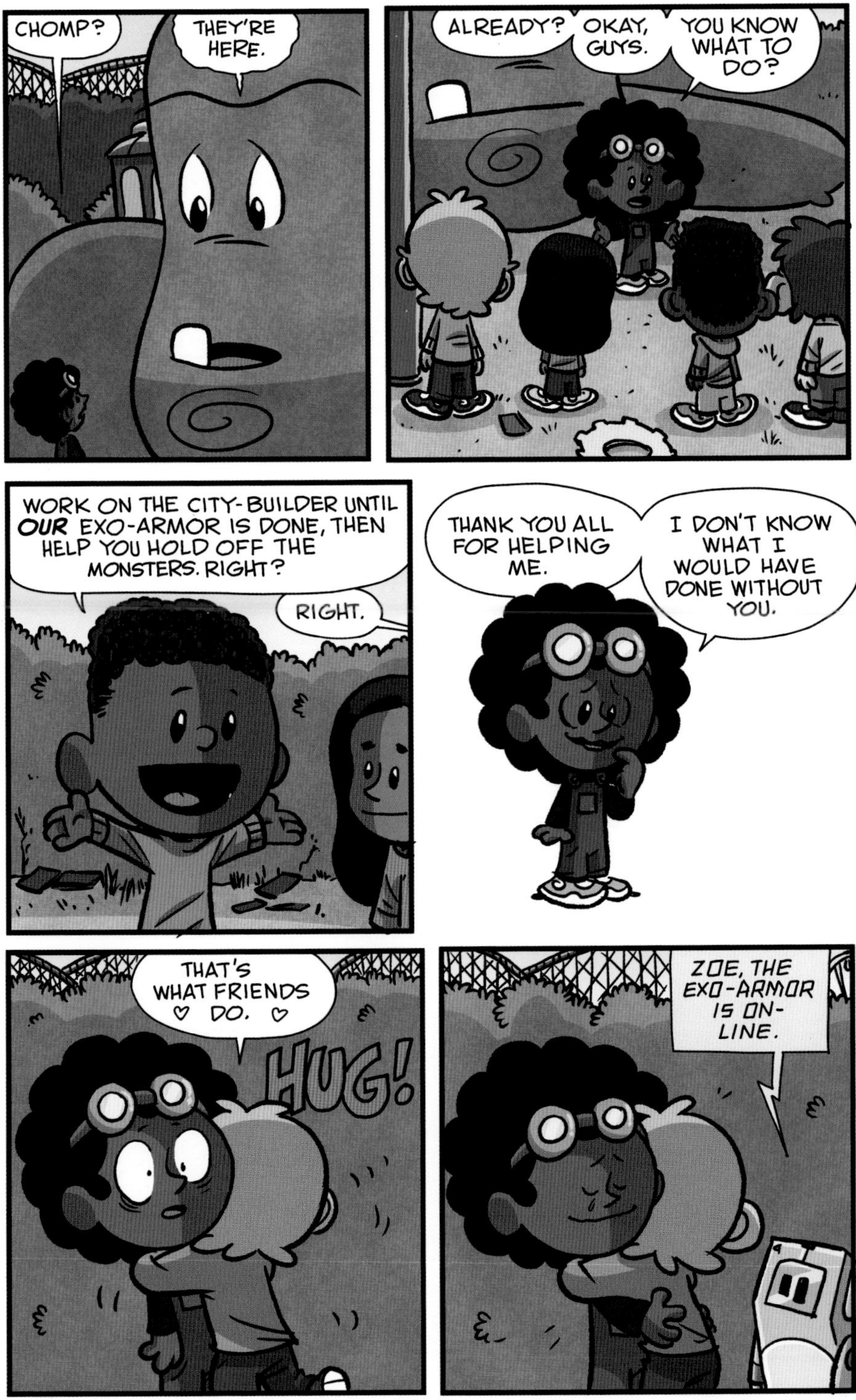
CHOMP?
THEY'RE HERE.
ALREADY?
OKAY, GUYS.
YOU KNOW WHAT TO DO?
WORK ON THE CITY-BUILDER UNTIL OUR EXO-ARMOR IS DONE, THEN HELP YOU HOLD OFF THE MONSTERS. RIGHT?
RIGHT.
THANK YOU ALL FOR HELPING ME.
I DON'T KNOW WHAT I WOULD HAVE DONE WITHOUT YOU.
THAT'S WHAT FRIENDS ♡ DO. ♡
HUG!
ZOE, THE EXO-ARMOR IS ON-LINE.

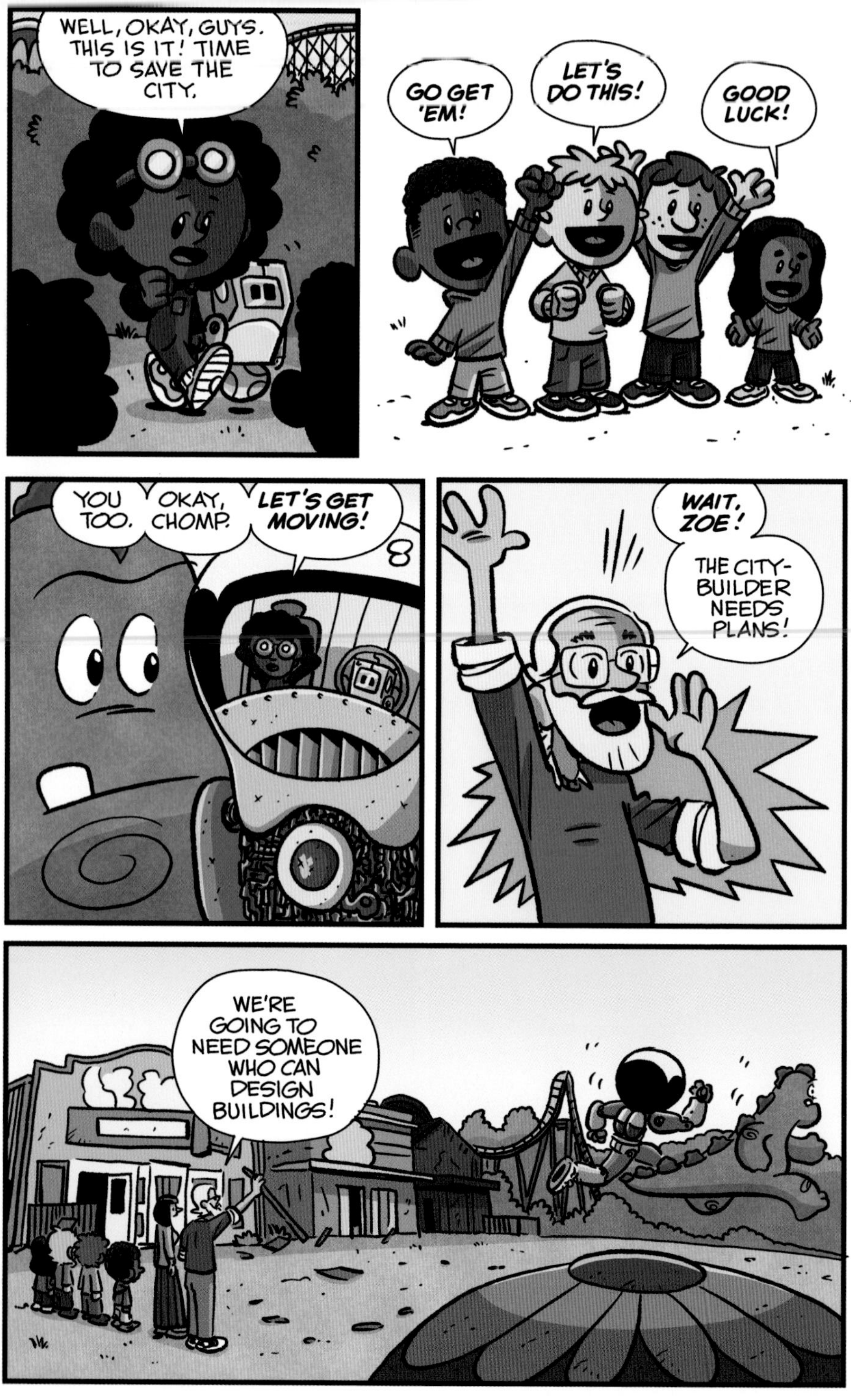
WELL, OKAY, GUYS. THIS IS IT! TIME TO SAVE THE CITY.
GO GET 'EM!
LET'S DO THIS!
GOOD LUCK!
YOU TOO.
OKAY, CHOMP.
LET'S GET MOVING!
WAIT, ZOE!
THE CITY-BUILDER NEEDS PLANS!
WE'RE GOING TO NEED SOMEONE WHO CAN DESIGN BUILDINGS!

CHAPTER 14 - BATTLEFRONT

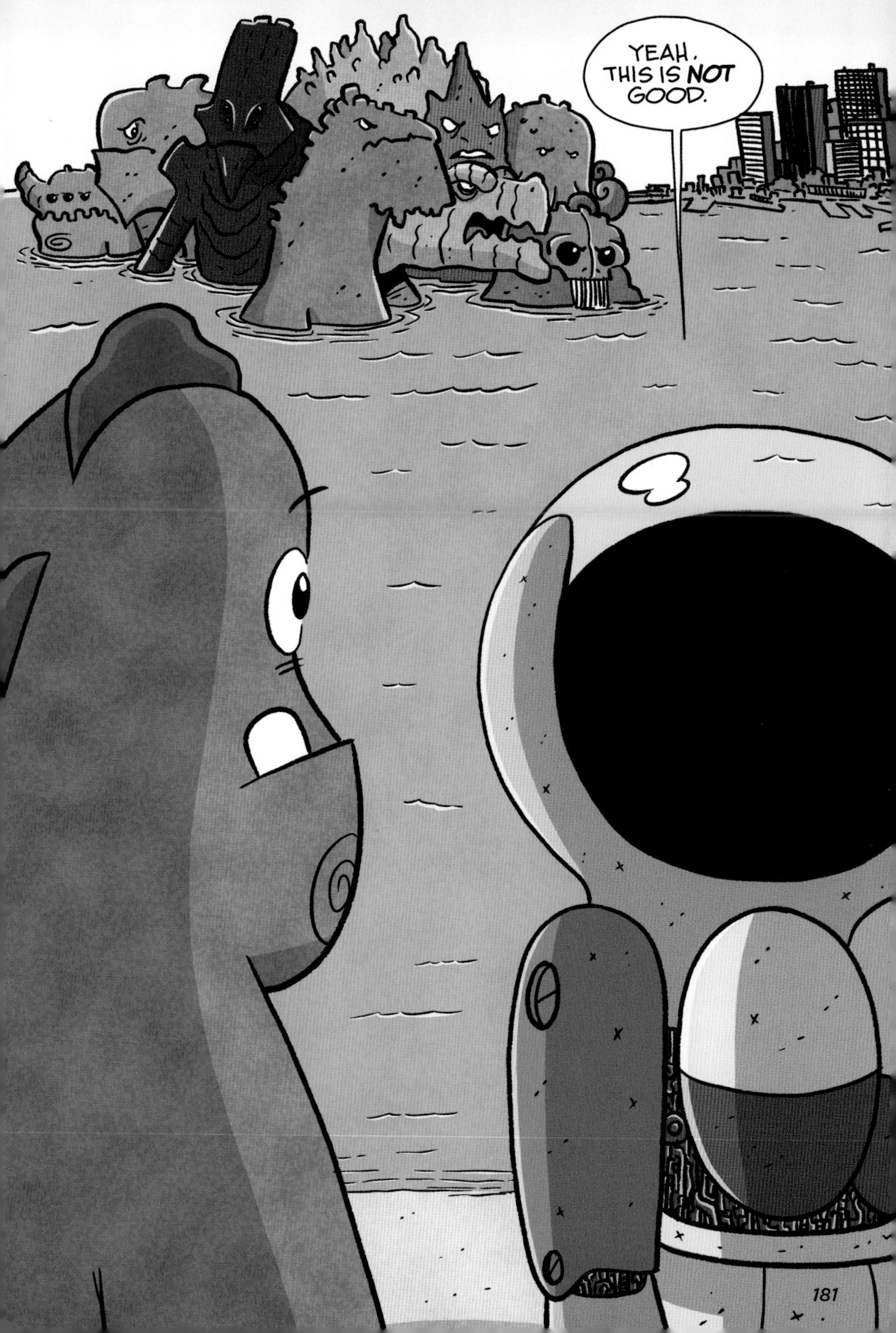
YEAH. THIS IS **NOT** GOOD.

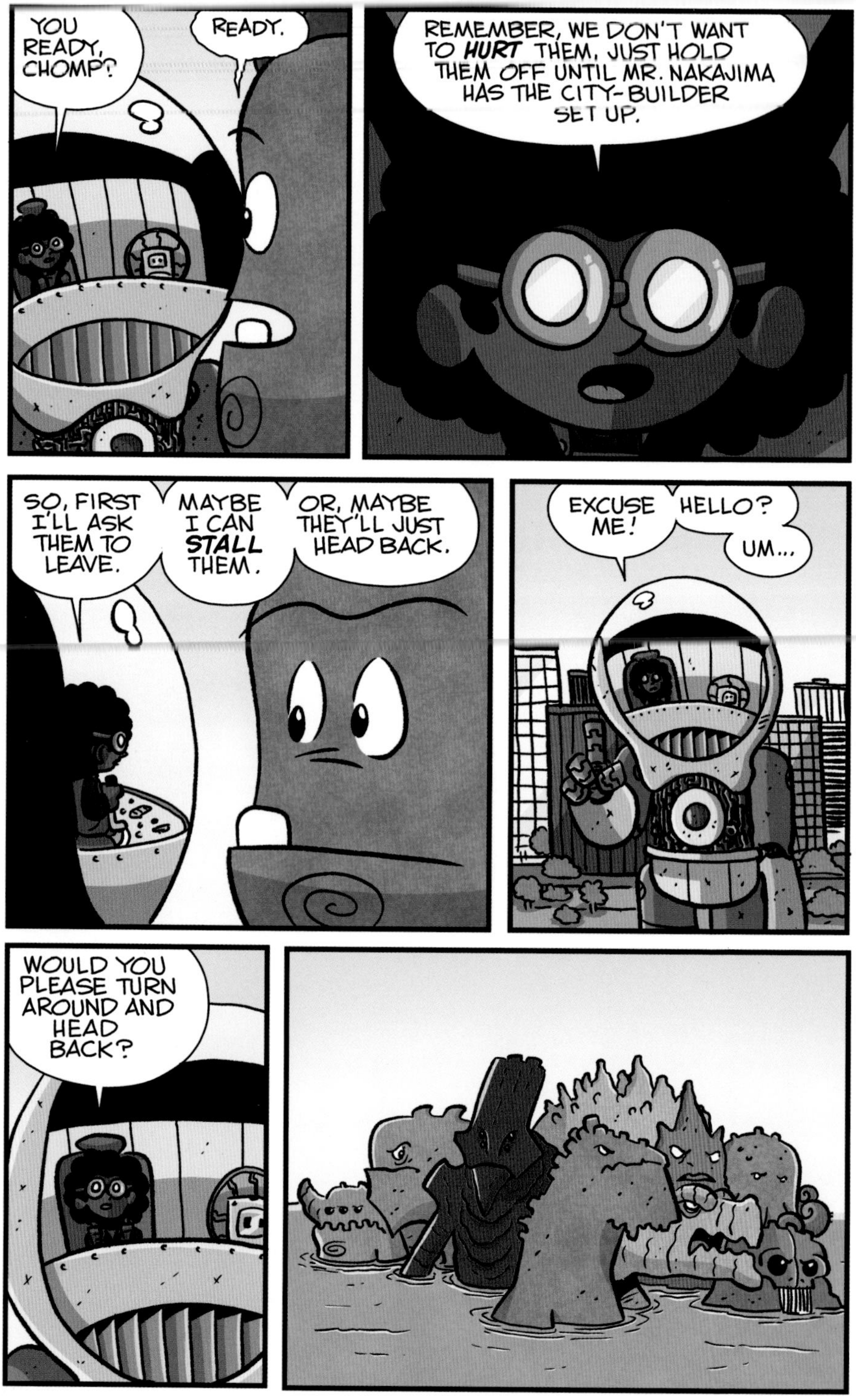
YOU READY, CHOMP?
READY.
REMEMBER, WE DON'T WANT TO HURT THEM, JUST HOLD THEM OFF UNTIL MR. NAKAJIMA HAS THE CITY-BUILDER SET UP.
SO, FIRST I'LL ASK THEM TO LEAVE.
MAYBE I CAN STALL THEM.
OR, MAYBE THEY'LL JUST HEAD BACK.
EXCUSE ME!
HELLO?
UM...
WOULD YOU PLEASE TURN AROUND AND HEAD BACK?

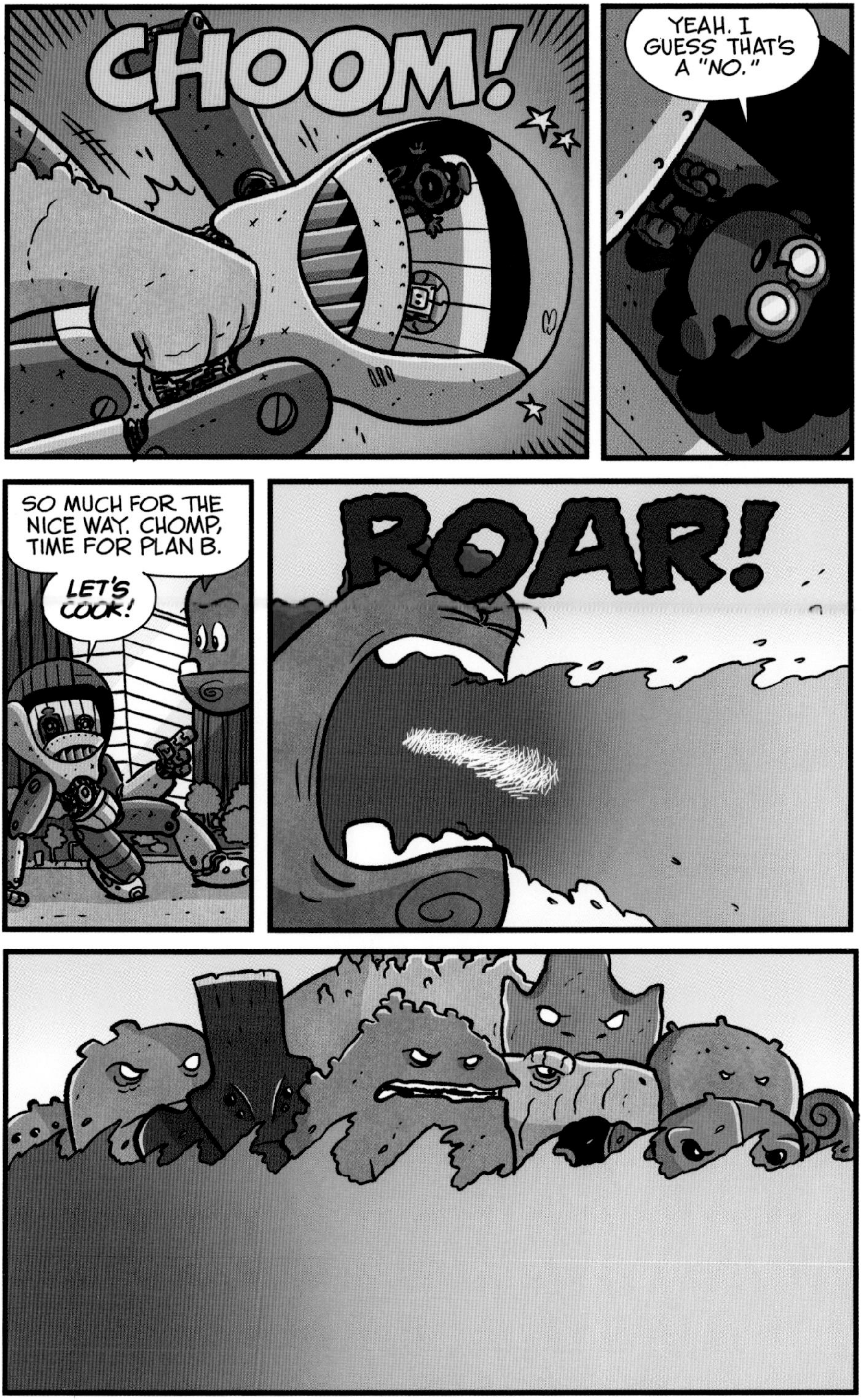
CHOOM!
YEAH. I GUESS THAT'S A "NO."
SO MUCH FOR THE NICE WAY. CHOMP, TIME FOR PLAN B.
LET'S COOK!
ROAR!

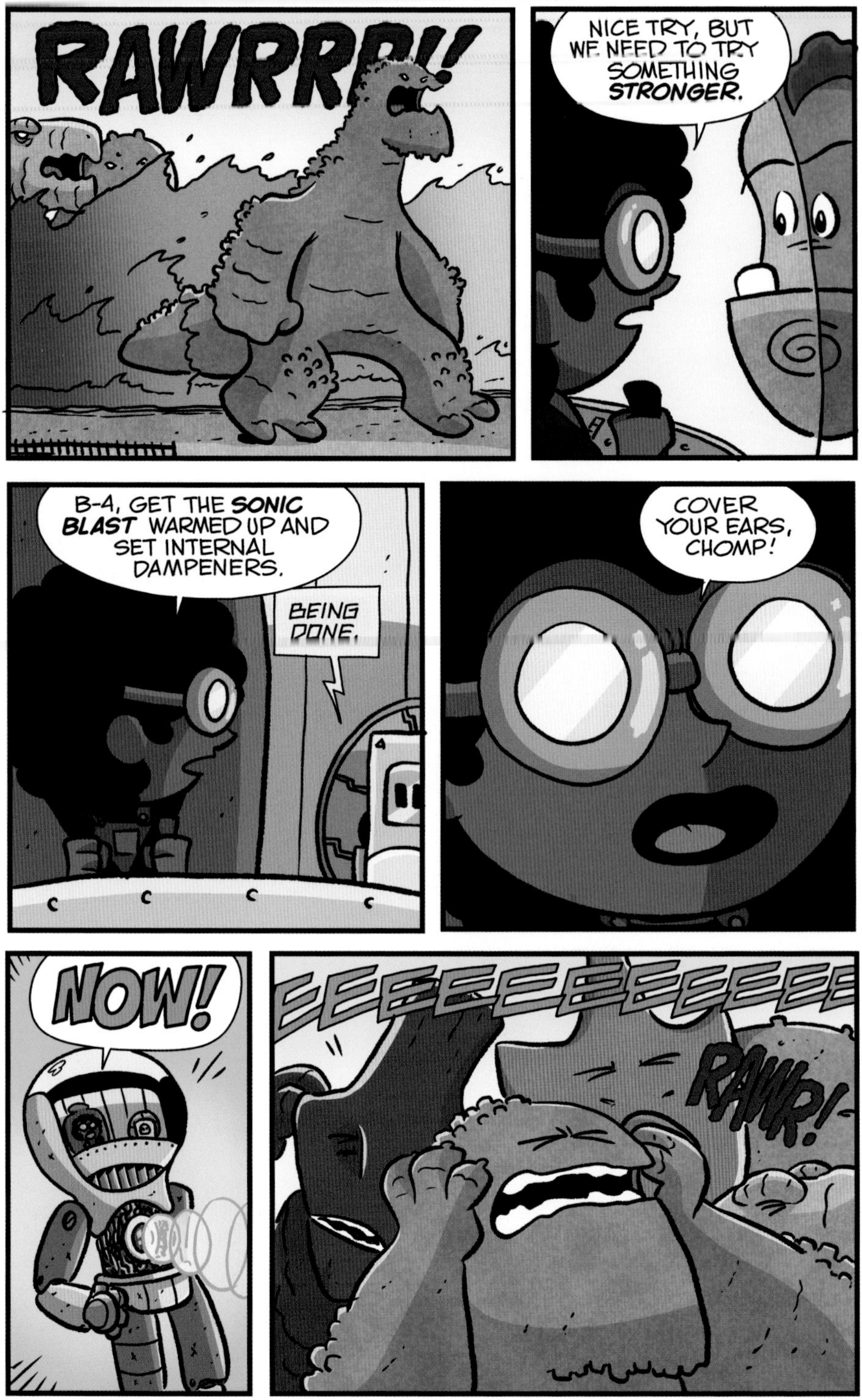
RAWRRR!!
NICE TRY, BUT WE NEED TO TRY SOMETHING STRONGER.
B-4, GET THE SONIC BLAST WARMED UP AND SET INTERNAL DAMPENERS.
BEING DONE.
COVER YOUR EARS, CHOMP!
NOW!
EEEEEEEEEEEEEE
RAWR!

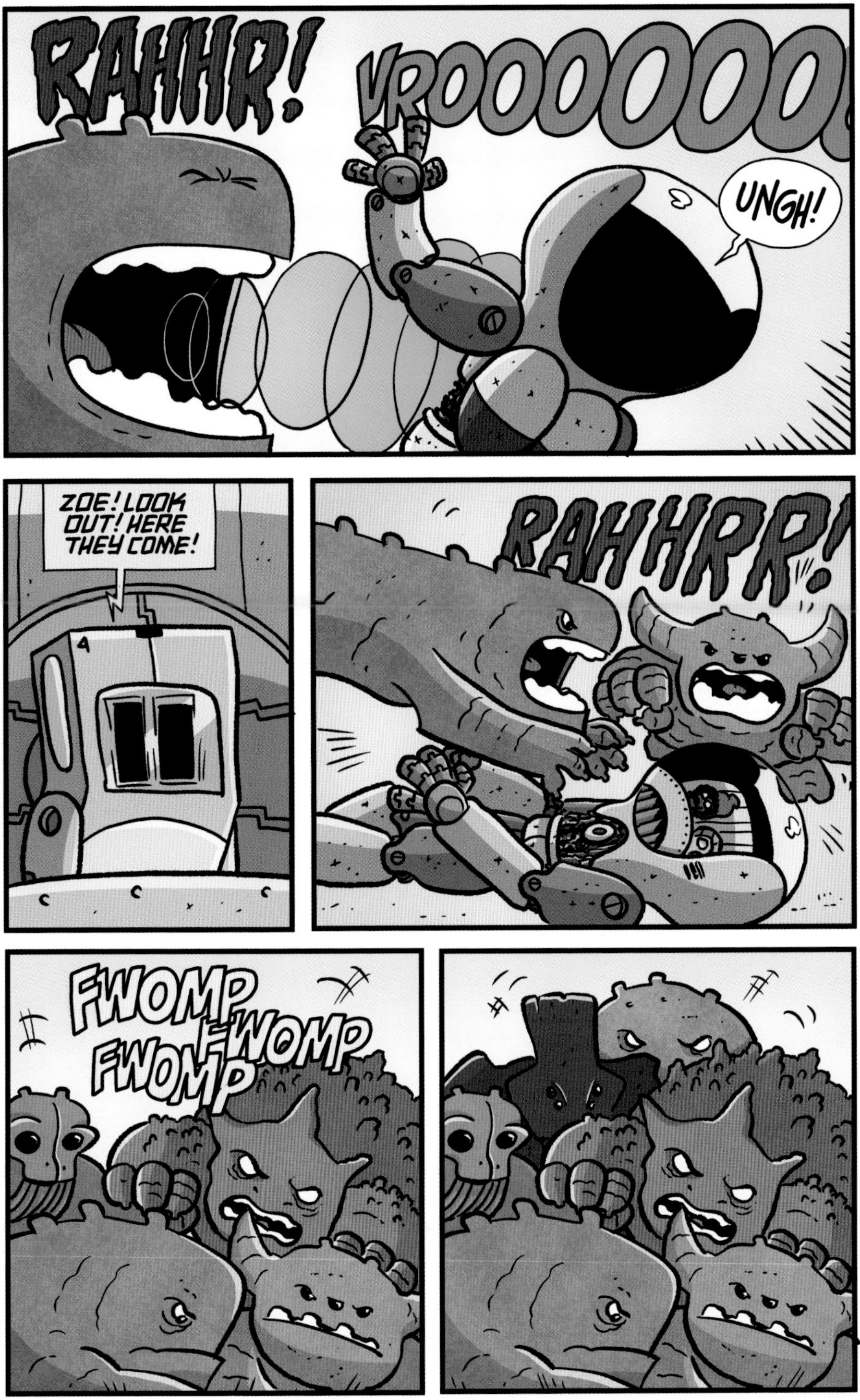
RAHHR!
VROOOOOOO
UNGH!
ZOE! LOOK OUT! HERE THEY COME!
RAHHRR!
FWOMP
FWOMP
FWOMP

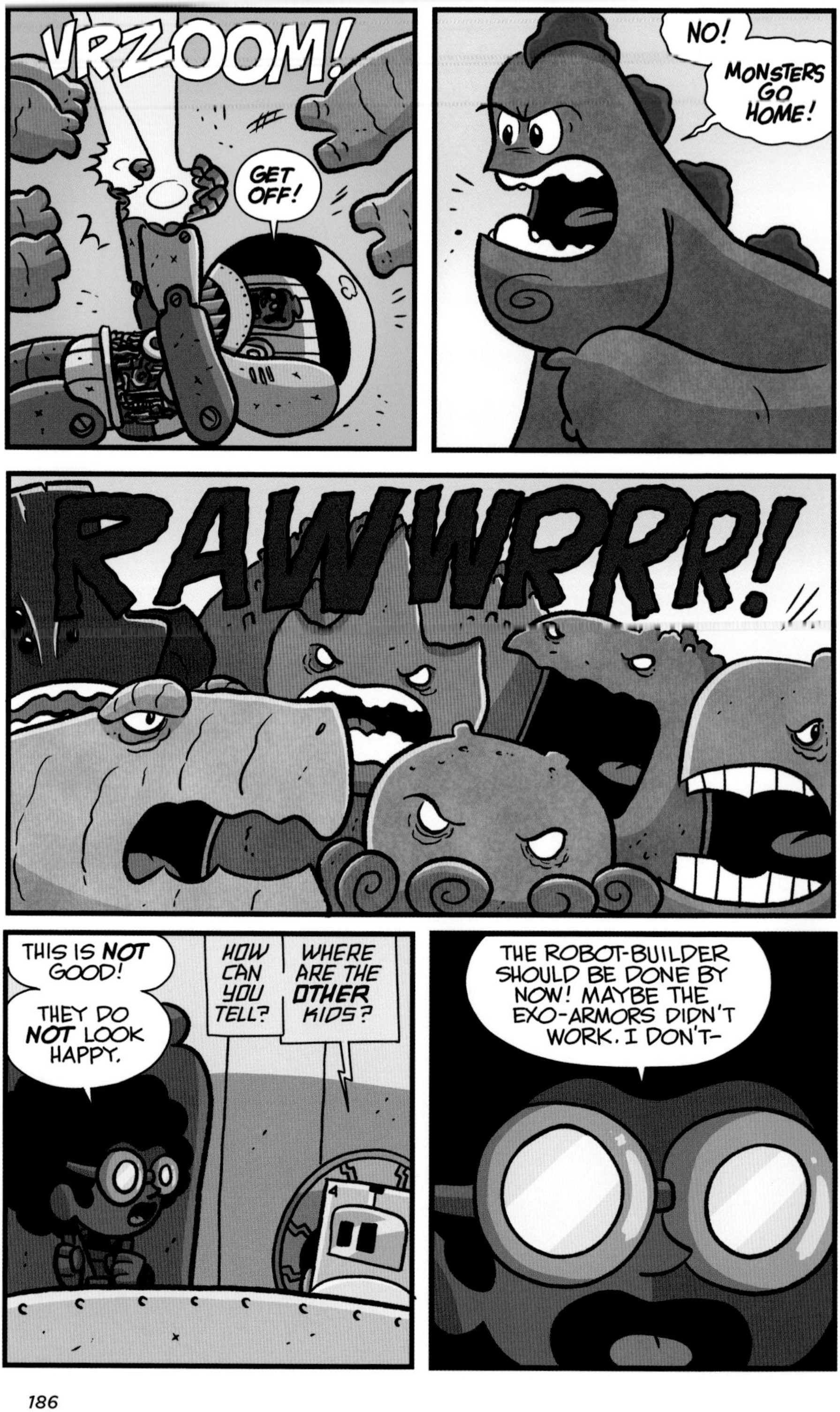

VRZOOM!
GET OFF!
NO!
MONSTERS GO HOME!
RAWWRRR!
THIS IS **NOT** GOOD!
THEY DO **NOT** LOOK HAPPY.
HOW CAN YOU TELL?
WHERE ARE THE **OTHER** KIDS?
THE ROBOT-BUILDER SHOULD BE DONE BY NOW! MAYBE THE EXO-ARMORS DIDN'T WORK. I DON'T-

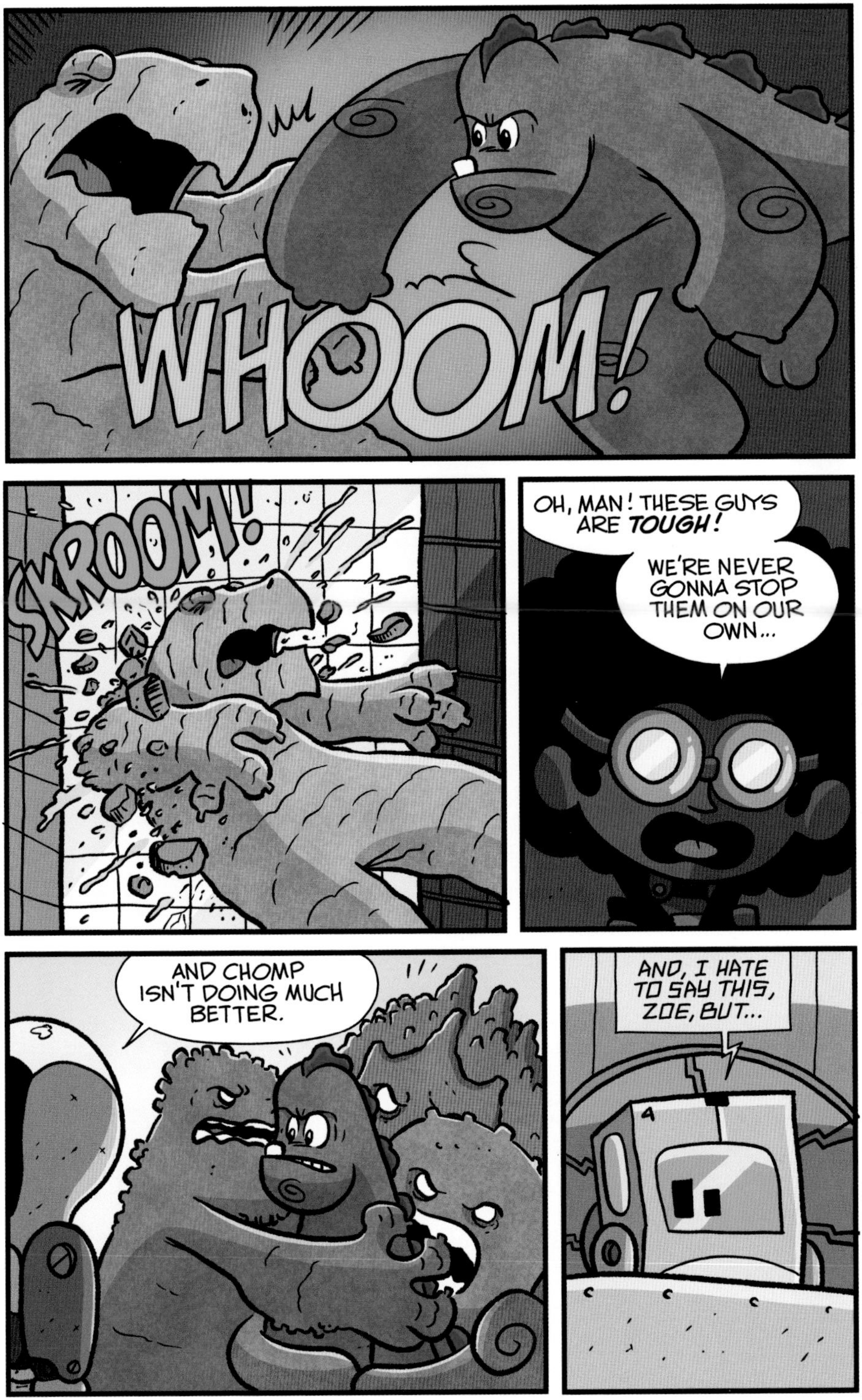
WHOOM!
SKROOM!
OH, MAN! THESE GUYS ARE TOUGH!
WE'RE NEVER GONNA STOP THEM ON OUR OWN...
AND CHOMP ISN'T DOING MUCH BETTER.
AND, I HATE TO SAY THIS, ZOE, BUT...

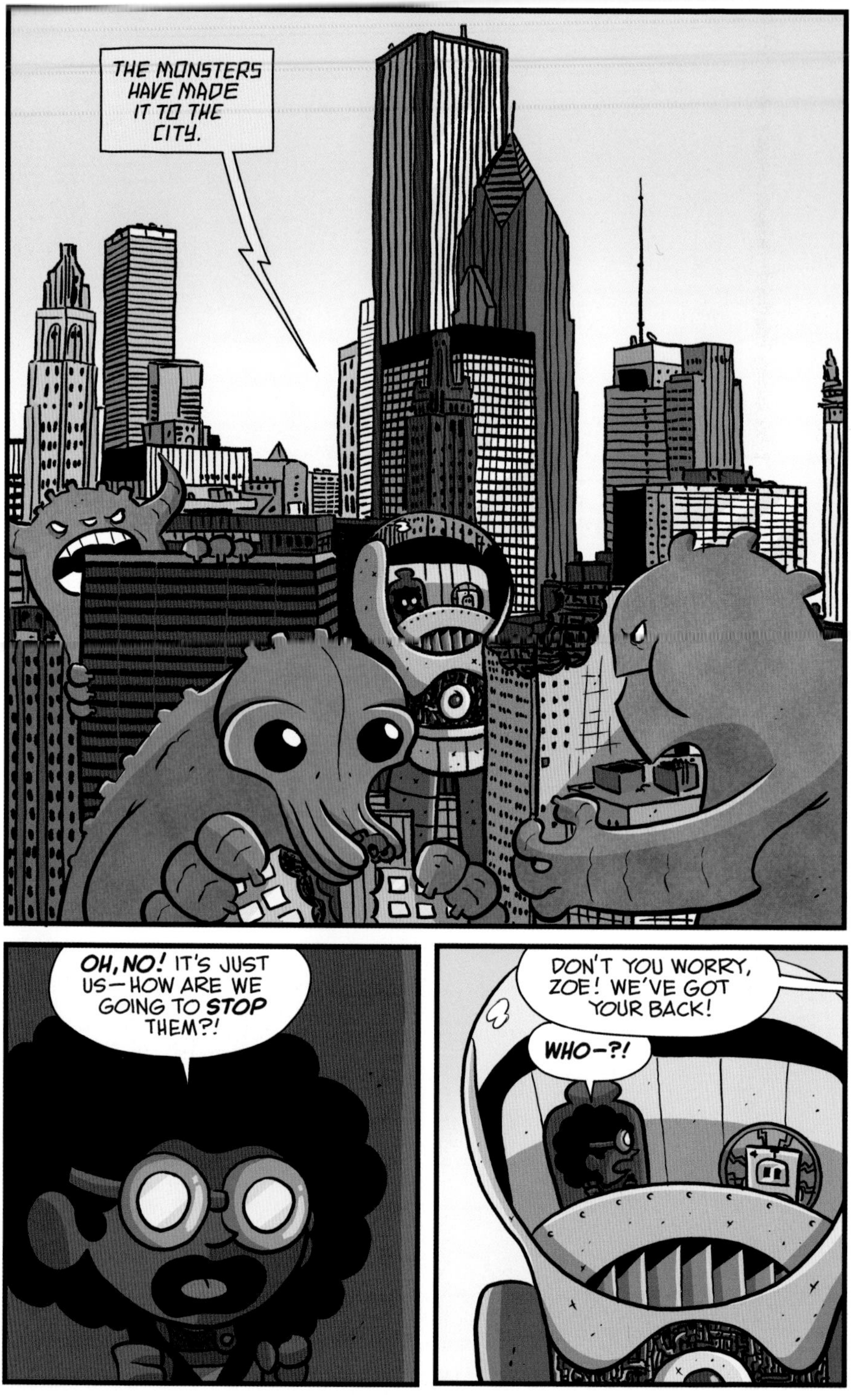
THE MONSTERS HAVE MADE IT TO THE CITY.
OH, NO! IT'S JUST US—HOW ARE WE GOING TO STOP THEM?!
DON'T YOU WORRY, ZOE! WE'VE GOT YOUR BACK!
WHO-?!

PUNCH! THANKS FOR THE COOL ARMOR!

WHOMP! IT WORKS LIKE A CHARM!

FWOOM! IT WAS SO NICE OF YOU TO MAKE THESE FOR US, ZOE!

NO PROB.

BUT, GUYS... DON'T *HURT* THE MONSTERS!

IN THE MOVIES, THAT ONLY MAKES THEM *ANGRIER!*

THEN HOW DO WE STOP THEM?

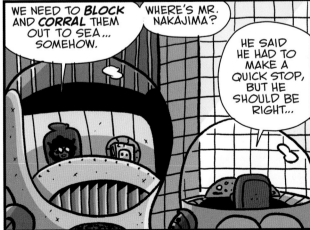

WE NEED TO *BLOCK* AND *CORRAL* THEM OUT TO SEA... SOMEHOW.

WHERE'S MR. NAKAJIMA?

HE SAID HE HAD TO MAKE A QUICK STOP, BUT HE SHOULD BE RIGHT...

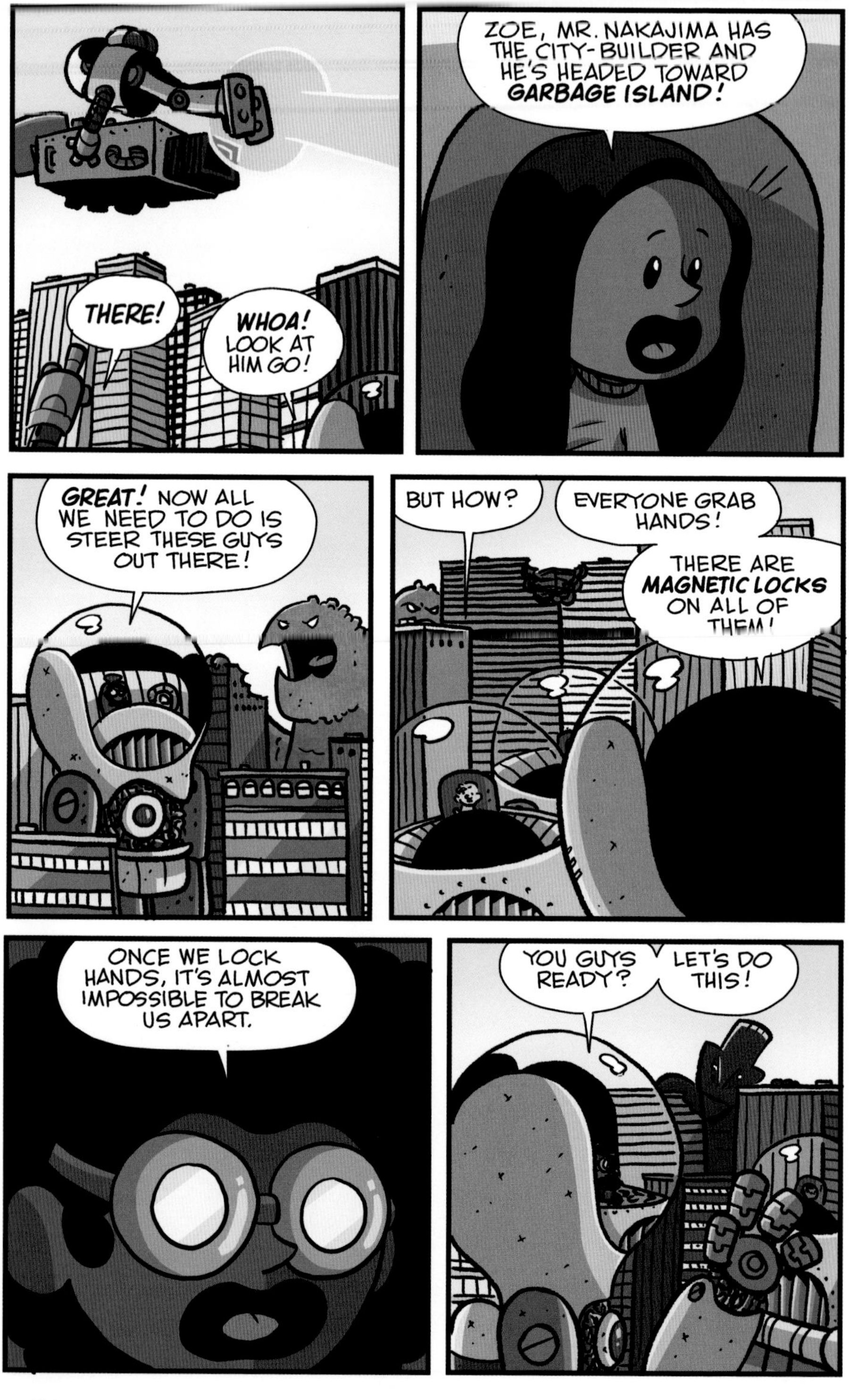
THERE!
WHOA! LOOK AT HIM GO!
ZOE, MR. NAKAJIMA HAS THE CITY-BUILDER AND HE'S HEADED TOWARD GARBAGE ISLAND!
GREAT! NOW ALL WE NEED TO DO IS STEER THESE GUYS OUT THERE!
BUT HOW?
EVERYONE GRAB HANDS!
THERE ARE MAGNETIC LOCKS ON ALL OF THEM!
ONCE WE LOCK HANDS, IT'S ALMOST IMPOSSIBLE TO BREAK US APART.
YOU GUYS READY?
LET'S DO THIS!

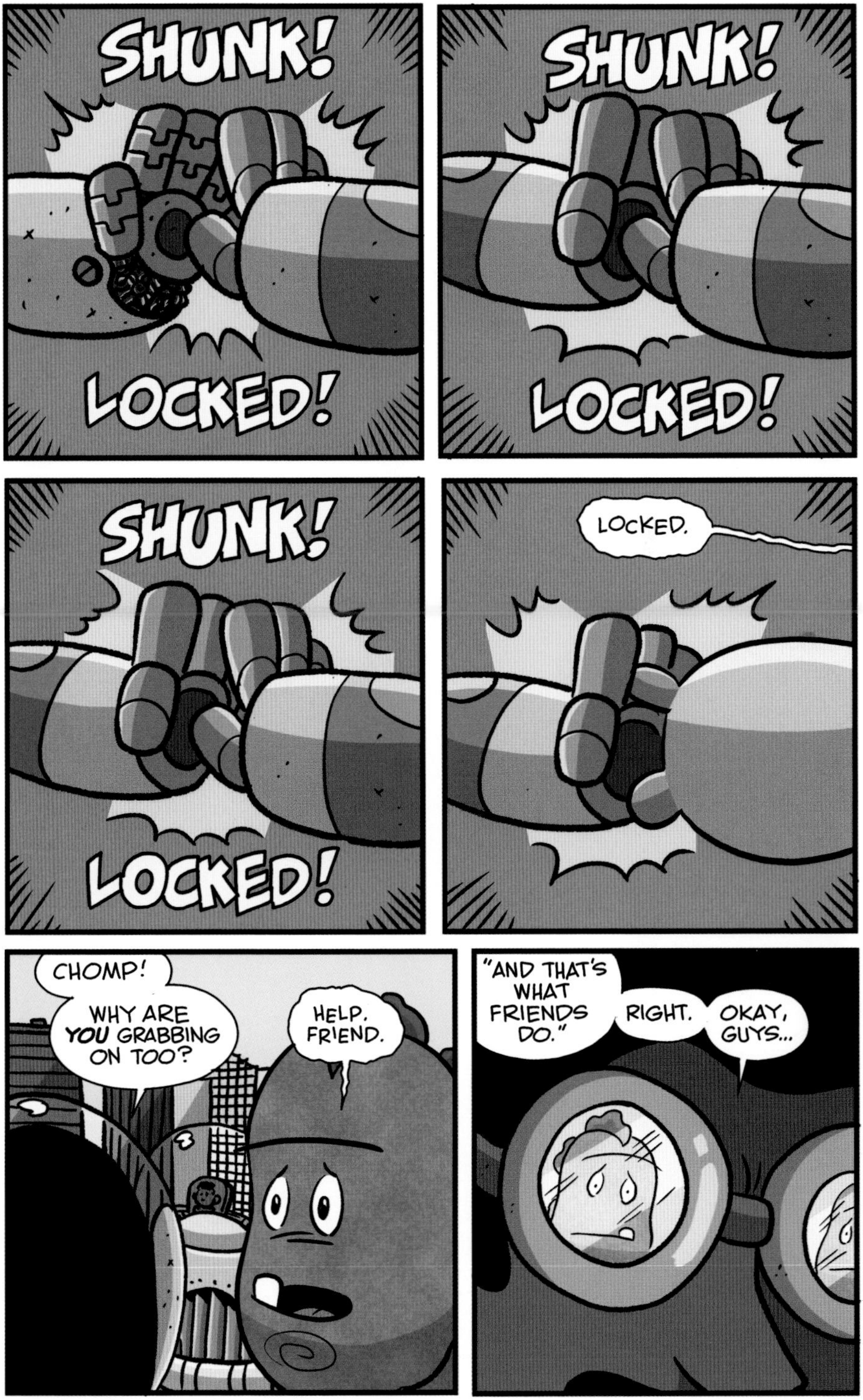
SHUNK!
LOCKED!
SHUNK!
LOCKED!
SHUNK!
LOCKED!
LOCKED.
CHOMP!
WHY ARE YOU GRABBING ON TOO?
HELP, FRIEND.
"AND THAT'S WHAT FRIENDS DO."
RIGHT.
OKAY, GUYS...

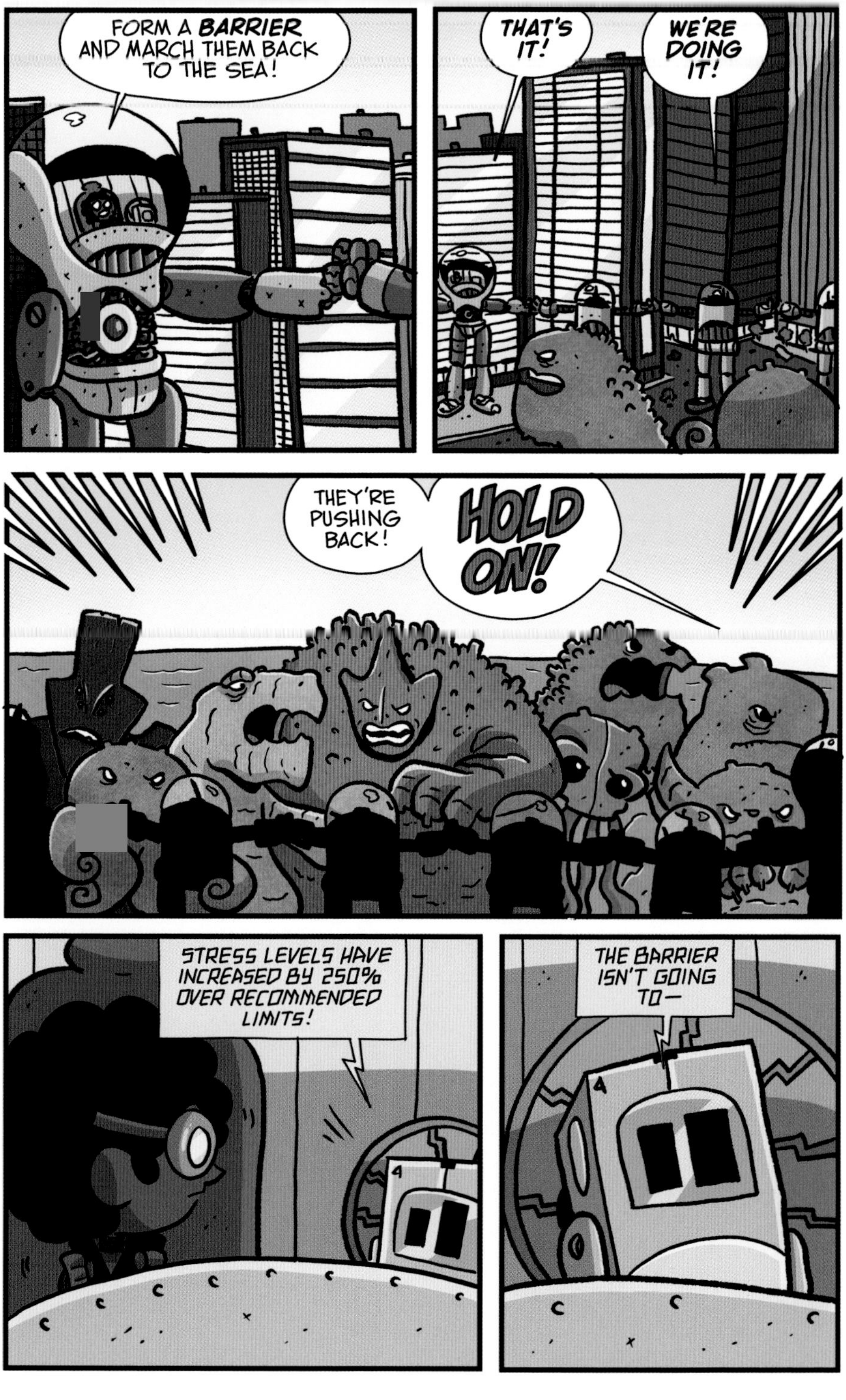
FORM A BARRIER AND MARCH THEM BACK TO THE SEA!
THAT'S IT!
WE'RE DOING IT!
THEY'RE PUSHING BACK!
HOLD ON!
STRESS LEVELS HAVE INCREASED BY 250% OVER RECOMMENDED LIMITS!
THE BARRIER ISN'T GOING TO—

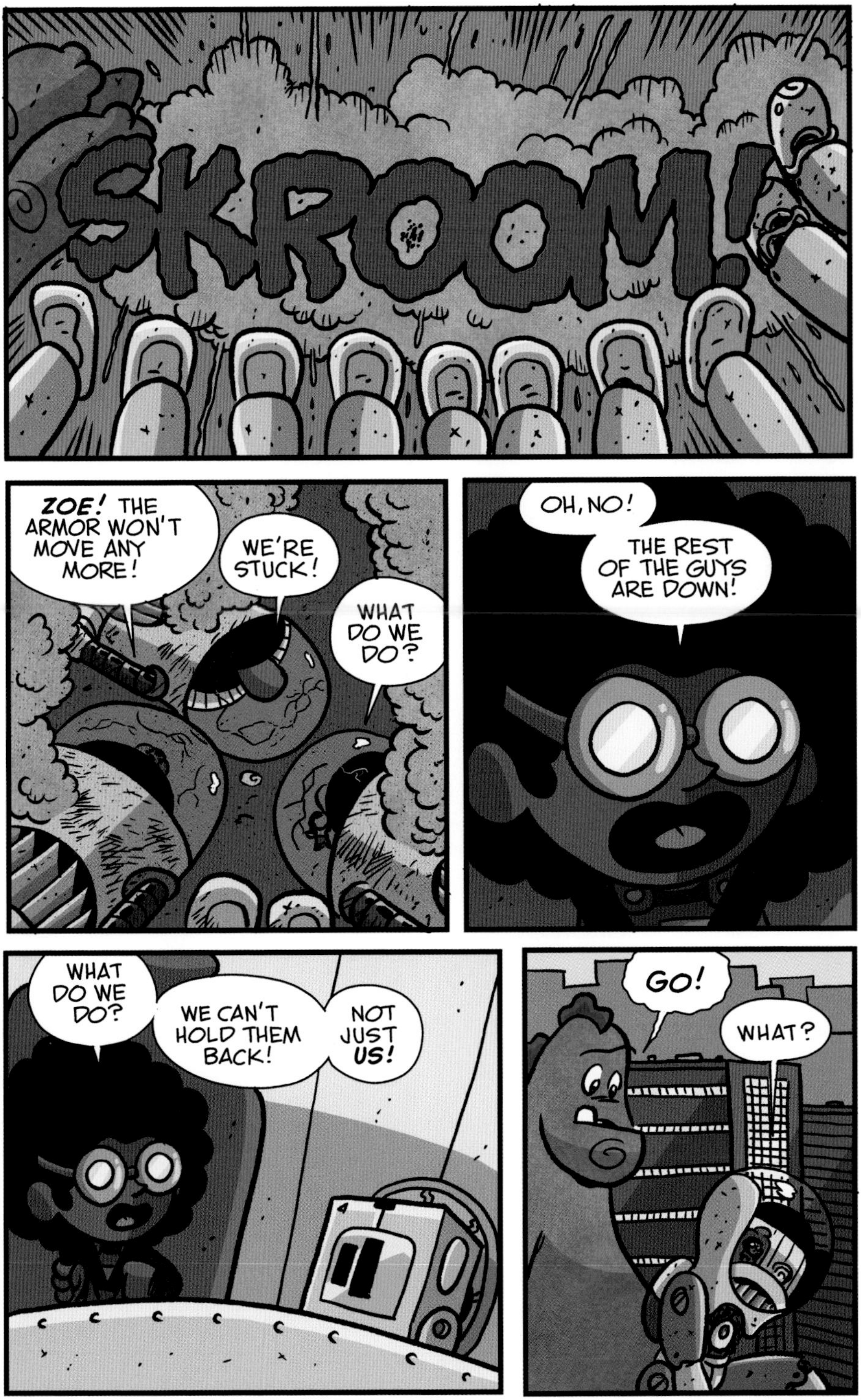
SKROOM!
ZOE! THE ARMOR WON'T MOVE ANY MORE!
WE'RE STUCK!
WHAT DO WE DO?
OH, NO!
THE REST OF THE GUYS ARE DOWN!
WHAT DO WE DO?
WE CAN'T HOLD THEM BACK!
NOT JUST US!
GO!
WHAT?

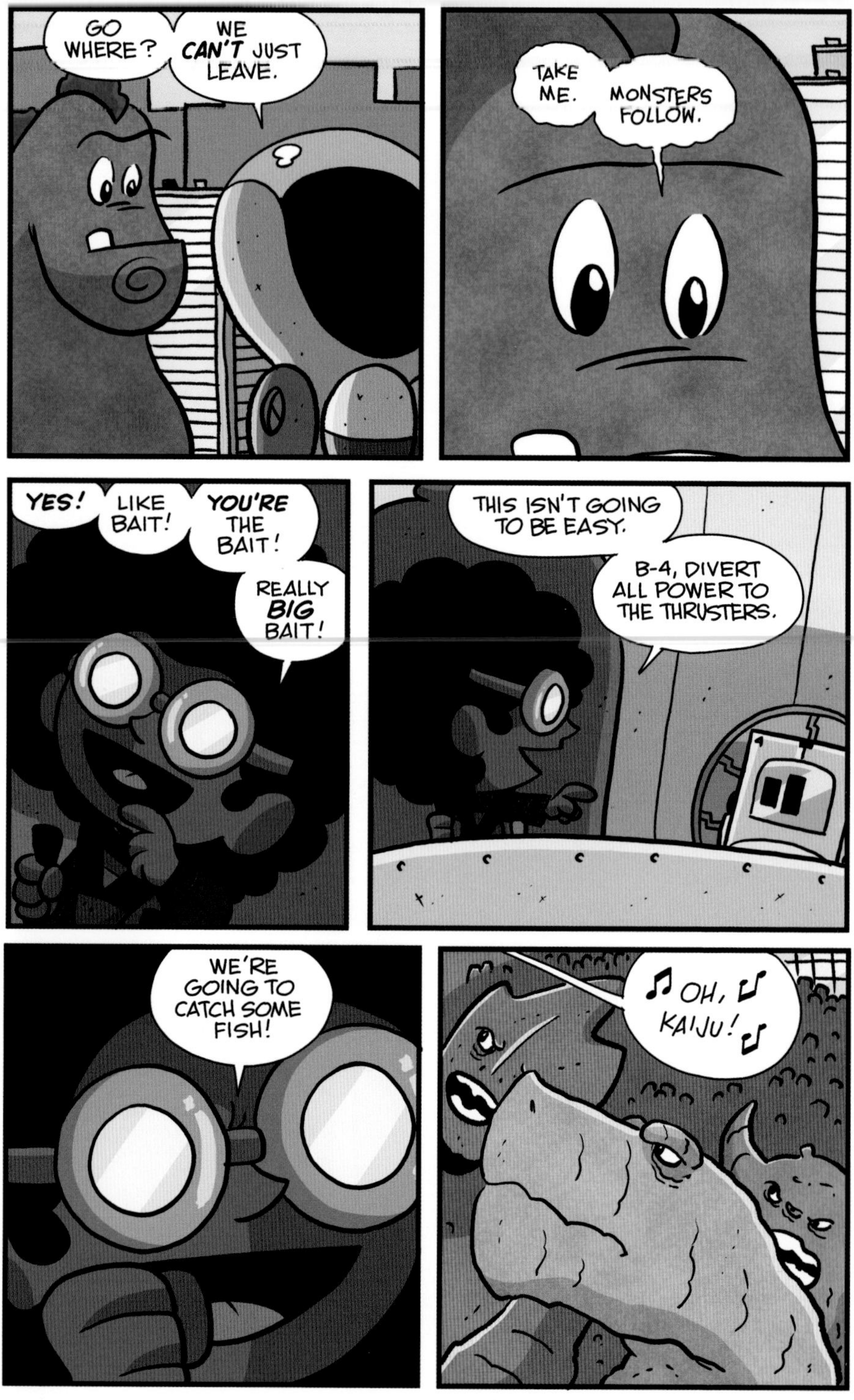
GO WHERE?
WE CAN'T JUST LEAVE.
TAKE ME.
MONSTERS FOLLOW.
YES!
LIKE BAIT!
YOU'RE THE BAIT!
REALLY BIG BAIT!
THIS ISN'T GOING TO BE EASY.
B-4, DIVERT ALL POWER TO THE THRUSTERS.
WE'RE GOING TO CATCH SOME FISH!
♫ OH, KAIJU! ♫

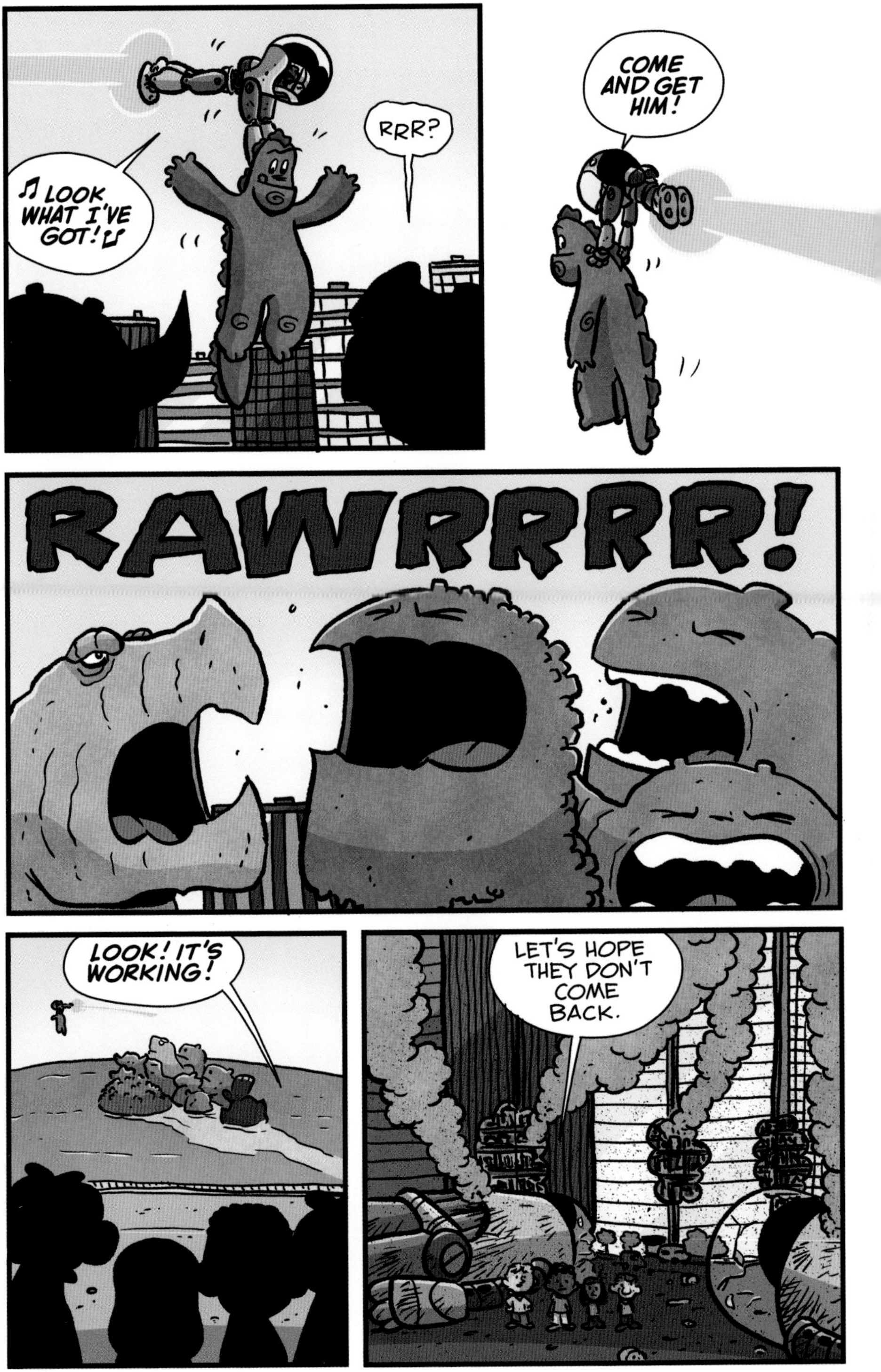
RRR?
♫ LOOK WHAT I'VE GOT! ♫
COME AND GET HIM!
RAWRRRR!
LOOK! IT'S WORKING!
LET'S HOPE THEY DON'T COME BACK.

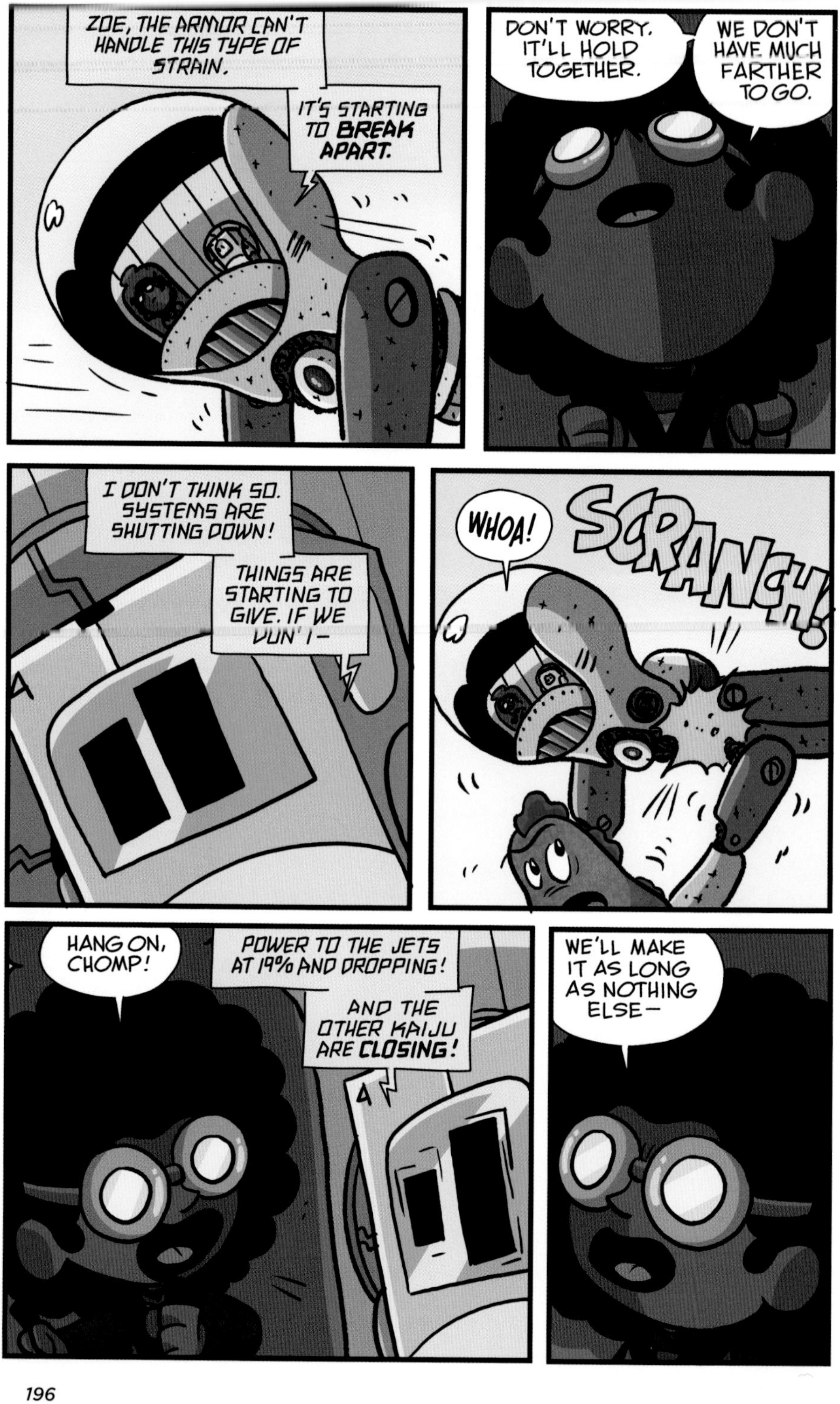
ZOE, THE ARMOR CAN'T HANDLE THIS TYPE OF STRAIN.
IT'S STARTING TO BREAK APART.
DON'T WORRY. IT'LL HOLD TOGETHER.
WE DON'T HAVE MUCH FARTHER TO GO.
I DON'T THINK SO. SYSTEMS ARE SHUTTING DOWN!
THINGS ARE STARTING TO GIVE. IF WE DON'T—
WHOA!
SCRANCH!
HANG ON, CHOMP!
POWER TO THE JETS AT 19% AND DROPPING!
AND THE OTHER KAIJU ARE CLOSING!
WE'LL MAKE IT AS LONG AS NOTHING ELSE—

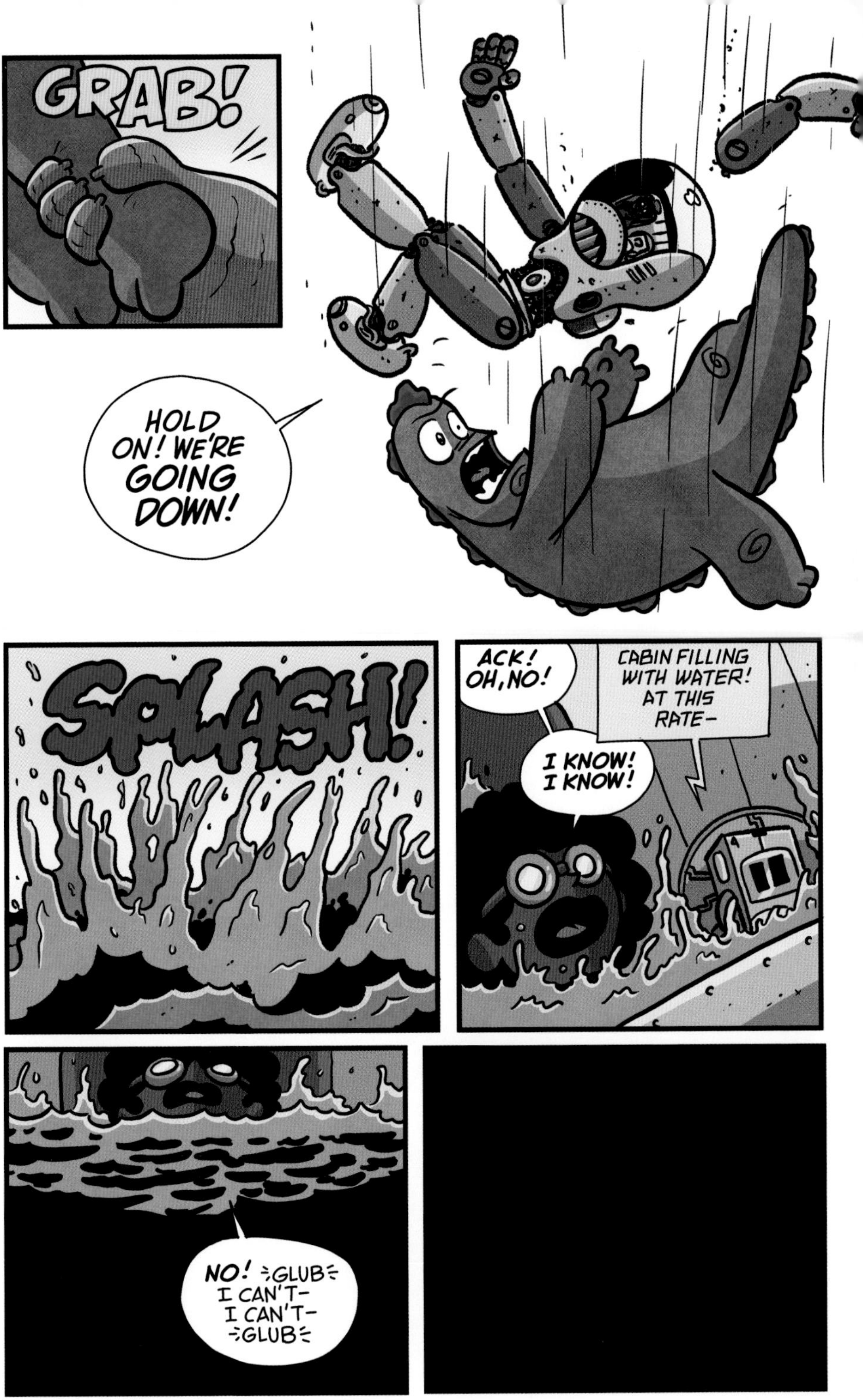
GRAB!
HOLD ON! WE'RE GOING DOWN!
SPLASH!
ACK! OH, NO!
CABIN FILLING WITH WATER! AT THIS RATE—
I KNOW! I KNOW!
NO! ⁼GLUB⁼ I CAN'T— I CAN'T— ⁼GLUB⁼

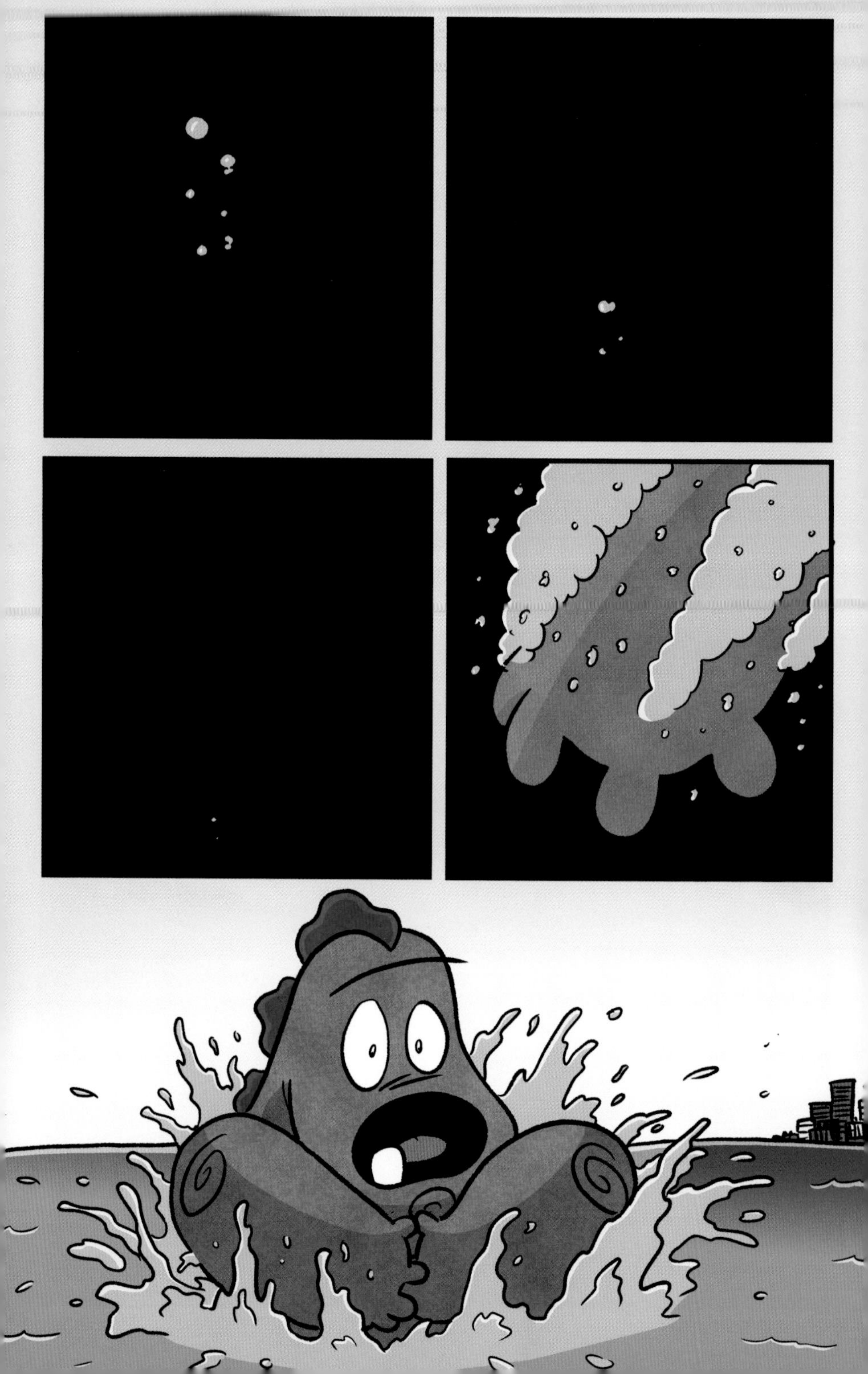

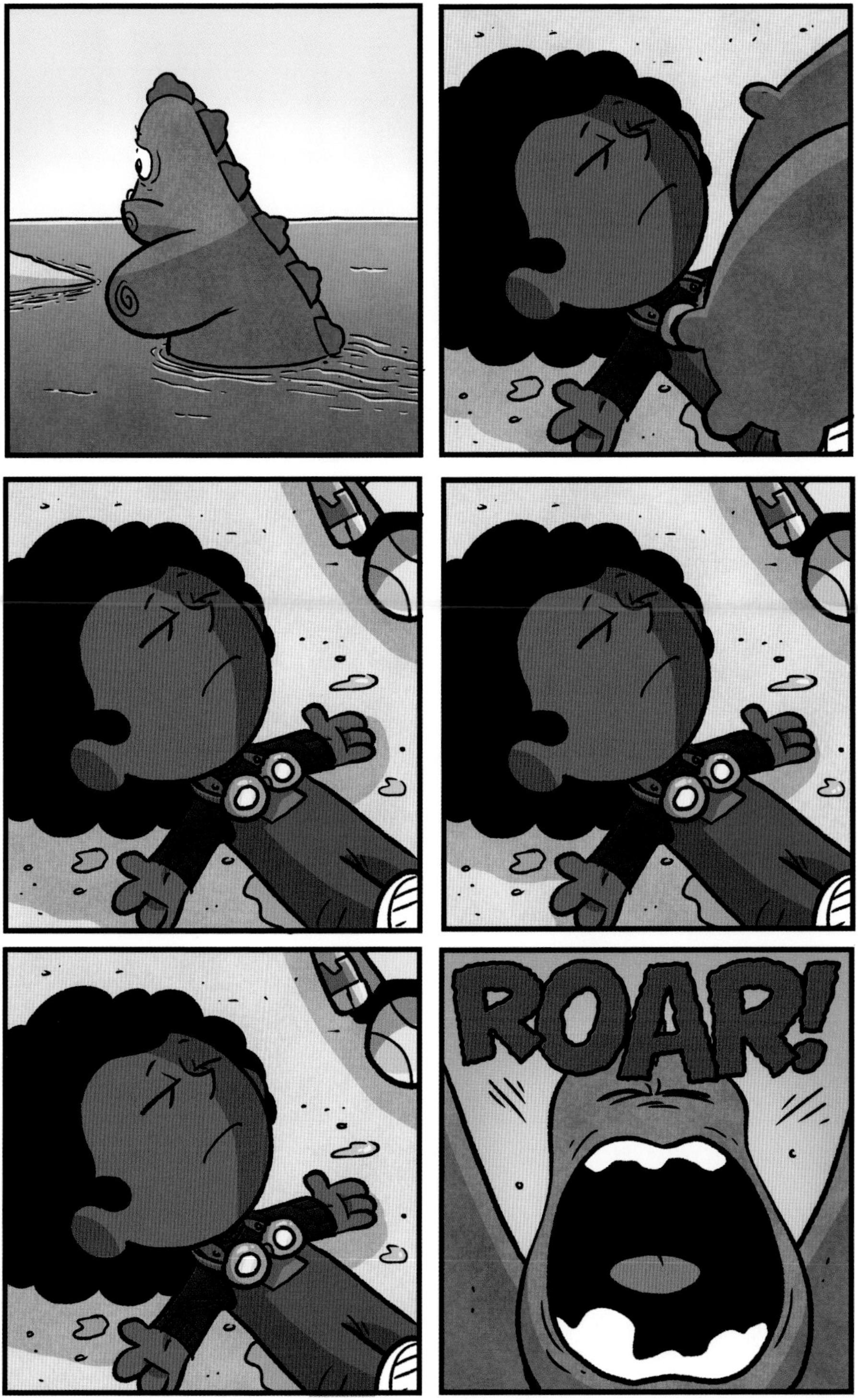
ROAR!

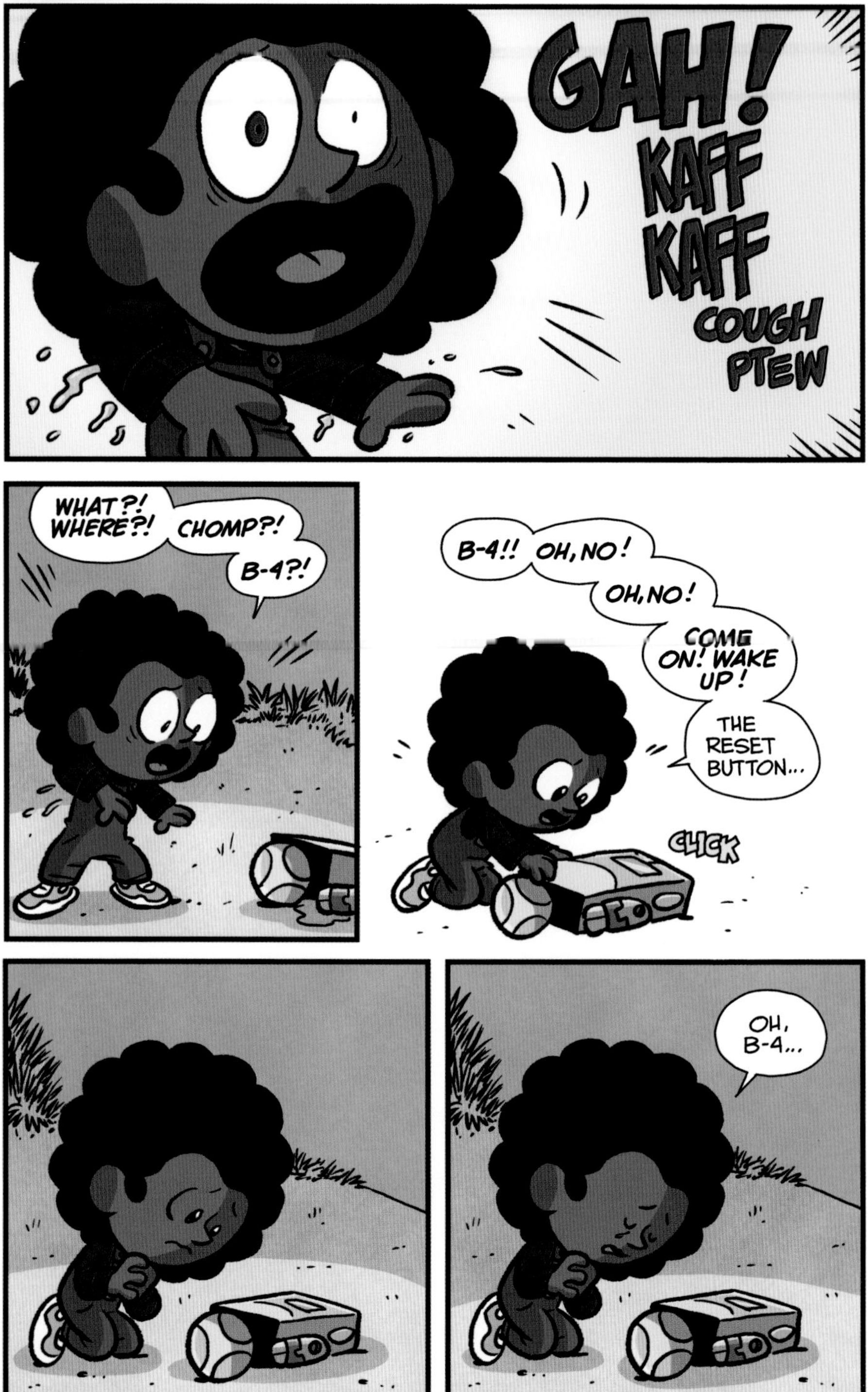
GAH!
KAFF
KAFF
COUGH
PTEW
WHAT?! WHERE?!
CHOMP?!
B-4?!
B-4!!
OH, NO!
OH, NO!
COME ON! WAKE UP!
THE RESET BUTTON...
CLICK
OH, B-4...

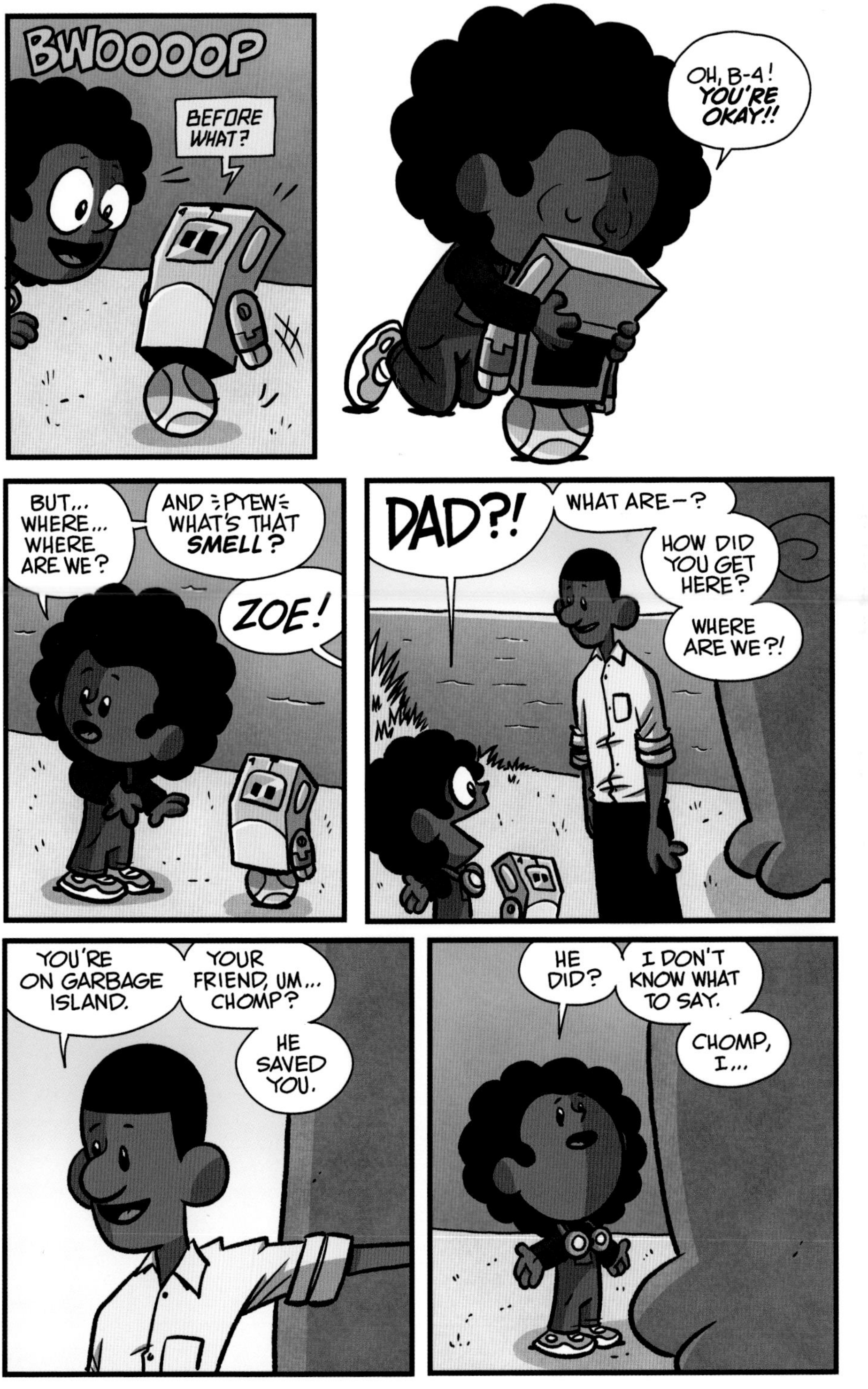

BWOOOOP
BEFORE WHAT?
OH, B-4! YOU'RE OKAY!!
BUT... WHERE... WHERE ARE WE?
AND PYEW WHAT'S THAT SMELL?
ZOE!
DAD?!
WHAT ARE—?
HOW DID YOU GET HERE?
WHERE ARE WE?!
YOU'RE ON GARBAGE ISLAND.
YOUR FRIEND, UM... CHOMP?
HE SAVED YOU.
HE DID?
I DON'T KNOW WHAT TO SAY.
CHOMP, I...

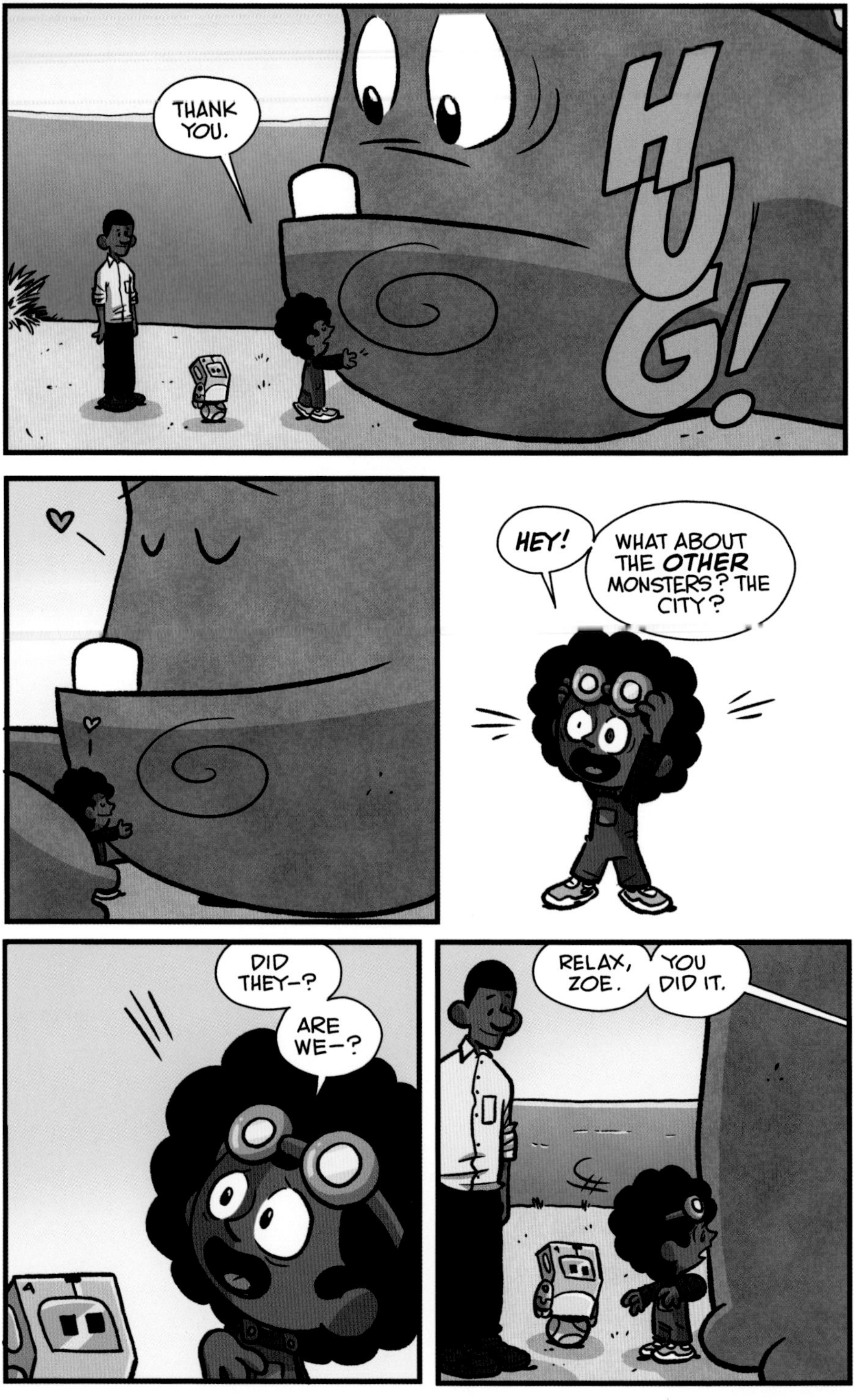

THANK YOU.
HUG!
HEY!
WHAT ABOUT THE OTHER MONSTERS? THE CITY?
DID THEY-?
ARE WE-?
RELAX, ZOE.
YOU DID IT.

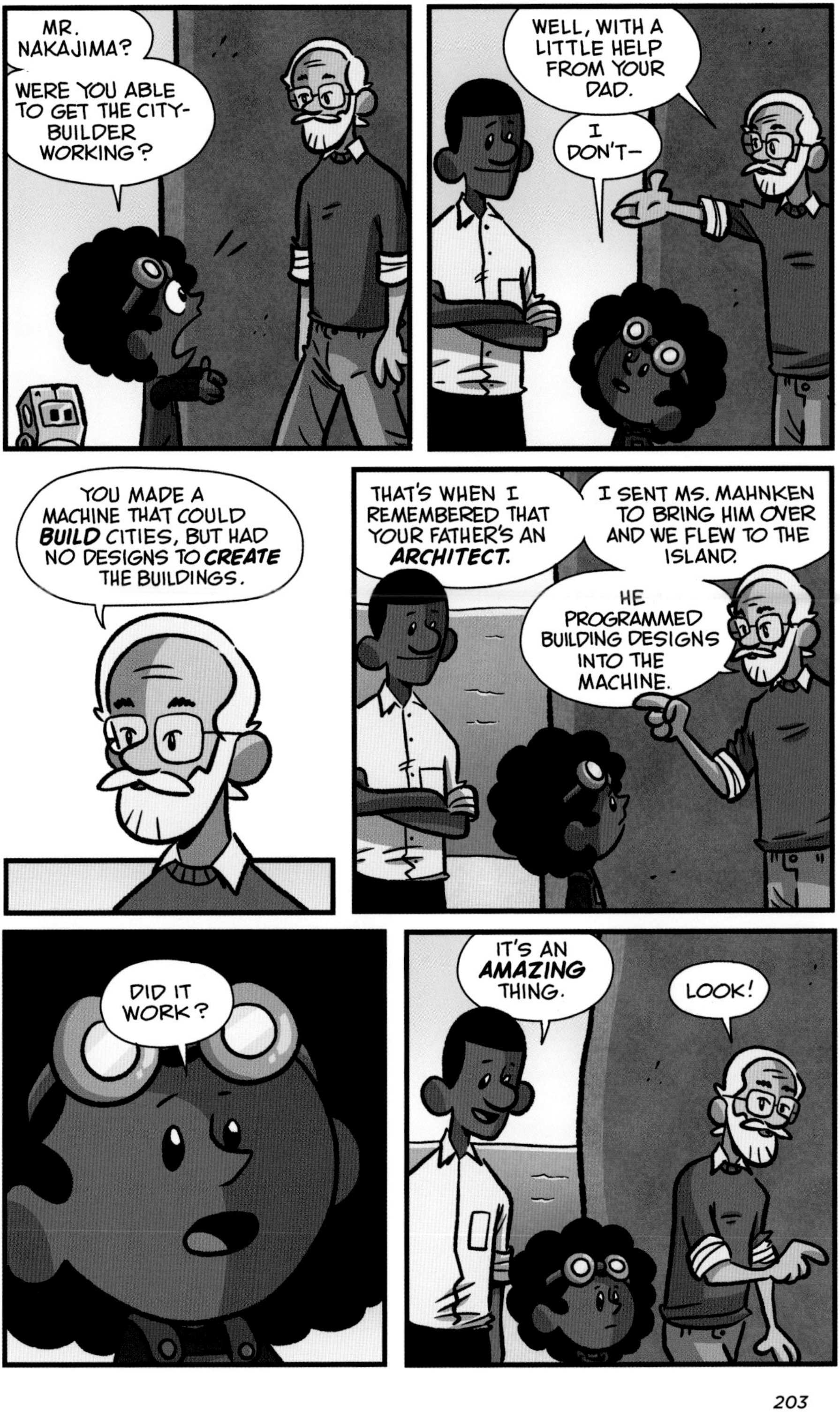
MR. NAKAJIMA?
WERE YOU ABLE TO GET THE CITY-BUILDER WORKING?
WELL, WITH A LITTLE HELP FROM YOUR DAD.
I DON'T—
YOU MADE A MACHINE THAT COULD BUILD CITIES, BUT HAD NO DESIGNS TO CREATE THE BUILDINGS.
THAT'S WHEN I REMEMBERED THAT YOUR FATHER'S AN ARCHITECT.
I SENT MS. MAHNKEN TO BRING HIM OVER AND WE FLEW TO THE ISLAND.
HE PROGRAMMED BUILDING DESIGNS INTO THE MACHINE.
DID IT WORK?
IT'S AN AMAZING THING.
LOOK!

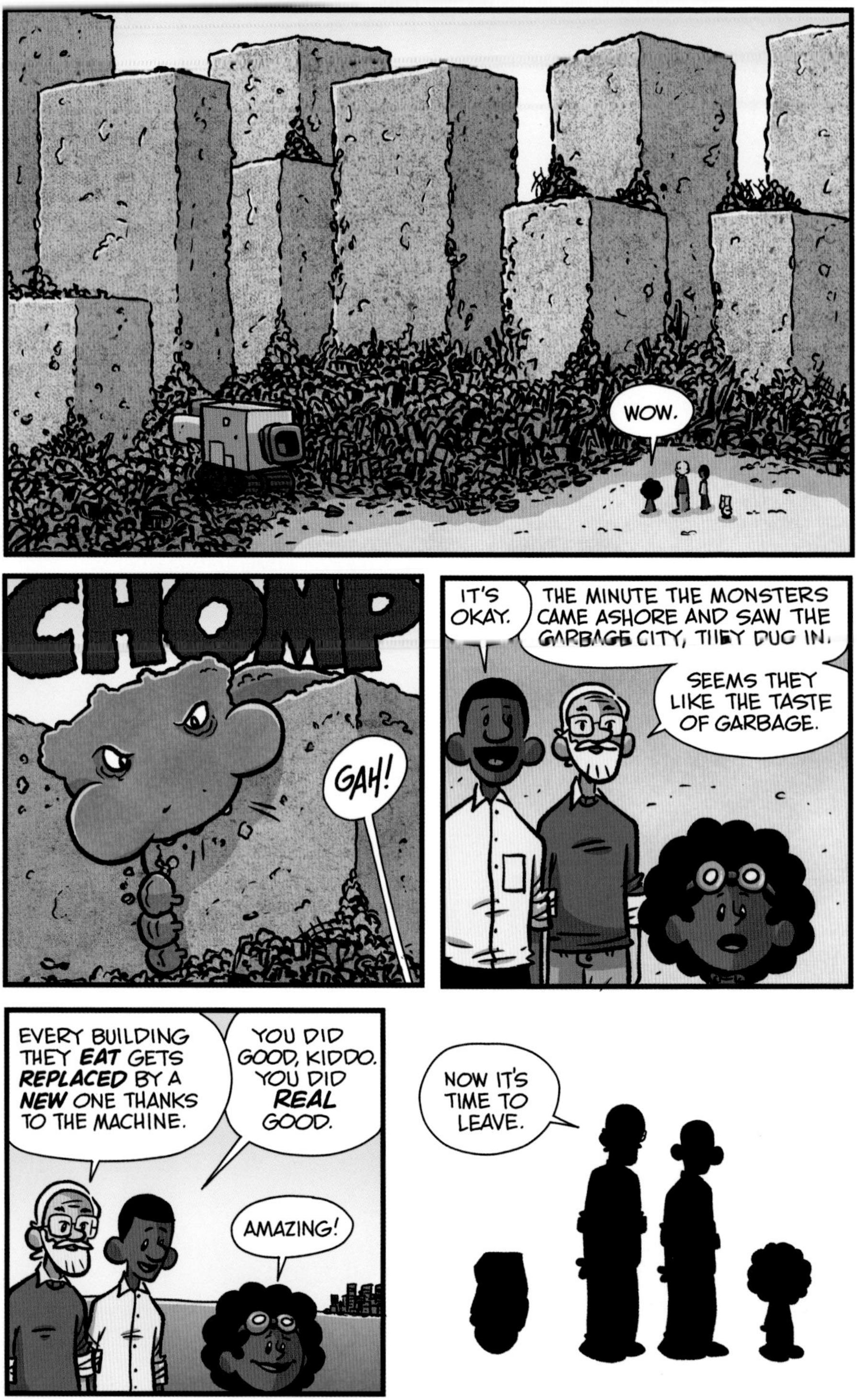
WOW.
CHOMP
GAH!
IT'S OKAY.
THE MINUTE THE MONSTERS CAME ASHORE AND SAW THE GARBAGE CITY, THEY DUG IN.
SEEMS THEY LIKE THE TASTE OF GARBAGE.
EVERY BUILDING THEY **EAT** GETS **REPLACED** BY A **NEW** ONE THANKS TO THE MACHINE.
YOU DID GOOD, KIDDO. YOU DID **REAL** GOOD.
AMAZING!
NOW IT'S TIME TO LEAVE.

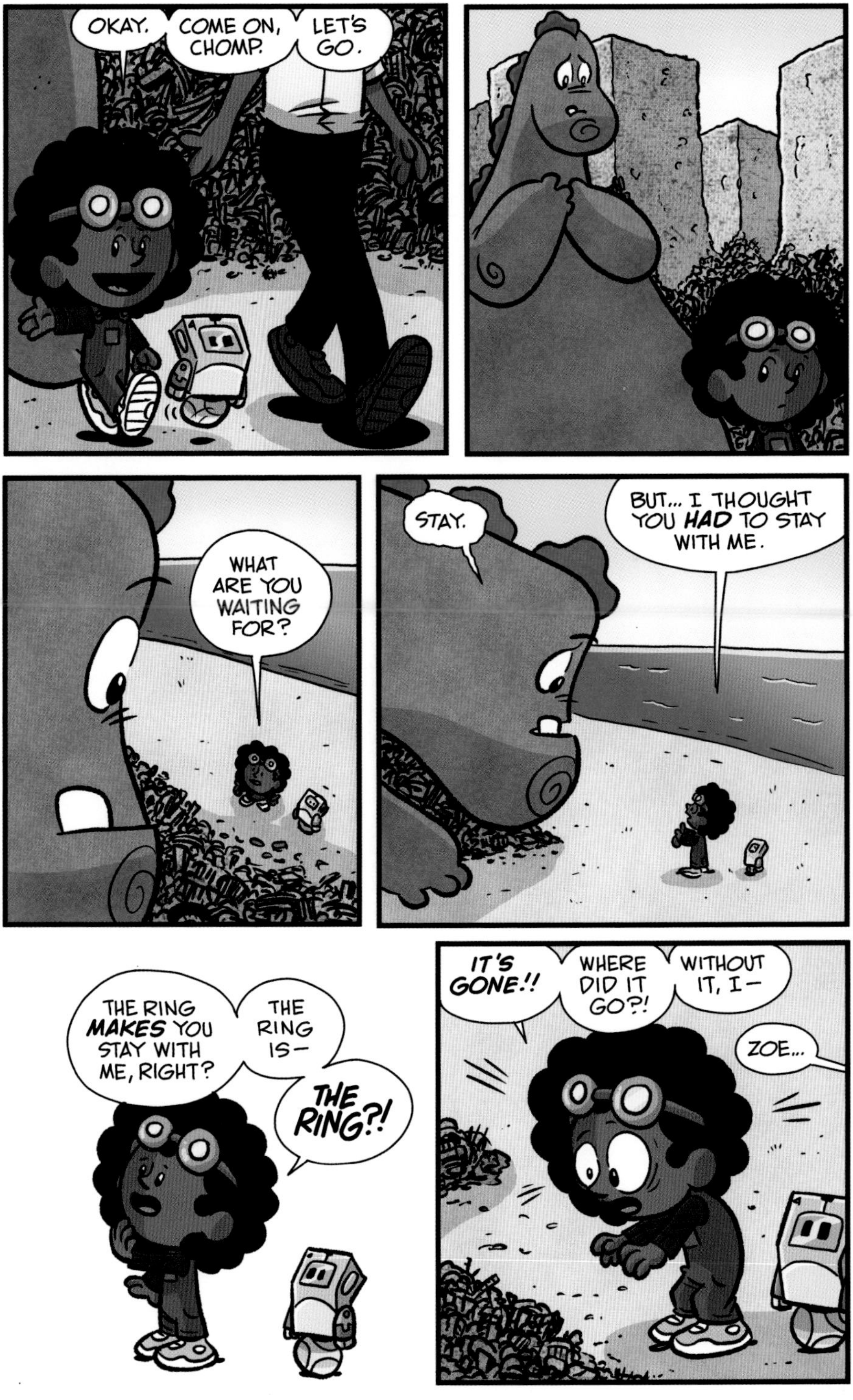
OKAY.
COME ON, CHOMP.
LET'S GO.
WHAT ARE YOU WAITING FOR?
STAY.
BUT... I THOUGHT YOU HAD TO STAY WITH ME.
THE RING MAKES YOU STAY WITH ME, RIGHT?
THE RING IS—
THE RING?!
IT'S GONE!!
WHERE DID IT GO?!
WITHOUT IT, I—
ZOE...

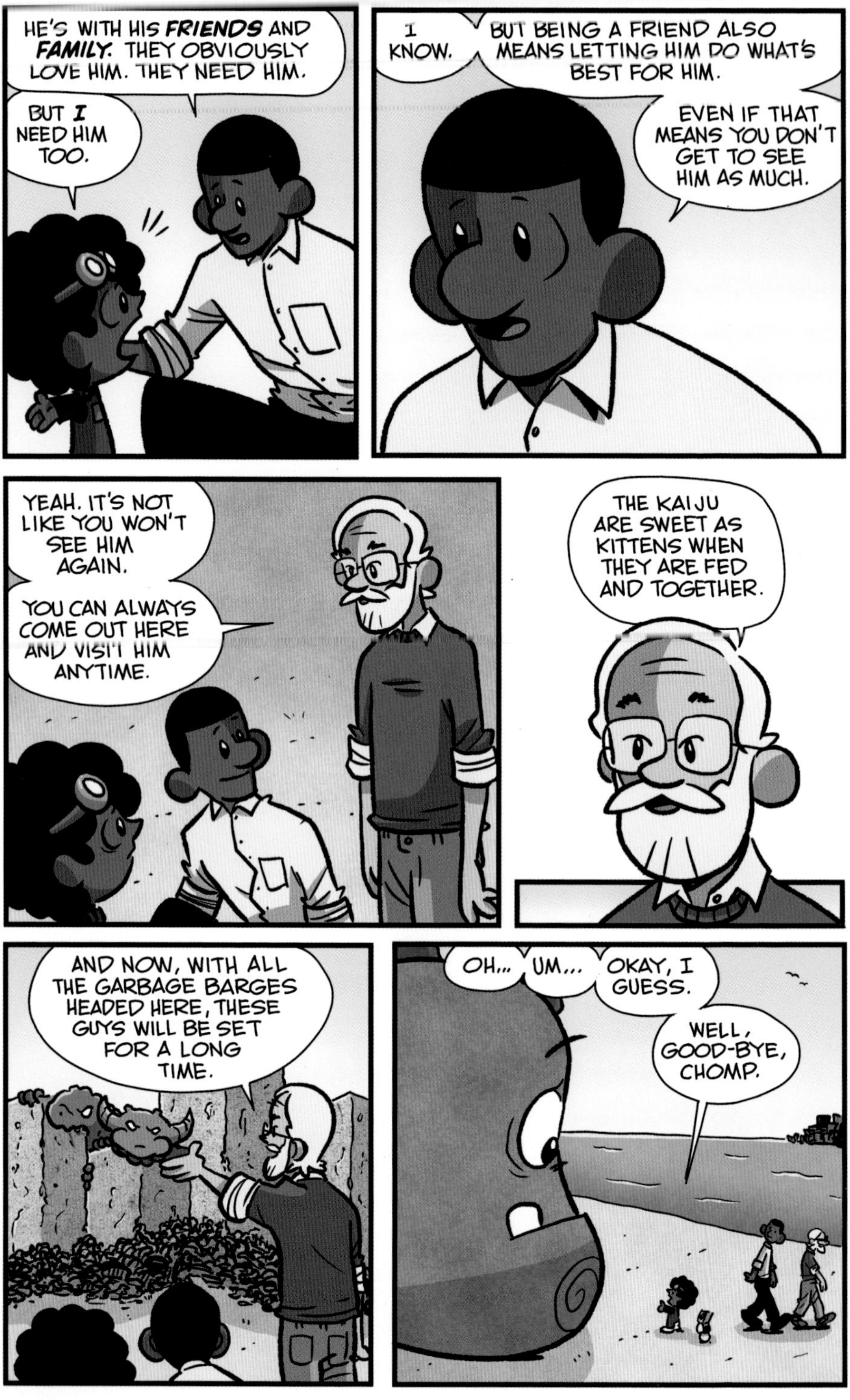
HE'S WITH HIS **FRIENDS** AND **FAMILY.** THEY OBVIOUSLY LOVE HIM. THEY NEED HIM.
BUT **I** NEED HIM TOO.
I KNOW.
BUT BEING A FRIEND ALSO MEANS LETTING HIM DO WHAT'S BEST FOR HIM.
EVEN IF THAT MEANS YOU DON'T GET TO SEE HIM AS MUCH.
YEAH. IT'S NOT LIKE YOU WON'T SEE HIM AGAIN.
YOU CAN ALWAYS COME OUT HERE AND VISIT HIM ANYTIME.
THE KAIJU ARE SWEET AS KITTENS WHEN THEY ARE FED AND TOGETHER.
AND NOW, WITH ALL THE GARBAGE BARGES HEADED HERE, THESE GUYS WILL BE SET FOR A LONG TIME.
OH...
UM...
OKAY, I GUESS.
WELL, GOOD-BYE, CHOMP.

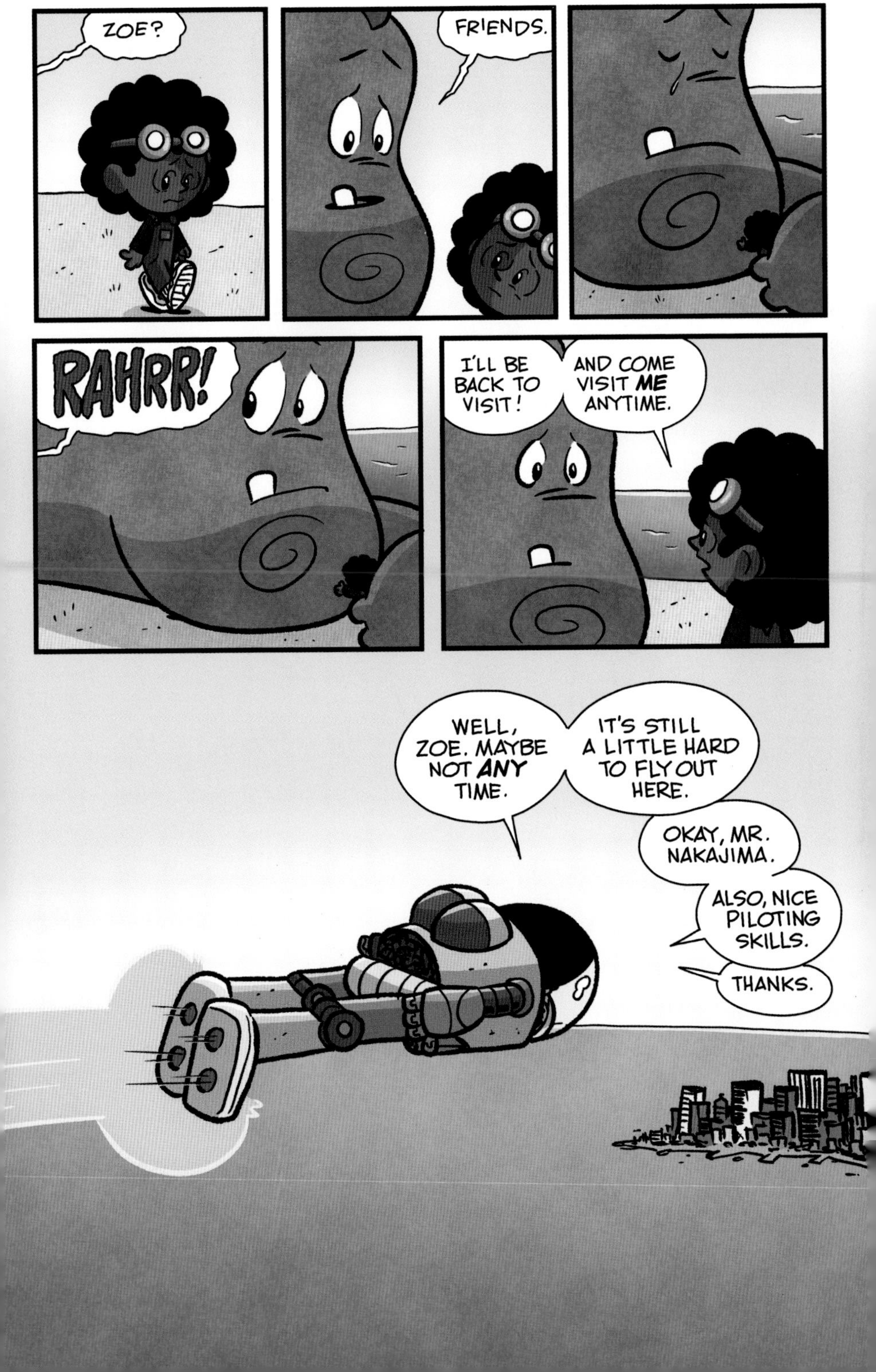
ZOE?
FRIENDS.
RAHRR!
I'LL BE BACK TO VISIT!
AND COME VISIT ME ANYTIME.
WELL, ZOE. MAYBE NOT ANY TIME.
IT'S STILL A LITTLE HARD TO FLY OUT HERE.
OKAY, MR. NAKAJIMA.
ALSO, NICE PILOTING SKILLS.
THANKS.

CHAPTER 15 - A NEW WORLD

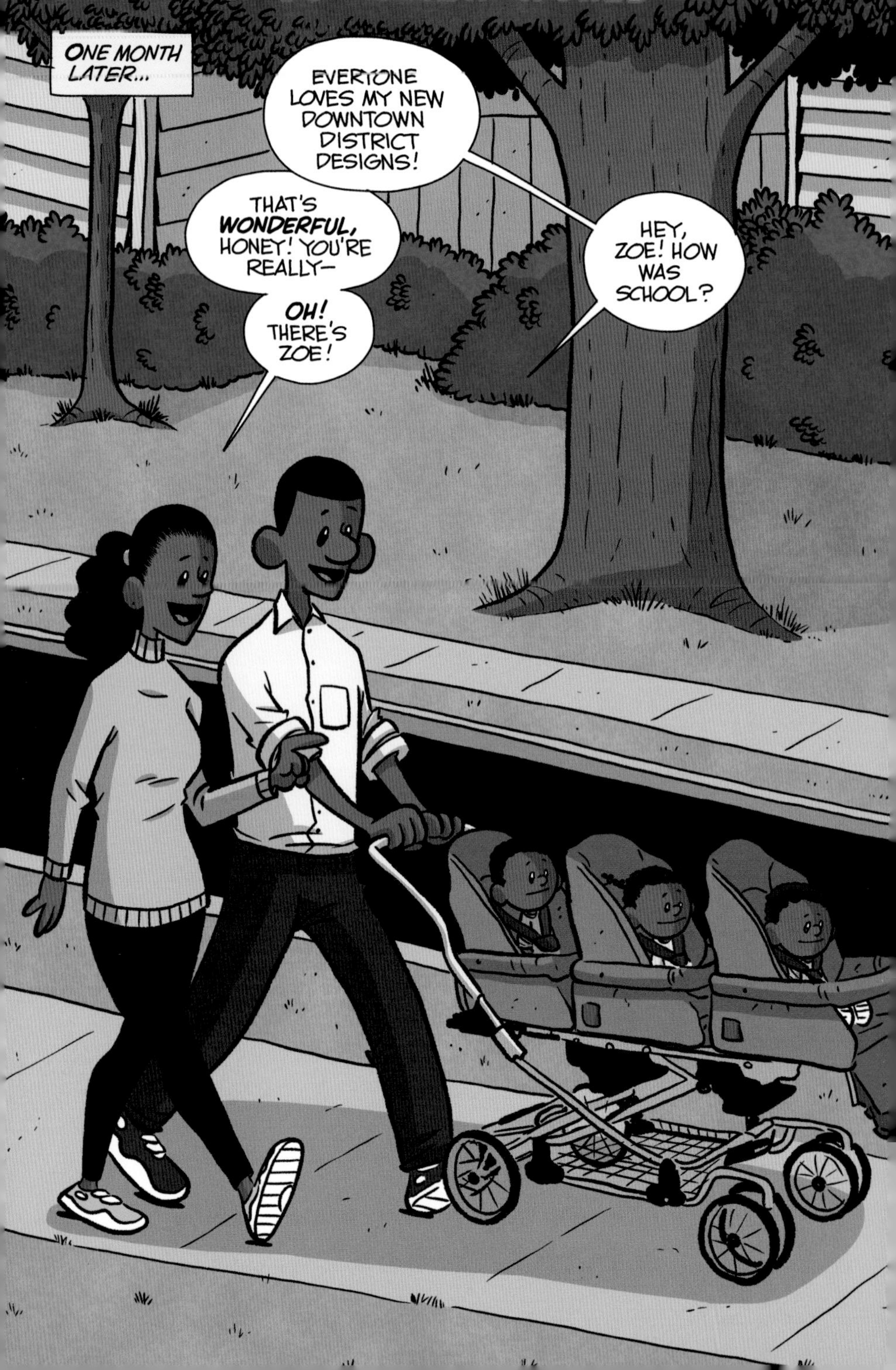
ONE MONTH LATER...
EVERYONE LOVES MY NEW DOWNTOWN DISTRICT DESIGNS!
THAT'S **WONDERFUL,** HONEY! YOU'RE REALLY—
OH! THERE'S ZOE!
HEY, ZOE! HOW WAS SCHOOL?

GOOD!

I GOT AN A IN ROBOTICS!

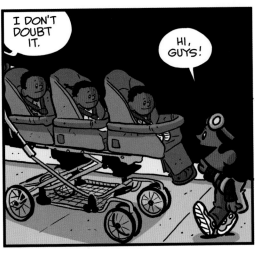

I DON'T DOUBT IT.

HI, GUYS!

≈SIGH≈

EVERYTHING OKAY?

YEAH.

I WAS JUST THINKING ABOUT *CHOMP*.

I MISS HIM.

I KNOW. BUT HE'S WITH HIS FRIENDS AND FAMILY.

HE'S HAPPY.

OH, I KNOW.

BUT HE WAS MY FIRST REAL FRIEND.

PARDON?

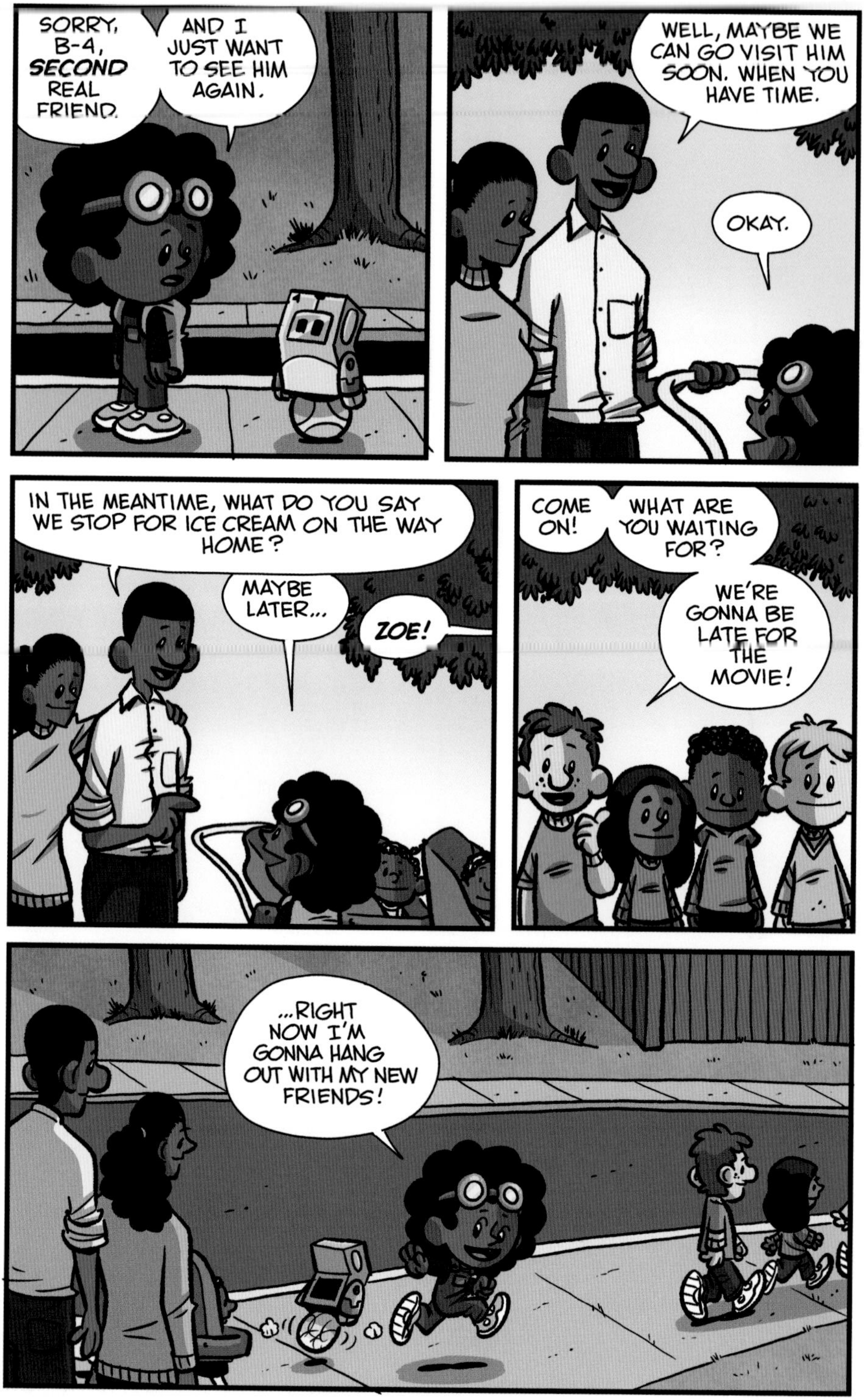
SORRY, B-4, SECOND REAL FRIEND.
AND I JUST WANT TO SEE HIM AGAIN.
WELL, MAYBE WE CAN GO VISIT HIM SOON. WHEN YOU HAVE TIME.
OKAY.
IN THE MEANTIME, WHAT DO YOU SAY WE STOP FOR ICE CREAM ON THE WAY HOME?
MAYBE LATER...
ZOE!
COME ON!
WHAT ARE YOU WAITING FOR?
WE'RE GONNA BE LATE FOR THE MOVIE!
...RIGHT NOW I'M GONNA HANG OUT WITH MY NEW FRIENDS!

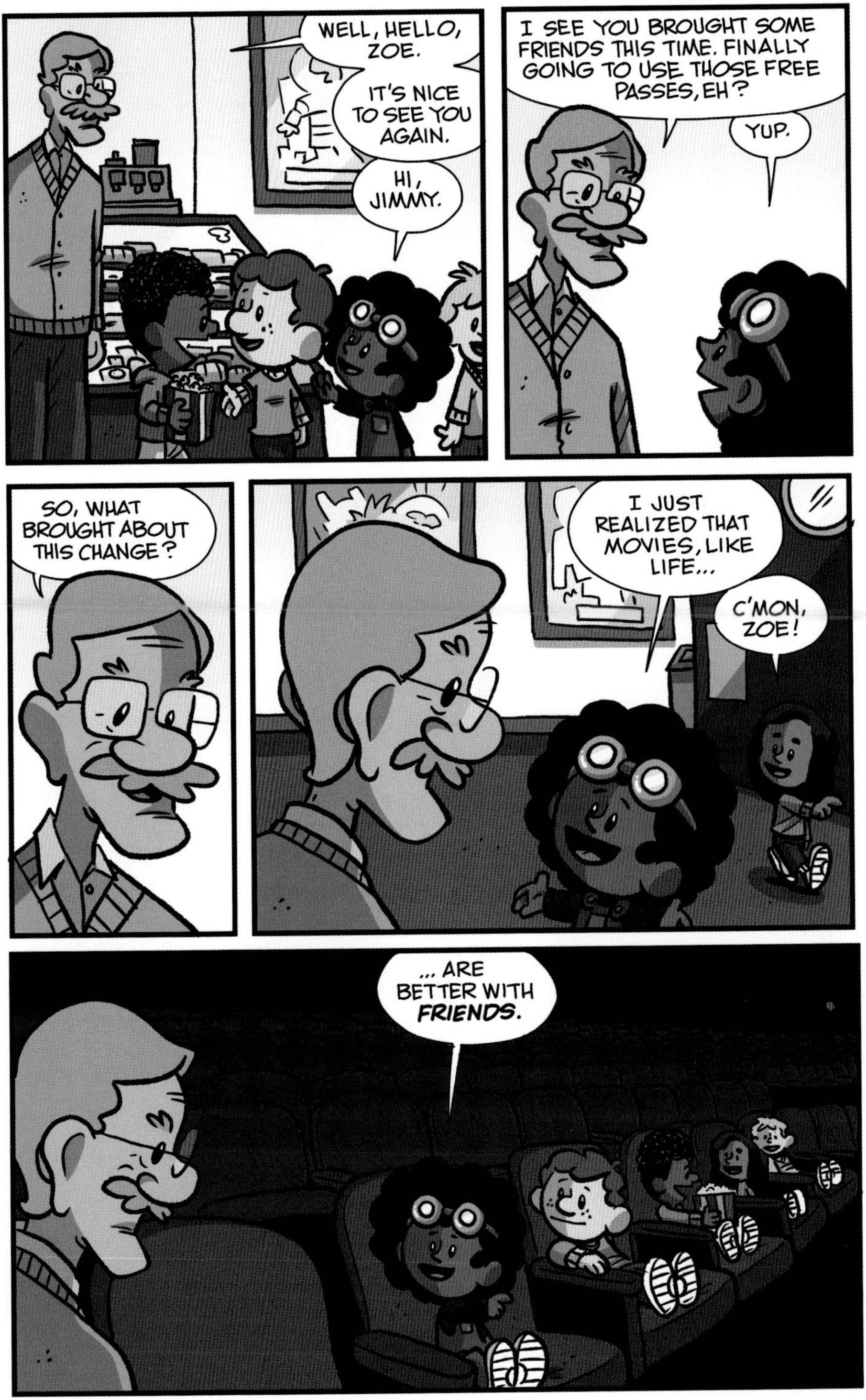
WELL, HELLO, ZOE.
IT'S NICE TO SEE YOU AGAIN.
HI, JIMMY.
I SEE YOU BROUGHT SOME FRIENDS THIS TIME. FINALLY GOING TO USE THOSE FREE PASSES, EH?
YUP.
SO, WHAT BROUGHT ABOUT THIS CHANGE?
I JUST REALIZED THAT MOVIES, LIKE LIFE...
C'MON, ZOE!
... ARE BETTER WITH **FRIENDS**.

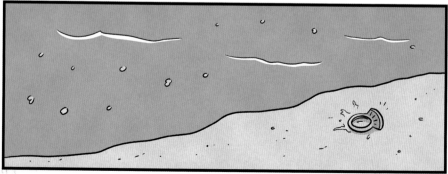

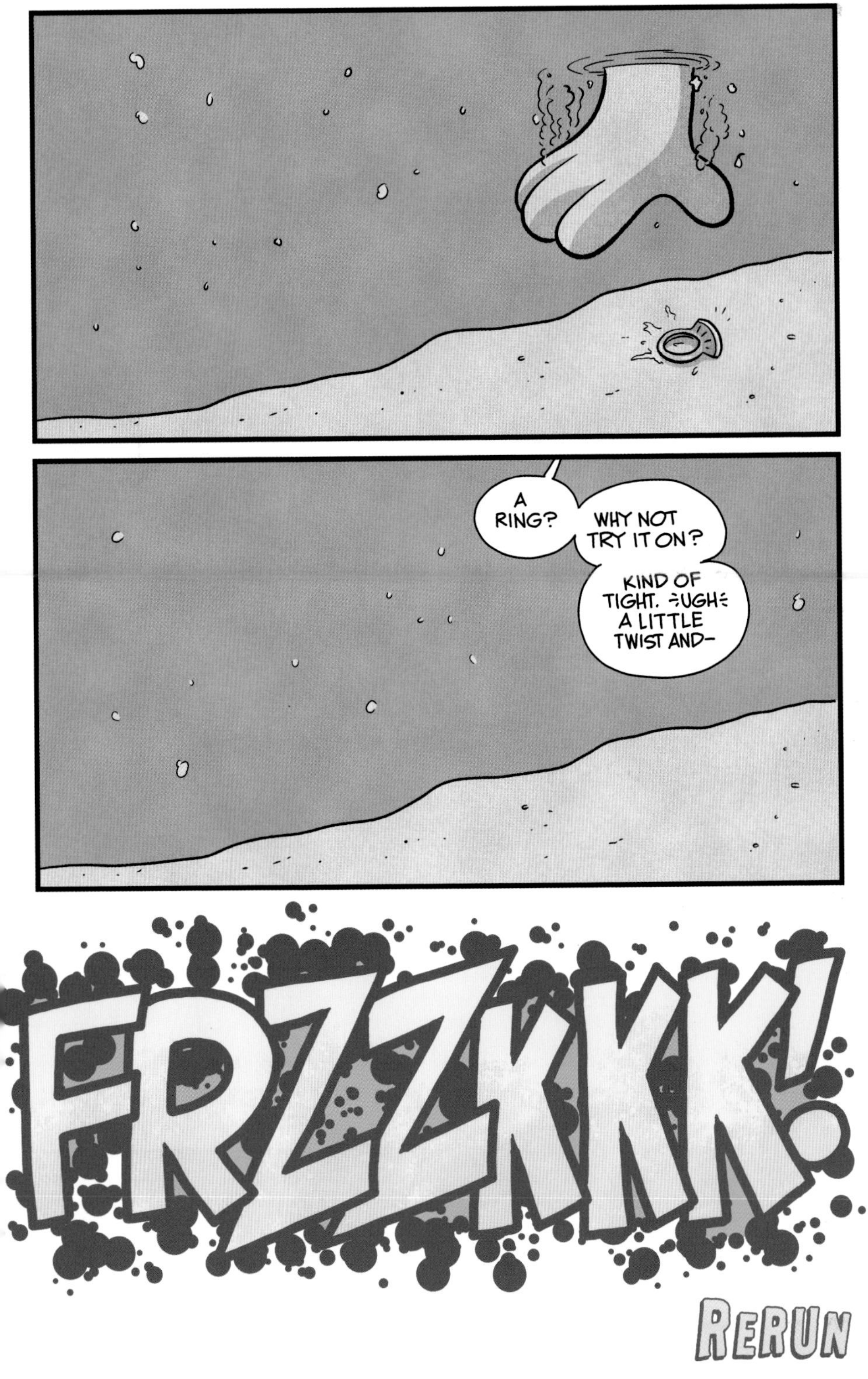
A RING?
WHY NOT TRY IT ON?
KIND OF TIGHT. ≑UGH≑ A LITTLE TWIST AND–
FRZZKKK!
RERUN

CHECK OUT THE FIRST MAGIC-RING STORY!

Jeremy is about to begin an amazing adventure when his cereal-box prize—a ring that grants wishes—brings his favorite video game to life, with Jeremy himself as the superhero who must defeat the villains. There's only one problem: Jeremy has never won in the final level of the game!

PRAISE FOR COSMIC COMMANDOS

"Near-nonstop action." —*Publishers Weekly*

"Emotionally complex and satisfying." —*Booklist*

"Fun for kids and hilarious for the adults who are lucky enough to get to read it to 'em!" —Patton Oswalt

"Originality, hilarity, and drawings so cute that they make your heart explode." —Judd Winick, author of *Hilo: The Boy Who Crashed to Earth*

CHRISTOPHER ELIOPOULOS started his career in comic books, writing and/or drawing books like *Franklin Richard: Son of a Genius*, *Pet Avengers*, and *Cow Boy*. He's currently the illustrator of the *New York Times* bestselling series Ordinary People Change the World, which is written by Brad Meltzer. He lives in New Jersey with his wife and identical twin sons (when they're home from college), and hates writing in the third person. You can find him online on Twitter @ChrisEliopoulos or at ChrisEliopoulos.com.

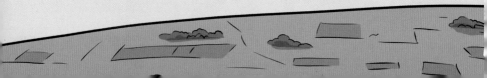

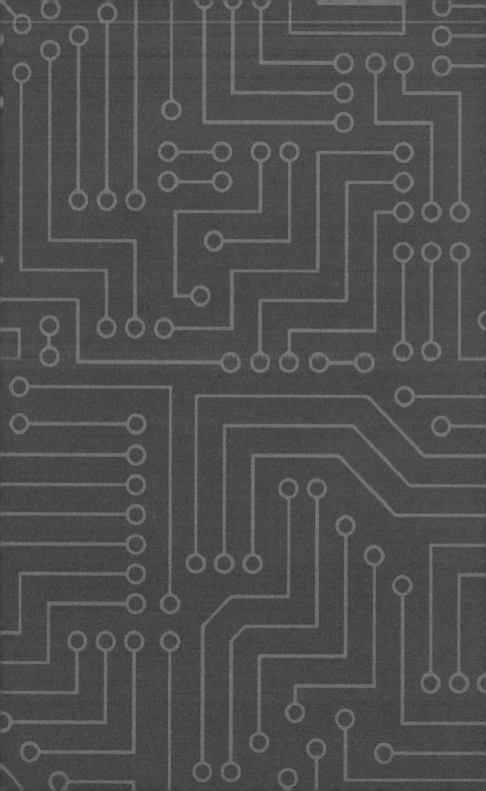